Born in England in 1932,
most major British television
is also an established scree
made movies in Europe and
first novel.

DEREK FORD

Panic on Sunset

GRAFTON BOOKS
A Division of the Collins Publishing Group

LONDON GLASGOW
TORONTO SYDNEY AUCKLAND

Grafton Books
A Division of the Collins Publishing Group
8 Grafton Street, London W1X 3LA

Published by Grafton Books 1989

First published in Great Britain by
Grafton Books 1988

Copyright © Derek Ford 1988

ISBN 0-586-20104-1

Printed and bound in Great Britain by
Collins, Glasgow

Set in Ehrhardt

All rights reserved. No part of this publication may
be reproduced, stored in a retrieval system, or
transmitted, in any form, or by any means, electronic,
mechanical, photocopying, recording or otherwise,
without the prior permission of the publishers.

This book is sold subject to the condition that it
shall not, by way of trade or otherwise, be lent,
re-sold, hired out or otherwise circulated
without the publisher's prior consent in any
form of binding or cover other than that in
which it is published and without a similar
condition including this condition being imposed
on the subsequent purchaser.

Part One

1

Panic hit George Schapner with a suddenness that caused his stomach to spasm and his skin to sweat. The stab of fear was so intense that when the traffic signal at the corner of La Brea and Sunset changed to 'Go', George couldn't move.

A model-T right behind him set up an impatient honking. It attracted attention but made no difference to George. Suddenly, he knew as a certainty that Galaxy Pictures were not going to renew Velma Torraine's contract.

Six months ago Velma would have been invulnerable. She'd just topped the box-office ratings for 1927 and was making as much money for the exchanges as Garbo and Gilbert combined. The exchanges couldn't get their hands on a Velma Torraine picture fast enough and he could have written his own ticket at any studio in town.

George had taken a skinny little street kid from Brooklyn and parlayed her into America's number one sex symbol. Few people could understand it, but George did. Garbo and Gilbert were great in their fancy uniforms and lavish palaces, Swanson terrific in her sophisticated-lady roles, but to the kids, they were figures in an unattainable dream world. Velma scored because her movies played against backgrounds the kids knew and recognized; her stories were extensions of their own fantasies. The kids were comfortable with Velma. With Garbo or Gilbert they wouldn't have known which fork to use. Now all this was jeopardized. All in the name of this latest fad for talking pictures.

Was George the only man alive who could see it for what it was? It was nothing new. People had been fooling around with it for years. Vitaphone had been putting out newsreels in sound for as long as George could remember. Nobody had gone nuts over those. It was just another gimmick to boost the falling box-office. George was confident it would soon go the way of Magna-Screen and colour.

'You mean to be here all night?'

George turned to see the cop bending low, peering into the interior of George's roadster, his nightstick resting menacingly on the door.

'No, officer,' George managed. 'I just didn't feel well there for a minute.'

The cop nodded. 'Been a hot day. How you feeling right now?'

George nodded. 'Better.'

'Any chance you can move on? You causing a traffic problem here.'

'Yeah. Feeling better.' George straightened in his driver's seat and put the roadster back into gear. 'Thanks!' he called to the cop.

The cop nodded and watched the Stutz pull away into the downhill traffic with shaking head. 'One day,' he said to himself.

George drove on down La Brea towards Rossmore and wondered how much longer it was all going to last.

Velma wasn't the only one in trouble: Charles Farrell, Edmund Lowe – even Mary Pickford! George saw it as a case of the crazies and he wasn't alone. MGM felt the same way. Unfortunately, Velma wasn't signed to MGM but to Galaxy.

Galaxy was pretty much a one-man operation and that one man was Wilbur Sterne – exactly the kind of maverick independent that was leading this manic rush into talking pictures.

George got the rest of the way home from habit. He pulled the roadster in front of his house and was immediately aware of the tar pits. On nights like this, the air was heavy with their nose-tingling pungency. There was a move by local residents to get them concreted over, but the city's answer was that the pits threw up the odd dinosaur bone.

Who needs dinosaurs, thought George as he fitted his key into the door lock and then hesitated.

Gillian!

Gillian was George's live-in girlfriend – a highly sexed and erotically creative girl, who, like Scheherazade, saw it as her role in life to come up with something new every night. What had once been a surprise and a delight was now becoming strained and tiresome. There were some nights he'd just like to come home, kick off his shoes and take a drink. Gillian considered any waking moment not devoted to inducing or enjoying orgasm as so much wasted time. George didn't feel he could handle Gillian tonight.

He took a deep breath and turned the key.

The house was curiously still, with no sign of Gillian, erotically disposed or otherwise. Maybe she was out shopping. George made straight for the table which, by means of a concealed catch, contained his illicit booze. As the catch sprang there was the flutter of a piece of paper falling to the floor. George poured himself a drink, picked up the paper and shoved it back on the table.

Sipping his drink he went through to the bathroom and started filling the tub. As he stood watching it fill he was suddenly discomfited at Gillian's absence. He hadn't wanted to get into anything lengthy and prolonged tonight, but he did want to have someone to tell his troubles to. He went back into the main room and spotted the note which seemed to be beckoning his attention.

> Dear George,
> It's not possible for us to continue this charade further.
> I'm leaving this afternoon for New York.

Stanley is meeting me there, and we are
going to be married.

Love, as always,

Gillian.

Charade? thought George. What charade? He read the note through again and noticed she'd even put the date: 'June 16th 1928.' Very formal. It was surprising she hadn't got a lawyer to serve him with it.

George carefully screwed the paper into a tight little wad and aimed it towards the waste basket.

He missed.

He must have been missing a lot lately.

Going back towards the bathroom he wondered at what point Gillian had decided to leave him. Shaking off his clothes he cursed her again and again. Dammit, he needed someone to talk to! This sound thing was getting to him. Maybe that was the problem. Galaxy had him worried. They were pressurizing him to get Velma to make a voice test before discussing her new contract. George was sure Velma wouldn't make it. She'd spent hundreds of dollars with these plummy voice coaches but it hadn't done a lot of good. Sure, she could manage 'The rain in Spain' with the best of them right there in their studios, but, two minutes after leaving, the Brooklyn was back in her voice as strong as ever. There was no way Velma was going to make it, and without Velma he had no agency.

George got into the tub and wondered how he ever got himself into this position.

Then suddenly it came to him. Erle!

As far as he could remember it had all started with the sinking of the *Lusitania*. Growing up in Maine, George had taken a big interest in all the transatlantic liners and their battle for the Blue Riband. When the *Lusitania* went down it was like losing an old friend. George hadn't realized then just how totally that torpedo was going to change his life. Within two years he was in the service and being shipped out. As a boy he'd dreamed of one day making a transatlantic voyage – but not like this!

He and a couple of thousand others had been shipped over in a German liner requisitioned by the government and renamed the SS *Mount Vernon*. Fulfilling a boyhood dream was one thing, doing it in a cockleshell in submarine-infested waters was something else.

After ten days of tossing and sea-sickness the green-faced doughboys had disembarked in France. It was at the dispersal camp that he'd met up with Erle.

Erle was the reason George had come out to California.

'When I get home,' Erle had been fond of saying, 'I'm going to take me out to California.'

'What's out there?' somebody, usually George, would ask.

'Don't know,' Erle would say, 'but it's as far as you can get from Europe without having to learn Chinese!'

Ten years later in a tub in California George smiled again at Erle's joke. It was pretty much Erle's only joke. He'd just retold it for the benefit of some replacements when, it being his turn, he'd lifted his head over the trench parapet for a looksee.

The sniper must have been zeroed in and waiting. Erle had fallen backwards from the trench step and lay on the muddy floor looking back up as surprised as George was looking down. The hole in the front of Erle's helmet didn't look as if it amounted to much but it had killed him.

When George processed out of the service he'd made his excuses to his family and boarded the first train west.

On the train to Chicago a grizzled old-timer had looked George over. 'Taking the train west?' he'd asked.

George had nodded, smiled and summoned up the ghost of Erle as he waited for his opening.

'Why's that?' duly asked the old man.

'Because it's as far as you can get from Europe without having to learn Chinese!'

The old man hadn't laughed. He'd looked steadily at George in a curious, puzzled way and then, after allowing a decent interval, had got up and changed seats.

It was hardly an earth-shaking incident, but George felt that he'd betrayed Erle. Erle had always got the laugh. It was the moment in which George's youth ended.

When the telephone started ringing George found himself sunk to his chin in the sudsy water. His first impulse was to ignore it, but then, realizing it might be a contrite Gillian, he hurriedly wrapped a towel about his sopping body and went out to pick up the handset.

It wasn't Gillian. It was a very Brooklyn Velma Torraine.

'George!' She always spoke with exclamation marks when excited. 'George! It's a disaster!'

'What is?'

'You're not going to believe this!' she warned him.

George sighed patiently. 'Velma, I'm standing here soaking wet from the bath. I'll believe anything.'

'It's Ronnie!' Ronnie was Velma's alcoholic ex-husband and the cause of much grief.

'He been arrested again?'

'I wished!' screeched Velma. 'George, he's here in the house! Dead drunk! Stark naked! In my bedroom!'

George sighed. 'Is that so terrible you have to call me?'

Velma put together a pithy stream of cuss words that probably had the birds falling off the wires in shock. When, for want of breath, she finally ran down, George managed to ask her what she wanted him to do about it.

'You get ten per cent of my money and one hundred per cent of my troubles, right?'

'Looks that way!'

'Damn right it does! It's you always saying it!'

'OK, but what am I supposed to do?'

'You get your ass over here, that's what you do!'

'Velma, it's been a long hot day, I just got in . . .'

Velma cut in icily. 'May I remind you,' she started out in patient tones, 'that you are supposed to be here, right now, anyway!'

'I am?'

'This just happens to be what may very well prove to be the turning point of my entire career. Tonight is the night I'm giving my dramatic rendition of *Paradise Lost* by John Milton to *Photoplay* magazine because, you tell me, I have to prove to the world that I can talk! You recall anything of this so far?'

George did and stood there feeling guilty. He knew why he'd forgotten it. Fear of the sheer foolhardiness of the event had caused him to block it out of his mind.

Meanwhile, Velma was using her most excoriating tone to continue. 'When, what I should be,' she was saying, 'is calm and collected, what I am is being harassed by a horny ex-husband who refuses to leave until I climb into the sack with him and, to use his delicate phrase, "Boff one up me!" Is any of this getting through to you?'

George sighed miserably to himself. He knew what he was going to have to do and his resistance was token. 'Loud and clear, Velma, but I still don't see what I could do even if I do come over . . .'

'You get that horny bastard out of my house! That's what you can do!'

George hastily considered. He'd made some money. Just a year ago he'd been able to take 25,000 dollars out of his bank account and put it into some RCA stock. Twenty-five thousand dollars was serious money. If he took it back east he could live well on it. Had Gillian been there to lend moral support he might well have told Velma that her game was no longer worth the candle, but Gillian wasn't there. She was on a train heading east to her Stanley. Abstractedly he wondered who the hell Stanley was. As it was he told Velma, 'OK, I'll come over.'

'You'd better!' she warned.

'Give me an hour.'

He hung the headset back on its hook, and went back to his tub.

The interruption had caused his skin to dry uncomfortably. He climbed back into the tub to damp himself down again.

Velma! It all seemed such a long time ago that it was an effort to relate all that had happened to a time-span of less than eight years.

Stepping down from the train in Los Angeles had been the beginning of a period of disillusionment with the Golden West. There was no gold and precious little dross to be found on the streets of Los Angeles. Up on the hills just visible across the bean fields, he was told, was a village called Hollywood. Up there were some damnfool easterners making photoplays and likely to hire someone like himself.

George got a ride up the dusty trail and within a day found himself back in a hole in the ground carrying a dummy rifle and wearing an authentically flea-infested army suit. The movie company had been looking for men who knew arms drill and that happened to be George's only qualification. He was hired for three dollars a day and lunch.

It had lasted all of three days but it had been enough for George to see that the prevailing methods of hiring people could use some improvement.

Back then it had been a haphazard business bringing in the extras needed for each day's work. Either you hung around the Hollywood Hotel – in Louie's coffee-shop if you could afford it – or else you got out early and hung around the studio gates. The trouble with the studio gate routine was that, at the first light of day, you had to commit yourself to one particular company which might be over-supplied with your type while, unknown to you, another company just a few blocks away might be looking for just your type.

What George did was to seek out the assistants that hired the extras and offer them a deal. George would establish a register of available extras along with any peculiarities, such as missing limbs, hunchbacks or midgets, and in return the assistant would supply him with a list of needs somewhere central. This enabled George to see the right people in the right place and save the unseemly studio gate scuffle that broke out as people fought for the available work.

The scheme had one major drawback from the assistant's point of view. Previously, in those God-like moments when they were deciding who was to work and who wasn't, they had been able to pick out one or even two of the prettiest girls for some after-work relaxation. George solved this by ensuring them a supply of hand-picked girls, and he was in business.

Soon he was renting an office. When he got his telephone installed business got even easier and faster.

Almost immediately George had imitators, but there was nothing like being first in the field. George's most serious opposition came when the Central Casting Corporation was set up in 1926, but George's reputation for reliability – and pretty girls – was well established, and he survived.

There was only one group which had, from the first, stayed out of this cosy arrangement, and that was the stunters. Those ex-cowboys hung around the junction with Cahuenga and weren't about to share their hard-earned pay with anybody. George had got too prosperous to notice.

When the Edward Small Agency moved west and opened an office just down the street from George he became aware, for the first time, that the big-money stars had 'agents', and realized that an agent was what he had become without even knowing what it was. His mind had turned from time to time to trying to represent some 'real' actors, but he had no idea how to go about it, let alone how to handle a negotiated contract. He learned when he had to. The cause was meeting Velma Torraine.

George had been making a rare visit to his old hunting ground in the lobby of the Hollywood Hotel when he saw one of the under-managers hustling a young woman out on to the street. Nothing unusual in that. The hotel's policy was that unaccompanied young ladies had fifteen minutes' grace in which to show they were genuinely there to meet someone. After that they were, politely or otherwise, shown the door. For no reason that he would ever be able to explain George found himself intervening. He'd caught hold of the girl's arm and cried, 'Where on earth are you going?'

The girl, sensing a saviour, had turned and looked up at him. George still remembered the reverberating shock of that first glance. Her wide open eyes had the colour and brilliance of polished emeralds. They danced as they locked on to his. Somewhere in the background the under-manager was mumbling that if he'd known the 'young lady was waiting for you, Mr Schapner . . .' but whatever he was saying faded into the distance.

'Did you say your name was Schapner?' It was obvious the name had meaning for her. '*George* Schapner?'

Later, over dinner, she told him her totally unoriginal story. She'd left her mother in bed with her latest lover and, stealing train fare and twenty-five dollars in stake money, lit out for Hollywood. She'd arrived thinking that the twenty-five dollars would tide her over until she found a job: 'Not movies right away, but I thought I might get something in a store or something.'

She found that there were a thousand girls ahead of her already in those jobs. She was down to change when, that afternoon, she'd gone to the hotel lobby.

'What did you hope to find there?' George asked.

'I was told a lot of important men were going through there, that's all.'

'And you were going to audition for them right there in the lobby?'

Velma's emeralds had flashed. 'I'd have done anything they wanted so long as they paid cash.'

He'd asked how old she was.

'Fifteen. How old do you have to be?'

'Fifteen's a good age, but not to be a whore.'

'Starving is better?'

'Where would your career be if you got pregnant?'

The laugh came direct from Brooklyn. 'Come on! I'm from New York not Goose Bend. There's rubbers and if the guy won't wear them there's the good old sponge soaked in vinegar. You have to remember! Mama was a whore!'

When he found she had nowhere to stay and suggested she could stay at his place she reminded him of her professional status and asked five dollars.

George handed her the five and then, with a sense of perverse virtue, gave her his couch, making it clear he intended sleeping in the other room.

Velma had summoned all the speculative philosophy the fifteen-year-old daughter of a whore could muster, and sighed: 'Mama warned me there'd be nights like this!'

George had lain awake for longer than he cared to remember, fighting the temptation her proximity presented, but had finally slept.

It was to prove, in an incredibly short span of time, the smartest thing he'd *never* done.

Velma of the emerald eyes.

A skyrocket closer to her apogee than she knew.

2

Beverly Hills was a fairly recent development, a parade of expensive but boringly similar houses in British mock-Tudor. It might look better, thought George, when the stumpy palms have had time to grow.

Velma's house stood about twenty feet back from the road, fronted by a half-circle sweep of gravel.

George swung his heavy tourer into the driveway to find himself impeded by a Ford parked right under the portico.

The press must have arrived early. Only magazine writers would have the nerve to drive a low-life vehicle like a Ford through Beverly Hills and park it right out in front of the house where everyone could see it.

As he parked he saw Velma's manservant, Manolo, appear on the porch. Obviously he had been detailed to watch out for George.

Approaching the house he had time to reflect that Manolo was suspiciously young and good-looking to be content with employment opening doors for a Hollywood movie star. His pants were too tight, his hair was slicked back in imitation of the great Rudolph of still fresh memory. All the Latinos dressed like him and it occurred to George that Manolo might be one reason why Velma was reluctant to give in to Ronnie and so save everyone a lot of trouble.

Manolo smiled a conspiratorial grin and waved George into the hallway which was dominated by an enormous chandelier. George never passed under it without remembering the day Velma had bought it.

'Four thousand dollars for a heap of glass?' he'd asked in amazement.

'It's Bavarian crystal!' Velma had responded. 'Lead crystal.'

To George it was still a heap of glass, and it didn't do too good a job of lighting the hallway either.

George could see well enough, however, to make out the flurry of feathers around Velma's thighs as she hurried towards him. She looked like an ostrich with a lion close behind.

'George!' she exclaimed on seeing him. 'They've come early! It's a disaster!'

'You mean you've already read them this Paradise thing?' asked George.

'No!' answered Velma furiously. 'I mean it's a disaster that they've come before you've got Ronnie out of the house.'

George had been half hoping that Ronnie would have given up and gone. No such luck. 'Still here, huh?'

Velma was impatiently scathing. 'Well, you don't imagine he'd *leave*, do you?'

George sighed heavily. 'OK, I'll go up and talk to him.'

'Talk?' gasped Velma. 'What good is talking going to do?'

'What the hell else do you suppose I can do?'

Velma's right hand left her body and floated around up, down, back and across her body in a series of helpless gestures. 'Something! Anything! Just get him out of here!'

George mounted the phony marble stairs and pushed open the door into Velma's 'boudoir'.

Ronnie was sprawled out on Velma's oyster-shell bed. His once fine-tuned movie star body was now a mound of wobbly flesh, beneath which hung Ronnie's one great talent – a monstrous object that went halfway from groin to knee. George had never had a homosexual impulse in his life, but he still took time out to register the magnificence of the thing – even in repose. The last time he'd seen anything like this it was on a horse.

Ronnie, whose interest had quickened when the door opened, threw his head back on to the pillow when he saw it was George and not Velma. Ronnie spoke through an alcohol-thickened throat. 'Come to renegotiate the wedding vows?' he asked, the English accent loud and clear.

George hesitated in his reply, while Ronnie turned an amused eye on him. 'Surely not to offer physical force?' he asked quizzically. He reached for a bedside bottle and pulled a swig. He cocked his talented eyebrow and smiled a deliberate insult. 'Central Casting has blundered again. You're not up to it, old boy.'

'Try me,' said George.

Ronnie seemed even more amused. 'No, thanks.' He lay back on the silk pillows with elaborate disdain.

George, provoked, reached forward intending to drag Ronnie off the bed, but soon realized this was easier conceived than accomplished. There wasn't a whole lot to hang on to when trying to move a wobbly-fleshed, naked drunk. Ronnie reacted with a sudden swing of his bottle which narrowly missed George's head.

'Piss off!' hissed Ronnie.

George stepped back to reconsider his strategy. Ronnie grinned in satisfied triumph. 'Besides,' he observed, 'you can hardly throw me out into the street bollock-naked, can you?'

'Where are your clothes?'

'Burned 'em!' said Ronnie.

George had noticed an acrid haze hanging about the ceiling of the room. Ronnie lay with an asinine grin as George, following his nose, checked out the bathroom. Sure enough, in the rose-pink enamelled depths of the tub lay a pile of smouldering clothes.

'You,' he told Ronnie on his return, 'are a raving loony.'

'It's all very simple,' said Ronnie. 'All I want to do is fuck my wife and be gone. Soonest done, soonest mended.'

'Velma is no longer your wife, and she doesn't want you.'

Ronnie grinned with satisfaction, and took another pull at the bottle, ignored a tributary of alcohol escaping his throat to stain the silk pillow, and tried to fix George with an uncertain gaze. 'You, dear George, have a capacity for stating the obvious which is positively stupefying.'

George was starting to feel that the situation was ridiculous. 'OK,' he said, 'I'll rephrase it. She isn't going to.'

Ronnie shook his head in disbelief, exuded a great sigh and lay back on the pillow. 'Can't understand it. Was a time when she couldn't get enough of it.' Ronnie began idly flipping his great dong back and forth with his free hand. 'Morning, noon and bloody night. Breakfast, lunch, dinner and dessert. Was at it till I feared she'd wear it out.' Ronnie roused himself to one elbow and fixed again on the blurred image of George. 'That's the trouble with quiff,' he philosophized. 'When it gets rich it gets fussy.' Ronnie lay back as if to recover from great exertion.

George felt they'd reached impasse. He had an uneasy feeling of sympathy for Ronnie. When Ronnie and Velma had met he'd been the Big Name and she a cute little ass in a bathing suit. It had been Ronnie's connections, as much as George's own efforts, that had put Velma on to the 'A' parties list, and it had been this exposure that had enabled George to negotiate the Galaxy contract. Now the positions were reversed and Velma, in the opinion of many, had simply off-loaded Ronnie as surplus to current requirement.

Velma, for all her simplistic jazz baby screen image, could be a cold-blooded bitch.

Realizing it was futile to stay, George went back down the 'looks-like marble' stairway.

Velma was waiting for him, demanding an answer.

'Nothing's changed. Either you go up or he stays.'

Velma, disappointed, sighed. 'What worries me more is if he decides to come down looking for me.'

Suddenly her voice was strident with petulance. 'There ought to be a law against it.'

George smiled. 'There is. There's also the newspapers.'

'Well, *think* of *something*!'

The idea struck George out of nowhere. It came fully fledged.

'Listen, Velma, would you mind if I brought someone over?'

Velma's eyes gleamed as if at the sound of distant bugles. 'You mean a doctor? You gonna have him certified?'

George shook his head to give himself more time. He was certain it could work, but it had to be put to Velma with some diplomacy.

'More of a therapist.'

He turned back and saw Velma looking at him blankly. There was no escape. It had to be said bluntly.

'A girl.'

Velma took on the expression of a bull lowering its head on a matador.

'You mean a *whore?*'

'Not just any whore. One of Madame Gregory's girls.'

Velma was wary. 'What's the difference?'

'Madame Gregory runs a house, but it's a very special and exclusive place. Her speciality is lookalikes.' Velma didn't understand.

'Madame Gregory specializes in girls that look like the stars.'

Velma's eyes opened wide. 'Are you saying that they got a girl up there – working – who looks like *me?*'

George found himself grinning. 'Two of 'em!' Just for fun, he added, 'One of them is much better than the other.'

'That's outrageous!' screamed Velma. 'They've got to be stopped, George! For God's sake, people might think it was me!' Velma suddenly broke off and looked at George strangely. 'How do *you* know one is better than the other?'

George shrugged. 'So I've been told!'

'*I'll bet!*' snarled Velma. 'Dammit, why's nobody told me about this before? No wonder I get such weird mail!' She paused for further furious thought. 'You'd better get me a lawyer, George. I mean tomorrow!'

'Now, Velma, think about it! It's a joke! A fantasy, and *very* discreet. If you were to take any action you'd only be publicizing your own embarrassment. Don't you think if I thought it harmed you I'd have stopped it long ago?'

Velma seemed to shrug off her belligerent mood. A wicked light of amusement was in her eyes. 'Who else is up there?' George shrugged, trying to keep it vague.

'Clara?' prompted Velma.

George nodded. 'Would you believe Mary Pickford?'

'Marion Davis?'

'Norma Talmadge?'

George felt they could go on all night. 'Let's say they got one of each.' Then some recklessness made him add,

'They've even got a Joan Crawford and she hasn't even starred yet.'

'Joan who?' asked Velma.

'Crawford, she's cast in Harry Beaumont's next picture.'

'A *talkie*?'

George flushed. He had to go and mention Joan Crawford! The whole town – producers included – were watching each other like hawks to see who was going to break ranks and leave the others, literally, speechless. This time George was able to reassure her.

'Added music is all.' Velma seemed to relax visibly. George pressed her. 'So what do you say?'

Velma's mind was elsewhere. Triggered by the reference to Crawford she had started thinking gloomily about her Galaxy sound test.

'About what?'

'About bringing this girl over to take care of Ronnie.'

Velma was dismissive. 'You think some cheap whore is going to fool my own husband?' she asked.

George trod carefully. 'Ordinarily it would be preposterous,' he agreed, 'but considering he's dead drunk, she might.'

A smile started to spread across Velma's exquisite face. The smile developed into a deep throaty chuckle. 'What a prank,' she finally burst out. The chuckle became an outright laugh. Suddenly Velma seemed entranced with the idea.

George stepped forward, nodding encouragement. 'I take it the answer is "yes"?'

Velma was struck with a sobering thought. 'Can you be sure she's "clean"?'

'What do you care?' he asked. Velma's chuckle rose again, this time dirtier.

'I've had stunt doubles before, but this is *priceless*.'

3

Madame Gregory spoke with an air of unequivocal finality.

'My girls never go "out". It's quite, quite out of the question!'

George leaned forward, aware that others in the room were straining to listen in on this corner conversation. 'It's just for an hour. An hour is all I ask!'

'You ask too much.' Madame was shaking her head with patrician dignity. 'It's my very strictest rule.'

'Not even for a hundred dollars?'

Madame Gregory flinched as if a noxious smell had been released under her nose. 'You are being crass, Mr Schapner!'

'But they have to go out *sometime*!'

Madame Gregory was actually vibrating with indignation. 'Not in their "faces" they don't! Never! You of all people should understand why. They could be used for fraudulent enterprises!'

George was getting out of his depth. This had been the last reaction he would have expected. 'But you know who I am. I'm her manager! I wouldn't do anything to injure Velma!'

Madame Gregory rose straight up from her chair as if impelled by some system of hydraulics. 'My rule cannot be broken,' she said as if pronouncing the edict of an empress. 'There can be no exceptions!'

Madame Gregory left no doubt that, this time, the interview was ended, and started to move away. George stood with the intention of pursuing her, but suddenly felt it was hopeless.

His eye was taken by a fabulously beautiful 'Louise Brooks', and he wasn't prepared for the arrival of a very real, grinning, Milton Bressler. Milton was a director of some of

Galaxy's cheaper programmers. There had been tension between them ever since George had blocked his assignment to a Velma picture. Milton's smiled greeting had all the warmth of a cobra about to strike. 'Hi, George. What are you doing up here?'

George was still trying to think of some likely story when his upper arm was suddenly clamped in a painful vice. George would have screamed but the pain seemed to have shut down his nervous system. Something nasty happened to his lower lumbar region and, vaguely aware that he was in the grip of Madame Gregory's ape-like bouncer, he found himself being propelled at full speed through a squealing crowd towards a very solid, and closed, front door.

A collision seemed inevitable, when a coloured maid, who attended to such things, managed to get the door open wide enough to allow him and Ape-man free passage into the chill night air.

The pain in his arm didn't lessen until, fighting for a foothold on the gravel driveway, he was spun carelessly away, to end sprawled on his left side.

George lay winded. 'I feel sick!' he murmured to a pair of size fourteen boots.

Ape-man reached down and with a one-handed grip put George on a low stone wall, thrusting his head between his knees.

'You'll be OK,' said Ape-man in a burst of eloquence and started to grind his way back across the gravel.

'Don't leave me!' called George. 'I think I'm going to pass out!'

Ape-man didn't falter, and went out of sight into the house.

George sat cocooned in misery and trying to figure out exactly what it was Ape-man had done to him. He hadn't felt the weight of any blow, merely a numbness which seemed to be still growing across his lumbar region.

The bilious feeling resolved itself into nothing more

alarming than a long and sustained belch. George was grateful he hadn't eaten before starting out on this lunatic enterprise. Sure now that he wasn't going to throw up, George tried flexing his back muscles before trying to straighten up. The pain was like that special punishment reserved for tennis players – but this was the devil's own version.

'Mr Schapner?'

The sweetly modulated voice with a hint of Britishness about it startled him. George looked up and saw Velma. He blinked as his head went into a series of loops. Everything about the girl was Velma – except the voice, which was better. Finally, he figured out who this girl had to be – after all, Velma had never called him Mr Schapner.

George reminded himself that he was seeing her in the dim light of the parking lot – maybe in full light the resemblance wouldn't be so convincing. She was certainly good enough to fool Ronnie!

'Madame Gregory suggested you might need this.'

'This', George saw, was something in a brandy glass. He took it and sniffed. It was genuine Courvoisier! George felt better, he downed it in one. His eyes snapped back into focus but the girl still looked like Velma.

'What's your name?' he asked the girl.

'Velma Torraine.'

'I mean your *real* name.'

The girl smiled a superior smile and was obviously not going to answer. George turned her towards the light coming from the house, and still couldn't fault her. She shrugged with that same fluttery sideways gesture of the hand. The flinty eyes were as green as the real Velma's – it was probable, though, that she was a few years older than Velma's nineteen.

Still, this was 'Velma'. The magic-time screen image Velma. The one that the public knew and would expect to see. There was another Velma that, thank God, neither the public nor this girl knew anything about.

'Does Madame Gregory know you're out here?'

'I wouldn't be here if she hadn't sent me.'

George felt strong enough to try standing. The girl put out a steadying hand until he got the hang of it again. He handed the glass back to her. 'Tell Madame Gregory thanks for the drink, and it's been a pleasure.'

George pointed himself in the approximate direction of his Stutz but had barely taken a step when the girl called out.

'Aren't you taking me with you?' she asked.

George turned back. 'That *was* the idea,' he said cautiously.

'Well then?' asked this Velma.

George wondered if the effect of Ape-man's handling had addled his brain. 'I just got thrown out of there making that suggestion,' he protested.

Velma sidled coquettishly closer to him. 'That was because she was afraid someone had overheard you. She didn't want anyone else making the assumption that they could get the same privileges.'

'Dammit, that guy *hurt* me!' George protested.

Velma smiled her famous smile. 'I suppose it had to look right. You've got me for exactly one and a half hours.'

George found this Velma's smile a lot more disturbing than the other Velma's.

He was also aware that this Velma's proximity was causing something of a stirring in his loins.

The other Velma had rarely done that!

The girl was completely unembarrassed.

'Dammit!' he heard himself saying, 'you *are* Velma!'

'Why, Mr Schapner! I did introduce myself!'

George fumbled forward and took her hand into his.

'Call me George,' he said.

This Velma chuckled just like the other one did.

4

George smuggled his counterfeit Velma into one of the guest bedrooms without incident.

Cautioning her to stay put, he started downstairs to report his success to Velma. He didn't get far.

Coming from the drawing-room was the unmistakable stridency of Velma's Brooklynese.

The words themselves were numbing enough but delivered, as it seemed, on a desperately rising cadence, they struck a chill in George's heart.

> The great Seraphic Lords and Cherubims
> In close recess and secret conclave sat,
> A thousand demi-Gods on golden seats,
> Frequent and full. After a short silence then
> And summons read, the great consult began.

Whatever these words might have meant to the magazine writers, they were totally meaningless to George. With a sinking heart he looked cautiously into the drawing-room.

Velma, dramatically posed with one declamatory arm raised, was at the centre of a stunned audience.

In the silence George had time to see that Velma had imported a clique of friends and hangers-on to swell the numbers. That this ploy had failed was obvious from the stony faces silently staring at her.

One of the braver, or possibly more learned, realizing finally that the dramatic reading was at an end, leapt to his feet with resounding bravos. Taking their cue, the others of the imported clique quickly recovered and gathered around Velma, showering her with congratulations.

The magazine writers distinguished themselves by remaining seated, glancing nervously at each other and their escape route.

Manolo saved Velma from the ignominy of their quick exit by making an appearance with a tray of brimming glasses.

The magazine writers gratefully descended on him and drank as if they felt they'd earned it. George edged himself into Velma's line of vision. She caught the movement and, pushing aside her clique, hurried out to meet him in the hall.

George pointed upstairs. 'Everything's arranged, she's here.'

Velma started worriedly gnawing on a knuckle.

George glanced towards the drawing-room. 'How did it go?'

Velma turned away, shaking her head. 'I don't know, George. After all my planning – all my work . . .' She broke off as distress engulfed her limited vocabulary. 'The thought of that monster upstairs – can you imagine what it's been like for me? I just don't know how I've got *this* far!'

George was alarmed. '*This* far? You mean there's *more*?'

'Screeds of it!'

George knew a disaster when he saw it.

'Velma, do you think that's a good idea? I mean, it *sounds* very impressive, but what does it mean?'

Velma stared at him. 'Mean?' she asked indignantly. 'What do you mean "What does it mean?"? It doesn't "*mean*" anything! It's *poetry*!'

George nodded. 'Oh, yeah, I forgot.'

Velma suddenly darted from his side and, glancing in at her guests, returned to George to whisper urgently. 'The trouble is,' she confided, 'it doesn't rhyme!'

'What doesn't?'

'This *Paradise Lost* by John Milton. It's *supposed* to be poetry – that's the section it was under in the bookshop, but there *aren't* any rhymes.' She drew George closer. 'What's worse, I think they *noticed*!' Velma gave another anguished glance towards her guests. 'They got quite restless at one point, I could sense it!'

George knew he was expected to say a few words of comfort. 'Well, anyway, it was good experience for you.'

Velma fixed her huge emerald eyes on him. 'Do you really think so?'

'Sure of it,' then, mindful of the time-limit imposed by Madame Gregory, he brought her back to the subject of her lookalike lurking above stairs.

Velma's upper teeth started worrying her lower lip and tearing off strands of her lip colour. 'Does she really look like me?' she asked.

George moderated his first impulsive thought of 'Better' into, 'Moderately. Superficially.'

'Where is she?'

'In the guest-room at the end – the one decorated all over pink.'

Velma seemed to be consumed with worrying thoughts. 'I don't know what to do, George. You tell me! What should I do?'

George shrugged. 'Listen, she's here. The way I see it, it's either her or you!'

That seemed to settle Velma's mind. 'The only thing is I don't want her – them . . . in my bed, so take him to her . . .' Velma broke off as if some impish thought entered her mind. 'No, better yet, move them both! Put her in the mirror room and take Ronnie to her there.'

George sensed there had been a sudden change of mood in Velma. It usually meant trouble. 'Any particular reason?' he asked.

'I'll explain later. Keep things going for fifteen minutes or so, and then I'll join you.'

George had started to move away before her meaning caught up with him. He turned back. 'What do you mean "join me", where do you suppose I'm going to be – in there with them?'

'Just do it! Get them both into the mirror room, and you wait in my room. Now do you understand?'

George threw up his hands. 'I hear what you're saying, but I'm damned if I . . .'

He broke off. Velma was already feathering her way back into the drawing-room.

'Listen, everybody,' she called out. 'Settle down and I'll give you my rendition of Book Two.'

George raced up the stairs two at a time, but not fast enough to escape Velma's opening lines.

> 'High on a throne of royal state, which far
> Outshone the wealth of Ormus and of Ind . . .'

'She's right!' thought George as he raced back into the pink room. 'It doesn't rhyme!'

What did rhyme was the other Velma. She was glowing in a roseate nudity which made the pink room the pinkest George could ever remember.

Confidently, conscious of the effect, she lay with one hand behind her head and one knee discreetly raised to offer the merest suggestion of concealment to an otherwise total display. Her smile faded the moment she registered George's presence.

'Where is he?' she asked peremptorily and, breaking the mood, reached for a whiff of négligé.

George's throat needed clearing before he could respond. 'Any minute now.'

'Velma' stood, drawing the non-garment about herself. 'I don't give freebies,' she said.

'I wasn't asking,' said George.

'You looked as if you might be about to.'

She crossed to a dressing-table and after a quick glance flicked an errant wisp of hair back into place.

'Did I hear someone reciting Milton?' she asked.

'That was Velma,' he said.

The girl turned with a deliberate studied movement towards George. '*That* was Miss Torraine?' her voice sounded incredulous.

George wondered why he felt defensive. 'Sure, something wrong with it?'

The girl paused long enough to register her surprise then, with a shrug, turned back to the mirror and started looking for some elusive imperfection. 'I always thought,' she murmured, 'that Milton was a much more original politician than poet. In any case, his work is totally unsuited to Miss Torraine's talents.'

George had a suspicion that she was putting him down. 'You some kind of expert on Milton?'

She shook her head. 'He wasn't my subject, actually. I took Anglo-Saxon literature, but then reading Caedmon naturally led me on to read Milton.'

She was sitting there, as close to dammit stark naked, waiting to be put to whoring, and parading her education. George felt that had there been the slightest hint of superiority in her expression he might not have been able to answer for his actions.

Whether or not she had deliberately thought through this double provocation mattered less to George than the subdued sense of anger she aroused in him. He dredged deep for some way to put her down. He said it as scathingly as he could. 'Tell me something. When you suck cock, do you swallow or spit it out?'

'Do you know,' she said amiably, 'I've never really thought about it. I suppose I just do what comes naturally.'

Now she did look in the mirror. The wintry smile on her face was of short duration. 'Mr Schapner,' she said, standing. 'This evening is costing you two hundred dollars, now it's immaterial to me whether . . .'

George interrupted. 'Now wait a minute. *Two* hundred dollars? The only figure I heard mentioned was *one* hundred dollars.'

The girl seemed politely surprised. 'Then there has been a misunderstanding. I'm sorry, but I must be quite firm. *Two* hundred dollars.'

This girl had the disconcerting talent of rousing him to anger.

'That's outrageous,' he got out finally. 'It's damn near blackmail. For two hundred dollars I could get . . .'

George cast wildly about in his mind for what he might get that would serve his purpose and, coming up empty, lamely broke off.

'*Yes*, Mr Schapner . . . ?'

George could see there was no alternative but to accept her price. 'OK,' he said grudgingly. 'You are here now. It's a stick-up, and don't think that'll go *unnoticed*. You do it in the mirrored room.'

The girl shrugged. 'The venue is immaterial. I take it we are agreed on the price?'

George could bring himself to do no more than nod.

The girl put out her hand. 'Then I'll take the fee now.'

'Jesus, you don't think I carry that kind of cash money around with me do you?'

'Your cheque will suffice,' she said sweetly, and then added with meaning, 'No one bounces on Madame Gregory.'

George almost tore his pocket ripping out his cheque book. He scribbled it payable to Madame Gregory – a small victory but a pleasing one.

The girl took the cheque and wafted it back and forth to dry the ink. She glanced upwards at George as she blew gently on its surface.

George found this glance unsettlingly erotic, and doubly so since she obviously intended it to be.

'You are a bitch . . .' he murmured.

The girl smiled at him.

'One of these days . . .' he went on.

The girl smiled again.

'Any time, Mr Schapner – now that we've established my

price. Try to get me before midnight, though. It's then I'm at my best.'

'Whore,' he murmured.

'Quite,' she answered.

5

'Look at that smug bastard's face!' cried Velma.

Velma stood in the closet watching, by means of a two-way mirror, the incredible sporting activity in the room next door.

George had had no problem in getting Ronnie to change venues. He'd got only halfway through telling Ronnie of the revised location when Ronnie was up and charging like a stallion in heat.

The liberal doses of alcohol seemed to affect his forward charge only marginally. A discretional correction here, a navigational adjustment there, and the stallion had been addressed to the ready and willing mare before George had had time to close the door on them.

If Ronnie had suspected the girl wasn't Velma then he'd given no sign of it. Ecstatically lodged, he'd roared and bellowed and given every sign of unquestioning gratitude for what he'd got.

'I thought only French whores did *that*!' called Velma.

Velma seemed entranced by the spectacle taking place in the next room. It was obvious she liked to watch, and presumably had had the mirror installed for that purpose. To George the whole episode was tawdry. His part in the staging of the show had been a sour reminder of the days when he had played the pimp, convincing young girls that their best interests lay under whichever assistant director was currently giving him business. The only difference was that, this time, he was paying.

Stag movies had never held much interest for George. The

real thing, without the barrier of the participants' anonymity, even less.

'Don't you think we've seen enough?' he asked the rapt Velma.

'Not half enough and you've hardly seen anything. Get over here, George.'

George moved closer, but was careful to keep distance between himself and his over-heated client.

'This is an education!' Velma was saying. 'How long have they been at it?'

'I've no idea, Velma. I left my stopwatch at home.'

Involuntarily, he found himself watching.

He had to admit to a certain jealousy, but wouldn't have sworn which side of the distaff it lay. The girl in there was beautiful but she was but a facsimile of Velma. The original stood close and apparently willing for him to get closer. Why then did he have the suspicion that Ronnie had the better part? The girl was undoubtedly beautiful, but she'd gone public. She was out to hire to anyone with the going price. A whore. Beautiful, but a whore. Why did he feel cheated? Why did he have this feeling of lost opportunity?

Then again, what the hell was he doing here watching this circus performance?

He'd had something like a seizure less than four hours before.

It wasn't the world that was crazy, it was the people living in it.

'Listen, Velma, there's things I have to do, maybe I should . . .'

Velma cut him short. 'Shut up and get over here . . . Will you look at that . . . ? Listen, do you really think she looks like me?'

'In this light, with him in that condition . . . ?'

'You're right! Sober, he'd know!' Velma's confidence was immediately overtaken by doubt. 'Still, he never went this long with me!'

George felt a compulsion to comfort her. 'Maybe you were more exciting.' Velma chuckled some, down deep around her diaphragm. 'If that's what you think, get over here, you horny bastard. I still owe you five dollars' worth.'

Velma drew George's hand to her thinly veiled breasts, and moved back against him. Her hand reached behind her and found his embarrassment with God-given instinct. George was desperately trying to remind himself that Velma was a client and that he had a strict rule about clients.

'It's years since I felt like this.' Velma sounded excited.

George was having dangerous thoughts about rules being made to be broken. 'Play with me some, George.'

George brought his other hand into play on the front of Velma's body, and this brought them into even closer contact. Velma's head was laid back on his chest, while her eyes remained firmly on the gymnastics next door. 'This is uncanny,' she was saying, 'it's like watching myself get screwed.'

There was now little between the thought and the act. George felt himself lost. One of the world's most beautiful women was moving her body against his. There were limits that no man could withstand.

George heard his father's voice: '*Wenn der Steckel steht, der Kopf geht!*' and was startled when he realized he'd just whispered it into Velma's ear.

'What does that mean, George?' she asked throatily.

'It means a man can't think when he's got a hard-on.'

'That's the trouble with men. They think too much.'

Both Velma's hands now reached round to pull him in even closer and George, closing his eyes, gave himself up to the moment.

'Oh, Migod! That's disgusting!'

George felt Velma suddenly straighten and move away from him. He opened his eyes to look into the room and see what could possibly have aroused disgust in Velma.

What he saw was the geyser-like culmination of all of

Ronnie's efforts. Disengaged, the girl was at the very apogee of the eruption and working her mouth down very quickly to engulf its source. A feat, given Ronnie's dimensions, which ranked among the most spectacular George had seen since watching a snake swallow an egg.

Whatever Ronnie's satisfaction, George was alone and feeling slightly foolish. Velma seemed to have forgotten all about their recent over-heated body contact, which still marked George like a branding iron.

'When you think where it's been!' screeched Velma. 'Jesus! They're at it again!'

George looked back to see that Ronnie, unlike him, was far from detumescence and ready for another bout.

'He's got to be super-charged!' breathed Velma.

George sighed. 'Listen, if it's been this much fun, why in hell didn't you go in there yourself?' George was aware of a certain petulance in his voice.

Velma turned to look at him as if he were an intruding stranger.

'On your way out, ask Manolo to bring me up a drink, would you?'

George was surprised. 'In *here*?'

Velma's throaty chuckle removed any lingering doubts he might have had about Velma's relationship with the Valentino lookalike downstairs.

'And don't forget Galaxy tomorrow,' she cried as George started out. 'Give 'em hell!'

6

Giving Galaxy Studios 'hell' wasn't easy.

'We gotta problem with you,' said Wilbur Sterne as soon as George was seated in his office. 'You been playing footsie with us and we don't like it.'

'How come, Wilbur?' George tried to sound as if he were innocent of all, as yet undeclared, charges.

'Your piece of quiff, Velma – why won't she take this voice test?'

'First things first, Wilbur. First we got to talk contract.'

Wilbur got up out of his chair to make himself more emphatic.

'I'm not about to get stuck with a contract artiste who can't talk!'

Standing up, Wilbur was a lot less impressive than sitting down. His egg-shaped, seemingly shoulderless body stood no higher than five feet. With his habitually enormous cigar stuck in his mouth he looked like a snowman with a suit on. Not half so friendly though.

George tried to get out a scornful laugh, but found it difficult in the looming presence of Milton Bressler.

In the ordinary course of things Milton was far too unimportant to be brought into this kind of meeting. To see his tall, lean figure here so soon after last night's encounter at Madame Gregory's was worrying.

'You know Velma can talk,' said George to Wilbur's restlessly roving roly-poly figure.

Wilbur grunted. 'I know she can *talk* – question is does she talk "*microphone*". I hear a lot of funny stories going about. Over at MGM they're having trouble with John Gilbert's voice. Nice enough guy to talk to. Wouldn't have thought there was anything wrong with his voice but the microphone just don't like him. MGM could be having to let him go. Now, when I hear the big boys doing that with one of their biggest stars I gotta consider Galaxy's position in relation to your piece of quiff.'

George felt himself getting angry, which was the last thing he wanted to do. 'You know, as well as I, that this "problem" with Gilbert is a personal thing between him and Mayer.'

Wilbur shook his head. 'That's not what I heard,' he said solemnly. 'I hear it's his voice.' Wilbur made an impatient gesture. 'Anyway, let's leave MGM their problems. Our situation is that we got nothing to talk about until, and unless, we get a voice test on Velma.'

George had the distinct feeling that Wilbur's hardened intransigence had something to do with Milton Bressler. A few days before they had skirted this issue and then it had seemed there was negotiating room. Now Wilbur's mind seemed made up. Was it bluff? They couldn't know about last night and, even if they did, it wasn't obvious what bearing that might have on Velma's box-office rating.

'Well, Wilbur, I have to tell you that Velma's been working very hard. Only last night she gave a reading to *Photoplay* magazine. They're doing a whole feature on her terrific diction and clarity.'

Wilbur glanced momentarily at Milton before looking back to George.

'Did they record this reading?' asked Wilbur.

'No, but . . .'

Wilbur pounced. 'Then it don't mean a thing! We got a guy used to train radio operators for the Cunard Company and he says what people sound like in real life is no guide to how they will sound to a microphone.'

George managed a laugh. 'Wilbur!' he cried, 'Cunard is a shipping company!'

Wilbur nodded. 'So?'

'Well, what in hell does a shipping company know about making movies?'

'What does any of us know about making *talking* pictures?' countered Wilbur. 'This guy cost us a lot of money. We gonna ignore what he says?'

George felt himself being backed into a corner. If he continued this blocking move to get Velma signed *before* the voice test, he would be revealing his own doubts about her ability to pass the test. This sound business was hanging over the industry like a storm-laden cloud. Nobody understood it or knew by what magic it was to be achieved, still less were they secure about its long-term appeal. There were many authoritative voices raised against it, a lot of humour being made at the expense of the established stars. The truth was that a lot of people, including George's one horse, Velma, were going to go under in the name of a craze that might last six months. George was grasping at straws.

'I'll tell you truthfully what's in my mind, Wilbur. I think that Velma has got enormous potential in this new talkie business. Now what happens if Velma turns out to be sensational for sound? Her value increases. Maybe I'll have to listen to other offers before signing with you.'

Wilbur nodded. 'What you're saying is that you're trying to do me a favour, right?'

George shrugged. 'You could say that.'

'Well, don't do me no favours!' said Wilbur. 'Do me a voice test with your Velma.'

Milton Bressler chipped in for the first time. 'I believe that Galaxy would be justified, in view of the amount of time and effort spent in developing Miss Torraine, to have a first option agreement depending on the outcome of the test.'

'Yeah!' said Wilbur. 'We want first option.'

George smiled. 'Then you want a contract?'

Wilbur's palm came slap down on his desk top. 'Options ain't contracts!' he said.

'In my book, they are,' said George.

'Then you been reading bad books. How's it going to look to any other studio if we don't pick up on Velma's contract? You think there's going to be a rush to pick up our leftovers?'

'I'll tell you how it'll look,' said George. 'It'll look like you've gone nuts! Velma's the sexiest money-making star in pictures today. You're lucky to have had her for four years. The way you're treating her now I wouldn't be surprised if she refused to sign with you notwithstanding any amount you offered.'

Wilbur flushed with anger and glared directly at George

for fully thirty seconds before his clenched face muscles relaxed and he studiously set about lighting up a second cigar.

'How did it go up at Madame Gregory's last night?' he asked between puffs.

George flashed a murderous look at Milton Bressler before answering. 'I was visiting a sick friend.'

Wilbur roared with laughter. 'Yeah! Like she was healthy when you got there and sick when you left, right?'

Wilbur lay back in his chair and gave a startling shout of laughter at the ceiling. George noticed that the normally sycophantic Milton didn't feel obliged to share his boss's mirth. Milton was suddenly in favour around Wilbur and George wondered why.

Wilbur came out of his self-induced paroxysm and was suddenly deadly serious. 'Show him the pictures,' he said to Milton. Milton reached into a documents case and withdrew a large buff envelope which he spun across the desk towards George.

George tipped the weighty envelope and out slid a dozen or so ten by eight glossy prints.

Any outsider not familiar with Madame Gregory's speciality would have immediately concluded that the photographs showed Velma Torraine in the company of two Latin-looking men, indulging in some pretty explicit sexual antics. George's shock was total. His laugh sounded hollow even to himself as he flipped from one picture to the next.

'That isn't Velma and you know it,' he said as he put the pictures back into the envelope with as much casual disdain as he could muster.

'Prove it,' said Wilbur.

George gambled hard. 'I can produce the girl in the pictures. I can get her affidavit, and I'll sue anyone that suggests that Velma Torraine would allow herself to be photographed like this.'

'Sure you can produce a girl that looks like Velma, and we

both know where you'll find her, but suppose, just *suppose*, these pictures got into circulation, say, in the Mid-West. Velma would be mutton by the time you got around to issuing affidavits and denials.'

George looked at Milton. 'This is a pretty shitty play, Milton.'

Milton looked suitably affronted to be so directly accused. Wilbur, to George's surprise, defended Milton vigorously. 'What "play"? We came by these pics legitimately, and OK, I'll agree that they probably ain't Velma, but we got to consider the possibility that we got ourselves an artiste who's some kind of pervert!'

George stood up. 'The only perversion in this room is in the mind of the man who dreamed up this blackmailing stunt.' He started towards the door.

'Where are you going?' called Wilbur.

George turned back. He was too angry even to give a thought to his percentage on Velma. 'I'm going,' he said with deliberate emphasis, 'to find a parking lot attendant that looks like *you*, and then I'm going to try and find a floozie so down on her luck that she'd fuck a face like that. Then I'm going to have some pictures taken!'

Wilbur was on his feet behind his desk. 'You're talking like a man with ambitions to be dead!' he spluttered.

George hoped his laugh sounded sufficiently scornful. 'If that's the kind of dialogue you are going to be using, my client is well out of it!'

The angry veins in Wilbur's forehead stood out like lines on a road map. 'You get that piece of quiff on our sound stage Tuesday or I'll destroy her – you too!'

George found himself staring fixedly at Wilbur. His mind was racing – desperately trying to dredge up a line that would get him out of the room with a semblance of dignity. Nothing came, and the silence, lasting a few seconds, seemed loaded with menace.

'Call me sometime, Wilbur,' he managed with a heavy voice. 'We'll have lunch! *Maybe!*'

George turned blindly for the door, and managed to get through it before the heavy ashtray on Wilbur's desk became a missile.

By the time George got to his car his body was a tight knot of tension-locked muscles. He sat there for fully ten minutes fighting to get control of his breathing. Maybe it was time to get out of this business. This town was getting too crowded. The Hollywood he'd first known was crowding in and there were buildings going up as high as four floors. 'Too many people in too little space,' was the way Al Klein put it to him.

Al Klein, it was generally agreed, was crazy. He was buying up thousands of acres of the north San Fernando valley. Some of the early lots he'd bought at a nickel an acre, but prices were now rising – sometimes as high as ten dollars. Crazy Al was getting ready for a housing boom he was sure was coming. He'd wanted George to put in some money, but George had reservations.

'There's no water out there, Al.'

'We'll pipe it in.'

'There's no transport, no roads, no way for people to get to work.'

'The trolleys have already extended to Burbank! We'll get them to put in lines all along the valley!'

Al Klein had defended his pipe-dream with one wild response after another.

Maybe this business was nuts, but at least it was real, established and making money. Crazy Al was expecting to house people where range cattle dropped dead from heat exhaustion.

George started feeling better. He even raised a smile at Al's expense. It was strange how somebody else's misfortune could make your own seem less tragic. That and the remembrance of the 25,000 dollars he had socked away in RCA stock.

George started the Stutz and pointed it west, along Sunset. Galaxy had him boxed in, there was no escaping that. What Wilbur had said about no other studio picking up on Velma was true. Even the majors would respect the no-poaching agreement with a penny-ante outfit like Galaxy. It was how they kept their own contract talent in line. In this business you needed every friend you could get.

George was surprised to notice that in his headlong flight from Wilbur's office he had snatched up the envelope containing the dirty pictures of the Velma lookalike.

He was certain he knew who had posed for them. All her high-falutin talk about poetry and education and she lent her body to pictures like those!

George pulled the Stutz awkwardly through the narrow gate that led into the courtyard of his shared office building. The building was built on two floors in the manner of a Spanish hacienda. George's office was on the upper floor, reached by an exterior stairway.

Four years ago, when George had moved in, the building had been new but already it was showing signs of ageing. It had been clap-built and the landlord didn't bother with maintenance. Still, it was affordable and central.

George was greeted by the Gimp. Nobody knew where he came from. One day two years previously he had just turned up in the courtyard with a bucket and wash leathers and set to, unasked, washing everybody's cars. He hadn't negotiated a price but had just hung around until going-home time and looked expectant. Most people didn't mind that first day. They tossed him 25 cents and wished him well. George witnessed one of the pikers who had just driven off without even a thank you. Feeling he had to make up for it, George had tipped the guy a dollar. Two years later and the Gimp was a fixture – and George was still stuck with a dollar.

'You got my beauty all dusted up and everything!' grinned the rheumy-eyed old guy.

'I may be going out again later,' George pleaded.

'I work fast, Mr Schapner!'

George smiled and nodded. 'OK,' he said.

The Gimp grinned with delight.

George had once booked the Gimp on a movie as an extra, but it didn't take. The Gimp was back in the yard before lunch. 'Them movie people are crazy!' was the only explanation he had offered for his brief career.

George found himself lingering out here in the yard. He needed to talk with someone. Not the Gimp; he lived in a humming world of his own. The tunes he hummed could drive a man crazy. Nobody could trace any kind of melody in them. It was just work-buzz noise, like a saw makes cutting through timber.

'You got a family?' George asked.

The Gimp stopped working as if he'd been struck. He didn't turn but just mumbled in a sad voice, 'Two boys and a girl.'

George felt that he'd intruded. 'Wish 'em luck from me,' he said and started up the exterior stairs.

He was cheered with the thought of being able to talk his troubles through with his secretary, Julia. Now that Gillian had gone to Stanley she was all he had.

Julia wasn't alone. Rising from the couch he kept for visitors was a rangy young man in a striped blazer holding his straw hat like a supplicant.

'Mr Schapner?' asked the young man.

'The books are closed,' George told him, moving swiftly through to his own office. Julia followed him in.

'George, he's been waiting hours!' she protested.

'Who is he?'

'He's Mike Traviss. He came by yesterday looking for a job ...' George started to raise a hand in protest but Julia talked right through. 'I do need help!'

'For what?'

'Filing, keeping track of things. Do you realize we are trying to work an operation here with nearly three hundred people on the books and one star!' Her tone held an element of reproof for the time he spent on Velma.

'That "star",' George reminded her, 'pays for everything else around here.'

'Good!' snapped Julia. 'Let's clear everyone else off the books and turn ourselves into a one-artiste management!'

George felt defeated. 'Not now, Julia. I got problems.'

Julia immediately dropped her defensive anger and sounded softer. 'Galaxy give you a hard time?'

George nodded. 'I think I just screwed our one client!'

'This sound business?' she asked.

George nodded. 'It's got Wilbur jumpier than a rat in a trap.' He looked up into her sympathetic face. 'Me too.'

Julia sat herself down across the desk from him. She tried to be comforting. 'It's just that it's all so new. They're having to re-write the book and nobody knows how it's going to end. Maybe given time, they'll settle down.'

George sat unresponsive.

'Look, George, there's nothing *wrong* with Velma's voice. It's New York, sure, but there's lots of people speak like that!'

George shook his head. 'They got a new language called "standard". They want English-English. It's like words are going to be holy or something. Good tits and a tight ass are not good enough any more. Suddenly actors have to sound educated. You know what the gateman told me? He told me Mary Pickford had taken a test and it was so bad they destroyed the negative and broke up the recordings!'

Julia leapt in. 'That shows how crazy they are! Pickford must have earned them 20 million dollars!'

They sat silently for a moment before Julia spoke. 'You want me to get rid of the kid out there?'

George shrugged. 'Listen, if you need help, take him on. You better warn him it could be the shortest career he's ever heard of, though!'

'That bad?' asked Julia. 'Look, you still got the extra business.'

George shook his head. 'No. If Velma's washed up I'll probably go back east.'

George was looking down at his desk top as he spoke, and became aware that Julia hadn't moved. Curious, he looked up to see her staring at him.

'I hope it doesn't come to that,' she said. 'I'd miss you.'

Julia turned and started out the door. George was startled by what he had seen in her face. Julia had been working in his office for over two years now. She practically ran the extra business herself. George felt that just a moment ago was the first time he'd ever really seen her. Smiling, feeling better, he picked up the phone that connected him with Julia. 'Get me Miss Torraine, would you?' He settled back in his sprung chair and the fleeting feeling of well-being drained out of him at the prospect of talking with Velma.

It was like having to tell the corpse it was dead.

Velma came on the line screaming. 'It's a disaster!'

'Ronnie still there?'

'Worse! He's come back! With flowers and candies! George, you've got to do something! He says he's in love with me all over again! You know why? Because of what that filthy tramp did with him last night!'

George's sigh was loud enough to carry down the line. 'It's hard to see what else I can do, Velma!'

'Well, you'd better think of something! This was all your idea in the first place! George, can you believe that he thinks it was me did all those disgusting things with him?'

George felt a momentary panic. 'You didn't tell him different, did you?'

Velma's voice screeched down the line. 'I don't take second billing to nobody!'

George couldn't contain the laugh that came out loud, but Velma wasn't amused. 'George! This isn't funny!'

George fought to keep the amusement out of his voice. 'She's a hard act to follow, that's for sure!'

'I have no intention,' Velma quivered, 'of following that particular act!'

George could hear her drawing breath for another tirade and sought to forestall it by getting in ahead of her. 'Galaxy insist you take the sound test next Tuesday.'

It had the desired effect. Velma fell silent for nearly half a minute, then: 'Tell them "No"!'

'I already have. They'll only listen to "Yes". It's either Tuesday for the test, or no contract.'

'Stall them.'

'They'll not be stalled, Velma. We're down to the wire. We got to go Tuesday or forget it.'

Velma was quiet for a record-breaking thirty seconds. When she did come back her voice was a whisper. 'What do you mean?'

'I mean that they are signing no contract, not even talking about one, until and unless you take the test. If they don't, you know as well as I, it isn't going to be easy anywhere else.' He let her absorb this for a moment before hitting her with the real frightener. 'Maybe this is the time you should go freelance.'

It scared her all right. 'You know I can't do that! I got commitments. The house, the car, the staff.'

'Consider cutting down, or take the test. Listen, Velma, we mustn't assume that you'll get a turn-down. A "no" we've got, let's try for a "yes".'

'I don't know.'

'What don't you know?'

'Which scares me more. The voice test or going freelance.'

George was debating how else to influence her decision when she side-stepped him with an emotional outburst. 'George! I'm in no condition to be making these kind of decisions! I've got a sex-maniac hammering on my door, trying to burst in and repeat dirty things I didn't do in the first place! I feel soiled!'

George's mind was elsewhere for a moment. 'What about some more coaching?'

Velma sounded thunder-struck. 'For sex?'

George wondered how often she thought about anything else. 'I'm talking about a voice coach!'

Velma wailed. 'George! I need you here with me. *Now!*'

George knew he couldn't face it. The day had started badly enough and it could only get worse at Velma's house. 'You know I can't leave the office! I got crucial calls coming through all the time!'

Velma wasn't impressed. 'Well! Lah-de-dah!' she crooned, and hung up.

Having Velma hang up on him was a routine part of their relationship and bothered him not at all. He wished he could as easily escape the liquid uneasiness that was occupying his stomach. He had a feeling that he could handle it if only he could pin down his problems to one particular worry. Every time he went over it the problem splintered into tiny fragments that couldn't be caught and held.

Julia startled him by bursting into the office. In her hand, brandished like a weapon, was the envelope from Galaxy.

'How long have Galaxy been making pictures like this?' she demanded.

George took the envelope from her. 'You should know better. They haven't and neither has Velma!'

'They're disgusting!' Julia seemed determined to pursue the subject.

'They're also fakes,' he told her.

Julia seemed partially reassured. 'Mike picked them up,' she said. 'I was embarrassed.'

'You'd better make clear to him what these are. Somebody's trying to put the arm on Velma. That's all there is about it, OK?'

George, determined now to follow up the photographs, was reaching for the phone.

Julia seemed affronted. 'You want me to get a number for you?' she asked.

George shook his head. He didn't want Julia calling up Madame Gregory. 'I'll handle it,' he told her.

Julia remained for a moment longer than necessary to emphasize her displeasure. 'It's OK,' he told her, 'I'll get this one myself.'

Julia finally went out, allowing the door to close with unusual force.

To George's surprise Madame Gregory came on the line directly.

'You're just the man I want to talk to! You owe me an explanation!'

'About what?'

'When I let Ailleen out last night it was against my better judgement!'

George interrupted. 'Ailleen! Is that her name?'

'You mean you didn't ask?'

George sighed. 'I did, but every time I did she said her name was Velma Torraine.'

Madame Gregory's chuckle was from somewhere down deep and came out dirty. It didn't last long. She suddenly snapped, 'What about this emerald?'

George was stunned. 'What emerald?'

'Ailleen came back last night with a thousand-dollar emerald in her tote. Now she says she's going to use it to stake herself to a new start!'

George's mind was racing. This girl was turning into a real peach. First the photographs, now she was raiding Velma's jewellery case.

'Where is she now?' he asked.

'Here. Where else?'

'Keep her there. I've got some checking to do.'

'She'll be here, never fear! My mistake was letting her out

in the first place!' Madame Gregory paused a moment. 'She didn't steal it, did she?'

'I don't know,' said George with truth. 'I'll have to check it out.'

Madame Gregory sounded concerned. 'I don't want any kind of trouble. You'd better come right over here and we'll sort this out.'

George promised and, disconnecting, immediately placed a call to Velma.

'On your way over?' she asked with a tinge of sarcasm.

'Later, maybe. Right now I want you to check your jewellery case. It's possible you're missing an emerald.'

Velma's reaction was to screech. 'What's all this about emeralds? Ronnie was spitting mad this morning because I didn't have his emerald on. The dumb bastard never gave me no emerald!'

It didn't take a genius to work out what must have happened. Ronnie, for all his drunken lechery, had come to Velma armed with a romantic gift. He must have handed it to Ailleen.

'I'll explain it all later,' he told her. 'There's nothing to worry about.'

Velma screeched again. 'Nothing to worry about? I'm here, barricaded in my bedroom, with a sex-crazed lunatic trying to break in and rape me, and my cockermamy manager tells me there's nothing to worry about!'

'I was talking about the jewellery!'

'And I'm talking about Ronnie! Get yourself over here, George. He's like a mad dog!'

George sighed. 'Velma, Ronnie is not a mad dog, and you are *not* to shoot him!'

He disconnected himself from Velma's social problems and, snatching up the offending envelope, made a run for the door.

Julia tried to block him with a pile of calls.

'Later!' he yelled at her.

51

Julia pursued him out on to the balcony. 'What'll I tell people? Where will you be?'

Breaking into the street, he called back, 'Out of my mind!'

7

Madame Gregory opened the door holding the emerald ring in her hand. 'Let's have no trouble,' she said by way of greeting.

George stepped into the hallway and looked closer at the ring. It looked worth every cent of a thousand dollars. It had occurred to him, on the way over, to wonder where Ronnie had got the money to buy a stone like this. It had also occurred to him that it could be a fake. He asked Madame Gregory.

She laughed at the question. 'I've not seen many of this quality,' she assured him.

'Where is she?'

'Upstairs. I'll take you.'

Following Madame Gregory upstairs George noticed the subtly different decor between the upper and lower floors.

Downstairs was formal with just a garish splash here and there lest anyone forget where they were but, in general, nothing to bring a blush to a maidenly cheek. Upstairs was different. Everything pointed in the direction of voluptuous promise. The canvases on the walls were flagrantly sexual in theme, some blatantly pornographic. The few pieces of statuary had been painted with pink nipples and added hair. Anatomically more accurate but probably not what the sculptor had in mind.

Madame Gregory led George into a large room which justified all the promise of the hallway, with added extras such as a mirror-canopied bed.

A sleekly-built dark-haired girl rose from a chair as they entered. Of the Velma lookalike there was no sign.

'It's mine!' said the girl. 'He gave it to me!'

George found himself fighting confusion. The girl had been totally unrecognizable until she spoke. She didn't look even remotely like Velma. What kind of alchemy was this?

'This is the girl?' he asked of Madame Gregory.

Madame Gregory was amused. 'You mean you don't recognize her? Well, that's understandable. She hasn't got her "face" on.'

George turned back to look again at the resentful Ailleen. With study he could see that she held a general resemblance in the shape of her face along with the set and colour of her eyes, but nothing even beginning to approach the stunning effect she had startled him with the night before.

Ailleen was defiant. 'I earned it!'

'What you earned,' George told her, 'was two hundred dollars, paid in advance.'

Ailleen may have continued in her spirited defiance but Madame Gregory stepped in to cut her off. 'This kind of thing is my reason for not letting my girls out in their "faces". It leads to trouble.'

Madame Gregory had advanced with some menace towards Ailleen as she spoke, now she turned back to George. 'However, you may rest assured that she will never again dream of doing such a thing.'

'I didn't "do" anything,' insisted Ailleen.

George found himself wondering why the ring would be so important to the girl. It was obvious that another thousand dollars never hurt anybody, but she was a top girl in the reputedly most expensive 'house' in the country. She should have been earning something between two to four hundred dollars a week, expenses paid, and well able to affort an emerald or two.

Pondering Ailleen's potential earnings reminded him of his other reason for coming.

He tossed the buff envelope to Ailleen. 'How much did they pay you for those?'

Ailleen looked puzzled as she pulled the pictures from the envelope. She took one look and shook her head. 'I've never done anything like those.'

Madame Gregory had been quick to take the photographs. She studied them more carefully than Ailleen had.

Madame Gregory looked up finally. 'Rowena,' she said.

George found himself wondering how simple it was to make a facsimile of Velma. Maybe there wasn't a 'real' Velma, just a parcel of cosmetics and hair.

Madame Gregory had meanwhile taken the photographs to the window for a better light. 'Definitely Rowena,' she pronounced. 'She was with me until a few months ago. If you look you can see by the nose.'

George joined Madame Gregory in the window, and looked as she pointed.

George saw immediately that she was right. The girl in the pictures had a perfectly straight nose, while Velma and, incredibly, Ailleen shared a slight bump to one side. It added camera interest to what would otherwise have been a somewhat blank beauty.

'What's your interest in her?' Madame Gregory was asking.

George decided to be straight. 'Someone's using these to put the arm on Velma. I have to find this girl and get a sworn statement that she posed for these pictures and not Velma.'

Madame Gregory was amused. 'What good will that do? In the first place the chances of finding her are zero. I had to let her go because she was drinking and drugging and totally unreliable. As a witness you'd do better with Genghis Khan.'

George knew that what Madame Gregory was saying was true but only if it came to court. What he needed was a statement that would frighten off Wilbur and Milton from trying to exploit the situation.

'Ailleen will sign,' said Madame Gregory.

George caught the quickly controlled look of protest that

rose in the girl's eyes. Ailleen obviously thought better of it, and said nothing.

'The real model would be better,' George said. 'Is there any chance you could find her?'

Madame Gregory sighed to indicate her displeasure at this additional chore. 'I can try. As I said before, the less trouble I get, the better I like it.'

Taking the photographs, she started towards the door. There she turned and spoke directly to Ailleen. 'I consider that you owe this gentleman an apology,' she said, and then, waiting only long enough to ensure that her message had been received, went out leaving a heavy silence behind her.

Ailleen glanced at George and then carefully, as if not wanting to look at him again, crossed to the bed. There she sat and placed one hand to either side of her as if their position had to be absolutely precise. Finally she looked up. 'You heard her,' she smiled. 'I have to make my "apologies". That's Madame G. for a freebie.'

George shook his head. 'That won't be necessary.'

Ailleen didn't seem overly disappointed. Instead she seemed concerned about something else. 'You have to make it right with Madame G. about the ring!'

'No,' said George. He tossed the ring in his hand. 'I think that matter is settled.'

Ailleen rose from the bed shaking her head. 'Oh no it isn't!' she said with force. 'I don't know if you have any idea how she punishes us girls, but that's what she means to do.'

'I didn't hear her mention any punishment.'

Ailleen smiled indulgently. 'Then you weren't listening.' She reached out and placed an inviting hand on his chest. 'Why not make it right for both of us?'

She was now very close to him but he found himself studying her face, and again wondering what kind of magic would transform her into Velma. Partially out of curiosity and particularly from a need to deflect a sudden urgency that she was provoking, he asked her, 'How do you do it?'

'Do what?'

'Look like Velma.'

Ailleen smiled. 'You want to see?'

George nodded.

Ailleen beckoned him to follow her. 'Come, follow me, and all will be revealed.'

Ailleen led him to a small adjoining room that was decked out like a miniaturized version of Velma's own room at the studio. George wondered where they got their information.

Ailleen was already seated before a light-bulb-encrusted mirror, and reaching for a hat box.

'Mostly, it's the hair.'

George had seen many wigs before, but this was something special. Gossamer light, even close to it looked real. Ailleen carefully lowered it over her own hair. The effect was remarkable. The whole shape of her face seemed to have changed. Suddenly it was possible to see Velma emerging.

'Then it's the make-up,' she said. 'I'll just do a quick job.'

George watched, amazed, as Ailleen's hand flew from one pot to another. A brush on the lips here, a streak on the eyelashes, a highlight there. She even added the fine white line down the centre of the nose which Velma had specifically developed to hide her bump.

It was obvious to George that none of this was accidental. Madame Gregory had good connections around the studio make-up departments.

'I had to see it to believe it,' said George as the final effect emerged.

Ailleen, pleased to show her skills, used Velma's famous hip swivel to walk across the room and back. Closing on George she dropped into the coy, sexually-provocative, tomboyish pose that was the focus of half a million adolescent dreams.

'Where'd you learn all that?'

'In the theatre.'

'You were an actress?'

Ailleen smiled Velma's smile. 'Don't tell me you hadn't noticed?'

George found himself more able to like this girl. She wasn't the girl in the photographs and he could understand her reluctance to surrender the ring.

'Would you like me to put on one of my Velma gowns?' she was asking.

George held up both hands to defend himself against further provocation. 'I'm convinced. It's really incredible.'

His next question was neatly anticipated. 'You're about to ask me how a nice girl like me got into a business like this.'

George was guiltily embarrassed and simply shrugged.

Ailleen smiled and sat herself before the mirror again.

'Sooner or later, everybody does,' she broke off with a tinkling laugh. 'Madame Gregory has given us the perfect reply. We turn the question back with: "What's a nice guy like you doing in a girl like me?"'

Ailleen enjoyed her own joke hugely, but George found himself not laughing. Ailleen was a very unusual girl to have got into this particular trade and, although he was old enough to have realized there isn't a regular 'anything', he was still intrigued enough to be curious about her.

Ailleen noticed he hadn't laughed. 'You don't think it's funny?'

'It's funny, but it isn't an answer.'

Ailleen registered disappointment and turned back to study her reflection. 'We aren't supposed to answer personal questions. Madame G. wants us to stay in character.'

She concentrated for a moment on scanning for flaws in her make-up. If there were any, they weren't apparent to George.

'I was really an actress, you know.'

'Where was that?'

'In England.'

It was George's turn to anticipate her next question. He let her ask it anyway.

'Do you think there's any chance for me in movies?'

George smiled. 'You're probably making more money here than you would in pictures.'

Ailleen picked up a brush and started teasing her wig. 'Madame Gregory keeps us short,' she said. 'It's a matter of practical policy. You know how much I shall get from that two hundred last night?'

George shook his head.

'Twenty-five, and even that's being withheld against "expenses".'

George didn't know much about the overheads in running an operation like Madame Gregory's, but he could see how it must run to a lot of money. What Ailleen was saying seemed a little harsh, but he wasn't about to get into a discussion which could alienate Madame Gregory. He needed Madame Gregory's co-operation and confidence more than he needed to take sides in a fight over money.

His silence seemed to provoke Ailleen into launching into her life history.

'My father didn't approve of my becoming an actress. He was rich in those days so had a hold over me. Suddenly he wasn't rich any more. Mother left him and he killed himself. Everyday story really.'

This last, well-rehearsed throw-away was obviously where the Johns were expected to gasp in sympathy and slip another twenty under the pillow. George wondered inwardly why he was keeping up this hard-nosed front. He was, after all, in Hollywood's top cat-house, he was with one of their top girls. He'd been invited to have one on the house but here he was playing the straw-hatted straight man.

Memories of his first meeting with Velma – the real one – kept reverberating through his mind.

'So you're an actress?' he salvaged from his thoughts.

Ailleen smiled and nodded. 'It's ironic, really. Everybody I went to see in London had this one idea of how the interview should end – me on my back like an upended turtle. I even grew the shell to go with the imagery. I played their game, and even started to enjoy it. Trouble is, it's addictive.'

'Sex?'

'Playtime sex. There came a time when I'd feel triumphant simply because I hadn't felt anything. Nowadays, either before, during or after, if someone starts getting romantic I find it hilariously funny. It never occurred to me that I was whoring.' She looked at him, more Ailleen than Velma. 'Don't you think it's ironic to start out as an actress playing the whore and end up a whore playing an actress?'

George didn't find himself qualified to answer. 'How did you meet up with Madame Gregory?'

'I won a lookalike contest on Venice Beach.'

'As Velma?'

'Funnily enough, as Clara Bow. It was Madame Gregory who saw the possibility of my "doing" Velma. She already had two Clara Bows.'

'And you like it?'

Ailleen struck a dramatic Velma pose. 'Dah-ling! I adore it!' then, reverting to her own voice, added with obvious seriousness, 'Actually, I do. I don't know why. It's the lack of guilt, I suppose. In this house there's no need to pretend. No one thinks it's unusual to go to bed with a stranger. That's what we're here for. It's all up-front. What it is, mainly, is honest.'

Quite suddenly she turned full square to him, spread her legs tight against her skirt and placed her hands on her head. The effect was electrifying, the more so since she looked so totally like Velma.

George was startled by the excitement that danced in her eyes.

'Go ahead!' she challenged. 'Tell me! Make me!'

George was relieved and grateful to hear Madame Gregory call out from the bedroom, 'I'm not interrupting anything, am I?'

The electricity flowing between them evaporated. Ailleen

relaxed into a more normal stance with almost guilty speed. George turned to Madame Gregory as she came circumspectly in.

'I had some luck,' she told George. 'Managed to contact a girl friend of hers. The last she heard of Rowena she was headed out of town with a man I know. He's a third-rate pimp. It's unlikely she'll be heard from again.'

'Dammit,' said George.

Madame Gregory was looking shrewdly from Ailleen, to George. 'I don't encourage personal relationships ordinarily but, I guess, today is different. You two made it up, yet?'

George nodded. 'You could say we've reached an understanding.'

Madame Gregory paced deliberately close to Ailleen, ensuring that every word reached its intended target. 'She tell you why she wanted to hold on to that ring?'

'You told me. To stake her to a new start.'

Madame's chuckle was a dispute. 'What she intended was to try to make it as an actress in the movies. Why don't you tell her she'd be wasting her time?'

George could have told her that simply enough, because, at root, that's what he believed, but something made him want to help Ailleen withstand Madame Gregory's pressure. 'I wouldn't do that,' he said instead, 'because it wouldn't be true. Matter of fact I was just about to suggest she came by my office where we could discuss just that possibility.'

'No chance!' said Madame Gregory emphatically. 'She has another five months to work out her contract with me.'

'Contract?' asked a startled George.

'You think I'm somebody's fool? Setting up these girls in their "faces" costs money, you know. You think I'm going to invest in them only to have the first love-struck producer take them out of here?'

George found the idea of Hollywood as a land of 'love-struck producers' amusing, and only marginally more so than the thought of someone trying to enforce a contract like that.

Madame Gregory saw his amused scepticism. 'My girls keep to their contracts.'

George could see that she wasn't a woman to concern herself overly with the legal niceties. 'I wish I could be that confident in my business.'

George caught a look of appeal in Ailleen's eyes that reminded him of the supposedly forthcoming 'punishment'. 'Listen,' he started as Madame Gregory eyed him steadily, 'I don't think we can really blame Ailleen for what happened. Ronnie did give her the ring – she didn't take it.'

Madame Gregory was unconvinced. 'My judgement on that incident is already made, and I'd like to remind you that I know best how to run my own business.'

George could do nothing more than agree with that. 'All I'm saying is, give her a break.'

Madame Gregory was scathing. 'I did that when I took her in a month ago!'

She was a tough one, and there seemed little point in pressing her.

George turned to find Ailleen's face made of stone.

He tried to soften her with a smile. 'Don't forget, when you've worked out your contract here, come and see me. We'll talk.'

Ailleen didn't even bother to acknowledge that she'd heard him. As he left the two women were facing off to each other like fighting cocks.

Going downstairs and through the hall George felt like some lower species of rat. If Ailleen didn't call 'bastard' to his fleeing back then he did it for her.

8

George got back to the office with the intention of sending Mike Traviss up the hill to return the emerald to Velma, but when he asked Julia where he was, he discovered that he was out trying his wings. 'Monogram sent out a call for a one-armed trick pool player. We don't have one listed so . . .'

'You sent him to find one?'

Julia shrugged. She had an almost-as-surprising message for George. 'Milton Bressler called. He wants to meet you.'

George was wary. Milton calling for a meeting should be good news, but George had an uneasy feeling that it might be in some way connected with Madame Gregory's.

'You mean just Milton? Me and Milton?'

Julia nodded. She'd been long enough in George's office to know what was bothering him.

Milton would not be likely to be making some play that Wilbur was unaware of – Milton didn't have the weight for it, unless . . . ? The trouble with living in a mythical place like Hollywood was that the natural order of things didn't apply. People could sky-rocket from obscurity to crushing power in the course of a day. That they could also go the other way was something nobody considered, just as normal communities don't dwell on death.

Maybe Milton had found the magic thread to fame and fortune, who could tell?

George wondered if the sometimes prescient Julia could enlighten him further.

'You any idea what it might be about?'

Julia shook her head long and slow.

George shrugged. 'Get him on the phone.'

Waiting for the connection, George had time to consider

that Milton's call, whatever else it might be, was an indication of Galaxy's continuing interest in Velma.

Wilbur wasn't likely to delegate Milton to tell him the deal was finally off. Besides which, he hadn't yet told them that the test on Tuesday was definitely off, even though he'd made up his own mind to it.

His reasons were simple. If Velma did take the test and the verdict went against her, he'd have no leeway to negotiate her anywhere else. The chances would move from slim to nothing overnight. If she didn't test, then it was possible he could find another producer on poverty row who'd be prepared to take a chance of getting promotion to a higher league, just as Galaxy had done.

George felt an obligation to give it an honest try on Velma's behalf. She was spent up to and beyond her salary. Even a six-month lay-off would spell financial disaster for her, and once the word was out that the skids were under, there would be no way he could bring her back from the edge.

Milton, when he got through, seemed to want to conduct his end of the conversation in monosyllabic grunts. George understood that he didn't want anyone his end of the line to know who he was talking to, but it didn't help the conversation any.

One thing was clear: Milton didn't want the meeting at Galaxy and wasn't about to come to George's office.

George found his interest in the meeting increasing. Milton's circumspection indicated that there was a game at hand. George found himself anxious to hear the ground rules and who would be playing. They managed to confirm that Milton would come to his house that night, but no time was set.

George hung up, and after a moment's thought called out for Julia.

'How would you like to play at being my girlfriend for one night?'

'Thought you'd never ask. Who're we fooling?'

'Milton Bressler.'

Julia nodded solemnly. 'I see what you mean!' and without further explanation or even agreement, she went out.

George went after her, feeling there was a lot she hadn't said, but ran straight into an excited Mike Traviss.

'Hey,' he almost crooned, 'you're not going to believe this. I found this pool player up at the pool hall, and you know what?'

George nodded. 'He had only one arm and could do ball tricks.'

Mike looked deflated. 'How did you know that?' he asked.

George shrugged. 'The woods is full of 'em. What else?'

'Well, I took him down to Monogram and they booked him. Three days starting tomorrow at six-thirty for make-up.'

'You fix a fee?'

Mike nodded eagerly. 'Twenty dollars a day plus lunch, and a cab ride since he's disabled.'

'And . . . ?'

Mike looked puzzled. 'And, what?'

'Where does the agency come in?'

Mike's expression again took a sleigh ride. 'Oh, gee . . . I forgot to . . . you know . . . Anyway, I'm sure it'll be OK. I mean, he'll know the score, right? I'll go down there and collect our percentage from him personally.'

George nodded indulgently. 'He'll know the score all right. If you haven't got him to acknowledge our agency then we ain't gonna collect.'

Mike looked to Julia as if for confirmation of what George was saying.

George wasn't finished with him yet. 'This one-armed pool player. Does he always travel by cab?'

Mike shrugged warily, looking for pitfalls and, finding nothing obvious, went on. 'Yeah. Well, I figured it best to get him right down there . . .' Suddenly Mike saw his error. 'Oh, I see what you mean!'

'You paid the cab, right?'

Mike nodded. 'Two-fifty. I had him wait to bring me back.'

'So we're out two dollars fifty and we don't collect. With your kind of business I could have gone broke years ago and saved myself a whole lot of problems.'

George remembered his intention of sending the boy up the hill with Velma's emerald, and decided against it. Mike was looking so downcast that George eased the hook a little. 'OK, kid, don't let it bother you. Get the two dollars fifty from the cash box and put it down to experience.'

Mike managed a smile. 'I'm real sorry, Mr Schapner. I'll make it my business to find the guy and put it right.'

George shook his head. 'Let it go. We all make mistakes.'

George was rewarded with a dazzling smile from Julia as he turned back into his own office. Worth two dollars fifty any day!

When Julia got to George's house that night she was toting a heavy valise.

'What's that for?' he asked her, pursuing her through to his bedroom.

'Things,' she answered enigmatically.

George suddenly feared she might have misunderstood his reasons for asking her over. 'Er – listen, the reason I asked you here was . . .' George trailed off as Julia turned to look at him with a steady, patient smile.

'I brought some things to spread around. You didn't tell me whether or not I was "live-in" so I brought some stuff to put in the closets.'

'You think Milton's going to check the closets?'

Julia shrugged. 'Fags notice these things,' she said.

George was surprised. 'Milton's a fag?'

Now Julia looked surprised. 'You mean you didn't know? I thought that's why you wanted me here – to make sure he didn't get any ideas about you.'

George turned out of the bathroom roaring with laughter.

Julia, looking hurt, followed him. 'Then why did you want me here?'

'To take some notes! You brought your notebook, didn't you?'

Julia sighed and looked almost disappointed. 'Oh,' she said, 'I should have known.' She started searching around looking for something to take notes with.

George found himself uncomfortably aware that he'd failed her in some way. For the first time since she'd applied for the job in his office, he noticed what an attractive girl she was. He wondered in that moment why she didn't have the same ambition to break into movies as everybody else he met.

Julia found a notebook on a side table. 'I'll use this.'

George nodded and poured himself a drink. Julia waited a moment and then went into a bedroom where, after some noises off, she called out, 'You haven't said whether I'm live-in or not.'

'Please yourself,' George called back.

George was enjoying some vintage Scotch when Julia emerged from the bedroom looking more ready for Madame Gregory's than an evening at home. She had loosened her hair and put on a flowing peignoir that promised much and concealed little.

George watched her as she walked about the room spraying perfume into the air from an atomizer.

George remembered his drink and hastily covered the glass with his hand. 'Why,' he asked, 'are you making my house smell like a Turkish brothel?'

Julia broke off and sniffed. 'Is that what Turkish brothels smell like?' she asked. 'I wouldn't know, since I've never been in one.' She went back into the bedroom and the door was firmly closed.

George sat, acutely aware of just how much sexual titillation he'd been subjected to lately, and just how little satisfaction.

Rising, he opened a window in the hope of dissipating a

little of the scented air Julia had left behind. Milton was late, he realized, and it might just give enough time for the air to clear.

He was sitting working his way through some New York trades when he remembered something. New York had all the trades, Hollywood none of their own. They had the *Filmograph* and the *Hollywood Spectator* but they, like the New York papers, were concerned mainly with the distributors. George was practically certain that the production side of the industry was big enough to support a weekly, or even a daily, devoted to their interests. He was about to call Julia in to take some notes, when he became aware of a curious scratching sound that came from somewhere near the kitchen.

Picking up a fire-iron, George went out to investigate, and was just in time to see a hand being hastily withdrawn from the kitchen screens.

Opening the back door cautiously, George found a guilty-looking Milton crouching beneath the kitchen window.

'We got a front door, Milton,' he told him.

Milton straightened up and brushed down his wrinkled suit. 'Don't you think I know that?' he asked.

George watched as Milton slid through the back door like a thief, and started out on an agitated tour of inspection.

George interrupted his progress before he got to the bedroom.

'What in hell's the matter with you, Milton?'

Milton turned towards him. 'We cannot be too careful,' he muttered, then, indicating the bedroom door, asked, 'Is there someone in there?'

'Sure there is, but I doubt that she's dressed!' George wondered why he had over-emphasized the 'she'.

Milton was pacing like a two-bit desk clerk anxious for his tip. It was an effort for George to remind himself how coolly he had disposed himself in Wilbur's office. Something was up, and Milton was holding cards.

'Like a drink?' he asked Milton.

Milton dismissed the suggestion with a gesture. 'I'll not beat about the bush, George,' he started then hesitated, as if trying to find the right words. 'It's like this . . .' Milton started pacing again. 'I want to produce Velma's next picture.'

Milton's words were music to George's ears. They meant, and Milton was in a position to know, that Galaxy were certainly intending to pick up on Velma and that there was going to be a 'next picture'.

George took time out to sip on his drink.

Milton smiled modestly. 'I'm big enough to know I'm not the world's greatest director,' he said, 'but as a producer . . . that's where my future lies.'

George nodded, inwardly unconvinced. 'What makes you think I could influence a decision like that?'

'If Velma asked for me, you could!'

George was feeling better by the minute. Not only was there going to be a next picture, but Milton had just indicated that Velma would be a powerful voice to be listened to.

George hesitated. Whatever he said or did now, he felt, was going to have a vital bearing on his own future.

Milton took his hesitation for doubt. 'Listen,' he said, coming so close that George could smell his perfume, 'Wilbur would probably assign me anyhow. I just want some assurance that there won't be any flak from Velma's end.'

George's look was deliberately non-committal. This was a whole new ball-game. Here was a company executive coming round asking favours from an agent. George had always felt that there was a higher status for agents; usually they were treated as damned intruders who had only one topic of conversation – money. George could feel a new and influential role beginning.

'Wilbur never assigned you a Velma picture before. What's changed?'

Milton smiled, as if armed with superior knowledge. 'Various reasons. I'm in really solid with Wilbur right now.

It's my chance to capitalize and I don't want anything going wrong.'

George was puzzled. Whatever it was Milton was supplying that Wilbur wanted, it certainly wasn't boys. There was no randier ram in all Hollywood than Wilbur.

George answered with played-out slowness. 'You put me in a difficult position, Milton.'

Milton looked alarmed. He was starting to worry in case coming to George had been a mistake. George let him worry a little longer and then went on. 'We haven't made any final decision on Velma's future yet. After that little show Wilbur staged in his office today, I've started wondering whether I should start listening to other offers.'

'You've had other offers?' asked Milton, and then, challengingly, 'Who from?'

George tried out his slow smile again. 'Obviously that's something I'm not going to tell you. Let's just say that some of them are pretty interesting. It's possible we might not sign with anyone, but just play the field picture to picture.'

Milton was shaking his head. 'Wilbur got a financial report on her,' he said. 'You know and we know she couldn't afford to.'

'Maybe she's got money you don't know about – an investor maybe?'

Milton was still shaking his head. 'Wilbur will destroy her if you try that. He's got the means to do it.'

'If you mean those dirty pictures, forget it. I've got the girl that modelled for them and she's agreed to swear out an affidavit.'

Milton chuckled just like Madame Gregory. 'What good will that do? People believe what they want to believe. All the affidavits in the world won't stop some of it sticking.'

'And Wilbur would be cutting his own throat. If the story was believed the theatre-owners would pull all of Velma's pictures. There's a lot of life in those pictures yet, and a lot of money.'

Milton laughed in his face. 'You really don't understand what's happening, do you, George? There aren't going to be any "old films". Talkies are going to wipe them out. It'll be like we never made a movie before. A whole clean sheet. The exchanges won't be taking a non-talkie even as a gift!'

George defended his own opinion. 'Six months from now it'll all be forgotten. Just like colour, just like Magna-Screen and all those other gimmicks people have come up with.'

Milton was still laughing. 'You're so wrong, George, it's pathetic! This business is going to have to grow up. We're going to need stories, we're going to need writers. Bringing in your favourite niece to write the titles isn't going to happen any more.'

It was hard for George to remain confident in the face of so much enthusiasm. Milton's positive assurance was beginning to scare him.

Milton, sensing George's shaken confidence, went on. 'Listen to me, George, we can help each other. This is a crucial phase for all of us. I can fix that sound test. It so happens that I can get a crew together that have had a lot of experience with Vitagraph. These guys tell me that they can make anyone compatible with the microphone.'

George was doubtful. 'That's directly contrary to everything I've heard.'

Milton was confident. 'There's a lot of horse shit being talked because there's a lot of people stand to make a lot of money if they can scare enough people. First they make the problem, then they get big bonuses for coming up with the "answer" to something that wasn't a problem in the first place. Listen, these guys are out to make what they can while it lasts. So am I. What I'm saying is that Velma can be made to sound right.'

George found himself warming to Milton. If what he was saying was true it might still be possible to dig a pot of gold from Velma. He looked at Milton with a thought. 'Does Wilbur know about these magicians from Vitagraph?'

Milton shook his head. 'I told you, I'm in it to make as much as I can, too. I'm only telling you so that you can see I'm on your side. I can get Velma through the test. I've already told you what I want out of it.'

George found himself on his feet and putting out his hand towards Milton, only Milton never saw it. George saw that Milton was staring slack-jawed past his left shoulder.

George turned and saw Julia framed in the doorway from the bedroom. The peignoir, if anything, was even looser now and left no doubt as to the quality of the goodies it so miserably failed to cover.

'Anybody want anything?' she asked.

Milton glanced nervously towards George as if for an explanation.

'I really have to run,' he murmured. He glanced again at Julia, and busied himself searching for his hat.

George found it and handed it to him.

'I hope my coming here wasn't a mistake,' he said to George in a confidential tone. 'I can get you Velma's contract, but I want that quid pro quo. Gentleman's agreement?'

George once again put out his hand and this time had it seized in Milton's own fleshily soft grasp.

Milton dazzled him with his dentistry and, with the briefest of acknowledgements to Julia, hurried out of the back door.

Julia sank into an overstuffed chair, allowing her legs to sprawl in a most unladylike way. 'I failed.'

George smiled. 'I didn't get molested, if that's what you mean!'

Julia gave him a furrowed brow scowl. 'I scared him off. I came in because I figured you needed an interruption to avoid making a commitment, but then you went and made it anyway.'

George felt suddenly secure and happy. 'You hear what he said about these sound guys?'

Julia nodded. 'I got it all down. You want me to read it back to you?'

George lay back and stretched expansively. 'Julia, it may well be that, in years to come, we shall look back on this night as the most important in our lives!'

Julia perked up with sudden interest. 'Really? Why?'

'Milton just told me a couple of things I didn't know. Firstly, that agents are getting to be more important around this town.'

Julia shrugged. 'I've seen that coming for a long time!'

'Yeah? Well, maybe somebody should have told me. The other thing is that Galaxy are getting anxious to get Velma signed up again.'

Julia seemed to be waiting for more. 'That's it?' she asked. 'That's what makes this the most important night of our lives?'

George took another look at Julia. It was obvious, clear across the room, that she hadn't a stitch under the peignoir. His first thought he sublimated. 'You want to eat?' he asked her.

Julia, looking at him intensely, nodded.

'What do you want to eat?' he asked her.

Julia took a long time building a smile and seemed to be giving the question deep thought.

'Well?' asked George.

Julia looked at him, and allowed her tongue to play across her teeth in a most disconcerting gesture.

'What I'd really like to eat,' she said, 'is you!'

9

The call came at three in the morning.

George, snuggled in tight against Julia's warm flesh, resisted the ringing bell. It needed a huge effort of will to break contact and reach for the phone.

A man, highly excited and speaking Spanish, dinned into

his car. George, still half-asleep, decided it had to be a wrong number and was about to hang up when, interposed in the stream of Spanish, he caught the name 'Velma'.

'Who is this?' George demanded.

'Is Manolo!' It took George a moment to register who Manolo was. Velma's live-in manservant. He of the tight pants and access to his mistress's bedroom.

George was instantly awake. That Manolo should call him at all was surprise enough. At three in the morning it meant a crisis.

'What's happened?'

'She is in hospital where I am speaking from!'

'Velma? What happened?'

'Mister Ronnie went berserk and attack her.' There was a heart-stopping pause before Manolo went on, 'I kill him!'

George's head was spinning. Had he heard right? Manolo had killed Ronnie Stillman? George was aware that Julia was awake and listening.

'What do you mean, "I kill him"? You mean you have killed him or you mean to kill him?'

'I mean,' said Manolo patiently, 'that I already did . . .' George's world once more stilled until Manolo went on, 'damn near, anyway!'

George felt they could go on floundering through Manolo's syntax all night. 'Now listen to me,' he said as firmly as he could, 'tell it to me straight. Is Ronnie Stillman alive, dead or dying or what?'

Manolo started in Spanish again until George brought him back to something he could understand. 'He's a fucking bastard, Mister George, he hurt Miss Velma pretty bad. He ought to be dead. Someone should kill him. Maybe me!'

George was shouting now. 'Will you calm down, Manolo! This is important. Velma is hurt, did I understand you right?'

Manolo agreed.

'Badly?'

'Pretty bad.'

This was getting nowhere. 'What I want to know is "pretty bad" and walking – or pretty bad and not walking?'

Manolo was under stress and finding it hard to concentrate. 'Her face, her beautiful face is all smashed up!' Manolo broke off and George was embarrassed to hear him sobbing.

George's blood was moving at such a rate that it seemed impossible to believe that only minutes before he'd been fast asleep. Now it seemed unlikely he was going to make it through the night.

'Now listen to me, Manolo. I understand you're upset, but listen! Are the police there?'

'No!'

'You're in a hospital. Which one?'

'It's more a clinic. My brother-in-law works there. It's called Santa Rosas.'

'In Hollywood?'

'No, downtown. Corner of Figueros and Flower.'

George was outraged. 'What in hell are you doing down there? We got hospitals closer than that!'

'Sure, you think I don't know? Maybe I should have called the cops too, maybe?'

'You should have called me!'

'OK. I wasn't thinking too good. Maybe on account of I was bleeding pretty bad too!'

'You? What happened to you?'

'I fight Mister Ronnie. He takes the knife out of him and stick it in me!'

George felt himself sway, and was relieved to realize it was only the movement of the bed as Julia got up and started dressing.

George realized that he would only understand what was happening if he went down to the clinic. He confirmed the address and then went on.

'Listen, stay where you are. Don't call anyone else. Don't let anybody else call either. Especially the newspapers, got it? Is there anyone there that has recognized Velma?'

Manolo was scathing. 'Mister George, *you* wouldn't recognize Velma!'

George hung up to find Julia already handing him his pants.

He felt it must have been providence that had engineered her to stay overnight. She was just as cool and efficient helping him to find his other shoe as she was in the office.

Taking his car-key she was behind the wheel with the motor running by the time he came out of the house pulling on a sweater.

The moment they stepped into the Clinica de los Santa Rosas, George could see that Manolo had done well. It was one of the many illicit clinics set up to deal with the pregnancies of girls who didn't have the money to cross the border. Doctors outside the control of the California Medical Board would slip into town for a few days, attend to their business, and be gone back to Mexico before the law even knew about them.

Some of these clinics were no better than ramshackle slums. This one was conducted on more professional lines, but even so, no one in their right mind would come here looking for a damaged movie star.

Manolo, heavily bandaged about the chest, met them in the lobby and led them up to Velma's room.

On seeing her George felt all the anger, and more, that Manolo had poured down the phone. Ronnie must have torn into her like a wild animal. Her nose was split. From her mouth to her nostrils was a wide bloody line. Her mouth was swollen, and it looked as if she might have lost some teeth.

Manolo had been right. Velma could have been Jane Doe at any casualty ward in town.

George was concerned to see that the lesion on her face was held together with nothing more than the surgical version of a paper clip.

He turned to the florid-faced man, presumed to be the doctor.

'Shouldn't this be stitched?' he asked.

The doctor looked uncomprehendingly at Manolo for a translation.

Manolo explained directly to George. 'I wouldn't let him. I think maybe somebody expert should do it.'

George nodded. Manolo, though wounded himself, seemed to have been thinking with remarkable clarity.

Julia spoke up. 'Who should we call?' she was asking. 'Syndal or Stevens?'

George gave it some thought. Either man could do the job; what he had to decide was which could he trust the most to keep his mouth shut.

'Try for Syndal first. If not him then Stevens. Don't mention any names. Just tell him it's for me and tell whichever one it is to bring down everything they are likely to need. We're not moving her.'

Julia nodded and went out.

George turned back and looked across at Manolo. 'You did good,' he told him, and then added, 'How do you feel?'

'I'm OK. Knife wounds is something they know about down this end of town.'

George gestured to Manolo to join him outside the room.

In the dimly lit hallway he turned to him. 'You want to tell me what happened up at the house?'

Manolo shifted uncomfortably. 'All of a sudden he comes crashing through the window!'

'Who? Which window?'

'Mister Ronnie. The bedroom window.'

'Velma's?'

Manolo nodded.

'And where were you?'

Manolo tried to avoid answering so George answered for him. 'You were there? In bed with Velma?'

Manolo suddenly lost his defensive stance and turned back, chin jutting with pride. 'Many times!'

George could easily visualize the scene: Ronnie, his libido

re-aroused and unassuaged, comes upon Velma rutting with Manolo. George could see how Ronnie would have gone in like a raging bull.

'What happened to Ronnie?'

'I told you. I stuck him with my knife.'

'No. I mean, where is he?'

Manolo gestured down the hall. 'Right here!'

'You brought him *here*?'

'Sure! Where else? I no damn fool. Anywhere else and they call the police, right? Velma is in the newspapers and I go to jail – deported even. You think I'm that kind of big fool?'

'Where's his room, show me.'

Manolo led George about four doors down and left with barely a contemptuous gesture of his thumb to indicate Ronnie's room.

It was identical to Velma's except in place of the attendant doctor a very overweight nurse was looming over Ronnie. George had chosen a bad time to come visiting.

Ronnie was vomiting into a kidney-shaped dish held to his mouth by the nurse. George knew, from his experiences in France, that this meant a chest wound. That Ronnie was able to bring up blood was a good sign.

The nurse was cooing reassuringly to him in Spanish, and after carefully wiping his mouth laid him gently on to his pillows. It was then that Ronnie saw George.

'Hello, old boy,' he smiled. 'Care for a tequila?'

George was shocked at Ronnie's paper-white face, but managed a smile.

'How are you feeling?'

Ronnie shrugged. 'Much as you see me. How would you feel if the mule that kicked you had forgotten to hone his hooves?'

'You look as if you'll live.'

Ronnie indicated the nurse. 'Much thanks to these kind people.'

There was a short, awkward pause while the nurse fussed about his pillows, and then, saying something in Spanish that neither understood, she went out taking the bloodied dish with her.

Ronnie looked anxiously to George. 'How is she?' he asked.

George shook his head. 'Don't ask,' he said, and then, seeing how stricken Ronnie looked, added, 'She'll be OK.'

Ronnie looked not a whit reassured. 'No excuses, old boy. Went totally jungle. Blood rushing to the head, that sort of thing.'

'Don't excite yourself. It'll work out.'

'Bitterly ashamed of myself,' Ronnie said with a sigh, 'but there it is.' Ronnie was deep into his misery. 'First time I've been sober in weeks. Ghastly feeling.'

'Just work on getting yourself better.'

Ronnie suddenly perked up and indicated the room. 'Mind telling me where I am? Wonderful woman that nurse, but she only speaks Spanish.'

'You've nothing to worry about. You're downtown. They got you to the right place – they know about knife wounds down here. The cops won't be involved.'

Ronnie nodded. 'Wondered why their heavy feet weren't pounding to my bedside.' He looked up and grinned. 'Not the first time, you know. Took a bayonet on the Somme, 1916,' adding ruefully, 'eighteen months before you chaps got there.'

George had run out of platitudes, and had to settle for an awkward smile.

Ronnie seemed content to ramble on. 'Damnable business. I love her, you see. Thought we'd got things together again. Bit of a shock. Not her fault. It'll be different after this. Done with the demon drink. Promised it to God if he saw me through. No going back on that, is there now?'

Feeling totally inadequate, George murmured further politenesses, and went out. He had a weird feeling that somehow this incident was going to be a watershed. There was the worry of how, or even if, Velma would come through, but the combination of Manolo's clear thinking and Ronnie's obvious contrition, combined with the good chance they could keep the press and police out of it, brought this particular crisis down to manageable proportions.

George was also guiltily aware that none of this was thanks to any of his actions. He had an uneasy feeling that he wouldn't have handled matters half as well as Manolo.

Julia had been looking for him, and found him in the hallway.

'I got hold of Stevens,' she said. 'He's picking up his theatre nurse and will be right over.'

Looking at Julia, George felt he had someone else to thank. 'What do you think, Julia? She looked pretty bad to me.'

'I spoke to the doctor . . .'

George interrupted in surprise. 'Manolo told me he didn't speak any English.'

Julia smiled. 'I speak Spanish.'

George was not particularly surprised. Gratitude was not a strong enough word for what he felt for her at that moment.

'What did he say?'

'He thinks the wound is clean, that there shouldn't be any secondary infection; as for the damage to her face, he is less optimistic.'

'Does he know who she is?'

Julia shook her head. 'I told him she was a photo model for *Vogue*, so the face was important.'

'But he doesn't think much for the future?'

Julia, sadly, couldn't reassure him.

George sighed. 'Let's wait and see what Stevens says.' He looked around.

'Any chance of getting any coffee round here?'

'They've got a kitchen downstairs. I'll make us some.'

Dr Stevens was with Velma for two hours, and when he emerged from her room he looked as exhausted as George felt.

'Should all heal normally. Don't expect to be able to put her on view for – let's say – six months at the earliest.'

'Even with make-up?'

Stevens nodded. 'Her nose was broken. I've had to reset it. I only wish I'd had more time.'

'Maybe we should have moved her to your hospital.'

Stevens shook his head. 'Not that. Splendid chap that Mexican. God! She took a beating. Who did it?'

'Her ex-husband. I'd like you to take a look at him too, he got stabbed.'

Stevens shook his head. 'Knife wounds are not for me. Besides, I doubt I'd trust myself with him. The man must be an animal!'

George found himself defending Ronnie. 'I have to say that he was provoked.'

Stevens held up his hand. 'Spare me the domestic details – I've enough of my own. Speaking of which I'm off back to bed to salvage what sleep I can.'

George delayed him a moment longer. 'Doctor, it goes without saying that . . .'

Stevens smiled tiredly. 'As you say, it goes without saying!'

Lifting a hand in salute, Stevens took his attendant nurse and walked away.

George was certain he could rely on Dr Stevens's discretion – and he was equally certain that it would be reflected in the doctor's bill.

George took another look in at Velma. She was sedated and sleeping peacefully enough. Manolo was sitting beside her holding her hand. He wished Manolo goodnight and added his gratitude.

'*Nada!*' smiled Manolo.

Julia drove him back home, but there seemed little point in trying to sleep. They passed the dawn hours discussing how best to handle Galaxy.

Julia finally came up with the most logical solution. 'My

father always used to tell me that the best method of defence was attack.'

'What does that mean?'

'It means you shouldn't give Galaxy any explanations. Just tell them you're not going to sign, that Velma is not taking the test, and let them worry about the reasons why.'

George could see this as one way out. 'What was your father?' he asked her, 'a general in the army?'

Julia shook her head. 'A poker player.'

10

George didn't feel like going to the office the following morning, but it was impossible not to. In the first place, Saturday was one of their busiest days as the studios decided the following week's schedule and put out their calls, and, secondly, it was essential that everything look as normal as possible.

George's preoccupation with the new Velma crisis was not helped by the ebullient Mike Traviss. He'd managed to track down his one-armed pool player and got his signature to an agency agreement. Obviously expecting to be showered with congratulations, he was disappointed by George's apparently grudging acknowledgement of his great achievement.

Mike had already got through detailing his triumph, when Wilbur Sterne astonished everyone by bursting into the office.

With no preliminary he made straight for George. 'Where is she?' he demanded.

George was on his feet. 'If you mean Velma, she's visiting friends.'

'That's not what I heard! What I heard is that she's dead!'

George was able to relieve his sudden fear by a shout of laughter. 'Whoever told you that is crazy.'

Wilbur reached across George's desk and put the phone down in front of him. 'Convince me. Get her on the line. I want to talk to her!'

George, feeling virtuously honest, spread his hands. 'I don't know the number, and anyway, where in hell do you get off coming into my office making demands?'

Wilbur looked round the room as if searching for traces of blood. 'You call this dump an office?' he growled.

George was now able to work up a genuine anger. 'You got anything else to say?'

Wilbur turned towards George and his gaze scanned George's face for signs of prevarication. Some of the anger seemed to leave Wilbur. 'People are talking all over town. I heard it from my own wife. She got it from our Spanish help.'

Inwardly George cursed himself. It was an angle he should have thought to cover. The fight must have disturbed Velma's bedroom – bloodstains, even – the maids would have gone in there this morning, found the mess, registered the fact that neither Manolo nor Velma was around and leapt to an emotional conclusion which, only by the grace of God, George was able to truthfully deny.

'Wilbur, do you seriously think that if my biggest client were dead I'd be sitting in my office going over next week's schedules?'

Wilbur watched a moment for any sign of weakness of conviction, and then, turning aggressive again, stabbed his finger into George's chest.

'I want from you, here and now, an absolute guarantee that Velma is going to be in my studio ready, willing and able to take that test Tuesday!'

George's first impulse was to play the card suggested by Julia, but now, with this 'dead' rumour floated, he needed something better, subtler and more convincing. At the same time he couldn't possibly give the guarantee Wilbur wanted. To have done so and reneged would have led to demands that Velma be produced for a press conference, maybe even lawyers would be serving papers. Anything could happen. He had to think, under pressure, of a ploy that would give him more time. He decided on the big lie, unattached to formal business agreements.

'Tell you what, Wilbur. I'm due to have lunch with Velma tomorrow. Why don't you come by? Bring a doctor to certify her still alive.'

Wilbur suddenly relaxed. 'Where's this lunch going to be?'

'The Beverly Hills.'

Wilbur nodded. 'I'll be there.' Wilbur was grinning now. 'Jeezus, what a town this is! Where do they get such stories from?' He turned to George. 'Seriously, though, you gotta consider getting yourself a better office – I mean, look at it . . .'

Wilbur, thankfully, started out the door, but George's pleasure at being rid of him was short-lived. Wilbur glanced into the outer office and was hurrying back to George to whisper urgently, 'That quiff out there . . .' George assumed he meant Julia, 'does she put out?'

George flinched in annoyance, but managed to smile through his reply. 'Only to her friends.'

Wilbur roared. 'And she doesn't have an enemy in the world, right?'

Wilbur went out again, this time laughing. He looked at the startled Julia and laughed again, then went off clattering down the exterior stone stairway.

'I hope you break your frigging neck!' George thought to Wilbur's back.

George turned back to Julia. 'Step into my office a moment, would you?'

Julia followed him in and then turned to close the door. Every time she did this it reminded him of their unreliable, as yet, new employee. George was starting to resent Mike.

'I'm beginning to wonder if that Mike Traviss wasn't one of my mistakes?'

Julia seemed surprised. 'He's willing to learn. Makes

himself very useful to me, and he did put that one-armed pool player right.'

George nodded and noted to himself not to start getting paranoid.

He gave it to Julia straight. 'I just promised Wilbur that I'd produce Velma for lunch tomorrow.'

Julia, looking stricken, sank into a chair. 'Oh, God! What are we going to do?'

'What I *was* going to do was call in with a twisted knee from tennis or something, but now I realize that won't work. Wilbur would still want Velma to come to lunch. We can't both call in with the same twisted knee.'

Irrelevantly Julia murmured, 'You don't even play tennis.'

George sighed heavily. 'Wilbur coming here just had me all of a heap. Rumours are flying about. Wilbur had heard that she was dead!'

Julia looked askance. George filled her in on his own embarrassment.

'The house staff! I should have guessed what would happen. They went in this morning, found the mess. Those domestics have got a bush telegraph that makes Western Union look like a bunch of Indian runners.'

Julia, he could see, was thinking hard and deep. 'If you need something that would cover them both — couldn't you hint that maybe Velma and Manolo have eloped?'

George roared with laughter. 'I like the "dead" rumour better than that!' Julia didn't respond.

'What we need is something simple, cute and convincing.'

They were still trying to come up with it when the phone started ringing. First it was the newspapers and later the radio stations. They'd all got some half-assed version of events but, thankfully, none of them was even close to what had actually happened.

George managed to field them all and, he hoped, kill any story, but with each succeeding call he knew he was going to have to come up with something more than an excuse for a missed lunch.

That night, after a fruitless day, he took Julia out to dinner.

They deliberately chose the noisiest, busiest place in town and made a point of laughing it up a lot. The idea was to make George as visible as possible out relaxing. Who could believe that a man as relaxed as this could have a major problem on his mind?

As effective as this was as a cover, it did nothing to solve the immediate problem. Lunchtime on the next day was starting to loom like Armageddon.

It was halfway through this charade that George was struck with inspiration. Pulling Julia close in the alcove he whispered his plan to her.

He could, with luck, tomorrow, pull the same stunt they were pulling that night. If he could get Madame Gregory to let Ailleen out again in her 'face' he could whisk her about some early-morning breakfast spots, make themselves visible all over, then stage-manage some 'accident' that would make the late afternoon editions and provide a highly public excuse for not turning up at the Beverly Hills Hotel.

Julia started shaking her head halfway through.

'What's wrong with it?'

'Tomorrow is Sunday,' she pointed out, 'there are no afternoon editions. To make your idea stick you'd need pictures in the papers – and there ain't gonna be none.'

'There's still the radio.'

'No pictures.'

George saw his idea crash to the ground, with nothing to put in its place.

He looked round the crowded restaurant. Suddenly the atmosphere was stultifying.

'Let's get out of here!'

Two and a half hours later they had got no closer to a solution. George was caught up with the notion of using Ailleen in some way that made 'Velma' visible.

'Couldn't she pass out in the lobby?' asked Julia.

'From what?' asked George. 'It might start worse rumours.'

'Worse?' asked Julia. 'What could be worse?'

'You're right,' he told her, 'but what would happen if, on the way in, she happened to run into an old friend and didn't recognize her? – or even if she didn't speak? Ailleen looks like Velma but, God knows, she doesn't talk like her.'

That objection kept them silent for another minute or two until Julia suddenly yelped, 'Bronchitis! You tell them she's got bronchitis. I mean she could croak something or other. It would also explain why she passed out in the lobby! Her fever! Also it gets you off the hook for Tuesday.'

'I'd have to get a doctor to swear to it.'

'You've got no problem there. Doc Stevens can honestly say that Velma is not fit to report for work, he doesn't have to give a diagnosis!'

George could only agree, but there still remained one huge problem – Madame Gregory. It was a simple enough idea, and drew strength from its daring. George reached for the phone.

'I told you I never let my girls out in their "faces". Look what happened last time.'

George protested. 'We've gotten that straightened out. Just one more exception? I wouldn't be asking but it's desperately important.'

There was a long contemplative silence from Madame Gregory's end. 'I've heard some stories,' she said finally. 'What's the truth?'

George took a deep breath. He had no reason to suppose he could count on Madame Gregory's loyalty. 'The lady has had a slight knock in an auto accident, but she's bruised and I have to produce her fit and well to scotch those rumours you've been hearing.'

Madame Gregory was not convinced. 'People can understand a few bruises, surely?'

George needed more story than he'd prepared. Suddenly

he found the answer. 'Someone else got pretty badly hurt. I'm trying to keep the cops out of it.'

If this story convinced Madame Gregory, she certainly didn't let on right away. 'OK,' she said finally, 'let me think about it. I'll call you back in fifteen minutes.'

For the next half-hour George and Julia sat hunched over the phone in a state of high tension. When it finally rang, both involuntarily lunged for it. George won by a short knuckle.

'I don't know why I'm doing this,' Madame Gregory was saying, 'but, OK. Come by not later than twelve. She'll be ready and waiting.'

George in his anxiety pressed just a little too hard. 'I'd feel better if I heard Ailleen say that . . .'

Madame Gregory's only answer was a dry-throated chuckle. Then she hung up.

George sat staring at the phone. The hurdle of Madame G.'s will-she-won't-she had momentarily masked the enormity of the stunt he was about to attempt.

If anything went wrong they'd stick his head on a pike. He turned to Julia for comfort, but she was as stricken as he was.

'. . . and all who sail in her . . .' was all she said.

11

George watched closely as Ailleen came down the front steps of Madame Gregory's. The half veil on her hat frustrated his attempts to judge how well she looked like Velma in full sunlight. Maybe the veil was a good idea.

'I hope you've got your Velma face on?' he prompted as she climbed into the roadster.

For answer Ailleen turned towards him and lifted the veil. There, large as life, was Velma's face before disaster and

Ronnie had struck. The plastic surgeon could have used it as a guide to restoration.

Aware that Ailleen had yet to speak a word, he let out the clutch and started the car rolling towards Beverly Hills.

'Something wrong?' he finally asked.

Ailleen shrugged and shook her head, still saying nothing. George pressed her.

'I don't like this business!' she burst out.

'What business? I'm taking you to lunch, that's all.'

Ailleen was still unhappy. 'It's out of context. I told you I don't mind being a whore and playing Velma in the house where it's expected. What I don't like is being paraded around wearing someone else's face.'

George felt that a tug on her rein would not be out of order. 'You make a lot of money out of that "face",' he reminded her. 'Now you can do a favour for the original.'

Ailleen remained silent for some time and George sensed some of the resentment leaving her, but enough remained for her to say: 'There is a girl inside here, you know!' She was pointing at herself.

George agreed with a smile. 'A very nice girl, as it happens.'

Ailleen, surprised by this sudden compliment, smiled. 'I'm sorry,' she said, 'please don't be angry with me.'

'About what? That you turn out to have feelings?'

Ailleen shook her head in wonder. 'I don't know what it is about you. You're the first man I ever met who made me feel like an actual whore. I mean, you know, a real one. With the others the real me was always hidden behind the fantasy. With you . . . ? I don't know.'

'Maybe it's because I haven't screwed you!'

Ailleen relaxed enough to be amused. 'That could be it!' Now she was laughing. 'I don't know many men who haven't.' She leaned in close and whispered as low as the roar of the motor would allow, 'Wouldn't consider pulling over and doing me a favour right now, would you?'

George laughed with her. 'Not on Sunset. They got a city ordinance against it.'

As George drove on towards the Beverly Hills he felt they had established a rapport, even the foundations of a friendship.

He was confident he could trust her, at least partially.

'One thing,' he told her, 'you've got bronchitis.'

She seemed surprised. 'Why?'

'Because the people we'll be meeting briefly know Velma's voice.'

Ailleen shrugged. 'So do I, now.'

George glanced across at her. She wasn't smiling. Looking directly at him she started to recite.

'The great Seraphic Lords and Cherubims . . .'

George brought the Stutz to a screeching halt by the kerbside, and sat staring at her while the powerful motor died to a patient throb.

'Do that again.'

Ailleen recited four more lines before George interrupted.

'That's uncanny . . .' he murmured. He felt very uncomfortable hearing Velma's voice coming from this close facsimile of Velma's face. If *this* Velma had been the one to give the reading to *Photoplay*, he'd have had nothing to worry about. She'd got the nasal breathing quality, even the squealed ending Velma put on many words. The rhythms had been different – but they were better.

'How do you do that?'

'I don't know. I've always been able to do it. Part of my actor's armoury.'

George found his mind seething with a whole host of possibilities. He reminded himself to be cautious. His ideas hadn't been all that good lately. Ailleen's newly-revealed talent seemed like a providential answer to his current problems – if he dared!

'You think you could keep that up all the way through lunch?' he asked.

Ailleen wasn't enthusiastic. 'I'd like to make some changes,' she said. 'Velma's voice hurts my throat.'

George continued looking at her while he worked through his idea. If he dared actually take her into lunch with Wilbur it would totally, once and for all, wipe out the rumours. It would be so much stronger than having her pass out in the lobby.

That idea had never much appealed to George. He had visions of an anxious and solicitous management insisting 'Velma' rest up in one of their suites. That would pin his imposter to one fixed position, with Wilbur, and possibly others, insisting on visiting with her.

It would be a much stronger hand to play – but, equally, far more dangerous.

'Voice lessons!' he said out loud.

Ailleen looked quizzically amused.

George went on: 'If anyone asks you why your voice has changed we'll tell them it's the result of your voice lessons. Velma's been spending a fortune on them.'

'Good grief!' said Ailleen. 'What in heaven's name did her voice sound like before the lessons?'

'Don't ask!' groaned George.

There was yet another side to this latest stunt. If he pulled it off and showed Wilbur Velma's new diction and well-rounded vowels it would scare the hell out of him. It might even resurrect the possibility of getting Galaxy to sign Velma *before* the voice test!

The prospects of success were exciting. The dangers were something George preferred not to dwell on.

'OK,' he said out loud to Ailleen. 'We go all the way.'

'Sounds exciting,' she murmured. 'I wish I knew what we were talking about!'

'I'm taking you out to lunch with the head of Galaxy Studios.'

If George had expected her to be impressed, he was disappointed.

'You do mean Mr Sterne?' she asked.

George nodded, pleased that she knew so much about Galaxy. 'Why do you know him?'

Ailleen smiled. 'He's one of my most regular clients.'

George stared at her. 'Oh jeezus!'

Ailleen wasn't the least disturbed. 'That makes things easier,' she said, 'he's told me a whole lot of things about them. Things of a highly personal nature that only he and Velma would know.'

George was intrigued. He knew nothing of any 'personal nature' relationship between Wilbur and Velma, except the early days casting-couch routine.

'What kind of things?' he asked.

Ailleen smiled. 'I couldn't *possibly* tell you that.'

'So there's no danger he'll mention something about Velma that you wouldn't know?'

Ailleen was smilingly confident. 'Madame Gregory keeps very detailed files on all her clients, and we have to keep up-to-date. It's all part of the fantasy. I'll bet she knows more about Velma than you do.'

George could only nod agreement. 'Velma,' he said, 'can be a very surprising girl.'

The car-hop at the Beverly Hills leapt forward to take charge of the Stutz.

'Morning, Mr Schapner,' he called as George stepped down. As George handed him the key he called across to Ailleen, 'And how are you this fine morning, Miss Torraine?'

'Feeling just great, thank you, Tony,' Ailleen cooed back in Velma's voice.

George found himself studying the car-hop's reaction. It had been their first test of Ailleen. They'd passed with flying colours.

George walked round the front of the car to join Ailleen on the kerb.

'How did you know his name was Tony?'

Ailleen sighed a patient sigh. 'I used to have dates, you know, even as plain old Ailleen Porter.'

As George walked her towards the double glass-doors he had the unsettling feeling that fiction was taking on an uncanny reality all its own. He could start to believe that he was handing the real Velma through the doors and into the lobby.

The murmur that went up from the lobby-loungers confirmed this feeling. Obviously they'd all heard the rumours, and there, right before their eyes, was the living denial.

So successful was their entrance that George had an impulse to call it 'enough' and cut and run. Even as he was about to turn Ailleen to the door he was stilled by an all-too-familiar voice.

'Sweetheart!'

Turning to face the inevitable, George saw Wilbur Sterne swiftly approaching with outspread arms and a curious crouch. Wilbur closed and grabbed Ailleen's hand to his mouth as if he were going to eat it.

Ailleen responded by leaning in to peck his cheek and was immediately enveloped into a bear-hug of an embrace.

Wilbur's words fell over each other with delight and, George suspected, some element of relief. 'You're looking just great, sweetheart!' he was calling out for the attentive lobby to hear. Stepping back, Wilbur held her at arm's length while he inspected her more fully.

'Put on a couple of pounds maybe, but all in the right places!'

Wilbur turned to George. 'Hey, we got to get this little lady back to work. We're crazy leaving the best cookie in the jar!' Turning once more to Ailleen, he tucked her arm under his own. 'Let's go eat!' he said, wagging his rear end like a delighted puppy dog.

George followed behind towards the garden restaurant.

They were over the first hurdle but it was going to be a long, long lunch!

The biggest hurdle loomed, literally, in the shape of Wilbur's wife Golda, who was shrewdly watching Wilbur and Ailleen's progress towards her.

George experienced a series of flash fears as they sat at the table. He had forgotten to warn Ailleen of Golda's possible presence at the lunch table, but he needn't have worried. Ailleen brushed cheeks with Golda as if she had met her a hundred times before.

As they sat, he realized he wasn't clear whether it was better to have Ailleen sit next to Golda, and so across the table from Wilbur, or the other way round . . . anyway it was all too late now. George decided that, whatever his fears, whatever the outcome, he was already launched and there was nothing he could do.

'Wilbur!' cried Golda as George sat down, 'she looks wonderful!'

Golda had this endearing habit of channelling all her conversation through Wilbur, as if this filtering process made for some kind of sanction for her words. 'Wilbur, you have to ask George what it is he's done with this girl. One thing is obvious – he's been feeding her!'

George was starting to get worried by these constant references to 'Velma's' increased weight. He hadn't noticed any significant difference between the two girls, but obviously others did.

The main consolation, however, was that Ailleen seemed, initially, to have been accepted by both as genuinely Velma. He could also see how well Ailleen was handling herself – especially the voice. She had started with a very close imitation of Velma's stridency, but as the conversation developed she was subtly moving into a more sophisticated cadence. She didn't go as far as becoming British, but became less New York and more East Coast.

The only disturbing factor was Wilbur. He kept leaning in

on Ailleen, and was holding her hand an awful lot. Wilbur seemed unaware of just how much close attention he was paying Ailleen/Velma. The easy atmosphere and exchange between them was having its effect on Golda who was practically ignored by her husband.

George suddenly realized that Ailleen's revelation that Wilbur was one of her most regular clients – a fact which had frightened him at the time – was probably working to his advantage. Wilbur, who obviously fantasized about Velma, would probably have merged his fantasy Velma with the real one and made them hard to distinguish one from the other.

That Golda was getting annoyed by the court Wilbur was paying to Ailleen also probably helped, since it diverted Golda's attention from any close scrutiny of Velma. In fact, she was doing her best to ignore the hand-holding by engaging in fervent conversation with George.

Wilbur, for all his hand-holding intimacy, had noticed the new cadence in Velma's voice. He leaned across towards George, interrupting, incidentally and without noticing, a long anecdote of Golda's, to whisper: 'I want the name of this voice coach, George. I want him working for Galaxy – I got others need working on. I mean, what this guy has done for Velma, it's unbelievable! What's his name?'

This totally unexpected question caught George without any easy answer. It should have been a simple question. 'I doubt you could afford him,' he finally managed.

Wilbur was offended. 'You *can* afford him, but I *can't*? What are you talking about?'

'Ah!' cried Ailleen, valiantly rescuing George, 'it might not be a question of money!'

Wilbur turned to Ailleen as if to protest, and then, from her expression, recognized the jokey innuendo. Letting go with one of his great shouts of laughter, he momentarily stilled all conversation in the restaurant.

It was at this moment that Golda's patience with Wilbur snapped. She rose abruptly and left the table, heading through the restaurant towards the ladies' room. Wilbur was so busy recovering from his burst of laughter that he didn't even notice his wife's departure.

'Tell you what,' he was saying to George, 'bring the guy by my office. We can talk.'

George agreed only to discuss the prospect with the coach. Wilbur resumed his close attentiveness to Ailleen.

It wasn't until they were serving coffee that Wilbur, turning to Golda for confirmation of some date or other, found her missing. 'Where's Golda?' he asked as if fearing she might have been kidnapped.

George told him he thought she'd gone to the powder-room. He didn't tell Wilbur that that had been over ten minutes ago.

Ailleen, obviously in need of respite, got up and announced her intention of joining her there.

Wilbur sat back peeling the wrapper from his cigar and regarded George with a smile of contented approval. 'I gotta hand it to you. I was beginning to suspect you was up to something. Some kind of stunt, maybe.' He puffed his cigar alight as George waited. 'You gone and got that girl totally made over. How'd you do it?'

George gestured his modesty. 'It's what agents are for.'

Wilbur shook his head with slow deliberation. 'It's what agents *should* be for – you're the first one I ever knew got off his fat ass and got the job done.'

George smiled his gratitude for the compliment.

'You know,' said Wilbur through the haze of cigar smoke hovering about his head, 'maybe there's things we could talk about together. I've often considered that there must be a lot of talent slips through the net. I've often thought that maybe Galaxy should set up some kind of agency to find and develop young talents. What do you think?'

'I think the kind of talent you're talking about comes cheaper than that.'

Wilbur looked puzzled so George went on. 'You're talking

about getting a harem started for Galaxy executives. It's an expensive way to get laid.'

Wilbur sat back with a passable imitation of hurt in his eyes. 'That's not it, George. If you knew what was happening in relation to Galaxy and Wall Street you'd understand better.'

'You going to tell me?'

Wilbur looked around the restaurant. Talking here was like broadcasting coast-to-coast. 'Big money!' whispered Wilbur with due reverence. 'Very big money is getting interested in Galaxy. Could be like the old days all over again. Galaxy could be a monster. Not just up there with the big boys, but *bigger*!' Wilbur sat back with the air of a man who feared he might have said too much. 'We going to rebuild the stages for sound. Maybe out in the valley.'

George laughed. 'You should talk to Al Klein!'

Wilbur carefully inspected the end of his cigar before looking up towards George. 'We already did. Al's offering us prime land for peanuts.'

'You're serious? Out in the valley?'

'Why not? It's good enough for the Brothers.'

George could see how Al Klein might not be so crazy after all, especially when Wilbur went on, 'Al Klein's going to be a very rich man, very soon.'

There was a sudden stir in the post-lunch hiatus and, looking round, George saw Ailleen returning to the table. Of Golda there was no sign.

'I'm afraid your wife has left,' she smiled at Wilbur.

Wilbur sprang to his feet. 'Oh-oh, I'm in trouble.' He turned to George. 'Tomorrow, my office. We talk!'

He pulled Ailleen into a grandstand play of a hugging kiss and, with a final cheery wave, fled to make his peace with Golda.

George collapsed back into his club chair, emotionally drained. Now it was over, he realized how much tension he'd been suffering. He smiled in gratitude at the calmly-composed Ailleen who smiled back with Velma's face.

'That man is disgusting!' she announced.

George quieted her with a warning gesture and indicated the open ears of the tables around them. It wasn't only the near tables. It was a known fact that the gossips hired lip-readers to hang around restaurants. The movies had bred a whole generation of people that could read lips!

'Let's get out of here,' he told her.

He called for the bill only to find that Wilbur had charged it to his own account.

Just getting out created further tensions. Someone would rise from each of the tables they passed, anxious to make contact with this made-over 'Velma' who was obviously back solid with Galaxy. Ailleen handled them all with easy grace, sprinkling 'darlings' at people whose names she did not know.

George didn't feel totally safe until he'd got Ailleen into the Stutz and was driving towards Rossmore.

He'd done it. Inwardly he exulted. All rumours were stone dead and Ailleen had managed to enhance Velma's reputation. It made a solid base for him to build a wall around Velma for the six months it would take her wounds to heal. Maybe a 'personal appearance' tour – Europe even.

Ailleen interrupted his thoughts. She had noticed the route they were taking did not lead back to Madame Gregory's.

'Where are we going?' she asked.

'My place,' he told her.

'Oh!' she murmured in a flat voice.

It was a minute or more before George realized the interpretation she'd put on his words.

'I want you to meet someone.' Ailleen remained silent. 'My girl and my secretary.'

Ailleen seemed to become more cheerful. 'That's two people.'

'Oh, no!' said George. 'That's *one* people!'

Julia was waiting in a high state of tension when they got

to the house. She took a little time to absorb the startling impact of Ailleen in Velma's face, and then turned to George. 'I've been so worried. You've been gone so long. I was sure something had happened.'

'Something did happen. We both had lunch with Wilbur!'

Julia stared from one to the other in horrified surprise. 'You did what?'

George could feel his excitement doubled in the surprise in Julia's expression. 'We had lunch with Wilbur, and I have to say that this little lady,' he was indicating Ailleen, 'was just tremendous. She carried the whole thing off beautifully. Neither Wilbur nor Golda noticed a thing!'

Julia's mouth was wide with delight. 'Golda? You mean Golda too!?'

'Golda, Wilbur and half Hollywood. Anybody trying to put out rumours about Velma is going to get the horse's laugh. No problem.'

Julia turned to Ailleen. 'I don't know whether to laugh or cry! What did you use? Hypnotism?'

Ailleen smiled indulgently. 'What I'd like to use is your bathroom. I'd like to get out of this wig. It's not my regular night-time wig, and this one itches.'

Julia led Ailleen to the bathroom and returned to take a celebratory drink from George. 'She's uncanny!' Julia said.

'Not only that, she's intelligent too. You should have seen how she picked up on everything! That girl didn't make a single mistake – not even half a one. I tell you, halfway through the meal she had *me* convinced she was Velma!'

Julia sipped her drink and seemed to be considering something. 'You know, it makes you wonder about things. It makes you wonder about identities and things. I mean, you and me. We think we're unique – different from anyone else. I tell you, it would scare me to think that someone could go in and pass themselves off as me, among people who knew me.'

George was nodding. 'You're right! Hey, there could be a

story in this. Suppose someone impersonated a bank president . . .'

Julia was shaking her head. 'I think this applies to women, mostly. Think about it. Women change their appearance. Wigs, make-up, clothes . . . nobody's surprised if today's fatso turns up, slimmed down, tomorrow. Hair colour changes, all these things, they're natural to women. Now Velma has a double, but mainly it's because people expect to see Velma. Who knows who Velma is? A moon shape blown huge by the movie screen, or the real life-sized one opposite you at dinner?'

George was nodding, but he had something he wanted to tell Julia before Ailleen came back. 'Listen, I want you to stay close to her. I've got an idea of how we could keep this charade going until Velma heals.'

Julia looked puzzled. 'How? That's likely to be six months!'

George was about to tell her his plan when Ailleen came back from the bathroom, her faced scrubbed clean of Velma. Julia had the same reaction George had had seeing her in her own face.

George invited her to stay for a drink, but Ailleen seemed anxious to get back to Madame Gregory's.

Julia, remembering George's injunction, immediately volunteered to drive Ailleen back. George agreed, since it was obviously not good business for him to be seen delivering Ailleen back so soon after producing 'Velma' at lunch.

Julia was gone more than two hours and George had become concerned as to what might be keeping her by the time she did return.

'Where were you?' he asked.

Julia was in a flippant mood. 'Chance of a lifetime!' she said.

'What was?'

'To see in a whorehouse. Unlike men, women get few opportunities!'

'You went in Madame Gregory's?'

'Certainly!' she smiled. Julia started swaying across towards the bathroom. 'Very, very interesting. Educational too!'

Julia disappeared into the bathroom and locked the door.

'You took a hell of a chance!' George complained through the door. 'There's people up there know you as my secretary.' He could hear her chuckling. 'Open this door!' he called. 'You owe me an explanation.'

Julia, despite his repeated demands, didn't open the door for a further five minutes. When she did, she was draped in a loose Mexican shawl that normally served as a table cover in the bathroom.

Before George's speechless gaze she sashayed across the room, dropped the shawl on her total nudity and, fluttering her eyes at him, drawled, 'Gonna cost you twenty, Blue Eyes!'

12

George had long been a believer in the brain's capacity to work out problems while the body slept. It followed then that the thought you had on waking was the one to be acted on first. That morning his dominant thought had been of Al Klein and his less-crazy-than-first-thought valley development scheme. George's second belief was, first things first. In this case, first raise the money to make the investment. George, against Julia's protests that there were other things to do, had placed a call to 'his' broker.

The broker had been gone from the phone for a long time before picking up on George again. 'Mr Schapner, you have to excuse me.'

'I do?'

'Yes, you see, when you first called I had difficulty in putting a face to your name.'

'That's understandable,' said George, 'we've never met.'

'Oh.'

The broker seemed to lapse into another long silence, during which George feared he might have lost his original 25,000 dollars by some default or other.

When the broker spoke again he seemed to be having difficulty controlling his emotions. 'Mr Schapner,' he began, 'this is a busy office, you know?'

George held his breath, wondering why he was being treated to this sermon.

'A *very* busy office!' the broker said again. 'Your holding was kind of put to one side and I'm afraid I didn't keep up to date on you.'

George became impatient. 'Are you trying to tell me something's wrong?'

The broker sighed. 'Mr Schapner, the way you've been acting is crazy!'

George gripped the phone hard. Now he was certain his nest-egg was gone.

'What's happened?'

'It's what's *not* happened that worries me,' the broker was saying, as if laden with guilt about something. 'Mr Schapner, your holding is currently worth . . . hold on a minute and I'll give the exact figure . . .'

George not only held on, he held his breath. Even above the static on the downtown line he could hear an adding-machine clicking. During that time, all kinds of figures ranged through George's head, from ten cents to a hundred dollars. The figure he hadn't hit on was the one the broker came back with: 'Two hundred and twenty-one thousand, one hundred and sixteen dollars and sixty-nine cents.'

'What's that?' asked George, not yet daring to believe.

'That's the present value of your holding as of ten minutes ago. It's probably gone up since then. Mr Schapner, do you realize that RCA is the hottest stock in the entire country?'

George was still struggling with the first figure. He asked the broker to repeat it.

'Two hundred and twenty-one thousand, one hundred and sixteen dollars and sixty-nine cents.'

George stared at the figure he had written down on his pad. It looked unbelievable. 'That's wonderful!' he cried down the phone.

The broker snapped back, 'That, Mr Schapner, is a disgrace!'

George was startled into silence for a moment. 'I beg your pardon?'

The broker sounded genuinely sad. 'Mr Schapner, if only you'd come forward and jogged my mind on your file! Listen, I've got clients on my books – and I'm talking about parking-lot attendants, who came in here a year ago with a hundred bucks that, today, are richer than you are!'

George began to suspect that the world had gone mad. 'What's so wrong about a quarter of a million dollars, Mr Beck?'

'What's wrong is we should be looking at two, maybe two and a half million, that's what's wrong!' Mr Beck sighed deeply. 'Listen, what's done is done. Now we're in touch again, I'll give your portfolio some thought. Take some profit, margin you into some more of a spread, and we'll catch you up. Jesus Christ, Mr Schapner, you'll be talking millions before the end of the year.'

George began to wonder if he had been connected with a lunatic asylum by mistake. It even crossed his mind to hang up and call back just to be sure. Mr Beck seemed to be overenthusiastic to say the least. There was one sure way to test him out and ensure that the figures he was talking could be liquidized into real money. 'Mr Beck, what I want to do is sell out.'

'*Sell out?!* You mean the whole thing, or, like I say, take a profit on some of it?'

'I mean I want the money. Sell everything.'

There was a pause during which George thought he had said something blasphemous.

When Mr Beck had caught his breath he murmured sadly, 'Mr Schapner, nobody's selling RCA. Like, they've gone up two dollars while we've been talking.'

George felt he was being treated like an idiot. He wanted the conversation over with and, if possible, his money in the bank where he could believe it. Stocks that went up like that might also come down. 'Mr Beck, I don't understand the first thing about the workings of the stock market. All I know is I had some loose money just over a year ago and a friend told me to put it into RCA...' Mr Beck interrupted: 'You should kiss the ground that friend walks on.'

'... but what I do understand is money in the bank. If you can sell my shares at what you say they're worth then I'll be happier.'

'You're seriously saying you want to pull out of the game when you're holding aces!'

'That's exactly what I mean. Mr Beck, I just don't understand how I've made that much money just holding paper!'

'It's the American way, Mr Schapner.' Beck went on hurriedly as if he'd just thought of a possible reason for George's behaviour. 'You *are* an American, aren't you?'

'Only if Maine is still in the forty-eight. Maybe that's my problem – where I come from, crops don't grow where you don't put seed, and money doesn't come out of thin air. Somebody had to sweat for that money you're telling me I've got. There isn't enough money in the world for everyone to be making money like that. It's crazy!'

Mr Beck's nod could be heard in his voice. 'There's something crazy all right, but you're the first man I heard complaining about making money!'

'I'm not complaining. I'm saying I don't understand it.'

'OK. I hear what you're saying, but you sure you don't want to think this thing over – talk to your friend maybe?'

'I know what I want to do. I want to sell my shares.'

'You *are* nuts!' said Mr Beck, and put down the phone.

George would have liked a moment to think through what

he'd just done, but Julia was in his office, and he knew at once that she was mad at him.

'George, what's got into you!'

George shrugged uncomprehendingly.

'There's things to do, George, and it seems to me that you're not doing any of them.'

'I'm doing things. Get me Al Klein on the phone.'

Julia sighed. 'I don't have that number listed.'

George searched around for Al's number and gave it to her.

The phone rang on his extension and, without thinking, George picked it up directly.

It was Wilbur Sterne. 'When we gonna talk, sweetheart?'

George cursed himself for picking up on the line. He wanted more than ever to get in touch with Al Klein now; going over to Galaxy would get in the way. 'I'd like to come right over, Wilbur, but I'm blocked in here waiting for a call.'

Wilbur was suddenly snarling. 'Who from?' he asked, then, without waiting for George, went on, 'You stalling me? If you're trying to sneak that girl into another studio you're going to get an awful lot of trouble out of me.'

George sighed. 'Wilbur, the call has nothing to do with Velma. Believe me!'

Wilbur wasn't prepared to believe him. 'We got phones down here, you know. What's it going to take you to get here – five minutes, maybe? When your call comes in, have your girl transfer it down here. Hell, I'll even step outside while you take it!'

George smiled. He could see Wilbur listening on the extension even now. There was little point in fighting the point further. 'OK, Wilbur, be with you in five minutes.'

George put down the phone. Five minutes. Five minutes in which to think of some way of not producing Velma for the test.

During the five-minute drive, George went over the ground. Wilbur had indicated that there was new money coming into the studio. It was difficult to see what there was to interest Wall Street other than Velma's contract. Galaxy's track record – Velma apart – was hardly distinguishable from any other similar outfit's.

Velma had to be Wilbur's showcase, and that meant he was going to be needing Velma's signature very badly indeed. It could prove the one factor in side-stepping this scheduled sound test.

By the time George had parked his car and was walking towards the executive block he felt he was going in to play cards, with a strong hand.

In the corridor as he approached Wilbur's office lurked the figure of Milton Bressler. George had the uncanny feeling that Milton was lying in wait for him.

'Hi, Milton, how's it going?' enquired George breezily, meaning to go right on by.

Milton stopped him cold. 'I hear Ronnie Stillman's in hospital with a stab wound,' he called after George.

George's stomach did loops. He turned back trying to look unconcerned. 'Where did you hear that, Milton?'

'Around!'

George was aware that Milton was watching him closely for reaction. George was careful to marshal his facial muscles in the hope that nothing showed. This was the first rumour that came anywhere near the truth, and it had to be based on something other than domestics' chatty conjecture.

George shook his head with deliberate slowness. 'How could a thing like that happen? Was it in the bar?'

'You telling me you didn't know?'

George could see the trap, and felt himself lurching into it just in time.

'How would I know? Ronnie isn't my client.'

'I would have thought Velma would have known.'

George managed a shrug. 'If she does, she hasn't told me – and why would she? None of my business if Ronnie gets into a brawl.'

Milton was still watching closely. 'It's not something that happens every day though, is it?'

'With Ronnie you never can tell. No, I'm pretty sure Velma doesn't know, we had lunch yesterday, she didn't say anything.'

Milton was suddenly smiling. Up to this moment George had been pretty sure Milton wasn't certain of the facts. Now, suddenly, he seemed more confident. George suspected that something he'd said had brought about this change, but his mind was racing too fast to search back for error.

Milton supplied him. 'So you knew enough to know it happened before yesterday?'

George managed to transform his startled loss of smile into a frown. 'Knew what?'

'That Ronnie got stabbed sometime on Saturday night?'

George spread his hands. 'I already told you. I don't know anything about Ronnie, and there's no reason why I should. Now listen, Milton, we can shoot the breeeze later, right now I've got Wilbur waiting to see me.'

George, wanting desperately to get away from Milton's grilling, turned away towards Wilbur's office and a meeting he'd rather run away from.

'George Schapner!' called Milton. 'You've either got the luck of the devil, or he's got your soul!'

George managed to call back, 'Stick around, Milton, some of it might rub off!'

If Milton had spread his rumour to Wilbur, it didn't show in the bounding effusiveness of his greeting.

'There's my boy!' he cried, and for a moment George was afraid that Wilbur was going to kiss him.

'Now listen, I got the whole switchboard alerted. Minute there's a call comes in for you, it'll be switched up here faster than you can lift the phone, right? So let's relax and talk Velma.'

Wilbur waved George to a chair, and paced up and down

a moment or two. 'George, I got a feeling that, one way or the other, this is going to be a day we'll both long remember.'

George felt that at this precise moment he could have got Wilbur's signature to anything, with or without the sound test, but just a few thin walls away glowered Milton Bressler with information that could destroy him. Probably the one thing that had prevented Milton going to Wilbur with what he knew was that he'd dared to take Ailleen in to lunch and pass her off as Velma. He could see now that if he had pulled the 'faint-in-the-lobby' stunt, he would by this time be cold turkey.

'We've still got one problem between us!'

Wilbur expressively dismissed this suggestion. 'Between friends there are no problems!'

'This one won't go away too easily. Velma doesn't want to take this sound test.'

Wilbur looked puzzled. 'Why not? What can she lose? Listen, George, I've got to level with you, before yesterday I had doubts. I did. But now – seeing what you've done with her – listen, I still want the name of that voice coach. Listen, you know what happened yesterday after I got home? Golda was mad as shit at me – she even thought I was paying attention to Velma, can you beat that? Anyway, mad as she was at me, she still said it was nothing short of a miracle. Like a different girl, were her exact words. Now, Golda's been around the business as long as me, and she's got something going for her which I ain't. You know what that is? Feminine intuition. Her very words to me yesterday, mad as she was, was "Wilbur, you gotta sign that girl!" What do you think of that?'

'I think that's great, Wilbur, and I think Golda's absolutely right – so why'd we have to horse around with a sound test?'

Wilbur spread his arms as if to embrace the whole world. 'Everybody's taking sound tests. No way is it the same thing as a screen test – *that* Velma don't need! It's a microphone test – a formality after what I heard yesterday. So what's the problem?'

'The problem is Velma. She's adamant that she won't take it.'

Wilbur was shaking his head in that hurt way that spelt trouble. 'You want to know what I think, George? I think you're playing some kind of cheap game to keep me dangling while you try to finangle a deal somewhere else. We haven't talked money yet, so I got to take it personal.'

'That's just not true, Wilbur!' George protested.

Wilbur was studying George closely, and with grave solemnity. Finally he spoke without the anger he'd previously used. 'I got to have that test, George. I need it for reasons I can't yet divulge.'

George was uncomfortably convinced of Wilbur's total sincerity, for the first time he could ever remember.

Wilbur was, uncharacteristically, making himself vulnerable, and he was too good a negotiator not to know it was going to cost money. Yesterday George had paraded 'Velma' as a living, breathing, healthy actress. It had scotched the rumours, and held off Milton, but it also left him defenceless in trying to delay the test.

A wrenched knee wouldn't do it. With Wilbur in this mood, they'd shoot it in a wheelchair if they had to. George was also acutely aware that, seen from Wilbur's side of the desk, Velma's hold-out would be totally unreasonable. George was on the rack and had nothing to say.

Wilbur had been watching him closely, drawing one deep breath after another as if trying to suppress his emotion. Finally, Wilbur seemed to reach a decision and, leaning forward, his eye still firmly fixed on George, pressed down his intercom. 'I didn't want to do this, George, but you leave me no choice.'

Into the intercom system Wilbur said, 'Send Hollister in!'

George looked at Wilbur sharply. Hollister was the head of Galaxy's legal department. It was Hollister who drew up all the contracts, and George had the distinct feeling that he was about to get his ass pinned to the floor.

Hollister, an unsmiling, ascetic-looking man, responded immediately. George realized that he must have been hovering, awaiting just such a summons.

'Mr George Schapner?' he asked needlessly of George. 'I hereby serve you these papers.'

George found himself holding a weighty sheaf of high quality papers. He didn't need to read them to know what they were.

George turned to Wilbur. 'You can't do this, Wilbur!' he protested.

Wilbur shrugged. 'Tell him, Hollister.'

Hollister cleared his throat as if about to launch into a courtroom summation. 'These papers, Mr Schapner, invoke Clause Six of your client's contract with this studio. Clause Six states, with clarity, that your client shall hold herself ready, at all times, to perform any reasonable request made upon her with diligence and to the best of her abilities, and to attend upon this studio or any other designated place . . .'

George burst out impatiently, 'Let's cut out this chicken shit! What you're saying is Velma has to be here or you're going to sue, right?'

Wilbur was shaking his head. 'Not sue, George. Destroy!'

Now George was good and angry. He had to be, he had no other defence. 'Wilbur, I think you've taken leave of yourself! How do you think Velma's going to react to something like this? You think you and I will be able to sit down and cosy up an agreement when you pull something like this?'

'Never thought we would "cosy up" anything, George,' said Wilbur with quiet confidence.

It was George who was shouting. 'Well, let me tell you, this little stunt is going to cost you an arm and a leg! You want Velma, Jesus, you're gonna pay!!'

Wilbur shrugged. 'I didn't want to do this, George. You forced me.'

George flourished the papers in his hand – he would dearly have loved them still to be trees so he could hit Wilbur with them. 'If you imagine you're going to get Velma Torraine into this studio to make movies for you – then you just blew it right out the window.'

Wilbur remained infuriatingly calm. On any other occasion he would have been answering George back in his own terms by now. George would have preferred an all-out shouting match. Wilbur's calm was not only infuriating, it was frightening.

George was aware that he was making a spectacle of himself, and he wished there was some way he could get out of the office. He needed time to think.

'Whatever happens in the future, George, is in the hands of the gods. What I do know is, Velma is going to be in this studio tomorrow morning for her test, or I'm going to break your ass from here to New York.'

George suddenly flashed up an exit line. 'That suits me fine!' he crowed, 'I'm from Maine!'

Turning blindly he somehow reached the door handle and got himself out of there.

When he got into the blinding light of the yard, he saw something that worried him. He knew it was Milton Bressler, and that Milton was talking to someone, but George, turning away, not wanting to get caught up, didn't absorb who the other party was until he was going into the office and there was an absence.

'Where's Mike?' he asked the worried Julia.

'He went down to Galaxy with some schedules.'

George froze. The other party talking with Milton *had* been Mike! It was unthinkable that Mike was a plant, or was it?

'What's the problem?' asked Julia.

George shook his head. 'I just saw Mike talking to Milton over at Galaxy.'

Julia seemed puzzled. 'Then why did you ask where he was?'

George gestured helplessly. 'Come into my office.'

Julia knew George's moods well, and she judged that their cover-up hadn't been totally successful before George spoke.

'The story's out,' he told her, 'half of it, anyway. Milton knows that Ronnie got stabbed.' He looked up at Julia. 'How would Milton have got that information?'

Julia looked bewildered.

'You think Mike knows anything he could have passed on?'

'Not from me, if that's what you're thinking.'

'I'm not thinking anything. I don't *know* anything!'

'How far has it got?'

'Not to Wilbur, not yet.' George heaved the papers on to his desk. 'That's what I got from Wilbur!'

Julia snatched up the papers and started scanning them while George thought things through furiously. He'd been taking each problem as it came. 'The luck of the devil,' Milton had called it.

Maybe. What had looked like solutions had just succeeded in getting them in deeper.

Julia looked up from the papers. 'There's no way! No way at all!'

George already knew that. 'There's just one last thing. The medical clauses. Right now, all I can think of is to take Velma's car out somewhere and run it into a tree, tell them Velma was in it, and let the doctors take a look at her.'

Julia was dubious. 'Wouldn't they be able to tell that the injuries weren't recent? You can't say it happened Saturday – you had her to lunch yesterday.'

George suddenly couldn't keep still. He got up and started pacing as if afraid that standing still would make it easier for God to strike him dead on the spot.

Somewhere along the way he'd lost the thread that would lead him out of this labyrinth.

'All we can do is check it out with Dr Stevens. It's our last hope so far as I can see.'

Julia wasted no time on debate and went out to her own office.

111

'Let me know when Mike Traviss gets back!' he called after her.

For fifteen minutes George sat reading through the papers and trying to think, but with each succeeding paragraph and codicil he felt more and more trapped.

Julia came back looking remarkably composed. 'Doc Stevens says that even a first-year nurse could tell the injuries weren't caused yesterday.'

'Even bandaged?'

'You know those studio doctors will want to see under the bandages.'

George nodded miserably. 'We'd better get them both out of town. God knows what's going to happen, but there's no point in making it easy for them!'

Julia nodded and made a note on her pad, then, looking up, said: 'That takes care of the walking wounded, what about the walking dead?'

George shook his head. 'I can't come up with anything.'

They looked at each other helplessly. Both knew that if they didn't produce Velma, they were cooked geese.

There came a noise of someone entering the outer office.

'Is that Mike coming back?'

Julia glanced at her watch. 'No, it's probably Ailleen, we're due to have lunch. I'll put her off.'

Julia was turned towards the door when George let out a yell so loud she dropped her pencils.

'*Ailleen!!*'

Julia, stooping to pick up the dropped pencils, saw George looming up from behind his desk with the desperate light of deliverance in his eyes.

'Ailleen!' George was saying.

'You can't be serious, George!'

'It worked twice already, didn't it?'

'Once with a drunk, and once across a lunch table. George, we're talking screen test. People who know her better than we do. Cameraman. Make-up ... Harvey Tilbury knows

112

Velma's face better than he does his own. Harvey Tilbury has lit every one of Velma's pictures. George, if she were a millimetre out of line, those people would know!'

Julia quailed before the messianic light in George's eyes, she could see he was serious.

'What else?' was all he asked.

13

The events of the next eighteen hours were to be a blur in George's memory. Each individual decision, taken against time, merged into the next desperate move, blended into one by the sheer sweaty tension of it all.

It started when he had Julia 'dog' Ailleen. Instead of taking her to lunch as planned, she took her to George's house, and there spent the time convincing and cajoling her into playing Velma one more time – for the cameras.

George had gone into the lion's den of Madame Gregory's easily aroused anger and, with the aid of five hundred dollars, managed to soothe her anger into cynical amusement at his audacity. He hadn't had to tell her why he wanted to use Ailleen again – she had guessed. Having contributed nine hundred dollars to Madame Gregory's pension fund in less than five days, he managed to come to an understanding with her.

George left her with the distinct feeling that he was going to have to pour more money on that particular smoulder if it were never to burst into flame. The last thing Madame Gregory had said as he left her was: 'Lucky for you I'm superstitious – I never mess with crazy people!'

Meeting up with Julia towards midnight he heard that they had Ailleen's co-operation – at a price. Ailleen had demanded that George arrange a screen test for her in her own face. Since she hadn't asked for a guarantee of anything coming out of the test, it was a simple enough thing for George to agree to. With luck he might even find someone willing to put film in the camera!

Having got the cast together, they turned their minds to more practical problems. First and foremost came the craft people – make-up, wardrobe and hairdressing. They had to keep them away from their counterfeit Velma at all costs. Fooling Wilbur was simplicity itself compared with the impossible task of fooling these people, so jealous of their skills. To exclude them from Velma's dressing suite was going to be difficult enough and was sure to lead to friction, but there was no way round that particular problem – they'd just have to meet it head on.

A bigger problem was going to be with the front office. Wilbur would be sure to want to welcome Velma to the lot – especially in view of the trouble it had taken to get her there – but he had to be prevented. They stood little chance of getting away with it unless they could present Ailleen fully made-up, costumed and ready to shoot before anyone got a close look at her. Once they had her on the floor, everybody would be distracted by their own problems and she, until the cameras turned, would be subject to far less scrutiny.

It all came down to smuggling Ailleen into Velma's cottage on the Galaxy lot early in the morning before any of the crafts were about. George called Madame Gregory's to warn Ailleen of their early start, only to be told by Madame Gregory that she couldn't come to the phone – she was 'busy'.

George managed to smother his angry reaction. He needed Madame Gregory docile and co-operative and if she was determined to squeeze the last ounce of flesh from Ailleen then they had to live with it.

George simply asked that Ailleen be told to hold herself ready at the house to be collected at five in the morning.

George looked at his watch. Even if Ailleen got 'unbusy' within the hour she'd have less than two hours' sleep.

Julia reminded him that this was a test of 'Velma's' voice and even if she did look puffy-eyed in the morning, that could be explained by a sleepless night due to worry over the test itself.

George just hoped that Ailleen's nerve was steelier than theirs.

During the remaining hours neither even considered sleep.

They concluded it would be too risky for George to go up to Madame Gregory's to collect Ailleen. Julia would do it in her more anonymous little Ford.

After going over the ground time and time again and scaring themselves half to death, they finally got the show started.

Julia went to fetch Ailleen while George went directly to the studio.

At that dark hour of the morning there was no one about but the gateman and the night security people. They seemed unanimously to resent George's early intrusion into their domain, and all his nervous efforts to engage them in conversation met with stony silence.

It was with relief that George saw Julia's little car arrive at the gate. The gateman seemed to take for ever to pass them through, peering as he did with great suspicion at the swaddled figure of Ailleen, who, unlike Velma, had failed to greet him by name.

It was the first of what George suspected were going to be half a hundred overlooked details, but it passed and the three managed to get safely into the dressing-room cottage without mishap.

Ailleen seemed the calmest of them, probably because she didn't appreciate the enormity of what they were about, nor would she take any knocks if things went wrong. Neither did she look puffy-eyed; in fact, George appreciated, she looked positively ravishing in her scrubbed clean, Ailleen, face.

She was also the most businesslike, setting about laying

out her armoury of make-up, and seemed to know precisely what it was she was about.

'I'm using this new panchromatic make-up,' she told George, 'it's Rosher. Now I know that Velma has been using Steiner's pink, but it just doesn't go with my skin colour. I'm a little lighter shade than Velma.'

George stared at her. 'How do you know so much about make-up?' he asked her.

Ailleen had stared at him, round-eyed. 'Didn't you know? Madame Gregory retains Siggi Allen as make-up consultant.'

Siggi Allen was the head of make-up at one of the major studios. What he didn't know about make-up was also unknown to Steiner and Rosher. George was impressed, even though he didn't understand a word the girls were talking about. They threw him out.

The studio was coming to life as more and more people arrived. As each and every one greeted him with some comment about being up and about early, George started to feel furtive.

He ducked into an open stage and found himself looking at a Spanish garden set clearly labelled TEST – VELMA TORRAINE. A couple of painters were wandering around, splashing dirty water on clean paintwork, but what took George's eye was the heavy felt drapes hung from floor to ceiling. That these were in some way connected with the sound element in the day's work was obvious from the way they sucked in any sound the painters made, adding to the light-headed sense of unreality that was beginning to haunt George.

He was about to leave when he noticed another unfamiliar addition to the jungle of lights and cables: standing dead centre of the stage was a curiously padded box on wheels. It looked like some kind of phone booth, and George went over for a closer look.

'Fella told me that's where they mean to put the camera.'

George turned and saw one of the painters had wandered over to stand next to him.

George was puzzled and looked for an explanation.

'Seems it's supposed to deaden the sound of the camera. Ask me, anybody who spends more than ten minutes in there ain't gonna come out breathing.' The old guy wandered off muttering about things not being what they used to be, and George could see how it might work to his advantage. Everyone was going to be jumpy working with this new technology, maybe they'd all feel unsettled enough not to notice some small thing about Ailleen. Maybe . . .

George stepped out in the fresh morning air, and immediately spotted the one man who could hold off the make-up and wardrobe crafts – the studio production manager.

He walked over to him and greeted him effusively, cursing himself for not waiting to find out the man's name before launching into his spontaneous plan.

'Listen, I need you to do me a favour.'

The production manager nodded and said nothing. He looked like a man who wouldn't do God a favour.

'Velma's trying out some new ideas she's been studying – like make-up and stuff – and I'd like you to tell make-up and wardrobe that they aren't going to be needed this morning.'

The production manager stared levelly at George. 'This been cleared with Harvey Tilbury?' he asked with the air of a man who already knew it couldn't have been.

George was puzzled for a moment. 'What does Harvey have to do with it?'

The production manager's look was scornful to the point of contempt. 'Any new ideas for make-up have got to be cleared with Harvey,' he said with an air of finality. 'It affects the way he lights. Unless you got clearance from Harvey, or Mr Bressler . . .' he was shaking his head dubiously and let his line hang over them like a threat.

George had to think fast. He still didn't fully understand what make-up had to do with camera, but this man did. 'Oh!'

117

George started as if seeing the problem for the first time. 'Listen, this has been cleared all the way up to Mr Sterne himself. All I'm asking you to do is pass on our decision.'

The man didn't look the slightest bit convinced. He let out an expressive grunt. 'You know what they're gonna say, don't you?' he asked.

George tried to reassure him. 'Put it diplomatically.'

The man sighed and looked off to where the lights were now burning in the crafts department. 'I just knew today was gonna be one of those days.'

George watched the man loping off towards the crafts department and knew it wasn't the last he was going to hear of it. As he watched, his eye was taken by a more immediately pressing problem. Milton Bressler was making his way towards Velma's cottage with a purposeful bunch of flowers. George hurried to intercept him.

George's greeting didn't cause Milton to lose a single pace. He tried again. 'If you're taking those roses in to Velma, let me advise you against it!'

Milton turned suspiciously to George. 'Why's that?'

George dissimulated. 'Surely you can understand. She's in a high state of tension – nerves, you know ...' Even as George spoke, he saw an opportunity to add to the fiction he was building. '... What with trying out this new make-up and all, she's excluding everyone. Even make-up and hair.'

Milton did stop now. He turned to George looking startled. 'She's *what*!?'

'Doing her own make-up and hair.' He added, 'Didn't Wilbur tell you?'

Milton was staring at George as if he were mad. George, realizing that he'd made another as yet unknown faux-pas, went hurriedly on, 'Well, what with one thing and another, I guess it slipped his mind.'

Milton was shaking his head now. 'George, what you just told me doesn't make the least bit of sense!'

George tried to stay calm. 'How's that, Milton?'

'The whole damn studio knows that today we're not only recording sound for the first time, we're putting a new stock in the cameras. There's no way Wilbur would allow Velma to do her own make-up, today of all days.'

George felt his knees giving out, but managed to stay outwardly calm.

'What new stock is that, Milton?'

'If I told you, you wouldn't know what I was talking about.'

'Try me.'

'Well, it's got more gradations than the old stock – better grey tones, less contrasty. Today calls for a whole rethink in terms of lighting and make-up. The test we're making is as crucial a test of this new panchromatic stock as it is of Velma's voice.'

The word 'panchromatic' struck a chord with George. Just in time he remembered Ailleen using that very same one. 'That's it!' cried George delightedly. 'Panco – what you said.'

'Panchromatic,' Milton said evenly. 'Are you telling me that Velma has already learned how to use it? How?'

'How? How would I know? You know women and make-up. Something new comes along, they've all got it before the first man hears about it.'

Milton was looking cautiously at George. 'This isn't something you buy in a store. We've had our own make-up chief away for five days finding out all about it, ready for today. Now you come by and tell me Velma's not only got it, she knows how to use it.'

Suddenly George spotted Harvey Tilbury, the cameraman, striding purposefully towards them. 'Women!' he cried into the startled Milton's face. 'Who can tell what they'll use to get up to date? Here, let me take those roses in to Velma for you. See you, Milton.'

George practically tore the roses from Milton's grasp, and hurried away before Harvey could catch up with him.

He didn't dare look round until he was on the threshold of Velma's cottage, and then it was to see Harvey making some expressive point to Milton, and from the way both of them were frowning in his direction, he didn't have to spend too much time working out what they were talking about.

George ducked into the cottage and felt like bolting the door.

Julia came up to him as he leaned against the wall. 'We've got a problem,' she said.

'Just *one*?' asked George.

'Who are the roses from?'

'Milton – he'll probably be here any minute. How's things going?'

Julia gestured him inside. Prepared as he was, he was still amazed at the transformation Ailleen could make into Velma. For all the world, there sat Velma, in her very own cottage, making a few last brush strokes of shading. She looked more like Velma than Velma did.

'Is that that new panco-what's-it make-up?' he asked as authoritatively as he could.

'Panchromatic,' Ailleen corrected him.

'That's good,' said George with confidence, 'because we're using the same kind of film stock today. As a matter of fact, I just found out that this test is more to do with the new stock than it is to do with Velma's voice.'

George didn't get the big reaction he'd hoped for. Ailleen just sat there looking at him steadily. George had the uncomfortable feeling that he was the only one in the studio who didn't know what was going on.

'Something wrong?' he asked.

Julia dumped the test script into his hands. 'That's what's wrong!' she said.

'What's wrong with the script? Velma had it six weeks ago. She didn't say there was anything wrong with it.'

'It's a stinker!' said Ailleen.

George chuckled without humour. 'You're kidding, of course.'

Ailleen stood up. 'I am not kidding. No grown woman is going to prattle rubbish like that.'

George felt himself on firmer ground. 'That's the point! Velma's image isn't a grown woman – it's this jazz-baby cutey-pie kid!'

Ailleen, holding his eye steady, walked round him to where the wardrobe hung on a rail. 'This,' she said, holding up a gown as if it were 'Exhibit A', 'is the gown I'll be wearing in the test.' Ailleen shrugged off the dressing-gown she had been wearing and without the slightest inhibition slipped naked into the test gown. Julia helped her zip it up and Ailleen turned to face him, and George got the full impact. The gown clung to every naked cleft and cranny of Ailleen's body while the neckline itself left half of her finely curved breasts completely bare.

'As you may notice,' she was saying, 'I'm bigger in some places than Velma and . . .' she reached behind her and took up the slack on the waistline, '. . . smaller in others. How does this dress fit your ingénue image? Am I going to sit in that Spanish garden mouthing platitudes or are you going to be the one to tell Galaxy Studio's wardrobe department that they don't know Velma Torraine's measurements?'

'I never thought about it!' he said.

The effect of that gorgeous body in that dress was nothing less than stupefying.

Julia stepped into the amazed silence from George. 'The moment we tried on the dress it was obvious the only way to play the scene was tougher, harder.'

George was still bemused. 'We got new film stock, we got new make-up, why not a new image for Velma?'

'Then you agree we should rewrite the dialogue?' asked Ailleen.

'Dressed like that I'll agree with anything you say. You make Theda Bara look like a boy!'

Julia sounded impatient. 'So you'll clear that we make the changes?'

George hesitated. He'd opened his mouth and fallen right through it enough already for one day. 'Listen, give me a few minutes while I try to work something out with Milton, OK?'

The girls looked at him with disappointment as he backed out of the cottage, only to run right into Harvey Tilbury. George hurriedly backed up against the door to block his further progress.

'What's going on, George?' he asked.

George tried to look as if he had no idea what Harvey was talking about.

'In what way, Harvey?'

'I hear there's some funny business about make-up. I got everyone screaming at me on the set – what's it all about?'

'It's nothing, Harvey. Velma just wanted to have first crack at this new panco make-up stuff. Naturally, anything she does is subject to your OK.'

Harvey huffed his dissatisfaction. 'Let me through, George, I'll check it out.'

'Can't do that, Harvey.'

'What in hell are you talking about?'

George still didn't move.

Harvey tried going round him. George blocked him more forcibly.

'Mr Schapner, will you get out of my way?'

George made a pretence of coming to a momentous decision. He grabbed Harvey by the arm and whispered with as much urgent confidentiality as he could manage. 'I'm gonna level with you, Harvey. The truth is, we are right in the middle of a shit-slinging row with the front office. Velma doesn't like the script, and she's making changes. If front office don't like it, then she's walking. Now we don't want that, do we?'

Harvey started getting mad. 'I don't give a goddam about what hassles you're having with the front office. I'm hired as cameraman. How she looks is my responsibility. You got troubles with the sound, don't bother me with them – you know what they're doing with my camera?'

George nodded sadly. 'I saw it. A guy can't breathe in that contraption.'

Harvey leaned in heavily. 'You can't damn well *move* it either!'

George was sympathetic. 'Listen, it's like it's tough all over. Everybody's on edge – nobody more than me. Now why don't we just let things take their course, and work together to solve our problems like we always do?'

Harvey was looking at George as if he might be about to throw up. George saw his earlier determination was wavering.

'Listen, Harvey, what have you got to lose? You know, and I know, that nobody's going to turn a crank until they get your say-so.'

Harvey backed off a little. 'Can I have that in writing?' he asked with a slow grin.

'I take full responsibility!' George declared.

That was too much for Harvey; he turned away laughing.

George watched him go. Laugh, you bastard, he was thinking, just so long as you keep walking away!

George thought it might be better if he went and hid on the stage. Sometimes a crowd was better cover than a locked room. The place looked like a beehive compared with how it had been an hour before. The first thing George noticed was the number of lamps slung and being slung from the roof. Inside it was already hotter than hell. By the time Harvey had finished lighting them all up, it'd be hard enough to breathe outside the cameraman's padded box, let alone inside it!

George was so taken with the innovations he could see at every turn that he didn't notice Milton sneak up on him until he spoke.

'What's this I hear about script changes?' he demanded.

'Velma wants changes. She reckons the present script is crap, and I have to say I agree with her!'

'She's had the damn thing for six weeks, for Christ's sake. How come she wants changes now?'

'Because it's only now we've agreed to take the test, let alone discuss its content!'

Milton was still not convinced. 'Has anybody OK'd the changes?'

George felt it was his turn to go on the offensive. 'What the hell does it matter what's in the script? We're shooting a test, for Christ's sake, it's not like it's going to play Grauman's, is it?'

'George, you really amaze me. You stride around shouting your mouth off about things you know nothing about!'

George bristled in response. 'Listen, Milton, maybe you're in with Wilbur right now, but you'd better consider which – out of you and Velma – Wilbur could most easily get along without!'

Now Milton was really angry. 'To hell with Wilbur! Have you checked this out with Mr Parker?'

Parker was a new name to George. 'Who is Mr Parker?'

'Mr Parker,' said Milton with laboured patience, 'is our director of sound recording. Wilbur hired him personally, and all script changes have to get his OK.'

George couldn't believe it. 'Is this the guy from Cunard?'

'The very same. You'd better come and meet him, George. You might learn something.'

Milton led George across the stage towards a small group gathered round a pompous little man in a wing collar. Milton pulled George to one side. 'Go easy on the *Titanic* jokes. He's very sensitive about them.'

George laughed. 'I can see how he would be! The *Titanic* wasn't a Cunard ship – she was White Star Line!'

'How come you know about shipping companies?'

'Maine, Milton! I'm from Maine.'

Milton frowned as if failing to see any connection, and led George through the adoring throng to where Mr Parker was holding court. 'Mr Parker, I'd like you to meet George

Schapner. Mr Schapner represents our major star, Miss Torraine.'

Mr Parker returned George's handshake with limp disdain. Here was a man catapulted from an obscure humdrum job to the very epicentre of Hollywood, to find himself treated like a latter-day demi-god. It had all been too much for Mr Parker.

'I'm very busy,' he protested, 'you'll excuse me, I'm sure?'

Mr Parker started away, taking his coterie of admirers with him. Milton stopped him cold.

'Mr Parker,' he called, 'Miss Torraine is insisting on making changes to the spoken words.'

Mr Parker turned and came back with an expression that was a mixture of horror and disbelief. 'No question of it!' he pronounced. 'Absolutely no question of changes to the spoken word at this late stage!'

Milton was almost a supplicant. 'I did explain that, Mr Parker, but you see the problem is . . .'

Mr Parker held up an imperious hand. 'It's out of the question!'

George found himself hating this little prick Parker. Any minute now Milton might fall to his knees and start begging forgiveness for even having suggested such a thing.

'Is there an explanation goes with this arrogance?' George asked of Mr Parker.

Mr Parker turned his mean little eyes on George. 'There is, but I doubt you'd understand it!'

'Try me,' challenged George.

Aware that his fans were hanging on every word, Mr Parker started. 'Each and every syllable of the spoken word has been checked with a fine-toothed comb for its microphone acceptability. For instance, there can be no question of sibilance.'

George was lost. 'Of what?'

Mr Parker was patient. 'Sibilance is the shushing sound

recorded when an actor might attempt to pronounce any "ess" sound. The microphone just doesn't like it!'

George was incredulous. 'You mean we're gonna have to make pictures that do not include any "ess" sounds?'

Mr Parker smiled in triumph, secure in his superior knowledge. 'It is obvious that you have not read the pamphlet which I prepared specifically to avoid such situations, entitled: "Notes for Directors, Writers and Producers."'

George pounced. 'You got four "esses" in the title!'

Mr Parker's smile was wintry. 'Are you being facetious, Mr Schapner?'

'Boy, there's another one! Facetious is a doozy!'

Mr Parker regarded George for a long moment and then, turning on his heel, marched away, the audience at an end.

Milton was stricken. 'Jesus Christ, George! If you've upset him, Wilbur is going to get good and mad at you!'

'The guy's nuts!' said George. 'Who can say a sentence without using an "ess" sound?'

Milton held up his hands as if to ward George off. 'Don't ask me! All I know is Wilbur hired the guy to be in charge of sound recording and, until I hear different, what he says goes!'

George suddenly saw that by creating the maximum of problems he might be able to derail the test and get himself off the hook of having to produce Ailleen. 'I'll tell you something, Milton, what may very well be going from this studio is Velma! Could be I'd be best advised to get her out of this mad-house before we all start hitting icebergs!'

Milton went white. He held up his hands to quiet George while looking round guiltily to see if the imperious Mr Parker had overheard. He turned back to George. 'I told you to go easy on those *Titanic* jokes!'

George turned on his heel and walked away. The sight of Milton cringing before that little shit from Cunard was sickening.

Halfway back to the cottage George could see that something was wrong. Standing outside the cottage door was Julia. In her hand she held a couple of sheets of paper. She seemed to be straining to hear something that was going on inside the cottage.

'What the hell are you doing?' George demanded of her.

Julia turned to him startled. 'Wilbur!' she said and pointed to the cottage.

George's stomach turned to ice water. 'In there? With Ailleen!? How could you let it happen?'

'How could I stop him? He just busted in! Listen, George, he owns the goddamned place!'

'How long has he been in there?' George asked.

'Five, six minutes. Almost as soon as you left.'

George tried to fight his nerves down to a more acceptable level. After all, he reminded himself, Ailleen had already passed the test with Wilbur. 'You couldn't hear anything?' he asked Julia.

Julia shrugged. 'I've been trying.'

'But why didn't you stay with them?'

'Ailleen asked me to step outside.'

'Ailleen!? What the hell is she playing at?'

Julia looked off into the distance and started blowing a silent whistle through her pursed lips. For a moment he thought she'd gone crazy, and then the thought struck him. 'You don't mean she's ... he and her, are ... ?'

At that moment the cottage door opened and Wilbur stood there. He looked like a man content with himself. His cigar jaunted out from his grinning lips. His eyes swivelled from side to side as he stood diminutively between Julia and George. 'Quite a girl you got there, George,' he said as he strode off towards the test stage.

Julia and George watched him walk away and then turned to look at each other. Then, as if out of a catapult, they both moved forward together and tried getting through the door. George finally deferred to Julia.

Ailleen was seated before the dressing-room mirror calmly redoing her lipstick.

'What happened in here!?' demanded George.

Ailleen looked at him through the mirror and raised an eyebrow. 'What a question to ask a lady!' she said dead-pan.

'Wilbur didn't notice anything different about you?'

'From when – Sunday?'

George stared at her as she carefully outlined her lips in grey lipstick. 'How can you stay so calm? You got ice water instead of blood or what?'

'What do you think we do up at Madame G.'s? Play pinochle? I tell you something – this . . .' she indicated the dressing-room with a sweep of her hand, 'is a whole lot easier than Saturday night up there.'

George stood there shaking his head.

Julia spoke. 'Let's look at the positive side. Wilbur is now one hundred per cent convinced that Velma is here and ready to work, right?'

George nodded.

Julia went on, 'Well, that's the ball game! You've sold it, George. Home free!'

George felt his muscles unlock. Julia was right, of course. With Wilbur smiling and happily convinced, who was now going to start making problems? 'You mean all this sneaking about has been for nothing? We could have just let them see her?'

Julia cautioned him. 'Now, that's not what I said. The craft people have got to see her yet. They could be trickier. The point is that if and when they go running to Wilbur they're going to get the horse's laugh, right?'

'Right!' said George with delight.

Ailleen spoke from between tense lips as she filled in the outlines of her mouth. 'So what happened about the script changes?'

George came back to earth with a bump. 'Yeah, well, there's problems I didn't even know about . . .' He was interrupted as Julia handed him the test script with the revisions pencilled in.

'Take a look at this,' she told him.

George scanned the pages hurriedly. 'There's an awful lot of "ess" sounds in here,' he murmured as he went through it.

Julia and Ailleen both looked directly at him. Ailleen spoke. 'So what?'

'"Ess" sounds create microphone problems. Can we get some of these out of here?'

Julia took the script from him and scanned it worriedly. 'Maybe we could make: "Let's hope we meet again . . ." into "There will come another day . . ."'

'Good idea!' said George.

'No!' screamed Ailleen.

George turned to her. 'Why not?'

'Because I'll throw up, that's why! Anyway, all this "ess" sound business is so much horse shit!'

George was condescending. 'Now you're an expert on recordings!'

Ailleen shook her head. 'No. I just listen to them – "ess" sounds and all!'

'Where?' challenged George.

'On my phonograph at home!'

George and Julia stared at her.

'You're right!' cried a delighted George. He took the script and turned to the door. 'You leave this to me!'

George strode back on to the stage in search of the shit from Cunard. He found him, once more the centre of an admiring crowd, this time supplemented with the presence of Wilbur Sterne. Wilbur looked as in awe as anyone.

George pushed through the throng and confronted Mr Parker.

'You ever hear of a song called "Sunshine Susie"?' he asked.

Startled, Mr Parker saw the trap he was walking into, and looked lost for an answer.

Wilbur pushed in and insisted on being heard. 'What's going on, George?' he asked worriedly.

'Try saying a sentence without using an "ess" sound!'

Wilbur was bemused. 'What's this? A quiz show?'

George pointed to Mr Parker. 'This so-called expert of yours has just been telling us that "ess" sounds will not record . . .'

Mr Parker came in forcibly. 'I said no such thing! I said they could only be recorded with difficulty and would be better avoided!' Mr Parker was near beside himself with indignation. 'It's a matter of sibilance!'

Wilbur took the cigar from his mouth. 'Sybil-who?'

Mr Parker rushed in to air his authoritative knowledge. 'Sibilance is the shushing sound you get when you attempt to record an "ess" sound. Mr Schapner is attempting to totally misrepresent what I said. What I actually said was – '

'Bull shit!' roared George. 'HMV got a record out called "Sunshine Susie from the Sunshine State" – you hear them telling their songwriters not to use "esses"?'

Wilbur looked from George to Mr Parker, who seemed close to tears, and then took George gently by the hand and led him away from eager ears.

'George,' he started, 'we're all of us on edge. It's understandable. We're all of us getting into something that none of us understands . . .' Wilbur, in reasonable mood, didn't suit George's purpose in getting a crisis started. He tried intervening, but Wilbur waved him to silence and went on. 'Now, let me tell you something. Getting hold of this equipment has been like drawing teeth. I kid you not, George, I've given blood to get this machinery on the lot, and we only got it because of a friend of Milton's . . .'

George suddenly realized the reason for Milton's sudden rise to pre-eminence – he'd worked the fagaele oracle trick!

Wilbur was still talking: '. . . now the fact is that a month from now, we're all gonna know a whole lot more about this sound business than we do standing here right now. When we do, we can get rid of schmucks like Parker but, until then, we gotta just roll with the punches.' Wilbur broke off and allowed himself a confessional sigh. 'I been taking shit from Parker and Bressler like you wouldn't believe. Only so's I could get this equipment on lot – now do you understand?'

George, disarmed by Wilbur's sincerity, made one last try to keep the fire stoked, but Wilbur would have none of it.

'Now I'm gonna tell you something I shouldn't. I already told you I got this big money interested in Galaxy? Right, well, it's like I show them a piece of footage of Velma looking great, like they already know she does, but in addition talking, like she now does, and I got my money. She don't and I'm washed up. You getting all this?'

George would have felt better if his only card in the game hadn't been the fifth ace.

George looked back at Wilbur. 'We're talking big bucks, right?'

Wilbur, for answer, nodded with great solemnity.

George was halfway back to the cottage when Milton Bressler caught up with him. 'OK, you bastard! Just what the hell are you trying to pull?'

With sinking heart, George turned to face Milton. 'You want to make yourself plainer?' he asked him.

'You know damn well what I'm talking about! I've got the whole story! Ronnie Stillman *was* stabbed – and not only Ronnie! I don't know who you've got stashed in that cottage but it isn't Velma Torraine!'

George took refuge in ridicule. 'You gone nuts or what?'

Milton smiled the smile of a rattler. 'Last night Velma Torraine was moved by ambulance to Pasadena. There she was put on a train heading East.'

'You're crazy, Milton!'

'She was bandaged practically head to toe, but hanging on to her hand was a Mexican who worked for her. He was bandaged too and it doesn't take a screenwriter to fill in the rest of it!'

George tried out his scornful laugh but it didn't even convince himself.

Milton was staring directly at him. 'What I want to know is who you've got in that cottage that you're trying to pass off as – ' Milton suddenly broke off. George, opening his eyes, saw that Milton was staring past him to the cottage door. George turned. Ailleen stood there – Velma to the life.

George didn't dare look at Milton as she came forward to brush his cheek. 'Oh, Milton!' she cooed. 'Darling, you deserve a big kiss for your flowers but it *would* spoil my make-up.' Ailleen, smiling beatifically, stepped back. 'What do you think of it?'

Milton could only stand and stare. Finally he managed to get out a choked off: 'Hi, Velma . . .'

Ailleen smiled again. 'Got to run, they've called me to the set. See you later, George.'

George stood and watched Ailleen walk away. Julia was walking with her. George wished Julia hadn't risked that wink as she had passed him.

George looked to see that Milton was still watching Ailleen's trim rear in the tight dress as she walked away.

Milton turned slowly to look incredulously at George.

'You were saying, Milton?' George asked.

George was startled to see Milton's face suddenly colour with rage. 'Those goddam bastards!' he yelled and started away across the hot concrete.

'Someone's in trouble with Milton!' thought George.

Suddenly he was drained. He knew he ought to go to the set but he couldn't face it. Wondering if Ailleen had brought any booze to the studio he went inside to investigate.

He searched her dressing-room, feeling like a character out of a prohibitionist's propaganda leaflet, when he heard the cottage door open and Julia and Ailleen laughing.

He straightened up guiltily and looked out. The two were holding each other and laughing. They saw George and went into more waves of laughter.

'What's so goddam funny?' asked George.

Julia could hardly contain herself. 'Your face when you saw Ailleen come out and confront Milton!'

George resented the joke being at his expense and so, straightfaced, asked why they hadn't reported to the set.

'Because we haven't been called!' said Ailleen.

Julia added: 'We saw Milton grab you and saw you struggling so we thought we'd take the pressure off!'

George was suddenly angry. 'I damn near died when you did that! Don't you realize the chance you were taking? Stepping out in full sunlight, for God's sake?'

'It worked, didn't it?' asked Julia.

George conceded that with a shrug. 'All I'm saying is you took a hell of a chance!'

'I thought that was the order of the day,' said Ailleen. 'I mean, this whole thing is hardly routine, is it?'

'You're making one big assumption,' said George. 'You're assuming that Milton was fooled! He could be looking for Wilbur right this minute!'

Ailleen and Julia started giggling again. Suddenly the humour went out of all three as they heard the unmistakable sound of police sirens screaming into the studio.

'They called the cops?' asked George hollowly.

They crowded round the cottage window and looked out. People were running, but not to the cottage – everyone was headed in a great state of excitement towards the sound stage.

'What's going on?' George asked of no one in particular, inwardly fearing that maybe Wilbur had had a heart attack on hearing Milton's news.

Julia was more positive. 'You stay here with Ailleen. I'll go and find out!'

She left no time for argument and was out the door before George could protest.

'What do you want me to do?' asked Ailleen. 'I mean, shall I get out of my make-up or what?'

George didn't know what to do, except shake his head.

'Let's just see what's happening. The one thing we got going for us is that Wilbur has seen you and accepted you.'

Ailleen smiled and nodded and went off into the inner dressing area.

'How about you?' she called back.

'How about me – what?' asked George.

Ailleen reappeared in the door. 'Have you accepted me?'

'*Have* I? I mean, what you're doing is saving Velma's career. Both of us are going to see you get taken care of when this is all over.'

Ailleen smiled and nodded without humour. 'Be sure you do, George!'

George nodded reassuringly, but he was worrying about what was happening outside. He went to the window and peered out. He saw Julia running back towards the cottage. 'Oh-oh!' he said. Ailleen joined him at the window.

'What?' she asked.

Before George could reply, Julia, breathless, was through the door. 'There's been a shooting!' she gasped. 'Someone got shot!'

'Who?' asked George.

Julia shrugged. 'I don't know. Apparently someone saw two men having a violent argument. They didn't see the shooting but they heard it. The story so far is that one of the men is dead – the other one got away!'

George was alarmed. 'You mean there's a killer loose on the lot?'

Julia shrugged. 'I hadn't thought of that!'

'Lock the door!' George shouted, and moved to do it himself. He turned back to see the two girls looking at each other.

'This'll take their minds off Velma's test,' said Ailleen.

George felt better immediately. 'That's right! Hey, listen, they'll have to cancel the test, right?'

They all turned as one as there came a rapping on the cottage door.

134

'You OK in there?'

George crossed to the door but made no attempt to open it. 'Yeah. Who are you?'

'Bennie. I'm assistant director on this test. Listen, you're doing the right thing. Stay put. There's a crazy guy somewhere out here with a gun . . .'

No sooner had Bennie finished speaking when there was the sound of more shots.

'Holy shit!' cried Bennie in panic. 'Open the door! Let me in!'

George turned the key in the lock and the young assistant came piling through the door. George jammed it shut.

'It's Mike!' yelled Julia from the window.

'What Mike?' asked George, moving to the window.

'Our kid, Mike. Hey, listen, he's being chased!'

George stared out the window and couldn't comprehend what he was seeing. Mike Traviss was running towards them, and behind him were two cops yelling something that didn't carry.

'What the hell?' asked George.

Suddenly, as they watched, Mike turned to face the cops. They saw him raise a revolver and heard the crack of it firing twice. The cops fired back, and Mike shot upright as if hit, did a slow turn and fell flat on his face. The cops ran up and stood over him, their own service revolvers pointing at arm's length down at the prone figure.

George was aware that Julia was screaming as he made for the door and fumbled with the lock, finally getting it open.

George stepped out into the direct heat.

The movement from the dark doorway caught the attention of the cops. 'Get back inside!' they yelled at him.

'I know that kid!' George shouted back. 'Is he hurt bad?'

The cops looked at each other. One of them knelt and turned the body over. 'He's dead!' he yelled.

Somehow George closed the distance between himself and

the cops round the body. Other people were starting to close in. The cops yelled at them to stay back.

George stared down at Mike. A boy he hardly knew. Dead. Like Erle.

The assistant director was at his side. 'Jesus. I know him. He used to work for you, didn't he?'

George nodded numbly.

'You can identify him?' asked one of the cops. 'Who was he?'

'Mike Traviss.'

'You know his address?'

'We'll have it in the office.' George felt himself swaying. He knew it was cumulative. He'd been through a lot today. Having Mike lie there like Erle once had suddenly made the day feel hotter than Hades.

'Jesus!' said the assistant. 'It must have been him that shot Milton Bressler.'

George turned to the assistant. 'Shot who?'

The assistant looked at him. 'Didn't you know . . . ?'

George turned away towards the cottage. He saw Ailleen standing there with a comforting arm round Julia. He had meant to ask Julia to give the cops Mike's address, but when he opened his mouth no sound came out. He started to raise his hand to her, but suddenly the asphalt was rushing towards his face at incredible speed.

14

George felt cold. Cold and confused. He knew he'd had a nightmare. Fragmentary images still floated about in his gathering consciousness. It wasn't an unpleasant feeling. Something like floating. He felt reluctant to surrender this intoxicating feeling of weightlessness, even for the sound of Julia's anxious voice.

'George? Are you all right?'

It seemed like a superfluous question. Of course he was all right. Matter of fact, he'd rarely felt better – especially of late.

It was strange the way Julia's face seemed to be floating above his head. She looked as if she'd been crying. George didn't feel able to figure out possible causes right then and there. It would have to wait until later. The urgent business in his mind was to figure out where he was.

'George?' Julia's anxious face looked strained. 'Can you hear me?' George nodded.

Then he realized where he was. That structure over Julia's head was the drop-head of his tourer. Turning slightly to one side he could see they were moving fast through Hollywood. The back of some stranger was at the wheel.

'Who is that driving?' he asked.

'It's OK,' said Julia. 'You passed out again. I'm taking you home.'

Home sounded good. Reassuring to know he had a home, that people knew where it was and Julia was taking him there. He decided he'd go back to sleep.

'Who did you say was driving?' he asked as he drifted off.

'Someone from the studio . . .'

The studio. George knew what it was but failed to relate it to his immediate situation. Something had happened there . . . Then he remembered. 'Where's Ailleen?' he asked.

Julia told him not to worry about that, and suddenly George felt fear driving adrenalin through his comatose veins.

He tried to get up, but Julia pushed him back.

'George, you should lie still.'

George eluded her anxious grip, and sat up. The studio driver looked as if he had the biggest ears in all Hollywood. Had George mentioned Ailleen's name? He turned to Julia. 'Where is she?' he asked, and only realized how loud he was shouting when he saw the sudden shock on Julia's face. 'Where is she?' he repeated, not bothering to soften his tone.

Julia gave an anxious glance towards the driver. 'She's at the studio.'

George found himself thinking that maybe Julia was crazy.

'You left her there? On her own?'

'George, I was thinking of you . . . I . . .'

George didn't waste any more time on Julia. He turned to the driver.

'Turn this damn thing round. We're going back!'

Julia was full of protest. 'George, you can't. Not in your condition. This isn't the first time you've passed out. Something's wrong, we've got to find out what!'

It was the mixture of anger and fear that caused him to speak so vehemently. 'I'll tell you what's "wrong",' he spat, 'I'm surrounded by idiots!'

They said no more as the driver made a U-turn and started back up the hill towards the studio.

When George got to Stage C he found his way blocked by a haystack of a security man.

'You can't go in there, mister,' the guard told him.

'Do you know who I am?' he demanded.

'Yes, sir, I do, but it don't make no difference. My orders are that nobody goes in nor out while they got that light on.' The guard pointed to a red light burning dimly in the afternoon sun. It seemed a puny enough excuse to bar his way.

'Well,' said George, 'those rules are going to have to be revised. Velma Torraine is in there, she's my client, and nobody is going to stop me seeing her. Now kindly step out of the way.'

The guard didn't budge an inch. 'I'm not meaning no offence, Mr Schapner, but the way they told it to me was that they can't have people going in and out the way they used to while they're making these new sound recordings.'

George looked again at the implacable red light, and turned towards Julia. Julia was standing a resentful way off, maintain-

138

ing the studied separateness she'd started in the car. 'Julia, you heard about this?'

Julia shrugged. 'I suppose it makes sense. If you open the door while they have the microphone open, they'll hear it on the recording!'

George shook his head. 'Damn sound!' he muttered. 'First no "esses" and now this damn nonsense.'

George looked back at the adamant bulk of the guard.

Julia came closer. 'George, why don't you wait in the cottage? I'll get you some coffee while you rest.'

George glared at her. Didn't she even appreciate that behind that damned red light was maybe a jury already bringing in his death sentence? All he had going for him on his side was an inexperienced Ailleen trying to pass herself off as Velma Torraine! He was having a nightmare while Julia was asking him to rest. He felt there was no way to explain how he felt, so he didn't try.

Across the open space between the stages, George saw Wilbur hurrying towards him, his short little arms waving frantically in the air. Wilbur looked agitated rather than angry.

'They told me and I couldn't believe it!' he shouted as he closed.

George had momentary doubts as to what Wilbur was talking about, but the way he was gathered into a bear-hug of an embrace was reassuring.

'When they told me Velma had insisted on taking the test I just ... I was just knocked sideways.' Wilbur was now clutching both George's hands in his own. 'You know what this means to me, George? After this I owe that girl my life! Where is she? I want to hug that lady!'

George, embarrassed, nodded towards the stage. 'They say we can't go in while that red light's burning.'

'What red light?' asked Wilbur.

George told him of the new rules and brought Wilbur

forward to where the red light should have been shining. It was off.

The guard, now standing to one side, coughed. 'It's OK now, sir. You can go in . . .'

As the guard spoke, the door flew open and Preston Daniel, the head director of tests, came out, surrounded by two excited assistants. Preston was doing the talking and the assistants were vociferously agreeing with him. 'Did you ever see anything like that? Anybody ever see a test like that?'

Wilbur was worried in case it was expensive. 'What?' he cried. 'What happened?'

Preston spread his hands wide as if to attempt to encompass the enormity of what he was about to say. 'Poetry!' he declaimed. 'Divinity!'

Wilbur glanced at George, who was daring to breathe again, then back at Preston. 'What?' he demanded. 'Who was divine?'

'Velma!' shouted a laughing Preston. 'Like an angel! If it wasn't recorded on film, I wouldn't believe it myself!'

Wilbur was half-afraid to believe. 'She's good?' he asked.

Preston stared at Wilbur. '*Good!?*' he scoffed. Preston turned to his assistants. 'Was she "good"?' he demanded of them, and then, without even a genuflection in the direction of his sole employer, moved away across the yard, still talking animatedly with his acolytes.

Wilbur and George watched them go before Wilbur turned back to George. 'I know that man,' he said soberly. 'If he says she's better than good, she must have been sensational. Come on, let's go find her.'

A bewildered George followed the bustling Wilbur into the stage itself. They both stopped short with shock in the sudden overwhelming heat.

'Jesus Christ!' breathed Wilbur. 'What is this?'

A sweating assistant had overheard and stopped. 'It's the draperies, Mr Sterne. We have to have them for the sound recordings, but they don't let any air in. People are near to dying from the heat!'

'What about the fans?' asked Wilbur.

'Same reason, sir. They let noise in, so they blocked them off!'

Wilbur shook his head. 'We're going to have to do something about that.' To the assistant he said, 'Get those fans cleared and start them up. People can't work in this heat!' The assistant nodded and rushed off, calling for some of the stagehands.

Wilbur was peering round looking for Velma. George grabbed a passing wardrobe lady. 'Do you happen to know where Miss Torraine is to be found?'

The wardrobe lady seemed to resent even being asked.

'I imagine,' she said tremulously, 'that she is in her cottage praying for forgiveness, and should you see her, you can tell her what I think of her!'

George stood stock still, aware of Wilbur's keen ear at his shoulder. The wardrobe mistress went on, 'I've never witnessed anything so disgusting in my life, and if this is what the movies have sunk to, then I, for one, am getting out!'

Both Wilbur and George stared after the wardrobe lady.

'What did she say?' asked a perplexed Wilbur.

George shrugged. 'Some bee in her bonnet. Come on, Velma's in her cottage.'

Velma was in the bathroom when they burst through the dressing-room door. 'Velma!' screamed Wilbur, 'get out here where I can kiss you!'

George watched, heart in mouth, as Ailleen stepped out of the bathroom. He needn't have worried. In a lookalike contest Velma herself would have come second.

Wilbur had taken her in a rush. He barely reached her neck, which is where he buried his lips. 'I hear you were sensational,' he mumbled through his flesh-filled lips. 'They tell me you were beautiful. I love you! I love you!'

Ailleen was looking over Wilbur towards George with a gleam of triumph in her eyes.

'What happened?' asked George.

Ailleen shrugged. 'It went OK!' She turned her attention to the vociferous Wilbur.

'Control yourself, Mr Sterne, or you might make me forget you're a married man!'

Wilbur gave a cry of something approaching ecstasy and, to George's astonishment, threw his diminutive bulk down on to his knees, clasped Ailleen/Velma about the knees and started cooing. 'I love you! I love you! I want your body!'

Ailleen laughed. 'Now let's not start that old thing again!'

'I was younger then!' Wilbur was blubbering. 'Give me another chance!'

Ailleen started gently disentangling herself from Wilbur's fervent grasp. 'No second chances, Mister!' Ailleen was saying good-humouredly, 'the last time you promised to make me a star!'

Wilbur looked up at her and started a heaving laugh which seemed to take for ever to reach his throat. When it burst forth, it roared out to fill the room.

George stared as Wilbur rolled over on his back like a puppy dog and started kicking his legs in the air.

Ailleen, with a slightly superior shrug to George, stepped over the animated studio boss and, leaning forward, peered into a mirror. 'You figure it went all right?' she asked in rhetorical irony.

George shrugged at her reflected face. 'I hear they're going to rewrite the manual. What did you do out there?'

'Played the scene my way, nothing more nor less.'

'What way was that, exactly?' asked George who, for no definable reason, was starting to get annoyed with Ailleen.

'Why don't you wait until tonight?' she asked, 'then you can see it all on the dailies.'

George smiled. 'You speak the language pretty good for a stranger!' he told her.

Ailleen merely smiled. George sensed there had been a change in her attitude. Always confident, she now seemed to have reached an attitude of arrogant disdain for what he might feel or think.

In the background, Wilbur was huffing and puffing his way to his feet. 'I'm getting on the tails of those guys in the processing plant. We don't get those dailies the moment they're developed, I'm gonna fire every last one of them!'

Wilbur blew kisses towards Ailleen all the way out of the door. Julia was coming in and they almost collided.

Wilbur even kissed Julia.

George pounced on her. If anyone could find out what happened, it would be Julia. 'Do you know?' he asked.

'Know what?'

'What happened on the test! Everybody's going nuts about it but nobody'll tell me what happened!'

Julia smiled. 'I know,' she said, 'but I'm sworn to secrecy!'

'Fuck you!' snapped George.

'Mr Schapner?' asked a voice from the door. George turned. The guy had the look of a cop about him.

George nodded. The man came forward holding out a gold badge. George barely glanced at it.

'What do you want?'

The man took a long time answering. He looked from one of the girls to the other before finally bringing his gaze back to George.

'Well, it's like most people seem to have forgotten it, but less than four hours ago, there was a double shooting on Stage C. It's my job to investigate those deaths.'

George nodded and waited for him to go on.

'It's my understanding that you knew one of the deceased – Michael Robin Traviss – and that he was until today employed in your office.'

George nodded again, but then, as the lieutenant seemed determined to go on, spoke hurriedly. 'Can't we discuss this some other time?'

The cop raised his eyebrows, and looked up at George through hooded eyes. 'You got something more important to do, Mr Schapner?' he asked laconically.

George's first instinct was to tell the man that he had, but the man's studiedly cold gaze caused him to think again.

'What I mean is,' George stuttered, 'that my office might be a more appropriate place.' The cop's steady eyes made George realize his words needed reinforcement. George waved a hand towards Ailleen and Julia. 'I think these ladies have been subjected to as much of this as they are likely to take in one day!'

That seemed to appeal to the cop's reason. He tipped his hat to both Ailleen and Julia, and indicated to George that he was ready to leave.

George hesitated. He wanted to warn Julia to keep Ailleen out of everybody's way until the test screening, but didn't want to do it in front of the cop.

Julia, seeing his hesitation, asked, 'You want me along?'

George decided he'd get the cop outside with a false exit.

'No. You stay here with Velma.'

Julia nodded and watched him join the cop at the door. He knew he'd been unfair to her earlier and wanted to tell her that too. But first he wanted to get the cop out of there.

He walked past the cop and out into the heat of the afternoon.

'You work with nice ladies,' the cop murmured.

George agreed and then went through the pretence of having just remembered something. Excusing himself he went back to the cottage. Later he was to wish he never had.

As he opened the door he saw Julia and Ailleen spring guiltily apart. They both stared at him like kids caught with their fingers in the molasses pot.

George couldn't think of a thing to say. 'Sorry,' he murmured and, turning, went back to the cop.

'Everything OK now?' asked the cop.

George didn't know how to respond to that either.

15

The lieutenant spent a long time looking straight at George. 'You movie people don't get moved by much, do you?'

George shrugged.

The lieutenant went on, 'What I mean is, there was a double death at the studio this afternoon. One corpse was well known to you all, the second, and possibly the killer, was well known to you, yet I'm having a hard time getting anyone to talk about it. Can you tell me why that is, Mr Schapner?'

George, while relieved to hear it, felt unable to offer anything but a shrug. 'Who knows?' he asked.

'Somebody knows, Mr Schapner. Somebody knows why a kid who worked in your office ups and shoots a prominent director–producer who just happens to be also connected to this office. Somebody knows why, Mr Schapner, and I intend to find that person and solve this crime.'

The lieutenant was on his feet by the time he'd finished speaking, and all George had to do was stick out his hand and the cop would have gone, probably for ever. George wondered why he didn't do that. Instead he spoke. 'Look, lieutenant, this is a very small town. The movie business is almost a village. Everyone knows everyone. You'd have a hard time finding anyone that wasn't connected with either one or both of the deceased.'

The lieutenant nodded. 'Except for one thing. Not all them people have motive to kill. When I find that linking motive ...' The lieutenant let his sentence hang, and George felt he didn't know quite how to finish it.

'Then ... what, lieutenant? As I see it, whatever the motive, the perpetrator is as dead as the victim. Why don't you let them lie?'

The lieutenant stood there a long moment, stroking the end of his nose. 'Wouldn't you be curious as to why this happened, Mr Schapner? Seems to me, if two people I knew were dead, I'd be interested, even if I wasn't a cop.' He paused. 'Always supposing I didn't already know, that is.'

George stood awkwardly across the desk from the lieutenant. Fervently hoping that his guilty flush didn't show in his eyes, George decided on a pious approach. 'I hope you're not implying that *I* . . .'

The lieutenant interrupted. 'I don't imply, Mr Schapner. I ask questions, I assemble facts, I get a warrant and I make arrests. It's as simple as that.'

'Just what crime, other than that between these two deceased, are we talking about, lieutenant?'

The lieutenant's face wrinkled into his first grin. Suddenly he seemed a whole lot friendlier. 'You got a point, Mr Schapner. You got a point.'

The moment the cop was out on the sidewalk, George raced down his back stairs and into his car. There was a more urgent mystery, capable of solution, up at Galaxy. George didn't want to miss it.

George was astonished by the mêlée outside the projection block. Technicians, directors and some famous names were jostling each other trying to get through the door.

The same security man who had turned George back at the entrance to Stage C earlier was one of the men sweating to hold them back. He was also the one to ease George through the protesting crowd.

'What's going on?' he asked the guard as he was pushed through to the front.

'Never saw nothing like this in my born days,' muttered the guard. 'It's like everyone has gone nuts. Some of these people don't even belong on this lot!'

George didn't have time to question him further because he was being propelled into the relative sanity of the projection theatre. He looked around. The room was filled to bursting. People were standing two deep round the walls, and George knew barely half the faces. Judging from the blank way they stared at him, they didn't know him either.

His eye was caught by someone deep in one of the middle rows waving frantically at him. In the half light he could make out Preston Daniel. Preston, bless the man, indicated an empty seat beside himself. On the far side of Preston sat Ailleen. George fought along the rows of people intervening to reach Preston. As he went he cursed himself for forgetting to tell Ailleen that Velma was well known for never going to see her own dailies.

'What's going on?' he asked of Preston when he finally reached him. Preston was in buoyant mood. 'It's all over town. Our little lady here is a sensation, that's all!'

Suddenly George remembered! These were the first sound takes shot on the Galaxy lot. That must be what all the fuss was about! He felt a little better. If Ailleen had done something totally un-Velma that people would notice, then he'd be in trouble. Realizing the fuss was as much about the recorded sound as the star made him feel a little better. Maybe people's minds would be more on the one thing and Ailleen's performance would slip by unnoticed. He said as much to Preston and was immediately disabused.

'We're not running the recorded sound!' Preston told him. 'Getting the sound synchronized to the lip movements is going to take a while. No, these people are here because of Velma – nothing more nor less.'

Preston thought George would be pleased. George *was* pleased – that the lighting was so dim Preston couldn't see how pale he went!

Ailleen, he fervently hoped, might have been good, but how could she survive this billing? Few people could. George slumped in his seat and felt depression settling round him like a trap.

It was the excited murmur greeting Wilbur's arrival that brought George out of his stupor. He couldn't afford to look like a man at a wedding who thought it was a funeral. He was standing ready to greet Wilbur, but Wilbur, in his rush to reach and kiss Ailleen, pushed past him, trod on his toes even, in his headlong dash to get to Ailleen's side.

'Sweetheart!' he crooned, loud enough for everyone to hear.

'I couldn't wait! I saw them on a moviola. Just say the word and I'll talk to Golda about a divorce!'

The laugh that went up round the room reassured Wilbur that he'd be quoted in the morning's papers. Wilbur, his eye sweeping his appreciative audience, finally noticed George. 'You!' he screamed, pointing an accusatory finger. 'You, I want to see in my office first thing tomorrow morning.' George nodded, aware of a rising feeling of exultation. He was home free! Wilbur had seen the footage and wanted to talk – it meant only one thing. George could afford to sit up and smile. Wilbur was standing and waving to the back of the hall to the projectionist. 'Roll 'em!' he was shouting and, as the lights dimmed, he shouted again, this time to the audience. 'Hold on to your hats, folks, you gonna be seeing history made today!'

The footage flickered and flashed until it settled down to the properly exposed section. This was material raw from the processing facility on the lot. Finally, the scene came into full, properly exposed, focus.

The scene was a moonlit garden. In the foreground a Spanish fountain gently played.

Preston started a commentary on the missing sound recording.

'The water sounds great!' he whispered urgently to Wilbur.

'What does it sound like?' asked Wilbur.

'Just like water, only maybe a little too loud.'

Wilbur grunted, but said no more since the first of the players was coming on screen.

The actor assigned to play opposite Velma in this test was

a well-known contract player. He walked down centre stage and elegantly produced a cigarette case, selected a cigarette and gently tapped it against the case.

'The tapping is fantastic!' cooed Preston. 'The trouble is going to be getting it into synchronization. I've no idea how they are going to do that,' he added, puzzlement in his voice.

'Then why don't we let "them" worry about it?' asked Wilbur.

George smiled in the dark. It was obvious that Preston thought this test was going to be the start of a whole new relationship between him and Wilbur, and it was equally obvious to George that Wilbur was already putting up his defences.

George started to get uneasy when this tiny bit of business went on and on. He began to think that Ailleen had missed her cue, when suddenly she appeared from behind a potted palm, crept up behind him and mouthed a big lip movement, which the joyous Preston interpreted as 'Boo!'

The actor on screen jumped with surprise, and the crowd in the auditorium roared with laughter. George smiled to himself.

Ailleen was going to be all right – they liked her!

Ailleen's lips moved: 'Why not?' quoted Preston.

It was then that George's blood ran cold. Ailleen suddenly turned her back on the actor and broke away, skipping lightly towards the fountain – and right out of the lit action area. Ailleen's brightly-lit figure disappeared into shadow, and the scene abruptly cut.

'I had to cut here!' said Preston with an astounding apologetic tone. 'Velma's move was so totally unexpected.'

George felt the earth opening beneath his feet. This was disaster. Velma would know better than to make an unrehearsed move that the cameraman hadn't allowed for. Ailleen, whose only experience was on stage, had ad-libbed! It was a 'page one' error.

It was all the more astonishing then for George to hear, as

take two started to play the same scene over again, Preston saying to Wilbur, 'Of course, as soon as Velma explained to me what she had in mind, I saw that she was absolutely right!'

'You bet your cock!' growled Wilbur.

When they came to the breakaway move this time, it was properly lit and Ailleen looked lighthearted and natural.

'I don't see why two people who love each other shouldn't do exactly what they want!' Preston was dubbing in missing dialogue again.

George felt his heart sinking at what happened next.

As the actor moved to come close up behind Ailleen, she swung her legs over the parapet of the fountain and, with abandon, kicked her shoes off over her shoulders.

The crowd roared as the actor, coming up behind, had to duck to miss the shoes flying about his head.

The roar of laughter blotted out the dialogue being supplied by Preston.

It was alarmingly unconventional, but even George, in his scared state, could see that Ailleen was bringing a zesty freshness to a stale and trite situation. George started blocking out Preston's explanatory notes to the dialogue. He was totally fascinated watching Ailleen's visual re-creation of Velma. If dangling her feet in the water was unconventional, what followed next made his hair stand on end. Ailleen, still with lips moving, was levering herself off the parapet of the fountain and into the water itself. The filmy ball gown she wore, already filled to bursting, floated up to the surface of the water and puffed up like a balloon. Velma/Ailleen's legs could be seen floating to the surface as she slid into a sitting position in the water.

That this move hadn't been rehearsed was obvious from the nonplussed look on the face of the usually suave stock player. He managed to carry on after only the minutest of hesitations. He was urging Ailleen's character to do something or other, but nobody was paying attention to Preston's dubbed-in dialogue. All eyes were on Ailleen; she was electrifying.

Preston was mumbling some justifying motivation for Velma's actions on screen. 'You see what she's doing, don't you?' he was asking urgently of Wilbur. 'She has managed to distance herself from this man's importunities, while at the same time making herself both unattainable and mercilessly brazen!'

'Who gives a fuck?' asked Wilbur in reply. 'She looks gorgeous!'

'Thank you, kind sir,' Ailleen murmured out of the darkness, and then squealed as Wilbur expressed his admiration in a more direct physical manner.

George watched the scene, and couldn't believe what he was seeing. Having thoroughly soaked the filmy gown, Ailleen, on screen, now suddenly shot upright in the water, causing an audible gasp from the audience as they saw how the gown clung to her body. She was still clad as she had been when the scene started, but in every man's mind she might as well have been stark naked.

The actor, poor guy, just stood there staring pop-eyed at this vision of Velma, never before seen in public. Ailleen, on screen, was extending a hand towards him. 'Won't you join me?' mimicked Preston, and the crowd roared as the actor on screen, obviously feeling that someone was making a fool of him, shouted something towards where the director would have been, and then stalked off the set.

Ailleen/Velma turned into camera and blew everyone a kiss, at which point the footage ended, and the house lights came up. Applause broke out around the auditorium. They were looking at Ailleen, and she stood and waved back at them as if it was the kind of thing that happened to her every day.

'Champagne!' yelled Wilbur through the tumult. 'My office!' This was greeted with a roar of approval from the crowded room until Wilbur shouted that he didn't mean them, and got a groan in response.

They fought their way out as the crowd outside pressed to get in for the second showing.

'You running them again?' asked an astonished George of Wilbur.

'We're going to get a riot if we don't!' he shouted back happily.

George finally fought his way free of the crowd and was checking the buttons on his jacket when Ailleen caught up with him.

'George,' she whispered urgently. 'You got to get me out of here!'

'Why?' asked the astonished George. 'You pulled it off – you're the star of the evening, relax and enjoy it!'

'You don't understand. I got to get to work.'

George stared at her. 'You mean . . .' He did a quick glance round to make sure no one was in earshot, 'up there . . .?'

Ailleen nodded. She obviously wasn't crazy about the idea either.

'Why?'

'Because it's the only way I got the day off today. If I don't show up tonight she'll break my legs.'

George's head was spinning. Here was a girl who had not only saved Velma Torraine's career, but had probably enhanced it to the tune of a million dollars or so, having to plead off her big night so she could resume her role as a fantasy garbage dump.

'You can't! We have to talk! There's ramifications here you haven't dreamed of.'

Ailleen was shaking her head. 'You got to get me out, George!'

Wilbur was already tugging anxiously at George's sleeve.

'Come on, you horny bastard, let's get outside some real champagne!'

George turned to him with a sinking heart. Wilbur took all his excuses personally and was obviously baffled and angry when they finally broke free, but George needed Ailleen's loyalty more than Wilbur's good offices right then. Wilbur could be brought round. Without Ailleen, George was dead mutton.

On the drive down Sunset, George's mind was racing. Ailleen was a valuable asset to him and, at the same time, dangerous. He needed control of her, control which was currently and firmly in the hands of a vicious whoremaster who not only knew which end was up, but had the power to rearrange things if they didn't suit her. At the same time George was confused at just how to handle the present situation. He hadn't dared think further than just getting Ailleen successfully passed off as Velma. Now that had happened – with a result beyond his wildest expectations – he didn't have the first idea what else he was going to do.

There were so many factors and so little time.

Velma wasn't likely to be in any condition to step back into her own life for some considerable time, yet, with this new sensation, he needed to be able to produce her from time to time or rumours – or worse – could get started again.

What was needed was sleight of hand of the highest order.

It seemed to George that the solution to one problem merely made way for even greater problems, to which the solutions got ever more elusive.

He felt Ailleen's hand on his arm. 'I'm sorry, George, I know how you must be feeling. If it helps, I want you to know you can count on me.'

At that moment it did help. George felt a rush of gratitude towards the girl. She was probably more scared than he was. At least he could bury himself in alcohol and wait for morning, while she, on the other hand, had been up since before dawn playing Velma and was about to start another night's work playing, still Velma, but in an altogether different way.

'We got to do something!' he told her grimly. 'I don't know what, but something . . .'

Ailleen nodded and withdrew the reassuring pressure of her hand on his arm.

Nothing better illustrated to George how confused he was getting than Ailleen's sudden cry of alarm as they neared Crescent Heights. 'George!' she called in startled tones. 'What are you doing?'

George slowed and glanced at her. 'What do you mean? I'm taking you to Madame G.'s.'

'George, what if someone were to see us? Somebody sees you delivering me, in Velma's face, right to the door?'

George stamped on his creaking brakes, and broke into a cold sweat. 'Jesus! What am I thinking about?'

'Drive!' said Ailleen positively. 'There's usually a cab standing around La Cienaga, I'll take it back to the house from there.'

'But the cabbie'll see your face ...'

Ailleen was shaking her head, and from her bag produced a veil, which she started hooking on either side of her hat.

'Cabbies notice less than you think,' she said.

Still feeling like the original hollow man, George let her off at La Cienaga and saw her duck into a cab. He sat there a long moment, feeling inadequately equipped for the game he'd invented himself. Somehow everyone seemed to know the rules better than he did.

He had intended to go down La Cienaga to Wilshire and take a left back to Rossmore, but he was passing Melrose when the big idea came to him. Suddenly it was there – all of a piece – the perfect solution!

The only problem was going to be getting it past Madame Gregory.

16

Madame Gregory handed George a drink. 'Hear there was some excitement on the Galaxy lot today.'

George nodded and carefully kept his tone neutral as he replied, 'You could call it that.' George wasn't sure how much Madame G. already knew or which particular 'excitement' she was referring to.

She seated herself opposite George and sipped her own drink.

'Nice enough guy, used to come up here a lot, but we never got close. Somehow there's always a barrier with pansies. Violence, too,' she added reflectively. 'Violence is bad for business, that's why I never catered for them.'

'Why do you suppose he came up here so much then?'

Madame G. shrugged. 'That was business. Milton had connections. You know, booze and a little giggle powder.'

George was genuinely surprised. 'Really? Strange. Milton always seemed such an educated guy.'

Madame G. smiled. 'Just because you're educated doesn't mean you're not stupid.' She looked down into her glass. 'I think he used to dabble more for the excitement than the money. Strange guy.' Madame G. seemed to tire of the topic of Milton. She looked directly up to George. 'Something you wanted to talk to me about?'

George took a deep breath. In his experience the opening of a negotiation was the most crucial. If you got the approach right, then the rest was easy. His difficulty in dealing with Madame G. was not knowing how much she already knew. He finally decided to assume that she knew, or had guessed, everything.

'I want to buy Ailleen out,' he said.

Madame G. looked at him for a long moment and then let

a slow smile spread across her face. She took her time arranging her spare arm along the back of the couch. 'Can it be that you've fallen in love with her?'

George managed to get off a laugh. 'No chance.'

Madame G. shrugged. 'Then we're talking business. Just like Paramount asking MGM for a loan-out.'

George nodded. 'I'll go with that. How much is Ailleen worth to you?'

Madame G. found a sudden interest in the fabric of her gown.

'That's hardly the question. The real question is: How much is she worth to *you*?'

George considered many different approaches but Madame G.'s shrewd eyes were watching his face for every sign of anxiety. This was a lady who had seen a lot of anxiety. Maybe it wouldn't hurt to let a little of it show.

'I'm in a fix,' he told her.

Madame G. laughed and raised her glass. 'I'll drink to that!'

George acknowledged the toast, and started in again. 'I got a star – Velma – who can't work, and a stand-in that pulled miracles out of hats for me. My problem is that having established that Velma is alive and working, I have to find some way of keeping Galaxy from demanding that she rushes into a series of programmer pictures. I don't have Velma! You see my problem?'

Madame G. nodded, listening attentively.

'Now, until about an hour ago I didn't have the first idea of how to go about creating this piece of magic. Then it came to me – a personal appearance tour . . . nationwide, you get it?'

Madame G. nodded. 'Using Ailleen?'

'Right. See how neat that is? The risk is minimal, since the public have only ever seen Velma in black and white – on the screen and in magazines – and they've never heard her talk!'

George sat back feeling nervous exhaustion setting in

rapidly – if Madame G. didn't buy this, there was no place else to go!

'It could work. It'd give my girl Velma a real chance at total recuperation, but to make it work I need Ailleen, and that's what I'm here to negotiate.'

'So what are you offering?'

George shrugged. 'I haven't thought it through that far, but we're both here, we both know the score. What do you want?'

Madame G. looked deep into her glass. 'I want to hear you open,' she said.

George took a deep breath. He hadn't been turned down, now it was only a matter of numbers. He began to feel better.

'The way I figure it is that Ailleen is worth, maybe, at the outside a grand a week to you, and she's got maybe twenty weeks or so to run on her agreement . . .' George made an open-handed gesture. 'In my book that comes out around 20,000 dollars.'

Madame G. rose and crossed towards him with a hand extended. George thought for a moment that she was going to shake on the deal, but he was disappointed. All she wanted was his glass. 'You want another drink before you go?' she smiled.

George protested. 'It's a fair offer.'

Madame G. shook her head. 'You're talking it round the wrong way. We're not talking compensation for what I already got. We're talking what her value is to *you*. The way I see it you're in a whole lot of trouble and I wouldn't want it to get around that I didn't take advantage!'

'It must never "get around" anyway,' he said.

Madame G. was nodding in agreement. 'Which makes my point for me. You're not just buying out Ailleen, you're buying me too – and I don't come cheap. Now do you want another drink or don't you?'

George handed her his empty glass and Madame G. moved towards where she kept the drinks.

George called to her turned back, 'OK. You name it. What do you want?'

Madame G. turned with the two refreshed glasses in her hand. 'I want . . .' she broke off while she walked the whole distance across the room, 'I want fifty thousand up front and a cut!'

George went hollow inside. 'You're crazy!' he told her.

Madame G. smiled and handed him his drink. 'OK,' she said. 'Finish your drink while we talk about something else.'

George took a deep dip into the drink, watching Madame G. infuriatingly composed and smiling. 'A cut of what?' he finally asked.

'Of Velma. The real Velma. You get ten per cent, I'll take two and a half. That leaves you seven and a half and you get to keep your "clippings".'

'I don't clip my clients!' protested George.

Madame Gregory laughed out loud.

'Well, not much, anyway,' muttered George. He looked up at Madame G.'s implacable face. 'Where do you suppose I'm going to get money like that?'

Madame G. shrugged. 'You picked up a lot of cash on your RCA deal.'

George stared at her. 'You got a ticker-tape in here?'

Madame G. smiled. 'My ticker-tape comes through this house, in a never-ending stream, and when it does it's got a hard-on. It talks plenty, does my ticker-tape. I bet I knew what happened at Galaxy today before you did – and I'm not talking about Milton Bressler.'

George's mind was confused, juggling these unfamiliar-sized numbers. Fifty thousand would have been an unthinkable sum before this afternoon's test. After it, he knew he wouldn't be offered any penny-ante contract for Velma. She was now the key to the whole of the studio's future. Set against that, fifty thousand didn't seem much. On the other hand, he didn't yet have a big-numbers contract signed. He'd be handing a sizeable proportion of his newly-acquired cash capital to Madame Gregory. Yet again, without Ailleen he didn't have a damn thing going for him.

'Your money won't grow in your hand like your prick,' offered Madame G. helpfully.

George nodded and stood up. 'OK,' he said, sticking out his hand. 'You got a deal.'

Madame G. smiled at the extended hand and for a moment it looked as if she would disdain it, but finally she took it and shook it without conviction.

'Don't forget the other business – we can do that legit, with lawyers.'

'How am I going to explain that?'

'You, me and the lawyers'll be the only ones ever to know.'

George shrugged. 'Since we're partners I can ask you this: I'd like to take Ailleen out of here tonight.'

Madame Gregory shook her head. 'No chance. Ailleen comes strictly COD.'

George persisted. 'At least let me talk to her before I leave.'

Again the shake of the head. 'She's busy right now, and likely to be the rest of the night. Hey, this'll give you a kick! I doubled her price tonight!'

George stared at Madame Gregory.

She laughed. 'When a property's as hot as Velma Torraine is right now, you can get any price you want. Could be a pointer for you when you go in to negotiate your contract.'

George smiled, and allowed himself a superior tone. 'Your clients are maybe a little more vulnerable than Wilbur Sterne!'

He got the superior tone back double. 'Would it interest you to know who is up there with her right this minute?'

'Who?' asked George.

'Wilbur Sterne!'

George didn't stop running until he reached his car. The irony of the situation escaped him completely.

17

George got back to his office from Galaxy just after three in the afternoon. The first thing he saw as he parked in the patio was Ronnie Stillman. He was sitting on the top of the stairs that led up from the patio, his feet up, head well back, soaking in the sunshine.

He looked asleep and for a moment George considered getting back into his car and driving off, but Ronnie was already stirring.

That morning George had responded to an urgent summons from Wilbur. Wilbur had been raving about how marvellous Velma was in the test, and they'd sat and watched it through – this time with the magical addition of the soundtrack.

George had been enthralled. Last night's viewing of this same footage had been startling, but Ailleen, at least to his guilty eye, had looked like just one more mime. Now that he could hear the dialogue there was a new dimension – naturalness. Ailleen looked natural. Gone were the exaggerations of expression and gesture that had for so long tainted the movie performance. Here was something the audience could respond to. If George had any remaining doubts about the difference sound was going to make to movies, they were now totally dispelled.

Through the many showings – Wilbur had wanted to check that this new-fangled system stayed in synchronization *every* time it was run – George kept recalling a phrase Ailleen had used the day before: 'If the movies are going to talk, at least let them say something.'

He was beginning to understand what she meant and, more, beginning to see how it was going to affect the entire industry.

He remembered Milton Bressler telling him how sound was going to cause a new demand for writers, 'not just someone's favourite niece writing the titles,' but along with that there was going to be a whole new batch of actors, and a lot of them were going to be stars very quickly indeed.

George said nothing of this to Wilbur. He was too busy working on ways he might attract this new influx of talent into his agency before the studios realized what it was they really had.

More immediately, there was Ronnie Stillman, raising the brim of his hat at George's approach. 'Hello, old boy,' he greeted in his plummy English tones. In that moment it occurred to George that he ought to sign Ronnie – his was the kind of voice they'd all be looking for soon.

'How you doing, Ronnie?'

Ronnie swung his legs down off the wall and stood up to extend his hand towards George. 'Never felt better. All the better for seeing you, George.'

George led the way into his office and found it empty. No sign of Julia anywhere.

It was Ronnie who explained her absence. 'Went to lunch with a girlfriend. Real smashing-looking girl, name of Ailleen – something like that. British too.'

Ronnie was looking directly at George who tried not to flicker a facial muscle, although all were quivering for action beneath his thick skin.

'You're looking good, Ronnie.'

Ronnie drew himself up to his full height, and smiled. 'New man!' he said with relish. 'Played a little gentle tennis yesterday.'

'Good for you.'

George got himself seated behind his desk and awaited the first real question. Ronnie came in right on cue.

'Where's Velma?'

George picked up a ruler from his desk and studied it minutely. 'Recuperating.'

Ronnie was silent. When George looked up from the ruler, he found Ronnie staring directly at him with a puzzled frown.

'How did you get her to work yesterday?'

George smiled. 'Guts and willpower.'

'I heard she never looked lovelier. What was that, some kind of medical miracle?'

George nodded. 'Courtesy of the make-up department.' George was anxious to get away from the subject of Velma if he possibly could. 'You heard about this new make-up and stock they're using?'

Ronnie shook his head.

'Marvellous!' exulted George. 'You know what it means, don't you? It's going to mean that the girls will be able to go on working until they are much older. No more scouting the country for unflawed fourteen-year-olds!'

'Like Velma was?' asked Ronnie quietly.

George decided that being Mr Nice Guy didn't suit his mood. He had a long hand still to play, and didn't want his fifth ace exposed unless it had to be. 'Look, Ronnie, you got to understand something. We've all got a lot invested in Velma – me, the studio, a lot of people. Well, you damaged that investment. I don't have to apologize for being cautious around you.'

Ronnie nodded in vociferous agreement. 'Perfectly understood, old boy. Absolutely. I – er – just wanted to see her, get a chance to express my apologies for what happened.'

George was nodding but giving no encouragement. 'This can happen, Ronnie, given time.'

Ronnie's eyes were becoming uncomfortably damp. 'Really am a different person, George. Absolutely top to bottom a new model Ronnie Stillman.' Ronnie's damp eyes were pleading for some indication from George that he was relenting. George remained poker-faced.

'I'd just like her to know how sorry I am about what happened. Damnably sorry and – well, you know, old boy, fair crack of the whip, that sort of thing . . .' Ronnie's voice was cracking as it trailed off.

'I'll tell Velma when I see her next.'

Suddenly Ronnie slapped his hand down hard on George's desk. 'God knows I'll never forgive myself, but if . . . if only . . .' Ronnie's voice broke again, and his tear-filled eyes gazed again at George.

George felt moved to get up from his desk and go round to put a hand on Ronnie's shoulder. 'I understand, Ronnie, I really do, and I'm sorry!'

Ronnie suddenly shot to his feet causing George to step back.

'Not pity!' he yelled full into George's face. 'For God's sake spare me your pity!'

Before George had fully recovered from this startling transformation, Ronnie had lunged forward out of the door and was racing down the steps to the patio two at a time.

Julia came in some thirty minutes later to find George sitting at his desk rhythmically slapping the ruler down on it.

Each contact caused a pistol-like clap to resonate throughout the hollow-bricked room.

'Anybody I know?' asked Julia.

'You, if you're going to take four-hour lunches!'

Julia smiled. 'I was with Ailleen,' she said as if nothing else need be said.

George nodded. 'I'm going up there to get her tomorrow night.'

Julia nodded. 'She told me. And it's not before time. Madame G.'s giving her a hard life.'

Julia started leafing through the pile of messages on his desk that he hadn't given a thought to.

'Had any thoughts about where she's going to stay?' she asked.

George looked up at Julia. 'To be honest I hadn't. How about your apartment?'

Julia shook her head. 'My room-mate's still there. Too risky.'

Julia seemed to be giving it considerable thought. George found himself strangely uneasy as she said: 'How about her moving in with us – temporarily at least?'

George looked steadily at Julia, feeling that his response was going to be important to her. Perversely he delayed. 'I don't know if that would work.'

'Well, it's your decision, but at least you'd know where she was and who she was seeing.'

George nodded. The suggestion made sense enough but he felt there was a whole lot more to it than Julia was allowing to show.

'Why don't we talk about it tonight?' he asked her, finally.

Julia seemed to accept that, but then surprised him. 'What did Morris Denny want?'

George stared at her. Morris Denny was top man at MGM. What was Julia talking about?

'Haven't you read any of your messages?' she asked testily, and reaching across the desk pulled a whole pile of them in front of him. 'While you were up at Galaxy, practically the whole of Hollywood was trying to reach you!'

George started leafing through the messages. Monogram and even Tiffany had called, and then, the most astonishing of all, Stephen Von Muller!

George yelped when he found that one. Stephen Von Muller was just about the biggest name in Hollywood directors, and, so far as George was aware, locked in tight at MGM.

'What did Von Muller say?' he asked Julia.

'Exactly the same as all the others. Where were you? When are you coming back, and when could they reach you?'

'And then you took a four-hour lunch!'

Julia looked at him steadily. 'I'm sorry about that. It wasn't intended. Time just ran away from us.' Julia was decent enough to flush guiltily before she went on the attack. 'But I never imagined you'd come back and ignore your messages!'

'Get me Von Muller at MGM. Make it sound personal . . .'

Julia, halfway to the door, stopped and turned back with a sigh. 'If I do that I'll not get through, you know what they're like over there.'

George gestured. 'Play it any way you like, just get him back!'

Julia nodded and went out.

In the interval waiting for the call, George's mind raced ahead. Von Muller probably wanted to use Velma in a picture. It could be the biggest thing that had ever happened to her, but he wouldn't be able to deliver her for, at the very earliest, a month or more. It would be surprising if Von Muller were prepared to hold on for her.

George snapped up the phone on the first tinkle.

'I want to talk with you,' Von Muller said, after the briefest of introductions, in a pleasant east coast voice which belied his Germanic name.

'Well, any time would be a pleasure, Mr Von Muller.' George couldn't rid himself of the excitement that just talking to someone as exalted as Von Muller gave him.

'Somewhere discreet,' Von Muller was murmuring, and then, after a slight pause, hit George sideways. 'I shall be frank with you, Mr Schapner, I am not happy where I am, and am considering a move. There are, naturally, several options but there is, in my mind, a possibility that could be of interest to you.'

George's mind was suddenly so full that he could barely bring himself to speak. Had he heard right? Von Muller was thinking of making a move? And wanted to speak to George about it? This was the stuff of dreams.

They set the meeting for that night at George's house.

George was getting slightly annoyed at the way people always referred to his location as 'out of the way'. As he hung up, he considered that maybe it was time to follow the crowd into the hills.

Julia came bursting through the door, having absorbed every word on the extension. 'Von Muller is coming to talk to you?' she asked, breathless with excitement.

George enjoyed a moment of fantasy. 'Why not? Listen, if Morris Denny can call up so can Von Muller.'

Julia was suddenly thoughtful. 'Hold it,' she said. 'You don't think this is a put-up job, do you? Morris Denny wouldn't have got Von Muller to call you to find out what plans you've got for Velma?'

George laughed out loud. 'Von Muller running tag for Morris Denny? Jesus, don't you know anything about Hollywood?'

Julia shrugged. 'Not *this* Hollywood! This Hollywood never called here before.' Another thought excited her even more. 'Maybe he wants you to represent him?'

George laughed even louder. 'Who ever heard of a director having an agent?' he asked.

'Times are changing,' cautioned Julia. 'The way things are going, anything is possible. Maybe even directors are going to need representation.'

George looked up at her bright, intelligent face.

She could be right. They'd reshuffled the pack and were starting the game over.

The thought of negotiating contracts for the Von Mullers of this world made George's mouth water. He tried to keep the excitement out of his voice as he murmured, 'We'll know tonight.'

18

Von Muller, on the telephone, had been cultured east coast, but here in George's house his whole bearing and appearance were one hundred per cent German. Teutonic was the word that came into George's mind.

Von Muller seemed unwilling to settle. He was pacing as he talked.

'As I told you, I am not happy with MGM. It is true that they are giving me everything – the best designers, writers, everything – except that which is most precious to me: control! Increasingly they interfere. Increasingly they impose rather than "give". Increasingly I find that I have less and less say in what is in the story, even less about the people that will play in it.'

George was nodding through all this, and trying to look intelligent, but he found himself paying less attention to what Von Muller was saying, and only marvelling that Von Muller was here in George's own house saying it!

'They allow me style – but there are limitations.' Von Muller took a dramatic pause. 'I have in mind to make a particular kind of picture which will uniquely encompass the true American values, allegorically presented so that it is at once acceptable and, of course, immediately comprehensible to the ordinary picture-goer. The coming of sound makes it imperative that I find a studio where I can make those statements!'

George was stunned. Von Muller wasn't on any fishing trip for Morris Denny – this was a twenty-four carat offer to George to represent him. The only problem was, George couldn't immediately see where he could help.

MGM's resources couldn't be matched anywhere in town. Paramount was always financially borderline. People were talking about a resurgence over at Warner's, but then the brothers had been bluffing for years past, and now they had gambled heavily on sound. If that failed, so did Warner's.

In any case, Von Muller would have considered all the obvious names. Surely he couldn't be thinking of Galaxy? A heavyweight like Von Muller could sink Galaxy, no matter how much money Wilbur hoped to raise on Wall Street. On the other hand, if it worked, it could sky-rocket them into the first rank of studios.

George sat there feeling inadequately equipped for this kind of front-rank dealing. He was also acutely aware that he hadn't said anything in a long time.

Von Muller was looking at him with a sympathetic smile. 'Are you wondering why I bring you my thoughts?' Von Muller asked.

George nodded. 'I have to be frank with you, Mr Von Muller, I think you're out of my league.'

Von Muller nodded. 'I appreciate your frankness, Mr Schapner, and naturally I knew a great deal about you before I called. I gave that call a great deal of thought – until today.'

George looked up. 'Today?' he asked.

Von Muller nodded. 'Today I saw Galaxy's test on Miss Torraine.'

George couldn't conceal his surprise.

Von Muller went on, 'I should estimate that there are some twenty copies of that test going the rounds. You seem surprised.'

'I am,' said George. 'Any idea where they're coming from?'

Von Muller shrugged. 'I don't concern myself with such things, but I had assumed that you had cleverly arranged for them to escape from Galaxy's security.'

George felt a surge of pleasure at the thought of Wilbur ordering a clamp-down on the test. It augured well.

'You're interested in Velma?' he asked.

Von Muller shrugged. 'Interested is a weak word for what I feel for that actress. For me she is the quintessential woman.

Watching that crude clip defined for me precisely the direction in which I wish to go, and precisely how I shall make my statements. For me, Miss Torraine is the Madonna!'

George stared at Von Muller. It passed through his mind that Von Muller was a raving lunatic.

George floundered but finally came out with something like: 'Well, Velma is a highly talented actress, but, frankly, Mr Von Muller, it escapes me how watching that sexy lady could make you think of the Madonna!'

Von Muller made a sound somewhere between a laugh and a raspberry.

'That you confuse motherhood with purity is a misconception you share with every mother's child.' Generously, he added, 'It should not embarrass you.'

George found his condescending, patronizing tone slightly insulting, but he bore it bravely.

'Is it not a fact that no mortal woman can become a mother without some measure of carnality?'

This sounded reasonable to George. He nodded.

'There you have it!' said Von Muller in triumph. 'It is something known to every woman, but few of their children. Like death, it is an obscenity not to be mentioned among the family, but the fact remains. My intention is to urge that subconscious realization to the fore, to use it to arouse and create emotions in the movie-goer that will be so strong as to be irresistible. I intend to disembarrass the world of the guilty secret. It will release such mainsprings of emotional response that the impact will be unimaginable. You must remember that it is the woman who decides which movie her husband, lover or escort will take her to. When we sell a ticket to a woman, we also sell one to her escort, even more if she is a mother.'

George was ready to agree, even if he didn't fully understand everything Von Muller was saying.

'I think I understand. I mean, I know women's pictures are

always good business, but these movies you want to make . . . would they *all* be about motherhood?'

Von Muller nearly exploded. '*None* of them!'

George sat back in the couch, blinking rapidly. 'Oh!' he managed. 'I – er – must have misunderstood!'

'No!' roared Von Muller. 'You did not misunderstand! You persist in confusing images with truth. This is what I am constantly up against. You will understand when you can see the movies I have not yet had the opportunity to make. At that moment everyone will understand!'

George found himself floundering, hopelessly lost. It occurred to him that Von Muller had come to him only after everybody else had turned him down. Maybe Morris Denny's call had been to beg him to get Von Muller off MGM's hands.

George needed time to think, so he filled in the gap with what he hoped sounded an intelligent question.

'Maybe I'd understand better if I could read something of what you have in mind? Do you have any actual scripts written?'

Von Muller crossed the room in three healthy strides to where he had left his briefcase. Reaching into it, he produced a bulky leather-bound volume the thickness of four bricks.

This he hurled across the room towards George. It slammed into George's stomach as he fumbled the catch.

'The Greatest Story the World has ever Known!' announced Von Muller to a literally breathless George.

George turned the leather-bound bricks over to discover that the missile was nothing less than the Bible. His most immediate thought was that Wilbur was Jewish – he wouldn't go for the New Testament!

'You mean *all* of it?'

'All of it!' cried Von Muller positively, then ameliorated his grandiose pronouncement with an added, 'Over the course of my career!' Von Muller came over to George so fast that George momentarily thought Von Muller was about to hit him. Instead, he towered over George and stabbed the air beneath George's nose. 'There are more scenarios in that book – more truth, more drama – than in all the studios in the world!'

'The Italians did a lot of them!' offered George. 'I remember before the Great War, they . . .'

Von Muller interrupted impatiently. 'Not with *sound*! Imagine the impact should an audience actually hear the word of God spoken from the screen? What will they think then?'

'Blasphemy' sprang to George's mind – especially if Velma did any of the talking!

Von Muller was going on. 'Think, will you, of all the great sermons that have been preached throughout the centuries. Think of your own Bible-belt preachers! Do they not use the word of God to hold countless millions spellbound! We now have it in our power to bring them not just *words* but images too!'

Suddenly George got it! Suddenly he saw the relevance of Ailleen's unscheduled dip in the Spanish fountain and this visit from Von Muller.

'Salome!' cried George.

'Bathsheba!' countered Von Muller.

'Cleopatra!' cried George before he saw the return of Von Muller's thin-lipped smile of condescension.

'Hardly biblical,' he said, 'but think of what we might do with the Roman Empire.'

George was excited now. He looked down at the heavy volume in his hand. 'Can I borrow this?' he asked. 'I haven't read it in years.' Von Muller nodded. 'You should read it, but first concentrate on my problems. I need a home to go to – one that will accept my terms. Freedom to create without interference and without constant harassment from the money managers.'

George nodded enthusiastically. 'Well, listen, there's going to be no problem getting almost anybody interested in a man of your reputation, but we're limited to the studios that have the money to give you that freedom.'

Von Muller was frowning dismissively. 'Finance is no problem. Where I go, the First National Bank follows.'

George wondered who else he knew who could talk in such sweeping phrases as Von Muller used.

George leapt to his feet as he saw Von Muller picking up his cape and heading for the door. 'There's just one thing,' he called after him.

Von Muller turned, the front door open, and looked patiently back.

'I'm going to look like the fool of all time if I start making some representations only to find you've already made a commitment somewhere else.'

Von Muller smiled. 'From this moment forth, at least until we meet again, you have my word that you are my sole representative.' He struck a dramatic hand to his chest. 'Not even *I* shall represent myself!'

George still felt nervous. 'There's one more thing. Your contract with MGM. How long has it got to run?'

Von Muller sighed. 'It has already "run" its course. Otherwise I should not have felt free to come here tonight. I am totally free of any commitment to anyone, excepting only yourself. Goodnight, Mr Schapner, I trust you will convey my warmest congratulations to Miss Torraine.'

George nodded. 'I certainly will, Mr Von Muller!'

Von Muller stopped short of clicking his heels as he bowed, but even as he turned away, he hesitated yet again. 'What is that strange smell, Mr Schapner?'

'Oh, that's the Tar Pits . . . La Brea Tar Pits.'

Von Muller looked puzzled. 'Carpets?' he asked.

'No. Tar Pits. Pits with tar in them. They keep turning up prehistoric relics. Ask me, they should have concreted them over years ago.'

'Whatever they are, they create a most unpleasant smell. How do you stand it?'

'After a while you don't notice,' shrugged George apologetically.

Von Muller's brows furrowed even deeper. George had an uncomfortable feeling that living close to the Tar Pits had somehow damaged him in Von Muller's mind.

'Well, again, I wish you goodnight!' said Von Muller.

This time he actually went.

George stood at the door waving him into his car and feeling slightly foolish. Von Muller didn't look back once, and it was with some relief that George saw the huge Mercedes take off down the street.

George turned back into his house to see an excited Julia staring wide-eyed at him. She'd spent the entire time listening through the bedroom door.

'Does he mean it?' she was asking incredulously.

'Did you get it all down on your pad?' asked George.

Julia nodded. 'George, if this comes off you'll be one of the most powerful men in Hollywood.'

George shrugged. 'You impressed?'

'With you and him both.'

Julia stood there, open-mouthed and excited. She had never looked more appealingly attractive to George. He took his time about pouring a drink. Julia just stood and watched him. She seemed excited beyond speech.

George brought his drink back to the couch. 'You understood him?' he asked.

Julia nodded.

'Then take your clothes off!' he ordered suddenly.

Julia flinched a moment before starting to reach for her zips. She gave an anxious glance towards the undraped windows. 'Shouldn't we close them?' she asked.

George shook his head. 'It doesn't matter,' he said. 'We're moving soon anyway!'

Some hours later they lay side by side in silent communion. Neither could sleep. George because he couldn't wait for dawn, Julia because she was afraid.

'George?' she spoke from the warm hollow of the silence. 'Were you ever afraid?'

George shifted restlessly. 'Every day of my life.'

'You don't show it.'

George said nothing for a long while. Even this conversation scared him. They seemed poised on the brink of something he didn't understand – as if he were about to learn something he didn't want to know.

Julia persisted. 'You haven't asked me what Ailleen and I talked about today.'

George was very still.

'Do you care?' she asked.

'Of course I *care* . . . I need you, both of you. Why wouldn't I care?'

'But you didn't ask?'

'No.'

'Why not?'

George suddenly sat up in bed. Julia reached out a hand to touch him, to prevent him separating himself too far from her. It wasn't necessary, George wasn't going anywhere. 'You want some coffee?' he asked.

Julia started out of the bed. 'I'll do it.'

She got as far as the door before she turned back to him. 'George, I'm afraid for you. This thing . . .' her hand fluttered in a vague gesture, 'it's getting to be a monster . . .'

George took refuge in anger. 'Don't keep asking me questions, Julia! I got more questions than I can handle right now! Money – I'm spending money I didn't even know I *had* . . . I'm running races against myself and I'm losing! Julia, I don't even know where I'm going!'

Julia, startled at the anguish in his voice, hurried back to sit on the bed and take his hand. 'George, there's nothing to fear. You're winning! You're doing nothing they can send you to jail for . . .'

George interrupted. 'Going to jail would be restful, Julia. Going crazy is what worries me. What worries me worse is why I'm doing it! I was doing OK. Velma, I don't know, we'd have made it somehow . . . there would have been others . . . Now I've got Von Muller bringing me the word of God, and I don't know which of us is the crazier – him or me.' Suddenly he pulled her to him. 'Don't load me with your thing with Ailleen as well.'

Julia tried to pull away from him but he held on. 'What are you talking about?'

'I can see it if you can't!'

'George! What are you saying?'

'You're in love with her, aren't you?'

Julia was silent.

George waited. 'I don't mind that. It could work for us on one level . . .'

'Are you saying you understand?'

George tried to lighten it. 'Sure. Why not? It could lead to some interesting mixed doubles play.'

Julia tore herself away from him now and glared at him in the dim night-lit room. 'If I thought you meant what you just said I'd hate you!'

George smiled at her. '*That*,' he said, 'I can't afford.'

Julia blinked at him. 'George Schapner, you are either the most cold-blooded opportunist I've ever known, or the biggest fool!'

George smiled. 'Or just plain running scared?' he offered hopefully.

19

Wilbur's cigar drooped from between suddenly lifeless lips.

'Von Muller? You mean *Stephen* Von Muller?'

Wilbur leaned forward over his desk, and the cigar, forgotten for the moment, dropped into his lap. 'You can bring Stephen Von Muller to direct Velma. Here? At Galaxy?'

George nodded, watching Wilbur closely.

Wilbur turned his gaze from George to stare unfocused at a corner of his office, sitting back in his spring-loaded chair.

'Not to make some low-budget flapper movie,' cautioned George.

Wilbur let his tensed chair go with a rush that almost catapulted him clear of the ground and on to his feet. 'Flapper movies!? Shit!' Wilbur spread his arms wide and started making circular movements like a slow-motion dervish. 'He'd cost us an arm and a leg!' he said as if to some unheard accompaniment. 'A fucking arm and a leg!'

Wilbur broke off his weird movements to stare at George. 'Von Muller directing Velma?' His tone was early shocked sepulchral. 'Theatre-owners would sue us for setting their screens on fire!'

'You know what his pictures cost?' asked George.

'Cost? Who cares what it costs! Think what it'll make!'

Thoughts were flooding in on Wilbur. 'The story! The story would have to be right. This isn't something we can rush!'

'Von Muller's got plenty of ideas. It's part of the deal that he gets to develop the story, start to finish, and controls casting. Artistic control has to be absolute.'

Wilbur nodded through all this, but George was certain he wasn't absorbing one half of it.

'But he wants Velma?'

George nodded.

Wilbur nodded. 'And you're going to sign Velma to Galaxy. Hell, you've as good as agreed that!' Suddenly he turned aggressive. 'I got Velma, right?'

George nodded. 'We haven't talked contract yet.'

'But you *do* have Von Muller?'

'Yes, if I can present him with the right deal.'

Wilbur dismissed this as a mere quibble. 'OK, so we can work something out. When do I get to talk to him?'

'You don't. You talk to me.'

Wilbur stared at George. '*You?*' he asked incredulously. 'You are representing Von Muller?'

George nodded, afraid for a moment he might have transgressed some unwritten Hollywood code of practice.

'Directors have agents, now?'

'Personal managers.'

Wilbur started pacing again. 'Call it what the fuck you like. Fact is we're here to talk business, right? Two old pals. We shouldn't have any trouble, right?'

George nodded carefully.

'So what does he want?'

'First thing he wants is Velma, so first thing we got to talk about is Velma's deal.'

'No problem,' said Wilbur emphatically. 'She gets a fifty per cent hike on the same scale, seven years with options.'

Wilbur wasn't looking when George started shaking his head. He only turned when George stayed silent. Wilbur's brow furrowed. 'Something wrong with your head? It's going from side to side when you should be down on your knees kissing my ass!'

'There's nothing wrong with my head, Wilbur. I'm saying no!'

'No? How can you say no? You worked out what ten per cent of what I've just handed you is?'

George shrugged. He hadn't and didn't want to.

Wilbur was getting really scary now. Maybe, George thought, he had overplayed his hand. Then he remembered Von Muller and he didn't want to go back to him looking like a horse's ass.

'So what *do* you want for your piece of quiff?'

'Half a million for three pictures.'

Wilbur stared at him. 'You mean half a million *dollars?*'

George nodded.

'For three pictures? No contract? Come on, George, you know better than that. When I sign talent I sign them to *time* not pictures!'

'Gloria Swanson got a million for three pictures.'

'We're not talking Swanson! We're talking Velma Torraine!'

'So is Morris Denny at MGM! So is Monogram. So is Tiffany . . . they all want to talk to Velma Torraine.'

Wilbur snorted. 'So go talk to them! Maybe they're as crazy as you are!'

George got to his feet. 'If that's your final word, Wilbur . . .' He started towards the door but found his knees getting soft before he got there. He turned back to Wilbur. 'Just remember, Wilbur, I brought you this deal first!'

Wilbur was scathing. 'Deal! What deal? This is no deal! This is blackmail! First you get me excited, then you kick me in the nuts! What kind of way is that for old friends to behave?'

George smiled, confident he had the upper hand again. 'Wilbur, I warned you what might happen if you tested Velma *before* putting her under contract. You thought I was bluffing, well . . . I'll let you work it out for yourself . . .' George again turned for the door knowing he would never reach it.

'George!' screamed Wilbur. 'Where the hell are you going?'

George, the blood coming back into his legs, turned and shrugged. 'Paramount, MGM, Monogram . . .' he tailed it off into another gesture.

'Why don't you throw in Fox and Warner's for good measure?'

George smiled. 'You think I'm bluffing again, Wilbur? Look what happened last time!'

Wilbur suddenly seemed to impact upon himself. His shoulders dropped, his arms hung forward and he looked a shattered man.

'Can you give me some time on this, George?'

George's stomach quelled. He couldn't take any more tension-filled 'waiting'. He shook his head. 'I'd like to,

Wilbur, but when I get back to my office I got to start taking some of them calls.'

Wilbur turned to his desk and started fumbling in his box for a fresh cigar. 'Well, dammit, George, I can't tell you now! I got to talk to the bank first.'

'Which bank?' asked George.

Wilbur was lighting his cigar as if his life depended on it. 'First National.'

George felt like a man who'd found the last elusive piece of a jigsaw puzzle. He walked back towards Wilbur's desk, laid down his case and picked up Wilbur's phone. Wilbur was watching all this like a man bemused.

'Who do you talk to there?'

'Marvin Barrington. What the hell are you doing, George?'

George spoke into the telephone. 'Would you get Mr Marvin Barrington at the First National Bank for Mr Sterne, please?'

George hung up.

Wilbur suddenly exploded with anger. 'Where in hell do you get off coming into my office using my phone to call my bank? You could screw up a big deal here! You know who Barrington is? He's the guy that's arranging this Wall Street finance. He wants everything on paper. The whole game plan. Cash flows ... numbers ... you think I can call him up on the telephone and say, "Send me three million, I've gone crazy"?'

The telephone rang with Wilbur's call.

Wilbur looked at it. 'What am I going to say to him?'

George picked up the phone and covered the mouthpiece.

'You're going to tell him that Von Muller is going to move over to Galaxy. That Velma's contract is going to cost you half a million for three Von Muller pictures and you need him to bank-roll you. Listen, let me know what time you get up in the morning and I'll come round and wipe your ass!' George thrust the phone into Wilbur's nerveless hands.

George was amazed to hear the shaken Wilbur repeating

almost word for word what he had just told him to say. Throughout his recital, Wilbur kept his eyes firmly on George, and when he'd finished looked ready to run.

As he listened to Barrington, Wilbur's face drained of colour. He fumbled the phone back on to its hook and looked, fish-eyed, at George.

'He said yes.' Wilbur stood beside his desk in shock. 'You heard me, George. I asked him for three million dollars, and he said ... What did he say?' Wilbur paused while he searched his confused memory. '"Yes, Wilbur, we'll back you on that!"'

Wilbur suddenly rushed at George and grabbed him by the lapels of his jacket. 'It took a goy like you to teach *me* how to borrow money? My mother, God rest her, is turning in her grave! "Wilbur," he says, "we'll back you on that!"'

The next moment George saw Wilbur's face suffuse with colour, and simultaneously felt Wilbur's full weight drag at his lapels. Wilbur was looking desperately at George as he fought for breath. George, fearing a heart attack, half dragged Wilbur to a couch and, meaning to get help, was halfway to the door before he heard Wilbur chuckling and crooning. 'On the fucking telephone he says to me: "Wilbur, we'll back you on that!" What's happened to me? Where am I? Am I dead and gone to heaven?'

George started back towards Wilbur meaning to calm him, but Wilbur was screaming in ecstatic excitement.

The door burst open behind George. Alarmed by the noise, Wilbur's executive secretary, a dignified lady of some fifty years with greying hair, rushed in.

She stopped short and stared through her pince-nez at Wilbur laying spread-legged on the couch, his belly rising and falling like a high swell off Malibu beach.

The woman looked from George back to Wilbur. 'Are you all right, Mr Sterne?' she enquired doubtfully.

Wilbur laughed uproariously and kicked his legs in the air.

'All right? You bet your sweet ass I'm all right!'

Suddenly he swung his legs to the ground and, standing, reached out his arms full stretch towards her. 'Miss Wilkins!' he yelled as he started forward, 'I want you to have my baby!'

Miss Wilkins yelped with shock and, turning, ran from the office slamming the door behind her.

Wilbur turned to George and spread his arms. 'Sweetheart!' he cried.

George spoke hurriedly before Wilbur could embrace him. 'We didn't talk about Von Muller's contract yet.'

Wilbur stopped dead in his tracks. 'What's he going to cost?'

George shrugged. 'I might get him to listen to an offer of around a million.'

Wilbur's lips went blubbery again. 'A million?'

'What do you care? Three pictures from Von Muller starring Velma Torraine will make you the biggest independent in town. The banks'll be trucking in dollars by the carload.'

Wilbur turned away towards his desk. 'I only just got over the price you wanted for Velma. You have to hit me again so soon?'

'Wilbur, if you had any sense you'd be taking them in as partners!'

Wilbur turned loose-jawed and stared at George.

'*You!*' he said, extending a quivering finger. 'You I should have as a partner!'

'If you'd said that a week ago I'd have dropped at your feet. The way things look now, I'm better off on my own. When word gets around of the kind of deals I have to hand, I'm going to be signing every top director and writer in Hollywood!'

Wilbur looked confused. 'Writers? What the hell do we want writers for?'

'The written word is going to be the key to this business, Wilbur. If the actors are going to speak, they're going to have to have something to say!'

Wilbur laughed. 'You have any idea how many theatrical plays there are in public domain? Thousands of 'em. Who the hell is going to pay writers when we got all that going for us for free!'

George was stunned. It had never occurred to him. Wilbur could be right, but this was no time to admit it. 'We'll see,' he said with as much conviction as he could rouse.

Wilbur advanced on him again. 'I'll tell you something else,' he started. 'You, George, with these ideas about managing writers and directors – you're going to be making a lot of enemies in this town. Powerful enemies!'

'Better to have enemies than no friends, Wilbur. By the time I'm through there's not going to be many people in this town who can afford me as an enemy!'

'A bullet costs five cents, George. Think about it – it's happened before!'

George smiled into Wilbur's face, and suddenly Wilbur dropped his serious hang-dog look and grinned. 'Not from me, though! Three pictures directed by Von Muller and starring Velma Torraine . . . which reminds me, when is she going to come round and see me?'

'I'm keeping her under wraps until the excitement dies down. Matter of fact, I'm sending her out of town on a coast-to-coast personal appearance tour.'

Wilbur stared at him. '*You* are sending her on a personal appearance tour? Don't I get a say in this? Didn't I just buy her?'

'No, you didn't, Wilbur. You bought her services for three pictures with Von Muller. It's going to take him at least three months of preparation to get the first one started, and I don't want Velma hanging around town while he does that.'

Wilbur looked desperate. 'Couldn't she knock off a couple of quickies while we're waiting?'

'No more "quickies", Wilbur. Let all the others burn themselves out in half-assed talking pictures. When we relaunch Velma it's got to be B – I – G!'

Wilbur's eyes narrowed. George could see him making a reassessment of the new George that stood before him.

'You! You bastard!' he said finally. 'I just realized something. You stand to make more out of this deal than Velma's entire five-year contract was worth a week ago!'

George smiled. There were a whole lot of things he might have said, but he felt like just standing there – and smiling!

20

George drove his drop-head back along Sunset, his emotions in turmoil.

He'd often wondered how people felt when they'd done a million-dollar deal. Well, he'd just done one, but he still didn't know how it felt.

At least one half of the deal was predicated on a fraud, and the other half was based on it too. He seemed to be getting away with it, but he still had to deliver.

First priority was to get Ailleen out of Madame G.'s and despatched on this cockermamy personal appearance tour. That was a sufficient smokescreen while the real Velma recovered. That brought up another problem. He had to get out to Nevada and talk with Velma. There was no way she wasn't going to go out of her mind when she heard what he had lined up for her – it might even speed up her recovery – but there was still the very real problem of her diction. She couldn't come back not talking like Ailleen. Maybe he could find someone to coach her during the next two months. By the time he got to his office, he was biting his lips raw.

Julia greeted him with a kiss and a whole pile of new messages. He brushed them aside. He had enough dreams and worries without trying to take on board new ones.

Julia was disappointed at his lack of reaction to some of the prominent names that had already called him, and, following him into his own office, immediately brought up the buying out of Ailleen.

'I'm working on it!' he shouted at her. 'Get me my bank . . .' Julia, blinking under his shouted response, hurried out to her own office. George couldn't rest. He paced up and down until the telephone rang.

He told them he wanted an armed messenger with fifty thousand in cash to escort him that evening. The bank seemed strangely hesitant and put him through to the manager.

'Mr Schapner, you have nothing like that amount in your account!'

George protested. 'But I sold my RCA stock. My broker told me I was credited – you mean you haven't got the money yet?'

The manager was apologetic and could only suggest George rang his broker.

With a sudden chill, George did just that, getting the number for himself.

'Mr Schapner,' the broker said in pained tones. 'Settlement day is still five days off!'

'What's settlement day?'

'The day they hand over the money they owe you. Look, don't worry, your stock is sold – incidentally, it's risen six point five dollars since, and you'll have your money in five days!'

George was yelling now. 'I need that money *tonight*! This is important! I can't wait five days, you told me the money was credited, so where is it?'

'Your account is credited, Mr Schapner, here within the company. We have not yet got your funds, but there's absolutely nothing for you to worry about. There's no way anyone's not going to buy RCA the way things are going.'

'I want the money today!' said George stubbornly.

The broker hummed and hawed a moment, then came up with a bright idea. 'Tell you what we can do. I'll get your sales contract round to your bank, that will enable you to arrange a bridging loan against the guarantee of the funds being deposited within five days. How will that suit you?'

'Fine,' growled George, 'if it works!'

George got his bank manager back on the line and found that, subject to seeing the franked contract of sale, he would be agreeable. George got him to start making arrangements for the messenger and the cash, and put down the phone with a feeling that he was undergoing some kind of crash-course in banking. Maybe he could use it to his advantage at some future date. But, then, with the closing of Velma's contract and maybe Von Muller's, would he ever need to?

'That's the trouble with information,' he told himself, 'it always comes when you don't need it.'

Next he called Von Muller, catching him at home.

George outlined the deal he thought he could make with Galaxy. Von Muller seemed totally uninterested in the astronomical sum of money, and far more interested in the amount of freedom and control he would have. George reassured him and Von Muller brightened considerably.

They fixed a meeting for when George had some draft contracts to show him.

Next he called a lawyer, and outlined the contracts he wanted drawn up, and this time got a satisfying whistle of surprise.

'Do I hear you right?' asked the astonished man.

George ran through the figures again, and he didn't miss the keen edge of excitement in the man's voice.

After warning him that all this had to be strictly confidential, George hung up, satisfied that the details of his coup would be all round Hollywood before the cocktail hour.

George was about to pick up the phone to ask Julia to trace a number for Velma when he looked up and saw Manolo standing in his door.

George was so startled he jumped to his feet. 'Manolo! How the hell did you get here?'

Manolo shrugged, poker-faced. 'I drove. It's Velma . . .' he said in such grave tones that George's heart skipped a beat.

'Nothing's happened to her?'

Manolo shook his head. 'She's downstairs in the car. She wants to know if it's OK to come up?'

George let his suppressed breath go with the sound of a bursting balloon. 'Great!' he said. 'I was just wondering how to get in touch.' Manolo nodded and went out.

George looked out the outer office to see what had happened to Julia. She was just hanging up the telephone. 'Sorry,' she called. 'I was on the phone and he just walked right in.'

'It doesn't matter. Matter of fact it couldn't be better.'

He went back into his office, rehearsing what he was going to say to Velma. Julia followed him in.

'The call was from your bank – they've OK'd the loan. The money and the guard will be ready any time after two.'

George nodded, and then turned as the outer door opened and Velma, swathed in bandages, her eyes hidden behind dark Klieg glasses, came in.

They exchanged embraces, while Manolo glowered in the background. Velma pulled back from the embrace and looked up at George.

'I hear I did a pretty good test the other day.' As she spoke she whipped off the Kliegs and fixed George with her gorgeous green eyes.

It was an awkward moment for George. 'I sweated blood, Velma. They backed me into a corner and I had to do something.'

'Did you use the same girl you used on Ronnie?'

George nodded. 'She used to be an actress once. That was a break.'

Velma smiled. 'I'm glad one of us was!' Her smile had made her bandages move, and George winced for her.

'How are things healing?' he asked.

'Good. Matter of fact I'm wearing these mainly for disguise. I get the stitches out a week from tomorrow.'

George got her seated and went behind his own desk. 'Can't be quick enough for me. We got to get you back to work – wait'll you hear what's lined up for you . . .' George broke off in the face of her raised glove.

'Stop, George. I don't want to hear it. I'm not going back to work!'

George stared at her, stunned. 'Velma – hear me out! This is something so big you won't believe it!'

Velma spoke in a carefully precise voice. 'I don't want it any more. I've had a taste of something else and I find I prefer it.'

George glanced at the impassive face of Manolo. Manolo looked down at the floor, avoiding George's eye.

George began to feel as if he'd had one drink too many.

His brain was beginning to soak up oxygen to the point where he was afraid it might float away. This was the point at parties when he stopped drinking. How did you stop breathing?

'You telling me you mean to retire? I mean, *now*, just when we got the business by the balls?'

Velma nodded. 'There's only one problem, George.'

'Just *one*!?' George's voice came out hollow.

'Do I have any money?'

George shrugged, overwhelmed with a feeling that this wasn't really happening to him. 'I don't know. What do you have in the bank?'

'Nothing I don't owe.'

Then George was hit by a thought of such compelling force that he started blurting it out before he'd even thought it through.

'You've given this thought? I mean, this isn't just some passing emotional . . .' he ran out of words, 'something?'

Velma shrugged. 'I thought it was. If I can raise enough money to get Manolo and me settled in Mexico . . .'

'Mexico?' interjected George. 'Why Mexico?'

'Land is cheap there. Manolo wants to buy a ranch or at least some land.'

George thought fast. 'How much would you need?'

Velma glanced at Manolo.

'Good watered land isn't that cheap,' he said. 'Place I got in mind could cost twenty, maybe thirty thousand dollars US.'

George looked back at Velma. 'What kind of living would a place like that give you?'

'*Gordo!*' exclaimed Manolo.

'Fat!' translated Velma. 'Like me, right now.'

George looked steadily at Velma, his mind assessing his sudden idea, looking for flaws. One thing was certain, he was burning bridges – he had to ensure he didn't make an enemy of Velma somewhere along the way.

'Velma, if this decision is final and irrevocable, then I have an idea, but first I have to be convinced you really mean what you're saying.'

'I mean it, George. I've gotten out of Velma's skin in these past weeks, the idea of stepping back in again – it's a nightmare thought. I don't want it!'

George nodded, taking time out to glance towards the impassive Manolo, who was watching him alertly.

'OK,' said George carefully. 'What I'd like you to consider is selling me your name . . .'

Velma's jaw dropped as far as the bandages would permit. 'My *name*?'

George nodded. Once launched, it all seemed perfectly clear.

'Not just your name, your identity – your power of attorney, everything of you, except your person . . .'

Velma sat stunned for a moment. Then she chuckled. 'I got to hand it to you, George, you're an original. You're the first guy that ever wanted everything of me *except* my body!'

George watched her carefully, aware that Manolo was

puzzling his way through this conversation along with them. Manolo could be an extreme danger to George if ever anything went wrong. He was also, at this precise moment, George's main ally in this final coup.

George prompted Velma. 'What do you say?'

She gestured, a little fluttering motion of her gloved hands. 'I don't know, George . . . I mean, you practically invented me in the first place . . . it just never occurred to me that you could sell your own identity.'

George shook his head. 'It's not your "identity" I want, Velma, it's the movie persona. You'd be walking away with everything you ever had before we met, plus a profit and Manolo.'

Velma smiled at that, she glanced round at Manolo who stood stoically against the wall, refusing to be drawn into it.

Velma looked back at George. Suddenly she got an insight into where this was all leading. 'You mean to go on with this girl?' she asked incredulously. 'I mean, make pictures with her . . . use her to take my place completely?'

George found that he was lying when he said: 'Only if you are sure you don't want it any more, Velma. Naturally, I'd rather you heard me out on the potential Velma Torraine has in this town, but if you are determined, then I think I can swing it the other way . . .'

Velma sat back and sighed. 'George, I'm worried for you . . . this thing you're trying to pull, what would happen to you if anyone ever found out?'

'That's *my* problem,' said George with more confidence than he felt.

'Well, how much am I worth?'

George thought of a figure, doubled it, sliced it in three, until like a roulette ball bouncing into a particular slot, he came out with: 'Fifty thousand dollars!'

'*Madre!*' breathed Manolo, as George and Velma held each other's eyes. George could read a sparkle in them that said 'yes', but she was more cautious. 'Have you got that kind of money?'

George nodded. 'I can get it.'

'My debts free and clear?'

George nodded.

'What about the house?'

'I'll take over the loan, otherwise that's included in my price.'

Velma hesitated only a moment longer. 'It's a deal!' she smiled. George moved round his desk and she, rising, embraced him. Even Manolo was moved to come forward and shake George by the hand.

'*Muchas gracias, señor,*' he murmured.

Velma smiled at Manolo, then turned back to George. 'How soon can we have the money – I mean some of it, anyway?'

George thought fast. 'Friday?' he asked.

Velma sighed. 'I really would like not to have to stay in Hollywood any longer than I have to.'

George couldn't see any danger in her being around with her face bandaged like that – on the other hand, there was Manolo. He might be spotted.

'Tell you what. Drive out to somewhere, say, Pasadena, let me know a number where I can reach you, and I'll call you as soon as I've organized the money. Maybe tomorrow.' Velma nodded. George went on, 'Meanwhile I'll draft some kind of agreement – I can't have a lawyer do it – and when I've got the money, I'll bring it out to you.'

Velma leaned in and kissed his cheek again, the bandages tickling his chin as she did so. 'I don't know what to say, George.'

'Then don't try. We said it all five years ago in the lobby of the Hollywood Hotel.'

She nodded. Her gorgeous eyes now had the added sparkle of a threatening tear in them.

Manolo had moved to hold the office door open, certain

the meeting was at an end. Velma turned to him. 'Manolo, could I have a few minutes with George?'

Manolo's eyes flashed quickly at George, and George quailed at the look that was in them before they softened into agreement. 'I'll wait outside,' he said and, turning, closed the door behind him.

Velma turned to George.

'Have you heard from Ronnie?' she asked.

George nodded. 'You got a problem there. He was in here yesterday asking about you. Says he wants a chance to show you he's a changed man.'

Velma smiled sadly. 'That must be about the tenth time he's become "a changed man". He'll never change, but he'll always frighten me.'

Velma scanned George's face urgently. 'Nobody must ever know where I've gone, George ... nobody. Getting away from Ronnie was what made me decide to get out altogether. If I were anywhere Ronnie could find me – I don't know ... I'd never be able to face him in case the nightmare started again!'

George nodded after Manolo. 'And what about him? You sure this thing is right for you?'

Velma nodded.

George went on. 'You couldn't have more different backgrounds.'

Velma's eyes widened at George. 'Are you kidding? George, are you forgetting what I was when you found me? That you, of all people, could say something like that is another reason I want out of this goddamned town! Round here they'd always think of Manolo as some kind of bloodsucking gigolo who got lucky. There's a whole lot you don't know about me, George, but for you to suggest that Manolo is less of a person than me ...'

George held up his hands to stem the passionate flow. 'OK, OK. You love the guy! Enough already!'

Velma laughed with him. 'Anyway, this morning Manolo

and I had a long talk. I told him I was broke, that with my face the way it was I'd probably never work again – but he still wanted me – scars and all!'

'OK. I just hope it sticks!'

Velma moved towards the door. 'It will. I've made up my mind!'

'And don't forget, once I pay you the money you stop being Velma Torraine, once and for all time.'

Velma paused, one hand on the door handle. 'The next time you see me I'll be Alicia Hernandez, how does that suit you?'

George moved after her. 'Been nice knowing you, Señora Hernandez. Don't forget to let me know where I can reach you!'

'Be assured, gringo, you'll be hearing from me later today.'

She opened the door then closed it again. She turned with an impish grin in her eyes. 'And another thing, you remember that stinky little one room you used to have on North Palmer?'

George nodded.

'Well, I always pay my debts. You can deduct five dollars from the fifty grand!'

Velma went out the door on a laugh.

The moment Velma and Manolo had cleared the outer office, Julia came bursting through the door.

'What happened?' she asked.

George exulted. 'I just bought Velma!'

Julia looked puzzled. 'Didn't they abolish slavery?'

'Maybe they did,' chuckled George, picking up the phone, 'but don't tell anyone – I'm getting rich on it.'

'Who are you calling?'

'The bank. I need an additional fifty grand.'

Julia hovered. 'When you get some time off from buying women, you might care to glance at your messages.'

George waved her to silence as the bank answered.

Julia went out, closing the door more firmly than was entirely necessary.

The bank manager hesitated only a moment before agreeing to load the guard's bag with an extra fifty thousand. George hung up with the satisfying feeling that the bank probably thought he was getting into bootlegging. They were certainly becoming more polite!

George was taking a moment off to review his crowded day, when he picked up the phone to find Al Klein on the other end. George had trouble remembering what it was he'd wanted to speak to him about, and when he did, it sounded to him like a hollow joke. Real estate? Who needed it?

He told Al that he'd had a proposition for him a few days ago, but that he'd found another home for his money.

Curiosity aroused, Al Klein tried to find out what this new proposition was. George fended him off. 'I'd be too embarrassed to tell you,' he said.

George hung up, not knowing then that he'd remember that call the rest of his life. He'd just hung up on thirty or forty million dollars but, right then, in the fall of 1928, it seemed to George that the sun shone only with his express permission.

He stood at the window and looked down at the mere mortals passing in the street below.

'This is *my* town!' he whispered to himself.

And he meant it.

Part Two

1

George rode the elevator up the four floors to the top of the building where his new office was located. The elevator was electrically driven, the hallways carpeted and the entire building serviced with cooled-air circulation.

The elevator came to a disconcertingly abrupt halt and George cursed. They'd promised to get it adjusted but nothing seemed to be happening. He made a mental note to get on to the owners again. He wanted nothing to spoil his new image.

Pushing open the frosted double doors that bore the legend: 'GEORGE SCHAPNER MANAGEMENT' he was the focus of three pairs of lovely eyes as his front office girls, already known as Schapner's Harem, looked towards him.

'Good morning, Mr Schapner!' they chorused.

'Good morning, girls. I trust your rabbits are all healthy?'

The girls tittered loyally at his gynaecological joke as he passed through to his own inner office to be greeted by his personal secretary, Sybil. Sybil was markedly different from the glamour line-up outside. They all looked as if they might have made the finals of a national beauty pageant – one of them actually had – but Sybil was all business. He'd poached her from the Morris Agency and who Sybil didn't know wasn't yet in town.

'I got calls backed up a mile back!' she greeted him.

George moved round behind his desk. 'Give them to me in order of importance.'

Sybil looked down at her notebook. George's heart sank as he saw she had to turn back five pages to get to the beginning.

'Two calls from New York. Operator 45 is waiting on your call back. That's from Julia and Velma Torraine.'

'Get them back for me. What else?'

'Mr Von Muller called from the studio, also Mr Sterne.'

'I'll take Wilbur right after you get New York. And?'

'Mrs Battershaw called and insisted you return her call today.' Sybil looked through her pince-nez reprovingly. 'She was quite rude about you not having returned her call yesterday.'

George nodded. He could imagine. 'Mrs Battershaw' was the telephone name for Madame Gregory. Having Madame G. for a partner was a pain in the proverbial. She was relentless in wanting to know when 'Velma's' contract was to be signed so she could start collecting her percentage.

'There're others but I think they can wait.'

George asked her to try for New York and Sybil bustled off leaving George with his thoughts.

Getting Velma's contract signed was no easy matter.

George held Velma's power of attorney but the studio legal department had insisted, because of the size of the commitment, that Velma sign it herself. Ailleen looked like Velma but there was no way she could sign like her! George could probably have found a way to enforce his power of attorney but that would only have given rise to speculation as to why he hadn't taken the easy route of simply having Velma sign. George had resigned himself to having to go down to Mexico and getting the real Velma to sign. The trouble was finding room in his schedule for what would probably be a four-day trip. Bringing Velma back to Hollywood was not an option he relished. Velma would have been sure to pick up the gossip on the size of Galaxy's contract and that could prove expensive.

The ring of the telephone startled him back to reality.

Sybil had succeeded in getting Julia back on the line. He could hear her shouting above the coast-to-coast static.

'This is a terrible line!' she was calling. 'Get a pencil and I'll read you the New York figures!'

George smiled. Julia had this theory that a great deal of the static on coast-to-coast calls was because the many operators on the myriad connected exchanges across the country listened in on the chance of picking up some newsworthy gossip. After all, people didn't call California from New York to discuss the weather. Julia believed you could shake off most of the eavesdroppers with boredom – like starting to read out the New York Stock Exchange figures. George had found it hard to believe, but it worked! Even now, as Julia started reeling off totally nonsensical numbers, the line started to clear.

Listening to Julia's voice reminded George of how badly he was missing her. She was the one person in the world who knew the true extent of his plans for Ailleen. Ailleen was, presently, parked safely out of town on the personal appearance tour, but time was rapidly running out on that safety ploy. Sooner or later he'd have to come to an accommodation with Ailleen and reveal to her that it was his intention to replace Velma with her permanently.

The tour itself had been an unqualified success. Acres of newsprint cuttings had winged their way back to Hollywood from around the country. The local press in every city they'd visited couldn't praise her charm, elegance and perfect diction highly enough. The exchanges were screaming for new, talkie, Velma movies. They all wanted to cash in on the interest the tour was stirring up. Velma Torraine had triumphed over the coming of sound and George Schapner got the entire credit.

With relief George heard Julia end her mind-bending numerical litany and get started on her 'real' call. She was bubbling over with enthusiasm at their reception in New York. Velma was going over big with the exchanges, the audiences and the press. Mischievously she added: '. . . and the airplane ride was sensational!'

George's stomach went cold. 'What airplane ride?' he demanded.

Julia chuckled again. She was well aware of George's fear of the fast-developing air transport system.

Julia, enjoying herself, told him that she and Velma had accepted an invitation from North East States Airways to ride on their inaugural flight from Philadelphia to New York. 'We got terrific press coverage on it!' shouted Julia.

'You could also get yourself killed! You stay off those damn machines – they're dangerous!'

'They're exciting!' Julia yelled back. 'We were thinking of flying all the way back to California.'

'Damn you, Julia, you take the train!' Julia's answering laugh was lost in the gathering static. 'Listen, we're losing the connection. It's important you get back here as soon as possible. I need you and Galaxy wants to get to work ...' Julia was silent so long that George thought they'd lost the connection. 'Hello?' he shouted across the nation. 'You still there?'

'Yes. I'm here,' said a muted Julia.

'Did you hear what I said?'

Julia was silent a moment longer. 'You really mean to go through with this, George? I mean, all the way?'

'What the hell else can I do?'

There was another pause. 'When are you going to tell Ailleen?'

'When you get back here, and – listen – say nothing to her yourself. Let me handle it when you get back. I don't want her starting to get ideas.'

'What will you do if she says no?'

'Don't even think it. Why would she say no? Listen, wind up the first you can in New York and get back here. I need you, Julia. There's nobody else. OK?'

'That's nice to hear.'

'Listen to all else I'm saying and get back here soonest possible. OK?'

200

'OK,' said Julia, 'but, listen. I've given your number to an incredible actress I met. Her name's Nadine Bourdon. She'll be calling you. Have you got that?'

George sighed. The last thing he needed was another actress. He hadn't bothered noting her name but let Julia think he had.

'I saw a picture she's over here selling.'

'What do you mean "over here"? Where's she from?'

'France. She's French.'

'That's all I need! Julia, nobody can sell a foreign actress in this town any more. You forgotten we're making talkies now?'

'She's different. See her, George. You won't regret it.'

'OK, but listen, you get back here. OK? Let me know when.'

Julia was still talking when the static suddenly intensified and drowned her out. He held on hoping it might clear but when it did the line was dead.

George hung up and started to feel as if he were heating up. Maybe the cooled-air plant was on the blink. Maybe it was that, and, maybe, it was the thought of having Ailleen back in town again. Just thinking about that increased the feeling of pressure.

That was one problem. The other was finding time to get down to Mexico. The four or five days it would take Julia and Ailleen to cross the country seemed to present the best opportunity he'd get for the journey. He buzzed for Sybil, meaning to have her find out the shortest possible round trip route but, even as he did so, he froze. Nobody, not even Sybil, must know about this trip. Everyone in Hollywood knew how fast things were moving for him. Nobody would believe he'd left town for anything other than something of vital importance. People might start wondering what there was outside of Chihuahua that rated that high. He needed a cover story – but what?

Sybil came in, apologizing for her delay. He told her not to worry about it.

'You did want me for something?' she asked.

George thought fast. 'Yeah,' he said. 'Get on to the owners of this building, will you? Remind them about the elevator.'

Sybil nodded and made a note in her book. 'Mr Sterne called and insists you call him back.'

'Get him back for me. Finally, I've got something to tell him.'

Sybil nodded and started to the door before remembering something else. 'There was another call from New York...'

'When?'

'While you were talking to Julia. I'm not sure since the connection was bad but I think he said he was Ronnie Stillman.'

George felt his stomach lurch. 'Ronnie Stillman? In New York?'

Sybil nodded and consulted her notebook. 'He asked if I knew which hotel Miss Torraine was staying in.'

George felt light-headed. This was something totally unexpected. 'And you said?'

'That I didn't know.'

'Good! And should he call again tell him they're in Canada or Nevada or any place else that comes to mind.'

'Will do. You want me to get Mr Sterne now?'

George nodded and Sybil went out.

When were these problems ever going to stop? Obviously Ronnie had read the press reports of Velma's tour and had pursued her to New York trying to find her. If he found her it would take some pretty fancy footwork for that not to be the end of everything! It was the one angle he hadn't figured, so naturally it had to happen.

The phone rang and George picked up on Wilbur.

'You! You bastard! I've been trying to reach you all morning!'

'You got me, Wilbur. What is it?'

'You know what your goddamned Kraut is doing to me? He's got two fucking stages blocked. He's got sets dressed down to the finest detail! The guy's taking me over. Now when is your piece of quiff going to get back here and start work? You tell me anything other than tomorrow I might have to go into bankruptcy. You any idea how many Velma Torraine starrers I could be selling right now?'

George took a deep breath. 'Listen to me, Wilbur. Everybody's rushing out talkies. Most of them are garbage and they're only selling tickets because of the novelty value. Make them wait for Velma. With Von Muller directing she's got to be a smash. Velma's first talkie will make you millions. Trust me!'

'Trust *you*!' Wilbur's scorn was enough to scorch the lines. 'I should trust you knowing what I know about your Kraut?'

'If you're referring to Von Muller, Wilbur, I'd like to remind you that his reputation is unassailable. Everyone in town is puzzling over how you got him to come to Galaxy. Don't forget he brought the money in with him. The banks aren't kicking, are they?'

'Not yet. But that's because they don't know what I know!'

'OK, Wilbur. I give up. What is it you know?'

'The guy's crazy! That's what I know! A Grade-"A" certifiable nut!'

'What makes you say that?'

'You get down here, George, and I'll prove it to you!'

Exasperation took George over. 'Wilbur, I can't leave my office right now. I got calls stacked up four blocks long. Listen, I'm sure there's some misunderstanding. We'll straighten it out!'

'Damn right we'll straighten it out. Either you get down here, right now, or I'm calling in Hollister and see if there isn't some way to break Von Muller's contract. An insanity clause, maybe!'

George tried one more plea, but finally found himself

asking if it was really that serious, and agreeing to come right over.

The moment he'd hung up, Sybil was in with a whole new list of messages. George stood and held out his hands to ward her off. 'Trouble,' he told her. 'I've got to run over to Galaxy.'

Sybil started protesting as he reached for his hat and went out the door. She was still trying to call him back when the elevator doors closed, cutting her off.

This George didn't need.

2

On arriving at the studio, George was surprised to find himself being conducted not to Wilbur's office, but to an obscure region of the studio where he had, to his knowledge, never been before.

'Where are we going?' he asked the car-hop, who was driving.

'Projection rooms,' the eager-faced young man told him. 'Mr Sterne's orders.'

George didn't pursue it. Wilbur had some bug in his head that would only be quieted with patience. Meanwhile George was enjoying his new status. These days he rated a car-hop whenever he came on to the lot. The car-hop's job was to keep moving his car around so that it would be instantly available to him no matter from which building he finally emerged.

George was shown into a projection room and annoyed to find Wilbur not yet there. Conscious of the stack of calls he had yet to return, George somewhat testily enquired of the projectionist where the studio head was to be found.

'Wilbur'll be along any minute now,' the man told him.

George was surprised that a projectionist should be on first name terms with his boss, but moodily returned to the empty rows of seats and stared at the blank screen.

George was about to demonstrate his impatience by leaving when Wilbur came bustling through the door looking pursued. Under his arm he carried a can of film.

'Glad you got here,' he told George and bustled through to the projection room. George went after him.

'Look, what is all this about, Wilbur? I really don't have the time to . . .'

Wilbur cut him off. 'You gotta make time for this! Word of this gets out and we could end up in jail!' Wilbur gave no time for George to speak but instead, turning to the projectionist, introduced him as his brother-in-law. 'With footage like this to show I couldn't trust none of the regular projectionists.'

George, his curiosity aroused, stared at the cans. 'What have you got there?' he asked.

Wilbur beckoned George to follow him into the theatre. 'Trust me,' he said in passing. 'It's dynamite!'

The lights dimmed even before they were properly seated. The scratchy front leader went through and then the first marker board showed. It told George pretty well everything he needed to know: 'SALOME – MAKE-UP/COSTUME TESTS.'

George groaned and turned to Wilbur. 'You brought me down here to watch tests?'

'Wait!' Wilbur cautioned him urgently.

George became increasingly restless as he sat through a series of portrait shots of actors in various make-ups. They were about as interesting as police mug-shots.

'Here!' Wilbur cried excitedly. 'Here it comes!'

George saw an actor in the costume of some kind of ancient warrior marching up and down inside the palace set as if on sentry duty.

'Watch this!' cried Wilbur.

George saw the actor on screen register discomfort and then, with a look one way and then the other, turn his back to camera, line up on a nearby urn and start, unmistakably, to show every sign of relieving himself into the pot.

'Can you believe that?' cried Wilbur. 'On my lot! He shoots a thing like that?'

George exploded. 'Wilbur! What the hell are you talking about? All he's trying to suggest is that even Roman soldiers, or whatever the hell he's supposed to be, are human. They got taken short too. I mean, you can't see *anything*!'

'Wait!' cried Wilbur. 'Wait and then tell me you can't see anything!'

There were some more apparently unconnected shots and then a board announced: 'TEST – HEROD'S COURT SET. SOUND & TRACK.'

The scene opened on a dozen or so extras milling around trying to look as if they had urgent things to do, and then the doors of the court were pulled back and a donkey was led into the main room. Riding it was a young girl with long hair combed down over her body. Von Muller tracked with the donkey, obviously intending to reveal the entire set. Suddenly the film crackled with sound. There was music and some rhubarbing from the extras, but there was so much crackle on the track that it was hardly distinguishable. What was interesting to George was that the camera was tracking with sound! All his information was that these new heavy cameras couldn't be tracked while recording sound.

'That's new!' said George.

'New!?' exploded Wilbur. 'New!? Is that all you got to say when we could all get arrested any minute!'

George was puzzled. 'What are you talking about?'

'You blind as well as stupid!? That kid is bare-assed naked!'

George took another look at the nervous girl on the donkey's back. She looked about fourteen or fifteen. He hadn't paid her that much attention and had assumed that, although appearing to be nude, she had some kind of skin suit on. Now he saw that Wilbur was right. Under the flowing long hair she was wearing precisely nothing.

Wilbur was standing up in the light of the projector and waving his arms at the projection box. 'Now tell me I've got nothing to worry about! What kind of nut makes movies with fourteen-year-olds naked on a donkey?'

George sighed. 'Are you telling me that you got me down here just for this?'

Wilbur stared at George open-eyed. 'You ain't concerned?' he asked as if astonished.

George shook his head. 'I'm not concerned, Wilbur. Von Muller shoots tests like that. Obviously he isn't going to use footage like that in the release print. You got to remember that Herod's court was a pretty decadent place.'

Wilbur came forward to jab his cigar end dangerously close to George's face. 'Yeah! But my studio ain't! George, you any idea what's going to happen to me if the banks find out about this stuff – not to mention the vice squad!'

George rose out of his seat to escape the threatening cigar. 'Wilbur, you're getting exercised over nothing. Von Muller is a genius.'

'He's a *nut*!' shouted Wilbur. Almost incoherent with conviction Wilbur waved his cigar at the now blank screen. 'You think that's *all*? You think that's the reason I brought you down here?' Wilbur paused to lend dramatic emphasis to his next words. 'You know what he's got on his desk?'

George had a mental picture of the cluttered pseudo-Bavarian hunting-lodge interior that Von Muller had built into his office. It was so full of boars' heads and trophies that it would take a team of experts a week to make an inventory. George gave up sooner than that. 'Tell me.'

Wilbur leaned forward and spoke in a conspiratorial whisper. 'On his desk,' he breathed, 'he's got a pair of tits and he says they belonged to the Queen of France!'

George laughed out loud. 'They did, Wilbur. Marie Antoinette was the Queen of France but that was a long time ago!'

Wilbur looked at him in astonishment. 'He told you the same thing? Well, if you're any friend of Von Muller's you'd better tell him to stop making dirty pictures on my lot and talking bad about queens and stuff. Them Europeans are very sensitive about that kind of thing!'

George spoke through the tail-end of his laugh. 'Wilbur, those "sensitive Europeans" you're so worried about cut off her *head*!'

Wilbur's jaw went slack. 'Her tits too?'

'No, Wilbur! Look, I know what you're talking about. What Von Muller has on his desk is a bronze casting of a plaster cast she had made.'

'The Queen of France had a cast made of her tits?'

'Sure! They did things like that in those days. What Von Muller's got is a very valuable antique. There's nothing wrong with it. Marie Antoinette also posed naked for some court painters!'

Wilbur was staring apoplectically. 'The Queen of France posed naked? You wouldn't kid me? I mean, I could have this checked out, you know!'

'Believe me, Wilbur, it's true. And another thing, any museum in the world would be proud to exhibit Von Muller's casting.'

Wilbur stared at George a long moment then, turning away, sank into one of the seats and gave every appearance of being lost in deep thought. George knew Wilbur well enough to know what had caused this sudden deep introspection. He cursed himself for forgetting the name of the Broadway writer Sybil had introduced to his office a week or so previously.

Wilbur spoke from his reveries. 'You know something?' he asked. 'That would make a hell of a movie. A queen posing naked and all that. I mean, there's a great scene when her husband, the king, finds out, right?'

Wilbur was on his feet now and suddenly animated.

George was still sorting through the turmoil of the past weeks trying to remember the guy's name. To fill in time he laid down his marker. 'And I've got just the guy to write it for you!'

Wilbur frowned. 'You representing writers now?'

George spoke with all the fervour of the recently converted. 'The written word is going to be the key to this business, Wilbur. Remember, I told you before. If the movies are going to talk they'd better have something to say.' George still couldn't remember the guy's name, so, to forestall any direct questions, he rushed on. 'Tell you what I'll do. I'll have this guy draft out a few pages on Marie Antoinette and drop them by. Right now, though, I really got to run. That test business with Von Muller? Forget it. The guy's a genuine genius, you'll see.'

George was turned for the door when Wilbur called him back. 'Wait! Hold on, what about this other business?'

George was genuinely puzzled. 'What other business?'

'This kid Von Muller tested.'

'What about her?'

'She could bring a suit against the studio. Suppose she starts shooting her mouth off about what happened here? We could get indicted for endangering her morals!'

'That's not very likely, Wilbur . . .'

'Maybe it's "not likely" but as head of this studio I got to consider it. Now, seeing as how it was you brought that Kraut to this studio the least you can do is help me out of the fix.'

'What can I do, Wilbur?' George asked tiredly.

'Sit down and I'll tell you.'

George sat down in one of the seats and watched Wilbur search his pockets. 'I had Casting check the kid out. They gave me her name – if I can find it . . .' Wilbur searched some more and finally came up with a tattered piece of paper. 'Here it is . . .' he scanned it and then spoke. 'Mary Davenport. Now, what I want you to do is find her and tell her you can sign her to a Galaxy contract. Make it fifty a week, five years with options.'

George got to his feet doing his best to show his

incredulity. 'Are you serious? You want me to negotiate a nickel-and-dime contract like that? You any idea what's happening down at my office while I'm here reminiscing with you? I got, maybe, John Barrymore and Adolph Menjou sitting in my outer office! You want me to call up this little girl and . . . !?'

Wilbur came pugnaciously and very angrily close. 'You got me into this with this madman! Now you're gonna get me off the hook!'

George stepped back in surprise. The anger in Wilbur's voice was real enough even if barely substantiated by what he'd seen on the screen. Most of the hopefuls turning up in Hollywood were fourteen or fifteen. Until the introduction of the new panchromatic stock any girl older than that had photographed like an aged crone. A girl child on the casting couch was no novelty, and one riding naked on a donkey for a Von Muller test wouldn't raise an eyebrow, so why was Wilbur putting so much energy into pretending fear of what this particular girl might or might not do? A glance at his watch told him that he was long overdue in his office. 'OK. I'll tell you what I'll do,' he said placatingly. 'I'll get one of my girls on to it.'

Wilbur seemed suddenly much relieved. 'Good!' he said.

George turned again for the door. 'Got to run, Wilbur.'

Again Wilbur refused to let him go. 'Hey, schmuck!' he called.

Wincing, George turned. 'Wilbur . . .' he started to protest, but Wilbur waved him down with the end of his cigar.

'I hear people talking about you all the time these days. You're getting to be a big man around town.'

'Nice of you to notice, Wilbur.'

Wilbur ducked his head in gracious acceptance of the compliment. 'Maybe you and I oughta sit down and have a serious talk one of these days?'

'About what?'

Wilbur made an encompassing, curiously coy gesture. 'Things. The studio, maybe. You and me go back a long way.'

'That'd be great, Wilbur, but the thing of it is, right now, I've just got to get back to my office.'

Wilbur nodded generously. 'You do that, and get your piece of quiff back here before that Kraut bankrupts me. OK?'

George nodded, and went out, both feet moving fast.

His car was waiting on the kerb outside the projection block. The car-hop leapt to his feet the moment he saw George and held the door open for him. George had a painful reminder of Mike Traviss.

Mike and Bressler seemed a long time dead these days. As George fumbled in his wallet for a suitable tip for the boy he idly wondered if the detective had got anywhere with his enquiries. In this case no news was most definitely the best news.

George's wallet couldn't come up with anything less than a five-dollar bill and he wondered where, in the studio, he could get it broken down. Then, in a sudden rush of guilt, he handed the whole five to the bug-eyed boy.

'Hey, Mr Schapner! Thanks a lot!'

The boy closed his car door with careful precision. You didn't slam the door on a five-buck tipper!

George felt good about it as he drove the car through the studio gates. Maybe when the whole façade he'd created came crashing down there'd be one voice out there speaking for him: 'Hey, he wasn't so bad. He once gave me a whole five-buck tip!'

Maybe it was a little like putting up an umbrella against an avalanche, but it was something!

3

The first thing George saw on getting back to his office was a startlingly beautiful girl. With her close-cropped black hair and cloche hat he thought, for one moment, that Louise Brooks had dropped in on him. Then he saw her interested eyes as she looked back at him. They were a clear, almost watery blue. Not Louise!

George exchanged polite smiles with the girl as he made his way to where Sybil was lying patiently in wait.

'Mr Schapner . . .' she started with 'that' tone in her voice.

George held up a hand to ward her off. 'I know! We got calls stacked up. OK. Tell me.'

Sybil flipped open her book with practised ease. 'Mr Stillman called again from New York. This time *very* angry . . .'

'About what?' asked George.

'He thinks you are avoiding him and that I am lying to him!'

George nodded. 'Keep up the good work. What else?'

Sybil sighed with the air of someone who knew she was wasting her time. 'Mr Von Muller called . . . a Mrs Davenport called . . .'

'Forget 'em,' George told her to stem the flow. 'Who's the girl sitting out there?'

Sybil flicked a page forward. 'She is Miss Nadine Bourdon. Apparently she was advised to ring you by Julia whom she met recently in Philadelphia.'

George nodded. 'I remember. Julia mentioned her. Tell her to call in and make an appointment. Try and find time for her.'

'She has already called more than four times. Mr Schapner, you're not taking any of your calls!'

'What the hell can I do? Wilbur Sterne needs nurse-maiding, he gets it. He's our most important client right now. French actresses with accents I don't need. Get rid of her.'

Sybil nodded and made a mark in her book. 'Other calls include Mrs Battershaw . . .' she looked up to get George's reaction. He dismissed Madame G. with a shake of his head. 'And,' Sybil went on, 'a lieutenant of detectives Marley.'

'Marley?' asked George. 'What did he want?'

'The same as all the others – to speak with you. That's the only reason anybody calls here, Mr Schapner.'

George thought that Sybil was beginning to sound like someone who wasn't happy in her work. He made a mental note to give her a raise.

'Shall I call him back for you?' she was asking.

Lieutenants of detectives George didn't need right now, but they weren't the kind of people to take 'no' for an answer. He would probably have to see him – but not yet!

'Let him come back. If he wants to talk bad enough he will!'

Sybil made one more note in her book and headed for the door. As she went George had a thought. He called her back. 'Wasn't it you who introduced that New York writer to this office?'

Sybil took a guarded step back towards him. 'Yes. What about it?'

'What was his name again?'

'Freddie Gross. What about him?'

'Have him call me, will you? There's a project out at Galaxy that might interest him. I gathered you knew him pretty well?'

Sybil smiled. 'I get his breakfast every morning!'

George looked up at Sybil with new interest. She had always seemed the epitome of the dedicated business type. Tall, slim, hair pulled back unbobbed, and plainly dressed; now he could see a glint in her eye that suggested a more vital personal life than he had suspected. 'It's none of my business,' he said, 'but I thought he had a wife back east.'

Sybil nodded. 'He does, but that's "back east" and you're quite right – it's none of your business.'

'OK! You're absolutely right, but have him call me.'

Sybil didn't need to make a note for that one and went out smiling happily. Maybe he wouldn't have to raise her pay after all!

Alone for a moment, with no phones ringing, George tried to count his problems. The trouble was they kept multiplying like mice.

He kept trying to tell himself that Ronnie Stillman happening to be in New York was no big deal. New York was a big city and there was little chance of an accidental meeting. On the other hand Ailleen, as Velma Torraine, was keeping a high profile and it wouldn't be that difficult for Ronnie to find her. If that happened the lid could blow off his entire artifice.

The thought jerked him to the other problem of the moment – Velma's real signature on the Galaxy contract.

He picked up the phone and asked for a direct line. The wait for the connection was interminable, and not made easier to bear by Sybil coming into the office and looking at him curiously, wondering why she hadn't been asked to get the number.

At one point his office door flew open and George, looking up expecting to see Sybil, was surprised to see the French girl standing there, trembling with indignation.

'I think you are a very rude man!' she said with shaking, angry tones. George was too startled to react immediately, and glad when Sybil intervened to lead her away.

It was at that point that he got the connection. It was a fiasco. So far as George's Spanish could carry him, he understood that he was not speaking directly to Velma's temporary home, but to some kind of feed store. He tried to tell them he wanted to leave a message for a Señora

Hernandez, but it seemed they had twenty or more Hernandezes in the area. George couldn't convey to them which one of them he wanted until he heard the magic word 'Americana'. George hung up feeling exhausted and far from certain that the message would ever reach Velma.

He still didn't know how he was going to get down there and back without attracting attention to his absence. Maybe he could get Velma to meet him halfway. Frontera, maybe?

It was one more loose end.

George was just considering a siesta on his couch when Sybil came bounding in with an excited light in her eyes. 'I managed to get hold of Freddie!' she told him.

'Good!' said George, reaching for the phone.

'No. He's here in the office. Shall I send him in?'

George smiled. Sybil's excitement left little room for argument. 'You keep him in a closet out there or what?'

'No!' she cried. 'He just happened to be passing!'

George chuckled out his disbelief. 'OK. Send him in!'

Freddie Gross's eyes lit up at the mention of Marie Antoinette. A tall, painfully thin man, his face was constantly shadowed by a virulent hair growth that refused to stay barbered. He was so like Sybil in build and general appearance that they might have been brother and sister.

Freddie had had a hit play on Broadway three seasons ago. MGM had bought the screen rights but then assigned one of their studio teams to write it for the screen. Disappointed by this, Freddie had come to George.

'But that's marvellous. I've been working on a play about Robespierre. I've researched the whole period. I probably know more about Marie than Louis did!'

George hadn't told Freddie that Wilbur's main interest lay in Marie Antoinette having posed nude for court painters. He found his mind wandering away from Freddie's enthusiasm by a thought that had just struck him. A chance remark had suddenly started to take concrete form and become a 'property'. George could see, with clarity, a theatre billboard.

It read: 'MARIE ANTOINETTE, starring VELMA TORRAINE, directed by STEPHEN VON MULLER, written by FREDDIE GROSS.' It was heady stuff. George was putting this whole deal together! It was a formula that he could repeat over and over again.

Just so long as a short-fused timebomb in the shape of Ronnie Stillman didn't go off and shatter everything!

George finally cut Freddie short with, 'Tell you what you do, Freddie. Put something down on paper, I'll get it out to Galaxy and, maybe, get you an advance and an option. OK?'

Freddie stood shaking his head and repeatedly thanking him. There elapsed only the shortest space of time between Freddie's departure and Sybil's reappearance. 'You don't know what this means to him,' she was saying. 'I know he's been fretting to get down to some real work!'

'Glad to be of service,' George told her and, on the wave of goodwill, said that he'd had enough for today and was going home.

Sybil smiled him all the way out of the door!

4

George had been slumped in the chair for over two hours, the only visible sign of life being the drink in his hand. He knew he should eat something, his stomach insisted, but somehow he couldn't summon the will to move. He was paralysed by the thought of the fragile edifice he had constructed about his own head.

Time and again he ran through his hit list.

Madame Gregory was held back only by the slenderest of restraints – greed. At some point that lady would realize that there was more to be gained from blackmail than adherence to their agreement. She was already getting restless about the signing of 'Velma's' contract. She was pressing for it, and the concomitant first payment of her percentage, harder than Wilbur whose whole studio now depended on it.

There was Ailleen herself. As the date for her return from Velma's personal appearance tour grew closer he would have to face the problem of what he was going to pay her. When he'd first decided to substitute her on a permanent basis it had seemed unthinkable that Ailleen would insist on the full amount he negotiated for Velma. Now, on her return, he would have to tell her what he had in mind, that she should continue to play Velma on and off screen, and, at that moment, he would make himself as vulnerable to her as to anyone else.

Mentally he moved his hit list up a notch – to include Ailleen, and even as he did so he suddenly realized that this wasn't just an addition to the list – it was the entire solution! Without Ailleen/Velma there would be nothing anyone could ever prove. In the sensation that the death of the young and beautiful Velma Torraine would cause it would be a strange mind that started wondering if she really was Velma.

Coroners' courts.

Big problem.

There'd be an inquest and investigation. Number one on the coroner's agenda would be identification. Fingerprints. The State of California had Velma's prints on file several times over. She'd been arrested on a drunk and disorderly warrant soon after he'd met her. She and some assistant director had been caught in the back of a tourer up on Mulholland.

The body would have to be the real Velma . . . unless . . . a car smash – a plane crash, even better, and a fire . . .

George suddenly suspected he was losing his sanity. He shot to his feet with a sudden sensation of nausea and, rushing through to the bathroom, threw up. Either his bootlegger was selling him bad Scotch or he should have eaten something.

George got back from the bathroom and, looking at the bottle, was surprised to see how far its level had shrunk. Alcoholism was something he didn't need right now. He had enough problems.

The telephone shrilled so loudly it sounded like a clarion call from a guarded rampart.

As he picked up the phone he was suddenly aware of how still and quiet it was around Rossmore that night. It reminded him of those mornings in Maine when he'd woken to find snow had fallen and the whole world seemed hushed and made over. There was no snow in California.

'Hello?'

Velma's voice crackled down the line. 'George! I got your message!'

George felt a sudden rush of warmth towards Velma. Of all the people he'd put on his hit list she had yet to figure.

'Hey! How the hell are you?'

'George? Are you drunk?'

'No. I just threw it all up. Punch drunk maybe. The world's going crazy around here.'

'George, listen, Manolo and I have found this dream of a ranch – the house is so beautiful you wouldn't believe . . . it's all coming so right . . . and you know what else? George! I'm pregnant!'

George was stunned by the avalanche of joy coming at him down the line from the Mexican feed store.

'That's wonderful news,' he murmured.

'So much for all those quacks in Hollywood who said I'd never do it, right?'

'It's marvellous news. Listen, I've been wondering . . . we have to meet . . .'

'We do?' Velma sounded suddenly cautious. 'What for?'

'I got a problem over this contract. It needs your real signature on it.'

George gripped the phone tightly when she didn't come back immediately. She might be going to hold him up for more money. Suppose she insisted on reading it and saw the numbers? George was relieved to realize that Velma was laughing. 'Oh, George! You know what? When you said we had to meet I thought you were going to ask for the money back!'

'No way!' cried George with relief. 'That's yours. All I want from you is a signature.'

'It'll be great to see you. When are you coming?'

'I was hoping we might meet somewhere halfway...'

Velma sighed down the phone. 'Oh, George. There's so much to do with the house, and Manolo's off buying stock and stuff we need, and what with the baby and all, I just don't want to leave here. Please, George, come down here, see what your lovely money is really worth!'

'OK, OK! I'll come. Trouble is finding the time. How would I get to you anyway?'

'Well, it's not easy from LA. You have to get the Southern Pacific to El Paso and then change to catch the Nacionales down to Chihuahua. I could meet you... No, wait a minute, I got a better idea. Quicker. There's an aerodrome quite close by us. Why don't you get one of those air mail pilots to fly you down here? You could make it here and back in a day if you had to, but I hope you'll stay over.' George's stomach had gone cold at the thought of chartering a plane. 'That's no good...' he murmured.

'Why not?'

'Renting a plane... people would talk about it. They'd wonder why, and the pilot might get curious too.'

'They wouldn't recognize me, if that's what you're worrying about. Tell him you've got a hot lady burning for you down here – or even better bring one with you and dump her in Chihuahua... wouldn't that explain the trip?'

George smiled down the phone. He suddenly realized that, since Julia's departure around the nation, he'd been living in

219

monk-like seclusion. There wasn't a girl that sprang to mind he could use to disguise his trip. It was, however, the one thing that most people would understand.

Flying was scary, but it would lend a raffish quality to the trip which might further serve to divert inquisitive minds.

'Anybody in mind?' he asked Velma.

'I'd volunteer myself, but circumstances, not to mention a jealous husband . . .'

'Husband?' interjected George. 'You're married?'

'Sorry I didn't invite you – a quiet ceremony, just half a hundred of Manolo's family and the entire village were invited!'

'But aren't you still married to, you know?'

'Not in Mexico, I'm not!' Velma's voice dropped in tone. 'Do you hear from him?'

'Not a word.' George lied for no particular reason.

'Let's keep it that way. Listen, it's impossible for you to call me – you have to put your name down at birth to get a phone installed out here! So what I'll do is call you the same time tomorrow night and you can let me know what you've decided to do. OK?'

'Fine, and thanks.'

'No problema. *Hasta la vista!*'

Smiling, George put down the phone. Velma was so obviously happy and fulfilled that it came out of the gloom like a beacon of joy.

The joy didn't last long. The thought of flying filled him with dread. As a doughboy constantly trying to find ways of burying deeper into the mud of France he had looked up and seen those lunatic airmen in their fragile machines lumbering around the skies exposing themselves to death with foolhardiness amounting to madness. He'd seen too many of them spiralling down towards the hard earth to have any confidence in the technology that had put them up there.

George made up his mind to two things. First, he'd take the train, and second, he'd go out and find something to eat.

He was about to leave the house when the telephone rang again. He snatched it up, illogically hoping it might be Julia, but it wasn't. It was Wilbur.

'How was she?' he asked enigmatically.

George was in no mood for games, and hadn't the least idea what Wilbur was talking about and told him so.

'You know . . .' whispered Wilbur.

George had a mental picture of Wilbur at home, probably with Golda in the next room, but he still couldn't guess what Wilbur was on about.

'The quiff on the donkey!' whispered Wilbur.

Suddenly George made connections. Wilbur must be talking about the under-age girl that Von Muller had tested.

'You mean this kid?'

'And her mother!' enthused Wilbur. 'I hear the mother is hot stuff, too. I gave her your number. Didn't she ring you?'

George gestured emptily and impatiently at his end. 'I think she did. I was too tied up to take the call. Is it so important you have to ring me at home? I was just going out.'

'Sure it's important. Kid like that could make a lot of trouble for us. Something we don't need right now.'

George sighed with impatient annoyance. Wilbur was right in one way. If the kid, or her mother, should be so imprudent as to take on a studio, it could make waves for him, the studio and the project. It wouldn't do Von Muller much good either.

'Listen, Wilbur, I'll talk to her tomorrow, right? As I understand it you want her bought off, and that's it. Right?'

'Yeah. Absolutely right, only I got to thinking . . .'

'What?'

'Well, there could be a return on the money. I mean, a kid like that showing everything and all, and her loving mother standing there letting her. Kind of sets the mind to thinking, don't it?'

'Wilbur, I thought you wanted to buy off trouble. You're talking like you're out looking for it.'

'What do you mean?' demanded Wilbur defensively.

'You telling me you want to meet her?'

'You trying to tell me you don't?' countered Wilbur with heavy inferences.

George was trying to formulate some suitably insulting remark when suddenly Wilbur's mood and voice changed up five gears into business-like briskness. 'Listen, George – give what I've said some thought, and let me know first thing tomorrow morning.'

Wilbur hung up abruptly giving George no time to make any response. It was transparently obvious that Wilbur had been interrupted at his end; probably Golda had walked into the room to find him whispering down the phone!

George let the receiver fall back on to its cradle and stood there, unaccountably depressed by the meaningless interruption. In Wilbur's mind George was still the five-dollar pimp he'd been when he'd first come to town. When he thought of the flimsy construction that was barricading him from that very recent past he was forced to admit that Wilbur could be right.

Dismissing the thought, George's stomach demanded attention.

There was a drive-in hamburger joint on Sunset and Vine that was as anonymous as he wanted to be tonight. The regular restaurants were haunted by table-hopping opportunists who, at the best of times, made him nervous. Tonight he felt their attentions could drive him hysterical.

He sat in the front of his car munching his way through the sauce-laden burger and fried potatoes and felt no better. Wheeler-dealer, the Coming Man, Big Bucks and what did it all come down to? Sneaking a hamburger and fries at a joint he could have afforded when he was back pimping five-dollar-a-day hopefuls. His life had been shit then, and it was shit now. When was the magic door marked SUCCESS going to open for him? Maybe civilians should adopt the army ways. In the service everyone wore their status on their collar;

whatever rank you were it showed. Here he sat, having made no progress in ten years but with the cold breath of driven fear blowing round his neck.

'Mr Schapner?' The pleasantly-accented voice startled him. He screwed round and peered out from the canvas hood of his tourer. Nadine Bourdon. He was struck by how beautiful she was. 'I saw you sitting there. I hope you don't mind my coming over?'

George smiled. 'You eat here, too?'

Nadine looked horrified. 'My God! No!'

George guiltily hid the remains of his fried potatoes.

'I live in the hotel across the street. I came out to get some cigarettes. Mr Schapner, may I talk with you?'

George shrugged. 'You mean, now?'

She shrugged back at him with added Gallic flair.

'Why not?'

Nadine walked round the front of the car and, as she did so, George was reminded of his monk-like abstinence since Julia's departure. He began to feel that this might prove an interesting encounter.

Nadine settled into the scuttle seat. 'I hope you don't think I'm presuming too much?'

George reassured her.

'I'm sorry for having called you "rude" this afternoon. Julia had told me so much about you that I felt I already knew you. That I had a right to assume things. Do you forgive me?'

'Forgiven.'

Nadine laid a hand on his arm and smiled warmly at him. George was beginning to feel presumptions of his own!

'You see, everything here is strange to me. Paris is like a club. Everyone knows each other. A director thinks of you for a film he is going to make and so he calls you. You have lunch and discuss things. Should everything be agreeable then you work together. If not, you part good friends resolved that there will be another time. Here everything is much more complicated.'

George nodded. 'It used to be like that here. Eight or nine years ago you could make a deal while out for an evening stroll. Times have changed. It's big business now!'

Nadine nodded and stared into her lap as if all this confirmed her worst fears.

George felt moved to add, 'You know, you've picked about the worst time for anyone to come to Hollywood. Everybody's running scared from this sound business. See, with someone like Greta Garbo, it's different. She was here and established. Whether she lasts or not, that's another question – the point is they are prepared to take a chance with her accent.'

Nadine turned her light eyes on him. For a moment George was afraid he could see tears in them. 'You think it is the way I speak?' she asked.

'Well, I have to admit that your accent is pleasant. You shouldn't have too much difficulty. The only thing is the moment someone knows you're from France they'll have an inbuilt reaction. "No accents!"'

'What about you? Can't you help me?'

It was George's turn to look away. 'I don't know what Julia told you about me, but right now I'm trying to consolidate what I've got . . .'

'And not about to take a chance with a foreign actress?'

George didn't answer. However, he felt a pang of loss when Nadine made every sign of being about to get out of the car. 'Tell you what,' he suddenly said, aware that he was merely making sentences to detain her. 'Tell me where I can reach you. If I happen to think of anything I'll call you.'

Nadine smiled. 'Thank you,' she said in a tone that suggested she knew he was being polite. 'I left my number with your secretary.'

George nodded and could think of no other way to detain her. Nadine smiled, laid her hand on his tingling arm again and stepped down from the roadster, smiled, waved and walked away.

George watched her all the way back to the Hollywood

Hotel and cursed himself. He needed someone to talk to tonight. Velma's telephone call had made him aware of his isolation. Wilbur's had depressed him. He wanted something to happen tonight. 'Dammit!' he told himself. 'I should have laid it on the line to her!' But he knew, deep down, that all he really wanted was Julia.

George, getting back to his house, was startled when the man detached himself from the shadows. 'Mr Schapner?'

Turning, he made out the face of the lieutenant of detectives. George wished he could remember his name. 'Oh, it's you!'

The cop came forward into the porch-light grinning. 'Sorry if I startled you. Fact is, I been trying to reach you at your office and, after tonight, I need to speak with you urgently.'

George saw he had little option but to invite the detective into the house.

Going through the door George apologized for not remembering the man's name.

'Marley,' he was told. 'Lieutenant Marley.'

'How can I help you?'

'You ever heard of a Nick, or Nicholas, Templar?'

George was able to shrug convincingly.

'He knew Mike Traviss pretty well.'

George opened his hands. 'I never met any of Mike's friends. I barely knew Mike.' George ended on a grin that, he was all too well aware, came out nervous.

Marley stayed unsettlingly quiet for a long moment.

George felt obliged to speak and break the silence. 'Would you like a drink?' he asked.

Marley smiled. 'A *drink*, Mr Schapner? I'm a police officer.'

George guiltily slammed his drinks table shut. 'Sorry! Naturally, I meant coffee!'

Marley nodded and, to George's relief, continued smiling. 'A drink would be just fine. You got any Bourbon?'

George poured him his best, added ice, and handed it to

Marley. Marley sipped on the drink appreciatively. 'Hey, this is the real thing! You have to give me the name of your bootlegger – and I promise not to book him!'

George smiled humourlessly. He was finding this interview, if that was what it was, difficult. There were a million thoughts fighting for space in his head. The primary one was survival.

Marley watched George sweat as he sipped on his drink. 'Why would Milton Bressler put a spy in your office, Mr Schapner?'

'I haven't the least idea, lieutenant.'

Marley turned away shaking his head. 'There's an element to this case that I can't put my finger on. So far as I can establish these two kids, Mike Traviss and Nick Templar, had been working with Bressler for years. Pretty smooth operation. Nothing big enough to bother too much about. Suddenly Bressler gets interested enough in you to plant Mike Traviss on you. Soon after that you start doing pretty good for yourself.'

George flinched under this direct accusation. He replied angrily, 'Listen, one thing has nothing to do with the other. I run a legitimate talent agency. I didn't know that Mike Traviss even knew Milton Bressler, let alone was in business with him!'

'OK!' Marley was holding up his hands defensively. 'I've got nothing on you or your business and I doubt there's anything I should know, except there's a connection here somewhere and I have to find it.'

Aware that his nerves were showing, George modified his stance. 'To tell the truth, lieutenant, I'd have thought you'd have closed this case down months ago.'

'It was closed,' said Marley. 'Until last night.'

'What happened last night?'

Marley looked up and smiled disarmingly. 'Last night we found Nick Templar's body. Somebody shot him, Mr Schapner.'

Staring at the lieutenant, George couldn't see how in the world this had anything to do with Milton Bressler's death. He told the lieutenant that.

Marley nodded, seemingly in agreement. 'It's hard to see, I grant you, but there's something been going on *after* Bressler's death that is, in some way, connected. I just thought you might be able to help me on that.'

George sat opposite the lieutenant but couldn't think of a thing to say. Marley was flicking imaginary cotton from his suit as he continued speaking with studied calmness. 'See, right after the shooting of Bressler this kid, Nick, went missing. Left his job, abandoned his belongings and just dropped out of sight. That is, until last night.'

Clearing his throat, George managed: 'I wish I could help.'

Marley nodded and drained his glass. 'Good booze, that. Well, thank you for your time, Mr Schapner.' Marley was on his feet and about to leave. Suddenly he turned back to the anxious George and smiled alarmingly. 'You know something? Ever since that day at the studio I been kicking myself!'

'Really?' asked George.

'Yeah. I mean there I was in the same room as Velma Torraine and I didn't get so much as an autograph!'

'Autograph?' asked George numbly. Panic-stricken, his mind was evaluating this apparently simple request. Fingerprints? Handwriting analysis? What did the lieutenant want Velma's signature for?

'She sure is a gorgeous-looking woman, Mr Schapner. If I had work where I could meet ladies like that all day I'd count myself a contented man.'

George was effusive enough, he hoped, to sound genuine. 'Well, perhaps you'd like to meet her sometime. She's out of town right now, but the moment she comes back . . .'

'That'd be real nice,' said lieutenant of detectives Marley. He looked round the house. 'Nice place you got here. Live alone, do you?'

George's heart-rate was increasing to the point where he was afraid it would become audible. Marley made him nervous, had him saying stupid things. 'Yeah, but lately I been thinking it's time I got married.' Even as he spoke George inwardly winced. What the hell had he said that for? Was he presenting his heterosexual credentials to distance himself from Bressler?

Marley started philosophizing. 'Been married myself fifteen years,' he was saying. 'Can't say I recommend it!'

Marley was holding out his hand. George shook it and he left the house.

George turned and raced for the drinks table and poured himself another glass. Bressler, Mike Traviss and now this latest shooting. Uneasily George was aware that somehow it all led back to Ailleen and Velma but, as the liquor stung his throat, he couldn't figure out how. George lay slumped on his couch feeling numbed, and totally disinclined to answer the telephone when it sounded out. Finally, as it became insistent, he lifted it to his ear.

'Mr Schapner?' asked a taut, nervous woman's voice.

'Who is this?' he demanded.

'My name is Mrs Davenport. I've had two calls tonight from Galaxy Studios telling me to meet with you now.'

Perplexed, George was beginning to suspect this was some kind of joke, when the name 'Davenport' connected in his mind. This was the mother of the kid that Wilbur wanted him to sign up and hush up. He was quiet so long that Mrs Davenport enquired if he was still on the line.

'Yes, I'm here, but I'm sleeping. Whatever it is you want, leave it until the morning and call my office number.'

George was about to hang up when he heard her starting to say something else. 'I did try to call your office, Mr Schapner, but couldn't reach you. Now this person at Galaxy keeps ringing to say I should get in touch with you immediately.'

'Well, the next time they ring, tell them I don't do business at home. Thank you for calling, Mrs Davenport, but I think you have been the victim of a hoaxer. Goodnight.'

George hung up before she could say anything else. The hand of Wilbur Sterne was obviously at work somewhere in the night. George wanted no part of it. He had enough problems of his own. Marley's visit had unsettled him.

It was as plain as day to George that the 'missing link' in Marley's investigation was the Velma/Ailleen switch. Bressler's death had saved his neck at the studio the day of the test, but his ghost was still hanging around. George would have given anything to have Julia by him to share these thoughts. She might have been able to put it all into perspective and calm him. He needed her. He needed Velma, and Ailleen and – shit(!) – he even needed Madame Gregory. There he went with his 'hit list' again!

Suddenly chilled to his toenails, George shot to his feet. Hit list! Madame Gregory! George grabbed for the phone.

Madame Gregory came on almost as if she had been expecting his call. 'I've been trying to get you for days!' she cried. 'How's our investment going?'

'Great!' said George. 'Listen, I've had a police lieutenant in my house tonight.'

'So what's new? I get them all the time. I give them a special rate.'

'You ever have a Lieutenant Marley up there?'

Madame G. was silent for some time before she said, 'I never talk clients' names, George.'

'Don't pull that crap!' said George angrily.

Then she said: 'Forget it!'

'Forget what? You mean, he has been up there?'

Madame G. got angry this time. 'You dumb bastard! You want to talk business over the phone? You want the world to know? Get your ass up here if you want any answers!'

George put down the phone with the sudden certain knowledge that Madame G. had 'hit' on Nicholas Templar. He lay down on the couch and wished he was on a train going anywhere. He got to his feet determined to drive up the hill and talk to her. He just wished he hadn't drunk so much!

He was on his way to a sobering shower when the phone rang again. Hoping for Julia he found himself speaking to Wilbur Sterne. Wilbur went right into a script of which George had no copy. 'All right, George,' he was saying. 'I've given it some thought and I'll be at your place in thirty minutes. Just make sure you have everything to hand. Let's waste no more time on this thing!' He hung up without George having said a word beyond his initial 'Hello'.

George stared at the phone and wondered if he had missed something earlier on. Could he be that drunk? On the other hand it was entirely possible that Wilbur had blown his cork. George hung up the phone carefully and started for the shower. Maybe the cold shock would sober him up. But maybe only a drunk could understand what the hell was going on.

He was still pulling on the other leg of his pants when he heard his front door bell ring. George stopped as if struck by lightning. Surely it couldn't be Wilbur?

George opened the door to an elegantly-dressed thirty-five-year-old woman. Beyond this first woman he saw a wide-eyed fifteen-year-old flapper and knew instantly who they were.

'Mr Pycroft?' asked the older woman sweetly.

'Who the hell is this Pycroft?' asked George.

The woman was as smilingly composed as if they had just been formally introduced. She came forward, forcing George back into the house, extending a gracious hand. 'Then you must be Mr Schapner. We spoke on the telephone. My name is Caroline Davenport!'

She was still holding out her hand but George couldn't take it. He needed both hands to hold up his pants. 'What the hell is going on?' he asked as both Mrs Davenport and her donkey-riding daughter forced their way into his house.

230

'I'm afraid I know little more than you, apparently, do, Mr Schapner. Mr Pycroft, as he finally identified himself, asked me to bring Mary ...' she waved an introductory hand towards the wide-eyed kid, 'my daughter, to meet him here.'

'Well, the hell he did! Listen to me, Mrs Davenport, I told you on the phone that you were the victim of a hoaxer. Now, so far as I know, there is no Mr Pycroft at Galaxy ...' George broke off as he suddenly saw the connection between Wilbur's recent idiotic promise to be 'there in half an hour' and Mr Pycroft. Wilbur would not have used his own name. George found himself staring towards the girl child that Wilbur had sniggeringly suggested they might 'get a return' on their money from. Wilbur's last call had been staged for Golda's benefit. Wilbur had pretended some kind of urgent crisis so that he could get out of the house to keep an assignation with Mrs Davenport and her wayward daughter. George realized with nausea that his house had become the favoured meeting place.

Mrs Davenport had been watching his silent confusion steadily. 'You were saying, Mr Schapner?'

George, disdaining to answer, turned away to his bedroom. There he completed buttoning his trousers and slipped on a sweater.

Mrs Davenport and daughter were still standing in the parlour when he came back.

'Are we to wait for Mr Pycroft here?' she asked.

'Do what the hell you like,' growled George. 'I have to go out.'

Driving up the hill George tried to get his mind off Mrs Davenport and her daughter and on to his own problems. Lieutenant Marley suspected something; seemed to think George knew something he, Marley, didn't know. The knowledge that he was right weighed heavily on George. The thought that people were dying for it was something hard for him to live with. By the time he reached Madame Gregory's he'd forgotten Mrs Davenport's existence.

Madame Gregory was drunk.

'Come in, you old bastard!' she greeted him as he stepped into her private drawing-room. 'Pull up a pew and have a drink!'

George refused the drink. 'What about this kid ...' he trailed off as he realized he'd forgotten the kid's name.

Madame G. filled it in for him. 'Nick Templar?' she suggested.

George nodded.

Madame G. sniffed inelegantly. 'You know who the kid was?'

George guardedly shook his head.

'Ambulance driver!' snorted Madame G. with triumph.

George's heart sank without trace. 'Don't tell me! He was the one drove Velma to Pasadena?'

'Got it in one!' crowed Madame G.

'How did you get to hear about it?'

'Milton Bressler got it from the kid. He came up here and asked what I knew about it. I wasn't about to tell him shit! All he knew then was some story about Ronnie Stillman.' She paused and took a pull from her glass.

'I know about that,' offered George. 'He came to me with it. So?'

'So Milton got the story about Velma being hurt. Then you *produced* Velma to Wilbur. Milton started going crazy. He was always paranoid, right? Now he doesn't know who to believe. He starts thinking his kid partners are setting up for something. He got convinced when Nick Templar asked him for five hundred dollars for the whole story. Bressler promised him the money if he would come to the studio the following morning. That was the day of the test. First thing the following morning the cops come knocking on the kids' door. The kids figure Bressler had sold them out. Turned out later that it was something else entirely, but that's what the kids thought then. The one kid goes out the back window while your kid stalls them – telling them that Nick was on duty with his ambulance. The cops leave and your kid goes looking for Bressler.'

'To the studio?'

'Right, but it turns out Nick Templar has had the same idea. He gets to Bressler first and ups the ante to a grand. Bressler, not knowing nothing about nobody any more, beats up on the kid and gets the whole story for nothing more than bruised knuckles. Enter your kid to find his friend and lover lying there bleeding. They got no money, the story's blown, and they got the cops at their back. Mike tells his friend he's "going to settle Bressler once for all" and leaves, looking for him!'

'Holy shit!' breathed George. 'I thought *I* had problems that day!'

Madame Gregory held up a thumb and forefinger indicating the tiniest space between them. 'You came that close! You must have the luck of the devil riding with you.'

George murmured, 'Milton told me that once.' Another question formed in his mind. 'But why did the kid come to you?'

'He used to make deliveries here. Booze, mostly.'

'In his ambulance?'

'You know a better way? I need the stuff in truck-loads. He ran here when he heard what his pal had done at the studio. He wanted dough to get out of town with. I tossed him a hundred.'

'He went?'

Madame Gregory nodded.

'But he came back?' he prompted.

Again Madame Gregory nodded. 'This time he thought he'd figured it all out. He could have made trouble. Trouble I don't need!'

George was solid ice, head to toe. 'So you had the kid killed?'

Madame Gregory's face was a taut mask. 'I told you once,

I tell you again, nobody makes trouble for me. They don't threaten me with it either!'

'Why?' groaned George.

'Listen,' started Madame Gregory pointing an uncertain finger in George's direction. 'By this time we're partners, right? OK, so you take advantage. Why not? I do, would and will, every fucking chance I get – so why not you? One thing I don't do is back down on a partner and I expect the same from them!'

George found words elusive, but finally managed to string some together. 'You could have sent the kid to me! Jesus, he was just a kid trying to get by . . .'

'"Get by" is one thing! Getting in the way is something else.'

He sat staring at her implacably set face for a long time before he could bring himself to speak again. 'You made me a murderer.'

'That's shit!' shouted Madame Gregory. 'Don't try loading me with that sanctimonious crap. We got a big money deal and it was about to blow up in our faces! I didn't shoot Bressler. Neither did you. Some mad twisted kid took revenge for his bed-mate – that's all it amounted to!'

'And this other kid? This poor fucking ambulance driver? First, he gets shit kicked out of him by Bressler, his friend gets killed by the cops, he comes to you for help and gets his head blown in! Jesus Christ, you could have sent him to me – I'd have given him five grand and he'd have been set for life!'

Madame Gregory was shaking her head from about half-way through until George ran out of words. 'You're forgetting something. I *did* give him a hand-out. Next thing he's back wanting more. Your way he'd have had the pot up to a hundred grand before winter! In the long run there's only one way to handle this kind of situation.'

George found himself on his feet. 'I don't believe that! Jesus, you are so wrong!'

Madame Gregory stayed calm and seated. 'So I'm wrong,' she told him. 'Sue me!'

George was out of the house, into his car and halfway down La Brea before he started getting any perspective on what Madame G. had thrown at him. He wished he'd never known. He reminded himself to stop asking questions when it was likely he wasn't going to like the answers. Nothing was worth all this!

He didn't remember any of the other strange events of the night until he saw the stranger's car parked outside his house. It had to be Wilbur! George had never seen Wilbur in anything other than a chauffeured limousine before. Obviously this was no occasion for one.

George marched up his own driveway determined to have a showdown with Wilbur.

Mrs Davenport looked splendidly at home in George's living-room. She had obviously served herself with the glass of cognac she had in her hand.

'Oh,' she cried on noticing George's aggressive entrance. 'You're back sooner than we expected!'

George looked round. Of daughter and Wilbur there was no sign. 'Pycroft show?' he asked Mrs Davenport.

Mrs Davenport beamed with delight at being asked such a question. 'They're discussing Mary's future at this very moment!' she said with pride.

'Where?'

'In there!' She indicated George's spare bedroom. At least they weren't using his bed! 'I hope you don't mind,' she added.

George crossed to the wide-open 'secret' table and poured himself a drink. 'Mind? Why the hell should I mind? You come into my house to prostitute your own daughter, help yourself to my booze! What in hell have *I* got to mind about?'

Mrs Davenport barely flinched. 'Mary is old enough to know what she is doing.'

'I'm damn sure she is. Question remaining is: are you?'

'I question myself on that, too,' she smiled with infuriating serenity. 'Some nights I worry about it, others, like tonight, I convince myself that it's the only way Mary is going to be noticed.' She paused and smiled down at her carefully smoothed skirt. 'I would worry about it more, except that she enjoys it so.' Mrs Davenport looked up directly at George, and smiled. 'Women *do*, you know!'

Coming so soon after Madame Gregory, George began to wonder about women. How could this mother imagine that a fifteen-year-old girl could enjoy having sex with a man like Wilbur Sterne? How could it be anything other than an ageing man cynically using a young body? This monstrous woman apparently was willing to believe it might be.

Mrs Davenport was smiling at him in a strangely detached manner. 'She really does, Mr Schapner. But then she comes from highly-sexed stock!'

George distracted himself from this laden remark by turning on his anger. 'How come you know my name? Everybody else around here is getting away with pseudonyms!'

Unshaken, she smiled as pleasantly as ever. 'It's no big deal,' she told him. 'It's on the mailbox outside.'

George turned away. He was getting out of control. He could tell because everybody seemed to be able to make a fool out of him without effort. It wouldn't have been so bad if they had to work at it once in a while.

'I'd be grateful if you, your daughter and Mr Pycroft would kindly get out of my house!' he told her.

'I do understand, Mr Schapner,' she soothed. 'You've been put upon.'

'Put upon' was not what George felt. George felt soiled. He felt 'shit upon'. He wanted to hit back. He turned back to her. 'Where do you get all these east coast words from? You don't fool me, lady! I hear Tennessee coming through loud and clear!'

Mrs Davenport smiled. 'Dammit, I thought I'd lost all

traces! I must be tired or something.' She paused, smiling, while George simply stared at her. Was she made of stone? 'It's a very interesting story,' she told him. 'Would you like to hear it?'

'No, dammit! I wouldn't. All I want is for you to get yourself out of here!'

'I do understand, but I can hardly interrupt, can I? They would be sure to be at a delicate stage in their discussions!'

She had the ability to reduce him to seething street-kid anger. 'You sicken me, lady! You really do!'

He walked out on her and into his own bedroom, forcefully slamming the door.

He lay fuming on his bed, not bothering to switch on the light. Big-Shot Agent! Jesus, he was in the same business as Madame Gregory, but not half so good at it!

After a long 'seethe', George became aware of the silence in the rest of the house. Cautiously he got up from the bed and, feeling like a sneak thief in his own house, put his ear against the inside of his bedroom door. Hearing nothing he carefully opened it and peered out.

The lights had been switched out. He stumbled across to the switch and threw it.

There was a note standing against a table lamp.

With relief he realized that the show had folded and the players sneaked off. He carried the note with him to the street window and peered out. Sure enough, Wilbur's borrowed car had gone. It was very un-Wilbur-like to just sneak off like that. Maybe the old bastard had some sense of shame after all.

George turned back into the room and read the note.

'Thank you for the use of your house,' it read. It was signed Caroline Davenport and gave a Vine exchange telephone number.

George carefully screwed the note into a tight ball of paper and then, to make doubly sure, went through into the bathroom where he flushed it down the toilet bowl.

He stood there watching it spin into oblivion and wished he could solve all his problems so easily.

5

George had been deep in sleep and dreaming of Julia with such intensity that he could almost feel her presence. He was angry when the telephone roused him but then, as he fumbled it to his ear, he heard operators' chatter; that meant coast-to-coast from New York and Julia. He wanted nothing more than to hear her at that moment. He had something very specific he wanted to say, something warm and tender and, he hoped, a comfort to them both.

When all the clicks and intervening voices had finally cleared the line he heard Julia but couldn't understand her tone.

'Listen to me,' she started. 'I'm not going to use any names – not even yours. Just listen! When I say "him" I mean the British, OK?'

George was numbed. She meant Ronnie Stillman. 'What's happened?'

'He's here!'

'I know. I heard he was in New York.'

'I don't mean New York. I mean *here*!'

'The hotel?'

'The *room* in the hotel!'

George groaned coast-to-coast.

'What happened?'

'We had just got back to the room. Suddenly there he was. I mean, he broke in, George . . .'

'No names!' snapped George.

'Sorry. It's just that I'm on edge. Look, he literally splintered the doorframe. He came in like some monster.'

'OK. Tell me what happened!'

'He just stood there and stared at her, I thought he was going to kill her from the expression on his face! Then, suddenly, he kind of dissolved. He went to pieces. He rushed at her, threw himself down at her feet and started sobbing like a baby!'

'What happened?'

'She and I stood there staring at each other over this crazy man and then she started crying too! George, it's the most beautiful thing I've ever seen!'

'Are you nuts?' he yelled at her. 'Get him out of there ... wait a minute, what time is it in New York?'

'Eight-fifteen.'

'In the morning?'

'Of course in the morning.'

George was fighting for some line of logical thought that was eluding him. He managed to come back to one pertinent fact.

'You mean he's still there? He's been there all night?'

'Yes, that's exactly what I mean. He's crazy about her!'

'About who? You mean he knows who she is?'

'No! That's it. He hasn't noticed a thing – not that I can tell anyway.'

'But what about her?'

'I don't think she cares. I think she's as crazy about him as he is about her.'

Coherence wasn't something George could find. To fill in time and keep the line open he offered, 'Crazy is right!'

'What shall I do?'

'What *can* you do?'

'Short of levering them apart with a crowbar I can't think of a damn thing!'

George found that his free hand was making strange involuntary gestures in the air. His whole body was shaking. He cursed the distance that lay between himself and Julia. He wished he had similar distance from his problems. He had to be decisive, but about what?

'Cut and run!' he told her. It wasn't a solution and he knew it, but he had to say something!

'He'll only follow!'

George began to think that, maybe, Madame Gregory's approach to problems had its merits, but he was in Hollywood and the problem was in New York. 'What can I tell you? Listen, you think he doesn't suspect?'

'I'm sure he doesn't. Not *yet*, anyway.'

'And her, what about her?'

'She looked happy like you wouldn't believe.'

'You think there's any chance she can keep this thing going?'

'Looks like it.'

'Then get back here. Close down everything. I don't care who gets upset or angry or any other damn thing, just get back here where we can handle it!'

'It takes four days on the train to get there, George.'

'What does that mean?'

'I mean it's four days when he might sober up enough to notice something wrong.'

'It might not last longer than Chicago. Just do as I say!'

Julia was silent a long time. George could hear the mush building up as the power boosters searched for a signal. 'Are you crazy?' Julia finally asked.

'Maybe,' said George. 'I don't know any more, Julia. There's nothing I can do from this distance. Get back here the fastest you can. Meantime, try to keep that lunatic distracted the best way you or she can think of.'

'That'll take no figuring out and I intend leaving it entirely to *her*!'

'Play it the way it works best. You hear me?'

'I hear you.'

'I love you,' he said out of nowhere.

'You what!?' screamed Julia.

'You heard me!' he yelled back and hung up.

George lay on his bed and stared at the ceiling. What the

240

hell was he playing at? He'd just played a scene from a 'B' programmer while the world was coming down around his ears. Ronnie and Ailleen locked in mutual deception. Was it possible that Ronnie was crazy? Ailleen had fooled Wilbur, had carried all those craft trades at the studio along with her. She'd seduced the press and publicity people. Could it be that Velma's husband couldn't tell the difference? Maybe the poets were right, could be that love was a state of insanity. Across the years George heard his father's voice again. '*Wenn der Steckel steht, der Kopf geht!*'

George winced at the memory of his father's voice. He'd never told anyone, not even admitted it to himself, but he would never recover from the last time he'd heard it.

On those first few days back from France his father hadn't spoken to him. Whenever George had approached him he'd turned his back and walked away. Haunted by his mother's sorrowing eyes George had finally cornered him in the barn and forced him to speak.

His father had turned angrily on him. 'You have killed German boys!' he'd said, and then added into George's confused and hurt face, 'Maybe your own brother!' It kept coming back to George no matter how he tried to forget.

George had watched his father walk away from him and known he was never going to turn back. George had returned his mother's last embrace and followed the ghost of Erle to California. Maybe this had all been for Erle. Maybe he was living the life that had been intended for Erle.

Mike Traviss. Julia. Milton Bressler. Velma. Ailleen. Nick Templar, who he'd never even met. Maybe they would have all known Erle. Funny thing, all the guys were dead and all the women alive. There might be some good philosophical reason for that, but George wasn't equipped to find it.

All George could feel was guilt. And pain. So why the hell had he said such a stupid thing to Julia at this, of all times?

George threw back the covers and got out of bed.

241

'Cut and run,' he had told Julia. The more he thought about it the better sense it made – as advice to himself!

George didn't normally eat breakfast but today was different. Someone had once told him that eating steadied the ragged nerves. That was one reason for coming in to the Hollywood Hotel, but there was another.

Once, in France, the army had pulled his unit back to a rest area in Normandy. That, too, had been a refuge from fear. There'd been a summer orchard heavy with swelling Calvados apples and there'd been a girl. She'd been no beauty. Her brows went in a straight uninterrupted line across her forehead. She'd had broad, stocky hips and thighs, but she'd smiled on him. Her dark luminous eyes had filled with joy as they'd lain together in that orchard. He'd not loved her but he'd never felt more safe or grateful in his entire life. It occurred to George that the Hollywood Hotel was a strange place to come looking for her, until he looked up and saw a smiling Nadine crossing the breakfast room towards him.

'Mr Schapner!' she cried in obvious delight.

George nodded to her and she sat down opposite him. 'What a pleasant surprise!'

They chatted about nothing much while Nadine ordered and bathed him in her smiles. George found himself halfway through telling her about Normandy and how he'd felt safe there.

Nadine's reaction to this was strange. She looked directly at him and asked, 'Are you saying that I should return to Paris?'

Startled by this lateral shift from his problems to hers, he found himself blundering into a more personal revelation than he'd intended. 'No. What I'm saying is that I'm thinking of going back there myself.'

Nadine's eyes sparkled with surprise. 'Do you speak French?' she asked him.

'I could learn,' he told her.

Nadine's laugh rang around the restaurant. 'But everyone in Europe is wanting to come here!'

George nodded and let it go with a dismissive shrug. He was aware, though, that Nadine was reassessing him. Somehow that pleased him. He wanted to please her. He had an impetuous thought.

'Listen, I have to run out to Galaxy Studios this morning to see Von Muller.'

'The director?' asked Nadine with sudden interest.

'I have to see him about a problem. How would you like to go out there with me?'

'Shall I meet Von Muller?'

'Only if you want to play Marie Antoinette,' George told her.

'*Merde!*' said Nadine.

Von Muller had less of a crisis than George had feared. The page delegated to them led Nadine and George to a building George had never been in before – the Wardrobe. Von Muller pounced on George and led him, with claw-like grip, to an area dominated by huge, square cutting-tables.

'There!' cried Von Muller.

George looked and saw a rack of costumes he immediately realized must have been made for the role of Salome.

'Look!' cried Von Muller. 'Look at this fantastic work!'

George nodded politely. Nadine took a closer interest and fondled the materials.

'Looks terrific!' said George. 'Is this why you wanted me out here?'

Von Muller raised an admonishing finger. 'No! But, as you see, we have the costumes – where is the woman that will wear them?'

George was bridling with resentment at Von Muller's hectoring tone.

'If you mean Velma, she's currently in New York.'

Von Muller made a gasping sound in his throat and turned away, apparently in disgust. 'As you see, we need her here!

Do you realize what is happening here? We have spent much money, even more time, in preparing what will undoubtedly be the world's first *talking* spectacular, and your artiste is signing meaningless autographs for nobodies in a city three thousand miles away. Here! Mr Schapner! Here! is where she should be! We can do nothing more until she gets here. Look! *Look* at these gorgeous gowns. Tell her of them! No woman yet walked the earth that could resist costumes like these!'

'Mr Von Muller, without those "nobodies", as you call them, there wouldn't be any movie industry. It just so happens that what Velma is doing out there with those "nobodies" is to ensure that this movie makes a million.'

'Three million!' snapped Von Muller.

George stared at him. 'You expect to make a three million gross?' he asked.

'Three million net!' Von Muller cried. 'Three million for Galaxy. Gross we shall do some ten million!'

George smiled broadly. 'I wish you luck. If you do that much I'll renegotiate your contract for sure.'

Von Muller sighed. 'All that is unimportant. All that matters is how soon I can have the privilege of working with Miss Torraine. Do you *realize*,' he asked with incredulous emphasis, 'that I have yet to meet her?'

George nodded, unaccountably guilty. 'I do realize that. As presently planned, Velma should be here by the end of next week!'

'Ridiculous!' cried Von Muller. 'Now I need her! *Now!*'

'Whichever way you cut it, it still takes five days from New York to Pasadena!'

'Then she should never have left.' Suddenly Von Muller's eyes left George and zeroed in on something beyond him. 'Who is that woman?' he asked.

George turned to see Nadine holding one of the Arabian Nights' fantasy creations against her.

'Nadine Bourdon,' George told him.

Nadine looked up as she heard the sound of her own name, and smiled as if caught doing something reprehensible. She looked from George to Von Muller. 'They are beautiful,' she said.

Von Muller brushed past George. 'You are French?' asked Von Muller.

Nadine nodded. 'It's a very great pleasure to meet you, Mr Von Muller. Of course I have seen your movies. I am a great admirer.'

Von Muller seemed not to notice the compliment. He started walking round Nadine, who, embarrassed, looked towards George.

'What do you know about Salome?' asked Von Muller as if accusing her of something.

'Salome?' asked Nadine in confusion. 'I thought you were making *Marie Antoinette*?'

George started forward, trying to head off Von Muller with whom the project had yet to be broached. He needn't have worried. Von Muller only heard relevancies. '*Salome*,' he emphasized. 'Well?'

Nadine glanced towards George and then, getting no help, turned back towards Von Muller. 'She danced!' said Nadine.

Again Von Muller raised the admonishing finger. 'More!' he demanded. Nadine shrugged. 'She danced for Jean Baptiste's ... er ...' she broke off pointing at her own head, fear having stripped her vocabulary.

'Precisely!' cried Von Muller. 'She danced for John the Baptist's head. But *why*?'

Nadine shrugged again. 'Mr Von Muller,' she protested, 'I am no *religieuse*!'

'Neither was Salome. She was a woman — so are you! Why did she dance naked for John the Baptist's head?'

Nadine shrugged. 'I don't know!'

Von Muller reacted as if he'd won a major victory. 'You see?' he demanded of George triumphantly. 'Nobody knows *why* she danced — only that she *danced*.' He turned back to

Nadine, who took a defensive pace backwards. 'That!' he cried, 'is the subject of my film!'

Nadine nodded enthusiastically. 'It will be very interesting,' she said.

George had a more mundane reaction. 'You haven't forgotten we've got a Hay's Office, have you, Mr Von Muller? I mean, this bit about her dancing "naked". You won't get away with it.'

Von Muller looked at Nadine speculatively and for a moment George thought his question was going to be ignored.

'You'll see,' he murmured quietly. He finally turned to George but pointed to Nadine. 'This lady,' he began. 'She is an actress, I can tell, but what has she done?'

'Some very fine work, Mr Von Muller. Nothing in the States yet, but I have every expectation that she soon will.'

Von Muller nodded. 'I agree. She is a superb-looking woman.' He paused a moment, then made one of his declamatory decisions. 'I shall test her.'

'For what?' asked George.

'Salome, of course. For the moment nothing else exists.'

George felt he had to pitch 'Velma'. 'But we have Velma Torraine already signed to that picture!'

'Salome had a sister. A voluptuous harlot. Decadent and depraved.'

George was surprised. 'She did?'

Von Muller nodded. 'She has now!' he said.

'And you want Nadine for that role?'

'It will be an important part of my structure. I see everything now with great clarity. Salome shall not be evil – not *as* evil! There will be a thread ... Salome is jealous of her sister, who can do no wrong while she herself is held on a chain amid the decadence of the court in which she lives. The sister becomes a convert to John the Baptist's teaching. Salome becomes fascinated with this man who took her evil sister and made her pure again. She too comes under the spell of John. Herod is furious. He always lusted after his step-daughter — both of them, but he's already had the one, now he wants Salome. The sister is arrested with John. Herod disowns her, refuses to help her. Salome's final sacrifice is to save her reformed and repurified sister. It is Salome's mother who, unknown to Salome herself, makes Herod think that Salome will only dance for the head of John the Baptist. Then at our climactic casting aside of the last veil, *two* salvers are brought to Herod — one carries the head of John the Baptist, the other that of the sister!'

'*Merde!*' said Nadine when he was all talked out.

'What does that word mean?' asked George.

'Excrement!' said Von Muller. 'And she is quite right. It needs work, but the seed is sown. I want this woman!' he told George.

Doesn't everybody? thought George, but smiled brightly and told Von Muller that he'd work something out with Wilbur Sterne.

Von Muller nodded and let them move away before calling after them.

'Miss Torraine! Here! Imperative!'

George reassured Von Muller that Velma was on her way and, grabbing Nadine's arm, hustled her out of the labyrinthine building.

In the courtyard he turned on her. 'Where do you get off using language like that? Don't you know who Von Muller is?'

Nadine seemed puzzled. 'Of course I do! But the word doesn't just mean that. Not only that. It can be an expression of surprise, of joy even.'

'It can?'

Nadine nodded.

'Like an American might say "shit"?'

'An exact comparison!' smiled Nadine. 'Excrement!'

'I like "shit" better,' said George and started her across the courtyard.

They hadn't gone far before they spotted the gateman running towards them.

'Mr Schapner! Your office wants you to call back!'

George took the call in the gate-house, not wanting to get into a conference with Wilbur. The only reason he could think of to explain this to himself was that he didn't want Wilbur seeing Nadine. Could this be love?

Sybil told him that he'd had a call from a 'Mrs Hernandez' long distance from Mexico. George remembered Velma telling him how difficult it was for him to call her.

'What did she say?'

'That she'd try again in an hour – that's fifteen minutes from now!' said Sybil excitedly.

George told her he'd come right back to the office, and yes, he was all right now.

The car was waiting for him, the car-hop smiling brightly at him in expectation. George remembered the five he had liberally donated the last time. Seems he was going to be stuck with it or called a piker.

Nadine was horrified. 'You gave that boy *five dollars?*' she asked him as they drove away.

George grinned at her. 'It's only money!'

Nadine looked away from him. '*Merde!*' she said so quietly George hardly heard it.

'There you go with that word again!'

'Are you crazy?' she asked him as she turned back.

George wanted to change the subject. 'Your English is good. You wouldn't happen to speak Spanish would you?'

'I love Spain,' she said.

'Yes, but do you speak Spanish?'

'Of course!'

'How'd you like to go to Mexico with me?'

Nadine looked puzzled. 'When?'

'Tomorrow. We'd fly down, of course!'

Nadine's eyes lit up. 'In an aeroplane?'

'Unless you know a friendly eagle!'

'That would be marvellous!' she said excitedly, then frowned. 'But tomorrow?'

'Problems?'

Nadine was silent for some moments. 'I'll have to think about it,' she said finally.

'Not too long,' chided George.

Nadine promised that she'd let him know later that same day. He let her off at her hotel and drove rapidly back to the office.

Velma was already on the line as he bustled in. He told her that he was coming down the following day and, lowering his voice, whispered: 'And I'm flying.'

'What?' screamed Velma. 'I didn't hear that!'

George cursed the phone system. 'I'm flying!' he yelled the whole way to Mexico.

Velma laughed joyfully. 'Great!' she yelled back. 'Check into the Hotel Republica in Chihuahua. I'll find you there.'

George was writing down the name of the hotel when he remembered something else. 'I forgot! How do I get a plane to fly in?'

Velma's laugh screeched down the line and into his ear. 'You lamebrain! Haven't you fixed that yet? Well, listen, write this down. Call the Hollywood Aerodrome. Talk to Mike Hammersfield. You got that? Mike Hammersfield!'

'Got it,' George told her, but that solution gave rise to another. 'Does this guy know you?'

'Of course he does!' she said, missing the point.

'Well, then, is that a good idea, considering?'

Velma was thoughtful for a moment. 'It's OK. Mike doesn't fly himself any more, so he'll assign someone else. Now this is important, George. Not Harry Coulter or Stevie Schultz.'

'Why not?'

'*They* know me too!'

George hung up laughing.

Now he was committed he found the idea of flying both

raffish and exciting. He'd never flown before, so, if he died on the first attempt, it would come as a blessing considering the problems he'd be leaving behind.

Sybil came into the office while he was still trying to find the number of the Hollywood Aerodrome.

'You want something?' she asked him.

'Just a line on an old friend.'

Sybil pursed her lips at him. She seemed to resent him doing anything for himself.

'Did you want something?' he asked her.

Sybil laughed. 'Boy, what an opening! No. I just wanted to say that Freddie's working on that project like a man possessed. The rate he's going he should have a draft outline by some time tomorrow.'

'Ah!' sighed George guiltily, 'I won't be in tomorrow,' and, as Sybil looked at him in surprise, went on, 'I'm taking a few days off over the weekend. Think I've earned them?'

Sybil shrugged. 'What about the calls? Just today we're behind about fourteen or fifteen.'

'You handle them,' George told her. 'As a matter of fact I've been meaning to talk to you for some time about taking more executive responsibility around here. Think you could handle it?'

Sybil beamed with inordinate pleasure. 'You mean until Julia gets back?' she asked.

George shook his head. 'No, I mean from here on. You and Julia would make a great team and I need help.'

'Have a great rest!' said Sybil happily.

George sat back in his chair. All his best ideas seemed to come off the top of his head. He thought of what Nadine might be doing right this minute. He thought of what he might be doing with Nadine by this time tomorrow!

Maybe this wasn't such a bad business after all.

6

They'd been flying for close to an hour and a half, but George didn't feel any more secure than when they'd first bucketed into the sky.

The plane had looked reassuringly big and sturdy when Jack Tobie, the pilot assigned to his charter, had shown it off.

'It's a Boeing 40A!' Jack had told him with obvious pride.

George had stood on bloodless legs and nodded. He felt as if he were looking over his own scaffold and regretted the idiocy that had caused him to gush to Velma that he'd fly down to Chihuahua. Especially when Nadine had backed out.

'I can't do it, George,' she had told him over the phone. 'I'm pleased and excited to have met Von Muller and I like you very much but I can't come to Mexico with you.'

'Why not?'

'Because of your kindness. I'm sorry, but if I were to go with you now it would seem as if I was paying you off. Like a *puta*.'

'That's ridiculous,' George had protested.

'Maybe, but that's how it would feel to me. I'm sorry, George.'

George had hung up on her feeling cheated. He'd only gone headlong into this flying thing because of her, because of some juvenile desire to impress her. Now here he was exposing himself to his worst fears on his own! Taking a drink hadn't helped. He'd just got angrier with her.

'Your first time up?' Jack Tobie had asked him with a knowing grin.

George had managed a paralysed nod in reply.

Jack had given him a hearty slap on the back. 'Nothing to it! You'll see.'

George had peered into the dark, cramped, little cabin

slung between the wings and failed to get any reassurance from its flimsy structure. Canvas chairs spread over a wooden floor. 'How long will it take to get there?' he'd asked.

'About six hours.'

'As long as that?'

Jack had shrugged. 'I got to put down for fuel somewhere along the way. This ain't the Spirit of St Louis, you know!'

And you ain't Lindbergh, thought George. Lindbergh had just the previous year flown fourteen hours non-stop across the Atlantic to France. Lindbergh was a national hero. George wondered if the national coward title was still vacant. He felt like the top contender.

George had found the take-off traumatic enough but the climb-out had been worse. The huge protruding motor up front had roared and he, in his canvas cabin, could hear every decibel.

The machine had seemed to labour mightily and achieve little as it fought for the height necessary to clear the mountains. George hadn't dared look out the window but couldn't escape the feeling that there was little between him and the ground, hundreds of feet below, except a wooden floor laid down, for all he knew, on flimsy canvas. The twang of the wing wires sounded like harp strings to George. Every muscle in his body was locked against the sudden impact he was sure was coming. He might have been more reassured if he could have seen the pilot, but, locked away down here in the aeroplane's belly, he could see nothing. The pilot could have parachuted out and he wouldn't have known it.

George hadn't been so frightened since France. There, at least, there had been mud to bury oneself in against the erupting shells. Here there was nothing. Nowhere to go but down. George decided this was worse than France. Solid earth was man's natural environment. Flying he would leave strictly to the birds!

When they finally put down in a dusty Texas field to refuel, George hadn't realized they had landed until the motor had cut. The sudden cessation of that thundering monster left him bewildered, his head thudding and bathed in cold sweat.

Jack Tobie helped his numbed legs drag him from the canvas shell. 'Don't you love it?' asked his tormentor, enthusiastically slapping him on the back.

'How much longer have we got to go?' asked George through anaesthetized lips.

'Two hours, maybe. See, I'm taking on extra gasoline. Your baggage is nothing and this baby is made to lift twelve hundred pounds of mail. We're making good time.'

'Faster than the train?' asked George.

'Trains!?' echoed Jack Tobie. 'Forget 'em! Flying is the thing these days!' Again George got slapped groggy on the shoulder. 'Don't you love it?' asked Jack Tobie.

George was too weak to argue. He let himself be led to the airfield's cantina where he forced himself to eat pork and beans. Still shaking he ate while watching Jack Tobie's sunburnt face with the two white circles where his goggles went. He wanted Jack Tobie's nerve to crack and admit they couldn't go on. George couldn't summon the will to say it himself. Nobody had charge of their own nightmares.

Jack Tobie didn't crack. He led George out to the aeroplane again. Every sense in George's body was telling him to run for it, but somehow he let himself be strapped in and that monstrous noise started up again.

George lost the pork and beans ten minutes into the resumed flight and then had to sit with its stench all the way to Chihuahua.

'Hotel lobbies are something of a speciality with us, aren't they?'

George looked up into Velma's smiling face. She leaned in and was kissing his cheek so she didn't see the flinch of surprise that George felt looking on her still badly scarred lips and cheeks.

'Been waiting long?' she asked as she slipped into the wicker chair next to his own.

George smiled and reached out a hand. 'You're looking great!' he lied.

Velma put a hand to her face. 'I know exactly how I look, George, you don't have to pretend. However, I'm here to tell you that I never *felt* better!' She leaned in on him. 'Aren't you the hero, though? I seem to recall you cautioning me about staying off those "damned dangerous machines".'

'Not that you took any notice.'

'Anyway, how was it? Change your mind?'

George shook his head. 'I'm just considering how long it would take me to *walk* back!' George looked around. 'Where's Manolo?' he asked.

'Out at the ranch. You should see it, George. I wish you had time to come out there. You'd love it, being a farm boy and all.'

'Sorry, I just can't make the time. I shouldn't have taken this much but . . .' he reached under his chair and lifted his briefcase into his lap. It had little in it except the contract and a pack of rubbers he'd intended using on Nadine. He sighed a passing regret at the night he had to spend alone in Chihuahua. Night was closing in and there was no chance of going anywhere until dawn. 'Dammit!' thought George. 'Dawn is when they shoot people.'

More immediately he flipped rapidly through the contract to the last page where Velma had to sign. 'Just there,' he told her, offering her a pen but holding on to the stiff legal paper.

Velma tugged the contract from him and watched him sweat a little before breaking into a smile. 'Don't fret, George. I'm not going to read it. It's none of my business any more.'

She took his pen and signed rapidly. 'There!' she said. 'Signing my life away blind!'

George took back the contract and put it away securely in his briefcase. Velma had made no attempt to peek at the colossal sum mentioned in the contract she'd signed. For that he felt immensely grateful and not a little guilty.

'You really figure you'll get away with it?'

Taking a deep breath George confessed he didn't know.

'That bimbo you're bringing in ... think she can handle it?'

George gestured again.

Velma sounded impatient. 'Well, you must have some idea! How did she react when you told her what you had in mind?'

'I haven't told her yet!'

Velma stared at him with exaggeratedly open eyes and mouth. 'You haven't told her yet! George, are you crazy? What you gonna do if she turns you down?'

'She won't!' said George as confidently as he could manage.

Velma still hadn't let go of her amazed look. 'You mean she's out on this cockermamy tour still thinking that's *all* she is going to have to do?'

George nodded.

'Jesus Christ, George. I thought you were a hero coming down here in an airplane, but *this* ... !'

They sat in silence for a moment, until Velma reminded him that Prohibition didn't extend to Mexico.

They remained silent until the waiter had brought their order.

'Here's luck,' said Velma raising her glass. 'I don't know anyone who's needing it more!'

'I can take care of myself,' said George.

Velma laughed. 'George! You are the one man in the world least able to take care of himself! I'm not complaining about what you did for me, understand, but the thought of you "taking care of yourself" ...'

Velma was silent for a moment. 'Is that girl Julia still with you?'

George nodded. He was remembering he still had the flight back to worry about.

Velma reached out and patted his hand. 'Then I'd say you were in with a chance. Why didn't you bring her down? She knows the whole story doesn't she?'

255

George explained that Julia was out on the tour with – he bit his tongue as he realized he'd just been about to say 'Ailleen'. The less anyone knew the better.

'You take my advice and marry that girl. She's got the shrewdest head on a girl I've ever seen.'

'Besides which,' said George, 'a wife can't testify against her husband!'

'A point worth bearing in mind!' agreed Velma laughing.

There was a bulky weight inside George's jacket pocket which was getting heavier the longer he and Velma sat there. In the envelope was five thousand dollars which he'd brought along as 'insurance' in case she had held him up for the signature. Now he didn't need to give it to her, but, bearing in mind the contract he had just negotiated, and which her signature ensured, he was beginning to feel a heel for the 'cheap' way he'd bought her out.

'How's things going?' he asked finally.

'Great. I told you. The ranch is dreamy. Little Pancho here . . .' again she patted her stomach . . . 'is just the icing on the cake.'

'No regrets then?'

'Are you kidding? You know something, George? Seen from down here my memories of Hollywood are a lot of strutting phonies each trying to impress the hell out of each other. I'm out of it – and glad I'm out of it. I got all I need right here. My Spanish is coming on too.'

'Glad to hear it,' said George. That envelope was kicking and struggling to get out into the daylight. 'How'd it work out financially?'

Velma shrugged. 'Things always cost more than you expected them to, but this is just the start – a fabulous start, thanks to you. We'll make it. Manolo is transformed. You should see him!' Velma broke off into a little laugh. 'Or maybe you shouldn't!'

'Why's that?'

'He's so jealous. The idea of me spending a night away from him was driving him nuts.'

'How far is this place of yours then?'

'Forty, fifty miles – they count different down here, I can't work these kilothings out. Doesn't sound far but there's no roads and I didn't want to bounce Junior, so I said I'd stay over, but you don't have to worry about it . . .'

'About what?'

'Me. I mean, if you want to go off round some of the places they got down here, that's fine by me.'

'What kind of places?'

'Bordellos. They got some of the greatest in the world.'

'Not for me. I exhausted all my nervous energy on the way down here.'

'Maybe you want to take in a show? They got some fantastic cabaret dancers.'

George shook his head. 'I just want to sleep.' In the silence he was struck by a thought. 'How do you know the bordellos are so great?'

Velma smiled wickedly. 'Where do you think I used to go with those fliers? The museums?'

George stared at her. 'Jesus! You were taking chances! You could have caught anything . . .'

Velma laughed. 'Don't be stupid! I didn't *do* anything – except with the fliers. I just used to watch. Don't tell me you've forgotten already?'

George hadn't forgotten. That night as he climbed exhausted into bed, he couldn't get the image of Ailleen, as he had first seen her, out of his mind.

Go to sleep, you crazy bastard! he told himself.

But sleep was elusive. He kept waking up in panic until he realized that the motor hadn't 'cut' and that he wasn't even in the damned flying machine.

257

7

George's charter plane got back to the Hollywood Aerodrome before four in the evening. George couldn't believe it. He was here, back in Hollywood, in one piece. That morning he'd woken in Chihuahua and, after a dawn take-off, two refuelling stops plus an unscheduled landing in a dusty field for a fuel blockage or leak or something, here he was back on the ground and resolved never again to leave it.

His nerves shattered, George hesitated about driving himself home – the office was out of the question – and considered taking a cab, but the complications of not having his car decided him against it.

Hollywood had never looked better to him! His admiration for people who did this kind of thing for a living was boundless. He didn't have to do it again, but they did it day after day. George couldn't figure out how or why, he only knew he was glad to get home and spring the lid on his secret table.

A soak in the tub and some pulls on his glass and he began to feel better. He was home safe. The contract was signed. One more problem met and surmounted. There were other problems but he decided to start worrying about them after a good night's sleep.

By the time he got into bed he was feeling light-headed. The booze or, maybe, the bath water had been too hot. He slept in fits and starts and counted it a triumph to wake at eight the following morning feeling refreshed and ready to start a new day.

It was an effort of will to remind himself that he'd been away only two days. That it seemed half a lifetime was less surprising when he reminded himself that in those two days he'd died a hundred deaths.

George drove to his office with a growing sense of unreality. There was something different about the town that he couldn't quite figure. The traffic seemed lighter for one thing.

Passing the Hollywood Hotel he was tempted to stop off again for breakfast, and smiled at the thought. *That* George had been in a totally different mood.

His feeling of unease grew when he noticed that the parking court at his new office building was very nearly deserted.

When the elevator delivered him to the fourth floor his sense of unease had grown into bewilderment. The office doors were locked. There was no sound of typewriters clicking. No telephones rang. Inside there were no people.

This place he knew so well was suddenly alien to him. Without his smiling 'harem' the place looked under-furnished.

Feeling like the sole survivor of some virulent plague George hurried through to his own office to find Sybil's home telephone number. She, if anyone, would know what had happened.

In the very act of asking Central for the number his eye fell on his diary. He'd left on Friday, stayed overnight, flown back Saturday. The explanation for George's isolation was there in his diary. Today was Sunday!

Hastily cancelling the call, George sat back in his swivel chair and settled under the weight of a profound depression. He had a whole day in which to do nothing. He could have stayed over in Mexico or, better, have taken a leisurely train journey back. Nobody had been expecting him today. Nobody, George felt, wanted him. During the week he felt significant. There was hustle and bustle and high pressure meetings. Problems to be solved. Crises to be overcome. Now all he had was this dramatic demonstration of just how isolated he really was. George began to fear the prospect of a day in which his problems would assert themselves when he had no possibility of being able to do anything about them.

Idly he went through Sybil's desk looking for his messages. There was little there either to reassure or distract him. Everybody wanted him to call them back. All the usual names figured. George threw them all down in disgust.

Going back to his own office he picked up the telephone and asked for Julia's hotel in New York. They told him the connection might take up to an hour.

George sat behind his desk impatiently waiting for the call to come through, feeling like an unharnessed steam engine. Frustrated by the inaction, George abandoned the call and left the office. Leaving his car in the court he started walking down Hollywood Boulevard towards Highland. He knew that he was vaguely headed towards the Hollywood Hotel but couldn't decide why. He told himself that he might feel better if he had breakfast but, as he studiously ignored the many breakfast spots that lay between him and Highland, he knew that wasn't strictly true. He wanted distraction.

The Hollywood Hotel wasn't what it had been when George had first known it. In those days they didn't even allow actors in. Later when they relaxed their policy it had become the favoured Sunday morning meeting place. Out here on the porch on a Sunday morning you might see almost the entire Hollywood hierarchy. Deals could be struck with Mayer, Fairbanks, Thalberg or Zanuck. These days they were more likely to be found downtown at the Alexandria or, even more likely, at home. The Hollywood was now the haunt of tourists, drifters and guys on the make.

Several of them greeted him as he settled down to watch the Big Red Cars go by. He suffered one man, who presumed not to introduce himself, overselling a fat, overly made-up little blonde. George smiled and nodded through the onslaught and wished the guy would go away. Had he ever looked or sounded like this when he'd been peddling Velma? George hoped not but suspected he probably had. Thankfully the man finally recognized defeat and went off with the brightly-smiling hopeful to buttonhole someone else.

He was through to his second cup of indifferent coffee when he saw Sybil coming towards him through the crowded tables.

'Mr Schapner!' she cried, wearing unfamiliar Sunday florals. 'You're back!'

George felt pleased to see her. 'What's been happening?' he asked.

Sybil switched back into her office manner with no apparent shift of gears. 'Several calls from New York. Julia seemed very anxious to talk to you. Mrs Battershaw. All the usuals including Von Muller and Mr Sterne. Mr Sterne seemed most annoyed you'd left town without telling him.'

George smiled and nodded. The world still turned on its axis. He became aware that Sybil was staring directly at him.

'I thought you were going away for a rest?' she finally asked in slightly pointed tones.

'I did!'

'You don't look as if you did. You look worse.'

George thanked her and Sybil went almost without pause into an excited run-down on what she evidently considered the most pressing of matters – Freddie Gross's progress on Marie Antoinette.

'Freddie's here with me. He just stopped off in the lobby to make a phone call, but I'm sure he won't mind me telling you that he's practically got a complete outline. I've read it and it's marvellous. When can he come in and see you with it?'

George shrugged. 'Listen, I meant what I said about you taking more responsibility. You work it into my schedule.' He waited while Sybil worked through her beaming approval of him before asking, 'Anything from New York? Have they made bookings to come back yet?'

'No. Julia indicated that there was going to be some kind

261

of delay but she would only speak to you about it. I think they intend to be back on Friday.'

'Friday? That means what? Leaving on Tuesday?' Sybil nodded as he paused. 'I'd better try and reach her.'

At that moment Freddie Gross came effusively to the table and treated George to a detailed run-down on what he considered the most significant events in the life and death of Marie Antoinette. George didn't absorb much of it, but noticed Freddie hadn't mentioned Marie's penchant for posing naked for painters. Knowing that Wilbur would be disappointed, George suggested he might include such a scene.

'Can we show a scene like that in a movie?' asked Freddie.

'I've seen the costumes for Salome,' George told him. 'If we can get away with those we can certainly show Marie Antoinette's bare back.'

Freddie reluctantly agreed that he would write such a sequence. George cautioned him not to get too involved with the politics of the situation and concentrate more on the splendour of the court and the mob scenes of the Revolution. Freddie seemed downcast by this but agreed he would 'get right on it' and, taking Sybil, went off down the boulevard.

'That was exciting!' thought George miserably. He considered asking at the desk for Nadine and was still struggling against the feeling of defeat this would induce when he suddenly saw her. She was stepping out of a limousine, incongruously wearing a fur wrap over a lamé evening dress. She waved happily to the driver and started up the steps to the hotel. George swung his eyes back to the driver who was temporarily held up in the drive by another car unloading baggage. As the driver turned his head to look back before pulling out George saw a famous face – John Gilbert! George felt an uncomfortable stab of anger at this. Nadine who, he fondly imagined, was his for the taking, had just returned from what was obviously an all-night affair with the famous star. George was aware that there was absolutely no reason for her not to have done, but nevertheless it moved his own opinion of himself down two or three pegs.

Marie Antoinette? Forget it!

Walking back towards his office to pick up his car, George again turned his mind to what he would do with this empty day. He considered something revolutionary, like going to a movie – but decided against it. He still had wobbly legs from yesterday's adventures.

Stopping off at a newsstand he picked up both the *Express* and the *Examiner* and just went home.

When he got there the phone was ringing. He snatched it up to hear a harassed operator telling him that she had a call from New York on the line. George held on hoping the mush would clear but it just got worse. He tried shouting: 'Julia?' down the line a couple of times, but that didn't work. Finally the defeated voice of the operator came on to tell him that they'd lost the connection and that she'd try and get it back.

George put down the phone and his sense of isolation closed in around him. He badly needed to know what was happening with Ronnie and Ailleen. Maybe his fraud was already front-page news! He scanned the pages of the papers he had brought home with him but they gave no sign. Could be that Ronnie had been run over by a bus on Fifth Avenue. He decided to hold on to that hope until he heard different!

He got himself a drink and settled down with the papers, but within minutes the past two days caught up with him and he slipped off into a doze.

An urgent rapping on his front door brought him to startled wakefulness. The newspapers had slipped from his lap and clung to his legs as he brushed through them to answer the knocking.

He opened the door to find the tear-filled eyes of Mrs Davenport's wayward daughter staring up at him. 'Is my mama here?' she demanded.

'Is *who* here?'

'My mama. She didn't come home all last night and I can't find her anywhere!'

'Why in hell should she come here? I haven't seen your mother and I wouldn't want to.'

The girl turned away in confused distress before turning back to ask, 'Can I use your bathroom?'

George started showing her the way to the facilities until she tartly reminded him that she already knew where they were.

By what stretch of the imagination Mrs Davenport's little girl could have concluded that her mother might be with him he couldn't imagine. His other confusion arose from the different picture this tearful kid presented to the composed young whore who had gone, so cynically, to bed with Wilbur Sterne! He was still reconciling these differences when there came another urgent knocking on his door. Going to answer it he found himself wondering if Nadine Bourdon had, by chance, any relatives in town! No. It was the same family.

'Is my Mary here?' demanded Mrs Davenport angrily.

George saw that a burly man was accompanying her. It was he who pushed past Mrs Davenport and into the house.

'What the hell's going on here?' he demanded. 'Look, all I know is ...' His explanation was interrupted when the bathroom door flew open and a half-undressed Mary rushed out and threw herself into George's startled arms. Immediately the burly man produced a press camera from behind his back and blinded George with an exploding flash-bulb.

Little Mary, her mission accomplished, separated herself from George and ran back to the bathroom and slammed the door. George stood blinking in the little black circles that danced before his eyes, but finally got them clear enough to see Mrs Davenport's triumphant smile.

George sank into an armchair to contemplate both the set-up and the carpet. He felt strangely detached as he heard Mrs Davenport drawing the photographer's attention to his unmade bed and asking him to get a shot of it.

Mrs Davenport and the photographer came out of the bedroom and stood staring at him. George felt called upon to say something. 'All finished?' he asked amiably.

Mrs Davenport pursed her lips but didn't deign to reply. The silence was broken when the refreshed Mary emerged from the bathroom.

'Take Mary back to the car would you, Bertie?' she asked the burly photographer.

'Bertie', who had stayed silent throughout the entire four-minute episode, took little Mary under his wing and steered her out. It crossed George's mind that he ought to do something dramatic like going after Bertie and wrestling the photographic plate from him, but he couldn't face the prospect of having to go through it all again at some future date.

He looked instead to Mrs Davenport. 'Shake down?' he asked her.

'Not exactly, Mr Schapner.'

'Paternity suit? Little Mary pregnant?'

Again Mrs Davenport shook her head. 'What it comes down to, Mr Schapner, is that you don't answer your calls.'

'I *what?*' asked George.

Patiently Mrs Davenport sighed. 'I have tried, many times, to telephone you. Mr Pycroft has assured me that he has authorized you to offer my Mary a contract. You, apparently, have been unwilling to do so. I've come to jog your memory!'

George was almost tempted to laugh. 'You think that little stunt is going to endear you to me?'

'Well, that's hardly the question any more, is it? Mary's under age. That would make it statutory rape.'

George was finally on his feet and angry. 'Listen, lady, the only person got raped round here today was *me*!'

Mrs Davenport didn't flinch. This might have been because she didn't know how close George was to hitting her.

'You,' she said evenly and unruffled, 'are the only one of

the four of us that knows that. The police might draw a different conclusion.'

Sudden awareness of just how ludicrous the situation was punctured George's anger. It had all been developed with such speedy efficiency that it was hard to believe it had happened. 'Are you telling me that you went through all this for some cheap fifty-buck-a-week contract?'

'Fifty dollars a week is a lot of money to some people,' she reminded him and then broke her first smile. 'Besides, be fair, it didn't take much. By the way,' she added, 'I think we would prefer it to be seventy-five dollars a week.'

'Why not?' asked George. 'It isn't my money! Why not make it a round hundred?'

Mrs Davenport smiled again with approving pleasure. 'I leave such matters to you, Mr Schapner. You are, after all, Mary's agent.'

George watched her, speechless, as she moved calmly to the front door. There she turned. 'Shall we say tomorrow morning at ten in your office to sign the contracts?'

'Fuck you!' yelled George wittily.

Mrs Davenport finally did flinch, but soon recovered. 'That's confirmed then. Good afternoon, Mr Schapner.'

George stood dead centre of the room and let out an anguished howl at the ceiling. Tiring of this he kicked shit out of the strewn newspapers for some minutes before sitting in his armchair and starting to laugh.

Even he, in his most desperate days, would never have thought of pulling a stunt like that! He tried to imagine who he could have set Velma up with but couldn't think of anyone. With his luck the photograph wouldn't have come out anyway! He spent some moments wondering about the kind of people that were coming to Hollywood these days. They were worse than him. It was entirely possible that if ever George's fraudulent conversion of Ailleen into Velma were found out they'd most likely elect him president of the Chamber of Commerce!

The telephone let out its shrill sound. Hoping it might be his interrupted call from Julia he snatched at it.

'Am I interrupting something?' asked Madame G.

'No. Just a regular Sunday. I got rolled and set-up for blackmail. What's new with you?'

'We got real trouble, George. I mean it. It's serious! You have to come up here.'

'Right now?'

'As of an hour ago!'

'You want to give me a hint as to what this is about?'

'Just get up here!' and she hung up on him.

George found his shoes under the pile of destroyed newspapers and fumbled his way into them as he tried to imagine what could have gone wrong this time. He was almost convinced it had to do with the 'hit' on the ambulance driver kid, but if that was it, why would Madame G. want to meet? The intelligent thing to do would have been to stay away from each other.

As George ran for his car he just hoped she hadn't killed anyone else!

Madame G.'s door was opened by the same black maid that had saved him having his head broken the first time he'd come up here. She was very good at opening doors!

He followed her through to Madame G.'s private rooms and the moment they were alone asked, 'What's this all about?'

Madame G. handed him a brim-full glass and had him sit down. 'You're going to need that,' she told him portentously.

George held on with nerveless fingers as she paced back across the room. 'What?' he asked.

Madame turned to him and spoke on the rush of a full breath: 'Velma Torraine just remarried Ronnie Stillman!' she said.

George had a flash of a happily pregnant Velma sitting in the lobby of the Hotel Republica in Chihuahua. 'You're crazy!' he told her.

Madame G. was shaking her head. 'That conniving bitch Ailleen,' she was saying. 'The moment you took her out of here in her "face" I knew there was going to be trouble.'

George just couldn't absorb it. 'You're telling me that *Ailleen* has married Ronnie Stillman?'

Madame G. still looked worried. 'If that was all, I'd say we didn't have a whole lot to worry about. What I'm saying is that Ronnie Stillman has married Ailleen *thinking* he's remarried *Velma Torraine*!'

'You're crazy!' said George.

'I got it from a newsman in New York less than an hour ago. It'll be on the wires any minute now. You can believe it, George!'

George couldn't, struggle as he might. 'How could a thing like that happen?' he asked, half of himself.

'It's the living truth,' said Madame G. with confident finality. 'What worries me is what's going to happen when the real Velma finds out what that silly bitch has done in her name! It could blow the whole deal right up in our faces!'

George, looking at Madame G., was startled to realize that she had, as yet, not the slightest notion of the breadth and scope of his plans for Ailleen. Her information, usually from impeccable sources, hadn't yielded the entire truth. It was comforting to know that he alone knew that the real Velma would, on hearing the news, laugh like a drain and count herself well out of it.

'What are we going to do about it?' asked Madame G. as George had remained silent.

George got to his feet. 'I can handle it,' he said with more confidence than he felt.

'Are you sure?' asked Madame G.

George, looking into her concerned eyes, remembered that Madame G. had a way with problems that wasn't to his liking. It might come to that, but he wanted to put off the day as long as possible.

'It's OK,' he assured her. 'Let me handle Velma. Just

remember that we're partners and do nothing that I don't know about first.'

Madame G. nodded. It was strangely comforting to George to get her acquiescence. For too long now he'd been running fast just to stay in second place on almost everything that had happened. For once he felt out in front.

George turned out of the door.

'Stay in touch!' she yelled after him.

8

George drove back towards his office knowing that he must speak with Julia.

That Ailleen had succeeded in marrying Ronnie Stillman was of less interest than *why*. There was always a justice of the peace who wouldn't bother too much with documentation, especially when the bride was, apparently, so well known! Ailleen's motive in exposing them all to such danger was something else. Julia had said that she was crazy about him, but that wasn't enough. Ailleen was no sentimental novitiate head over heels. His impression was that Ailleen was a cool, calculating lady. She'd proved that over and over again. So what was the angle? George was certain there was one. Less sure that he'd ever find it until, as things tended to do these days, it crept up and socked him one.

George jumped lights and broke the speed regulations getting back to his office. When he got there he wished he hadn't bothered.

Every connected line in the entire place was ringing! It didn't take much imagination to guess it was the press hot on his heels. He wouldn't have wanted to speak to them anyway, but, knowing nothing, he had even less reason. He fought his way through the cacophony to his private office where, thankfully, his private lines were not ringing. The press hadn't bribed the right operator, yet!

He got behind his desk and called Sybil, told her something of what was happening and begged her to come in to the office. Sybil, loyal as ever, promised to be there in ten minutes.

His next action was to go round the office and lift each of the phones in turn and then hang them up just long enough to break the connection and then leave them off the hook. The operator's desperate cries down the open lines were a lot less distracting than the shrill of the bells.

Without much hope of a connection George placed a call to Julia's hotel in New York. He remembered, bitterly, his own impatience earlier in the day when he'd abandoned just such a call.

All he could do after that was sit and wait.

Sybil turned up with Freddie Gross in tow. Freddie volunteered to man the phones in the outer office. George cautioned him to say nothing. 'I don't know anything!' protested Freddie and happily went off to relieve some of the pressure on the phone lines.

George asked Sybil to call the railroad company and find out if and when any reservations had been made by Julia on the Chief. Sybil went off to find a free phone.

George's New York call came through in what seemed like record time. Asking for Julia he heard that she, and Mr and *Mrs* Stillman had checked out to an unknown destination.

'That wouldn't be Los Angeles, would it?' he asked hopefully.

They repeated that they didn't know and further confirmed that they had made no train reservations for them.

George hung up just as Sybil came into the office.

'The Southern Pacific have two reserved parlours on the Wednesday night Chief out of Chicago in the name of Torraine.'

'That means they intend staying in New York until Tuesday night . . .'

'*If* they're still in New York,' Sybil reminded him.

'Whatever way, the press are going to get them in Chicago. They got a five-hour stop-over between trains, right?'

Sybil nodded agreement but seemed puzzled by George's problem.

'We've got to figure some way to protect them from the papers during their stop-over. Trouble is, knowing what.'

Sybil seemed to be struggling with her restless puzzlement. 'Why would you want to protect them, Mr Schapner?'

George looked up at her ready to explode at her for being so obtuse when the expression on her face stopped him cold.

'I think this is the most beautiful thing that could possibly have happened. I think that two people getting back together again is a wonderful story!'

In Sybil's shining, smiling face George saw revealed a whole different facet to this problem from the one he was concerned with. His trouble was he was caught up in his own lies. The fact that one more gigantic fraud had been added to his own was something the rest of America didn't know! They would see it simply as the repledging of marriage vows. The women of America would love it. He also saw that in marrying Ailleen Ronnie had put the final validating seal on her new identity. Pushing aside the question of how, or if, Ailleen could possibly sustain the deception, he found himself able to return Sybil's smile. 'You're right!' he told her. 'God knows they've had enough practice in handling the press these past few weeks!'

'So is it all right to give out the information about Chicago?'

'Let them have it,' said George. 'Why not? They're going to find out anyway!'

Sybil turned happily for the door.

'Also,' George called after her, 'it just might get some of them off our backs so that Julia can get through!'

'If you don't mind me making a suggestion,' said Sybil

looking at her pendant watch. 'Julia would most likely be trying to reach you at home at this hour on a Sunday.'

He knew she was right but found himself reluctant to leave the office. 'Can you stay on here?' he asked her.

'No problem.'

George started moving out. 'Look, if by chance Julia does call here tell her I'm home and I'm not moving until I get to speak to her. As double insurance, if she rings here get her number and tell her to stay put until I can get back to her. OK?'

Sybil nodded. 'You want me to ask her what happened?'

'The rate we're going we'll read it in the papers the same as everyone else.'

After stopping off in the outer office to thank Freddie for his help, George went home.

The phone there was quiet. All the way home he'd been revelling in the possibilities of this new situation. If the rest of America's women reacted the way Sybil had, it could be the best thing that ever happened for them. His big worry remained Ailleen. Could she keep up this most intimate of deceptions? The whole thing was either a tribute to the skill and duplicity of women or the monumental stupidity of men. George couldn't make up his mind between the two.

The phone did ring but it was Madame Gregory anxious to know how 'things' were going. George reassured her that he thought he had every angle covered and that they were going to keep the lid on the pot.

Madame G. was silent for some time after hearing George's reassurances. 'I got to admire you, George,' she said finally. 'You get away with more than anyone I know. I figure if you'd been on the *Titanic* you'd have *walked* home!'

Towards evening George started to feel hungry but, true to his promise to Sybil, didn't feel able to go out to eat. After a search of his meagre food supplies he came up with a tin of beans and had just cut his finger opening it when the phone rang. Hastily wrapping his cut hand in a towel he raced through, sure it would be Julia.

It wasn't.

'What the fuck are you playing at?' asked Wilbur Sterne.

George didn't want Wilbur at that moment. His finger was starting to throb and the only person he wanted to talk to was Julia. 'What is it, Wilbur?' he asked.

'You know where I am, schmuck?'

'Wilbur, I'm in no mood for guessing games!'

'You, you bastard, *you* get to be home Sundays. Me, the head of a studio, I'm in my office. Why didn't you tell me about Velma and Ronnie Stillman?'

'Simple. I didn't know. They're in New York and I'm stuck here with you.'

'Well, you want to know what I think?'

'You're going to tell me anyway . . .'

'I think your piece of quiff is a genius, OK?'

'That's perfectly fine with me, Wilbur.'

'You want to know why?'

'You're going to tell me anyway . . .'

'The reason I'm in the studio is because every goddamned theatre owner and *all* the exchanges are screaming down the phone to know when they're going to get their hands on a Velma Torraine picture. You any idea what we'd be grossing if we had something to toss them right now?'

'Ten million. Von Muller told me.'

'Damn right! Now you get that Velma back and let's get to work. I want that picture the worst way, George, and, by the way, I love you!'

'I love you too, Wilbur,' grinned George.

He hung up the phone and looked down at his towelled hand. Unpeeling it he saw that the blood was still pushing its way out of his skin. Suddenly he didn't care. Laughing, he went back to the kitchen and tipped the beans into the garbage can, and poured a celebratory drink instead.

The next time the phone rang it *was* Julia!

'Now before you start yelling at me,' she began, 'it all happened so fast I didn't have a chance to get through to you.'

'OK, but how the hell are we going to handle this thing?'

'It's "handled". Don't worry about a thing. It's going to work out. I can't go into details on the phone. Enough to tell you that the press are round her like puppies at the teat. She's a miracle, George.'

'What about him?'

'The least of your worries. Never saw a happier man in my entire life.'

'Where are you?'

'We're at this lake resort in Illinois, about a couple of hours from Chicago.'

'What are you doing there? I hear you got reservations for Wednesday. Can't you take the train tonight?'

Julia chuckled. 'You ever heard of a honeymoon? Listen, if I put them on the train in their present mood we'd probably be asked to leave. Up here we got coyotes coming down out of the hills to complain about the noise!'

'They have coyotes in Illinois?'

'They do now!'

'So everything is OK?'

'Couldn't be better. Honestly, you wouldn't believe it!'

'I do believe it. I do *believe*!' George counted on his fingers. 'So you'll be in Pasadena Friday?'

'Right! You going to be there?'

'Me and the entire Hollywood press corps!'

Julia was silent a moment. 'There's only one thing,' she started ominously.

'What's that?'

'You got big trouble.'

'Why's that?'

'Because when I get back there I'm going to marry you!'

'Hey, wait a minute . . . ' George started to protest along with his laugh, but Julia had hung up on him.

9

Pasadena, noon, Friday, was a riot.

Those colonnaded Spanish walls had seen some stage-managed, publicity-boosting homecomings in their time, but nothing like this!

In the two and a half days since the first news stories filed from Chicago, the story of the reunion of Velma Torraine and Ronnie Stillman had become a monster.

Galaxy's publicity department was there to a man, but the story had a life of its own, it didn't need stage-managing. America couldn't get enough of this story of repledged love! George, for his part, couldn't get anywhere near the Chief as it hauled to a stop.

Newsmen rushed forward to jostle for an advantageous spot near where they'd been briefed the car would stop. George, craning over the crowds, caught a glimpse of Julia standing on the top of the steps, and then judged that Velma and Ronnie must be there from the splendorous explosion of massed flash-bulbs being centred on one area.

Voices were shouting hysterically for a word from the couple, but George still hadn't seen them when the tight knot of jostling humanity started moving towards the head of the platform. Julia he saw step down and get cut off from the main progress, but it didn't matter. Velma Torraine and Ronnie Stillman were invulnerable now!

The heaving mass was still as dense when they approached George. He'd found a baggage car to stand on, but still could see little other than the feathered top of Ailleen's hat, and the top of Ronnie's fedora. He stood on tiptoe but nothing helped. It was obvious that he was never going to get near them.

'What are you? A parrot?'

George looked down and saw Julia grinning up at him.

George, stepping down, caught the heel of his shoe in the edge of the baggage car and nearly toppled on top of her. Julia laughed and put her arms around him, and they kissed long and hard.

George and she looked into each other's shining eyes.

'We did it, George!' she said happily.

'Let's get the hell somewhere where you can tell me *how*!'

Julia nodded and, cosily locking her arm into his, they started towards the screaming, hysterical bunch round the couple.

'You didn't forget to get a limousine for them, did you?'

George laughed at her. 'Damnation, I knew there was *something*! What the hell? Let them get the bus like regular folks!'

Julia leaned in on him as they fought their way forward to the sun-blinding exterior.

'Where are you having them taken?' asked Julia.

'Their house,' said George. 'Where else?'

They still hadn't been able to say as much as 'Hello' to the happy couple, and didn't look likely to, so George steered Julia to where his own limousine waited with uniformed chauffeur standing cap in hand.

Julia pulled a face at him as she realized this was for them. 'Fancy!' she said.

'Where's your baggage?' he asked her.

'It's all labelled. Let Galaxy handle it. Come on, let's go home . . .' She dived into the back of the cushioned limousine, and turned, bouncing happily, waiting to pull George to her.

'God! How I've missed you!'

'Missed you too!' he told her.

'I'll just bet!' she told him but cuddled up close as the driver took his solemn place up front.

'As planned, Mr Schapner?' the driver asked.

'Right!' said George.

'What's planned?' asked Julia.

'I thought we'd go up to the house and welcome them home.'

Julia went still. 'Why not leave that till later? It's been a long time.' George reassured her with a kiss. 'Restrain yourself.' He indicated the rigidly-turned head of the driver. 'We are not alone!' Julia lay against him, holding so tight to his arm he thought he'd lose the circulation, until she nudged him and indicated that she wanted his ear.

George leaned down.

'You know what?' she whispered.

George shook his head.

'I'm hotter than a two-dollar pistol.'

'So what else is new?'

'You wanna know why?'

'Tell me.'

'Travelling three nights listening to what those two have been doing. God, George, if I don't get laid soon I'm going to burst!'

'You mean they really are a "couple"?'

'No way! What they are is two sides of one thing. George, they've not stopped from Chicago to here!'

'I'm still trying to figure it out.' He glanced towards the stiff neck of the driver. Despite the glass partition, which was now solidly closed, he still felt the need for caution. 'Ronnie doesn't suspect a thing?'

Julia sighed heavily. 'Ronnie wouldn't care if she turned out to be a shaved orang-utan. The guy's besotted. He only sees what he wants to see. Wait till I tell you how this all got started!'

George laid a cautioning hand on her. 'Not now. Later!'

George had expected, or at least hoped, that the press would have had their fill at the depot, but no such fortune. Velma's house was besieged.

They had newsreel cars double-parked along the narrow

road, and reporters and photographers were trying to climb in the windows and overspilling into the neighbours' gardens.

The neighbours were reacting in different ways. Some were just standing there grinning, others were at their doors shouting at the newsmen to 'get the hell' off their lawns. Getting grass to grow in California was a painstaking, expensive business – these people weren't about to see their investment trampled underfoot no matter what.

George looked out at the mess and shook his head. 'I never dreamed it could get this big,' he said.

'You should have seen them in Chicago!'

George saw a woman chasing a reporter with a broom. 'We're going to have to call the cops to cool this thing down.'

'In Chicago it would have taken Al Capone,' smiled Julia, holding tightly on to his arm.

George pulled her to him and smiled down at her. 'You really are pleased with yourself, aren't you?'

Julia leaned in and kissed him. 'Why don't we give up and go to your place?'

George hesitated. He couldn't believe it was safe to leave 'Velma' alone with Ronnie, on the other hand he couldn't see how they were ever going to get into Velma's house in one piece.

'OK,' he told her. 'You win.'

He gave the driver the new directions and sat back to a congratulatory hug from Julia.

'Scrumptious!' she told him snuggling close.

Arriving back at George's house they went straight to bed and mutually out of their minds in an orgiastic reunion.

Several hours later, out of a stunned, exhausted silence, George murmured: 'Now I know how Ronnie must be feeling!'

'Quitter!' Julia chuckled back. 'It's going to take a week before I know how *Ailleen* feels.'

'Hold on, you don't imagine I can keep this up for a week, do you?'

Julia chuckled meaningfully and slid down the bed. 'You don't have to! Keeping it up is my job, all you got to do is use it. The only thing is,' she added, 'it's going to cost you.'

'Five dollars a throw?' he asked.

Julia looked up at him from a most delicious angle. 'More than that!'

'How much more?'

Julia suddenly grabbed him in an extremely painful manner. George shot up in surprise. Julia, grinning, released the more painful grip but kept her hand moving deliciously over the more interesting part. 'You're going to marry me, you bastard,' she told him. 'You're going to marry me and fuck me full of babies!'

'I couldn't have put it more romantically myself!' said George.

10

'Woof!' whined Ronnie Stillman.

'Woof! Woof! Woof!' Ailleen barked back.

George stayed silently amazed.

They were seated by Velma's pool. George had come for his first face-to-face with Ailleen since her return to Hollywood as Mrs Ronnie Stillman.

Julia had prepared him for some part of the bizarre relationship which existed between the two, but being a witness to it was, to say the least, embarrassing. Ronnie, having apparently received instructions, trotted off into the house leaving them, finally, alone.

'Why did you do it?' George asked her.

Ailleen stretched her naked body in the sunshine and smiled. 'We're having one of our dog and bitch days. We only talk "doggie".' Ailleen chuckled. 'Guess which one is the bitch! Does it bother you?' she asked.

'Listen, it's your relationship. You play it any way you want so long as it works.'

'It works,' sighed Ailleen. 'I have to say that he is probably one of the most disgusting men I've ever known, but he has his points.'

'Which brings me back to my original question: Why did you do it?'

Ailleen turned her eyes towards George. 'Oh! You mean marry him?'

George nodded.

Ailleen turned her head back into the sun. 'Simple, George. You've probably forgotten, or never given it a thought, but until my marriage I was an alien. British. You get it?'

George cursed himself. He'd never thought of that. If he'd sent Ailleen into Canada he could have been in real trouble. He sat back in his lounger and silently whistled out his relief. He sat back up again as he remembered something. 'But Ronnie's British, too, isn't he?'

Ailleen was shaking her head. 'Took out citizenship when he came over here.' She turned towards him again. 'Don't worry, George, what you don't think of, *I'll* remember.'

Once more George reminded himself that he was dealing with a very sharp mind. He started to feel insecure about his main reason for coming here to Ailleen, who was under personal contract to himself as Mrs Ronnie Stillman – a name she could now use legitimately.

'You figure you can keep this up? He doesn't suspect a thing?'

Ailleen was lazily shaking her head. 'During the entire time of their marriage Ronnie was in an alcoholic stupor. Not any more. Any differences he notices he'll put down to being sober.'

'Is that wise? I mean, wouldn't some boozy confusion work for us?'

'The booze was killing him. Did you know that? I may be

using the guy, George, but with that, I figure, come obligations. I've got him straightened out. He gets his fantasies. The guy's obsessed. While I keep him that way, I keep control. *Total* control!'

'Whatever you're doing, it's working. The last time I saw Ronnie he was a tub of lard. You've got him back in great condition.'

'Good diet, regular exercise and keeping his nose cool.'

'I just hope he stays cool – all over. That guy's got a pretty terrible temper as I know to my cost. You'd better bear it in mind and not provoke him too much.'

Ailleen smiled and waved a dismissive hand.

'Speaking of provocation,' said George, 'you wouldn't consider putting some clothes on would you?'

Ailleen turned her head to look wide-eyed at him. 'Don't tell me I'm starting to interest you, George? You a newly married man and all?'

'Newly married men are the most susceptible, or hadn't you heard?'

Ailleen cast a hand down her body. 'I'm doing this for the picture. Salome must have been dark-skinned and from what I see of the costumes I'm supposed to be wearing I'll be exposing ninety-eight per cent of it!'

'OK. Just remember that the sun ages the skin.'

Ailleen sighed. 'You came up here to talk about my body?' she asked.

'Nope.' George reached into his briefcase. 'I've had the contracts drawn up. The top sheet is a summary of all the rest.'

Ailleen, suddenly interested, swung her legs down between the recliners on which they were sitting. 'About time!' she murmured as she eagerly scanned the top sheet. 'I'll be under personal contract to you?' she asked.

George nodded.

'In the name of Mrs Ronnie Stillman!'

'Clever bastard,' she murmured, reading on. She found

the numbers section and George held his breath as she read through them. Ailleen looked up at him. 'Five hundred a week?' she asked.

'Plus I pick up your house expenses and pay your taxes.'

Ailleen looked down at the contract again and seemed to be studying it closely. 'I hear some different figures being spoken about Velma Torraine's contract.'

'Maybe you have, and maybe they're exaggerated and maybe you should bear it in mind that it *is* Velma Torraine we're talking about, not Ailleen Porter!'

Ailleen looked up at him. 'I could blow you out of the water, George!'

'Sure you could, but why would you want to commit suicide?'

'Madame G. have anything to do with this?' she asked.

George, reluctantly, nodded.

Ailleen's tone softened. 'Well,' she started. 'I guess it isn't so bad.' She pursed her lips as she rescanned it. 'What about the cars? You going to pay for them?'

George shrugged and nodded.

'Just how much are you making on this deal, George?' she asked him.

'About half enough to compensate me for the trouble I've gone through to get you this far!'

Ailleen smiled. 'You got a pen?'

George handed over his Parker and watched, relieved, as Ailleen scribbled down her new married name.

Handing it back to him she asked him never again to use the name Ailleen Porter. 'I'm Velma Torraine from now on!' she said, laying herself back down in the sun and closing her eyes.

George, rising to leave, leaned over and planted a chaste kiss on her forehead. 'You never looked lovelier, Velma.'

The new Mrs Ronnie Stillman smiled her thanks with closed eyes. 'When's the baby due?' she asked him.

'Early November.'

Ailleen laughed and started counting on her fingers.

'Don't bother,' George told her. 'We're going to say it was premature!'

'Give her my love!' she called to him as he walked away round the house.

George waved back and went to his car. He took a moment, before starting up, to exult. This was the third in a series of vital contracts he'd got signed. Velma, Nadine Bourdon and now Mrs Ronnie Stillman. What with Von Muller's contract bagged he could start to feel that he had some legal bricks around his straw house. Even if they did run him out of town he wouldn't run poor!

He drove the few hundred yards uphill to his own home. The new house was keeping Julia pretty busy these days and left her little time to come to the office. Today she'd made a point of staying home with fingers crossed that all went well with Ailleen.

She ran out of the house as he was parking the car.

'Did she sign?' she called excitedly.

'Like an angel!'

'See!' Julia crowed. 'And you wanted to pay her seven hundred and fifty dollars a week!' Julia pulled him into a hug and kissed him. 'So it's all over then?'

George nodded. 'Except for one detail.'

'What's that?'

'We have to shoot the picture!'

11

Salome started shooting 16 March 1929.

By June the assembled footage was starting to look like the smash hit everybody had been predicting. The 'new' Velma was delivering a performance to scorch the screen.

Von Muller strode around the studio like a proud parent

and astounded Hollywood. He had the reputation of being a foul-tempered martinet but, with the new freedom which George had negotiated for him and Wilbur pouring everything he owned or could borrow into the picture, Von Muller had come home. His stature around Galaxy was god-like. Even Wilbur was prepared to admit that 'the guy had something'.

Everyone, although agreed about Von Muller, was split into two camps over the relative merits of Velma Torraine and Nadine Bourdon. There were those that would kill to maintain their belief that Nadine was the most beautiful creature on God's earth and those that argued that Velma Torraine remained the undisputed queen.

George was able to remain aloof from these fiercely fought arguments. Not only both ladies but also Von Muller were under personal contract to himself.

It had been George's idea to gouge the anxious exhibitors for cash advances against first-place bookings on the picture. This had placed the movie into something approaching profit before they turned the first camera and accounted for Wilbur's quiet contemplation of the mounting production costs. Wilbur's enthusiasm had carried him along to the point of putting *Marie Antoinette* into pre-production to provide Nadine with her first starring vehicle. Unfortunately, Von Muller had refused even to read the script. Apparently it wasn't in his Life Plan.

George, with his stock around Hollywood soaring, had had little trouble in snaring Soloman Rice to direct. Rice loved the project and, rumour had it, was crazy in love with Nadine. Not that anybody blamed him.

On George's personal horizon there remained but two small clouds: Madame Gregory and Ronnie Stillman.

Madame Gregory, on realizing the true extent of his plans for Ailleen, had upped her price for silence to a full ten per cent of Velma's Galaxy contract – *and* she meant the real Velma Torraine contract – of which, with her awkward walking ticker-tape, she had obtained details down to the fine print. George had been able to afford it but it still rankled.

Ronnie Stillman was something else. George found his obsessive slumber akin to a snow-capped volcano. It looked quiet enough from a distance but George felt it could blow its top at any moment without warning. Time and again Julia had assured him that Ailleen's non-stop psychodramas were enough to keep him quiescent but George couldn't understand it.

He felt better when Madame Gregory, a lady who knew what she was talking about in such matters, accepted that it was as well to leave things as they were. Madame G. had initially been all for taking Ronnie off the board altogether. When George had hastily repeated what he'd been told about the way things stood, Madame G., to George's relief, had accepted it. If Madame G. was happy then why not George? The doubts still lurked somewhere in the back of George's mind, though.

An army of post-production technicians got the picture ready for its premiere by Labor Day.

Nobody had much doubt. The sneak previews had returned cards showing the audiences were stunned with delight. The only changes made were suggested by Von Muller himself. They took out some draggy footage from reel four but, other than that, the one that went to Grauman's Chinese was pretty much the one seen at the 'sneaks'.

It was a night (rumoured to have cost Wilbur 35,000 dollars) that the industry was never to forget. Police estimates put the early crowds at 120,000 – bigger, even, than for the *King of Kings* which had marked the opening of the theatre itself.

The boulevard was filled by sweeping parades of bands and a hundred girls in oriental costumes. Between them they kept the roads open for the limousines to start rolling up.

Searchlights fingered into the sky, and radio interviewers broadcasting coast-to-coast had whipped the atmosphere into frenzy by the time George got there with Julia. George eyed the narrow red-carpeted track, bordered by screaming fans, and feared for Julia's safety. It looked more like a punishing gauntlet run than a reception ramp.

'You going to be all right?' he shouted above the noise.

Julia, bearing her pregnancy like a badge of honour, nodded excitedly. Holding tight to each other they ducked and ran into the theatre. Few of the people that reached out to touch them knew who they were. The fact that they had tickets was enough to make them important.

The crowds broke the police lines when Velma arrived with Ronnie Stillman. Velma got caught and it was only by a supreme effort from a wildly lashing Ronnie that she was wrenched free and dragged into the more protected area of the lobby. There they found that her gown had been ripped and was a rag round her waist. Ronnie had whipped his cloak over her, but not before some press photographers got pictures. The pictures couldn't be printed in the papers but, later, there were reports of them being sold round the country at two bucks apiece!

George, already seated, got the story from an excited Wilbur.

'Jesus, if they could have held her for five more minutes they would have raped her! George, I swear to God that this picture is going to be so big you won't believe it!'

Before George could respond to his boundless excitement Wilbur got swept away in a flurry of well-wishers and four-flushers.

George was happy to sit out the delayed start of the picture holding hands with Julia. Von Muller finally got up on stage to make an opening announcement before the lights went down. 'Ladies and gentlemen. I welcome you to the first showing of *Salome*. All I ask is a little kindness . . .'

He went off to rapturous applause, the lights dimmed and the reels started to unspool.

There was absolutely nothing to worry about.

When the audience got their first look at Salome there was a suppressed gasp, followed by a quick intake of breath which everyone seemed to hold in for the next twenty minutes.

Nadine caused as big a sensation – especially in the orgy scene which she dominated.

'Is this legal?' asked Julia at one point.

'I don't know,' George whispered back, 'but I would bet half the men in the audience would be embarrassed to have to stand up right now!'

It was then that the usher's hand fell on George's shoulder. George looked up to see an anxious face peering down at him. 'Urgent telephone call, Mr Schapner.'

'Now?' asked George.

The white gloves fluttered in the half light and George realized he was going to cause more of a disturbance by staying than by going. He excused himself to Julia and, bending low, ducked as fast as he could to the back of the auditorium.

Julia started getting restless when she realized that George had been gone more than twenty minutes. Carefully she levered herself out of her seat and went to look for him.

She found him in the manager's office, slumped forward in a chair, a glass of Scotch held, with both hands, between his knees.

The manager's stricken face told her that something was very seriously wrong.

Julia called out to him softly, almost fearfully. When George lifted his head to look at her she was shocked to see tears in his eyes.

She flew to him.

'What is it, George? Tell me!'

George took her hand and silently held it against his forehead.

The manager mumbled something apologetic and withdrew, leaving them, finally, alone.

'For Christ's sake, George! *Tell* me!'

George was shaking his head in a tired, unfocused way. 'She was just a kid,' he said. 'Just a kid I met in a hotel lobby.'

Julia was stricken. 'Velma?'

George nodded. 'She died yesterday. They couldn't even save the baby!'

Julia pulled his sobbing head against the bulge of their own unborn child and held on very tight.

George didn't say any more until they were in the limousine headed home. He turned from looking out at the strings of lights lacing across the Basin.

'You know what life needs?' he asked her.

Julia shook her head.

'What life needs is a damn good rewrite!'

12

George came awake to find Julia shaking him.

'George! Wake up. It's started!'

'What has?' asked George.

Julia patted her swollen stomach. 'Junior!'

Instantly awake, George rushed towards the telephone. 'Where are you going?' she called after him.

'An ambulance. We got to get you to the hospital!'

Julia followed him out of the bedroom laughing. 'Put the phone down, you idiot. I said it's started, not coming.'

George hung up the phone and stared at her. 'There's a difference?'

Julia sighed. 'The difference is that we have plenty of time for you to drive me down there.'

George came back towards her unconvinced. 'You're sure?'

'Positive. Now do something sensible like make yourself a cup of coffee and I'll finish packing my bag.'

George held her to him wondering how she could be so calm. She was facing pain and she seemed happy about it.

Julia nestled against him. 'I know what you're thinking, George, and you're not to worry. This is Beverly Hills, not some isolated ranch in Mexico.'

George felt a stab of guilt at Julia's words. He hadn't been thinking of Velma at all. Now he was. 'I'll go make the coffee,' he said.

Waiting for the pan to boil George looked down across the wakening Basin. The sun was just clearing the San Bernardinos and burning off the mist. The oil stacks were poking their heads out like nervous gophers. Inside those stacks were the donkey engines, working away like the living heart of the city.

It was a dawn Velma would never see.

Julia's words had cut him deeper than he cared to dwell on. There should have been adulatory obituaries. There should have been eulogies and a mass weeping of fans at Forest Lawn. She should never have been giving birth in that Mexican ranch in the first place!

George had cheated her, and now he was exploiting her ghost.

'You haven't got time for that now!' yelled Julia through the kitchen door. 'They're coming quicker!'

'I got to get dressed yet!' George yelled back and, hurrying through to the bedroom, found Julia wincing with her latest pains. 'Is this normal?' he asked her as he struggled into a pair of pants and a sweater.

'How the hell would I know?' asked Julia. 'I never did this before!'

By the time George had her hustled out of the house and into the car Julia seemed calmer. George wasn't. He had trouble getting the car started, crashed the reverse gears, ran over the kerb and started off down the hill on the wrong side of the road.

'Will you take it easy?' pleaded Julia. 'What's the matter with you?'

'*I* never did this before either!'

Julia started laughing while George glared at her. 'Anybody would think it was you having the baby!'

'I *am* the father!' said George feeling the need to stress his rapidly diminishing role.

'Don't mean beans!' said Julia happily. She sighed and went on, 'Shame he couldn't wait till Saturday, though.'

'What's special about Saturday?'

'You mean you haven't noticed all those heavy hints I been dropping about October 30th?'

George searched his memory while Julia glared at him and waited expectantly. In the very nick of time he remembered. 'It's your birthday!' he cried triumphantly.

'Congratulations!' said Julia. 'The governor's reprieve came through just in time!' She sighed and sat back, hands clasped contentedly on her distended stomach. 'Anyway, it doesn't matter. We're just about to get the best gift anyone could ever hope for!'

From the moment he delivered Julia to the hospital reception he could see that what she'd said about fatherhood not meaning beans was true. She was whisked off into smooth, sterile mystery while he was consigned to the visitors' lounge.

George paced up and down feeling slightly resentful. He felt that expectant fathers should have a higher status than mere 'visitors'. But somehow this didn't seem the time to be offering constructive criticism.

George was left there, exchanging vacuous, furtive, even guilty grins with the other imminent fathers until a white-starched mountain of a nurse came to tell him that Julia was 'comfortable' and that nothing was expected to happen for at least ten hours.

George, more irrelevant and somehow culpable than ever, left them his office number and slunk off.

He was halfway down Sunset before he realized that he wasn't yet dressed for the office. Making a U-turn to return home, he found himself inconvenienced by some carelessly parked cars. Outside the Hollywood Savings and Loan was a whole mob of people impatiently banging on the doors. George considered that the bank must be giving away some pretty fancy dishes to have attracted this kind of a crowd.

When he got to his house he found Ailleen's car parked outside. Today she should have been at the studio. Obviously not. Maybe she'd come to call on Julia and waited for news.

He barely had time to get through the door before Ailleen was on him. 'What's going on, George?' she demanded.

'I just drove Julia to the hospital, that's all. Junior decided to come a little early.'

Thoughts of Julia had been far from Ailleen's mind. 'I'm talking about the studio!'

'The studio?' asked George.

'Yes, George, the studio! I was down there this morning having fittings for the new picture when these men arrived and said we all had to leave!'

'What men?'

'I don't know. They had papers and everything. I called the front office and they confirmed it. What's going on, George?'

'That's crazy!' said George and started for the telephone.

Ailleen pursued him through the house. 'I've tried that. It's no good. You won't get through!'

George obstinately pursued this with the operator only to have it confirmed. Frustrated, he asked for Wilbur's home number.

Ailleen hovered, nervously anxious. 'What can it mean, George?'

George shrugged her question off. He was fighting his own mounting feeling of dread.

Wilbur's home phone was picked up by a familiar voice that George couldn't immediately place. When George asked for Wilbur the voice identified himself as Hollister, Wilbur's financial and legal executive. 'You'd better get up here George!'

'What's going on?'

Hollister's reply was testy. 'This isn't something you discuss on the phone!'

In all the years that George had known Wilbur he hadn't once been invited to his home. George had to ask for the address. 'Is it serious?' he asked while writing it down.

George found the phone had been taken by a tearful Golda. 'George!' she started. 'Wilbur's always telling me you can work miracles. Please, I'm begging you, we need a miracle. Come as fast as you can?'

'What is it, Golda? Can't you tell me anything?' But George found he was speaking to Hollister again. Hollister would say nothing on the phone.

Hanging up, George had to face a thoroughly frightened Ailleen. 'Don't tell me it's all over?' she pleaded.

'You'll know the minute I do,' George told her, moving out of the house. 'Stay where I can reach you!'

'I'll be at home!' Ailleen yelled after him.

George's run back down the hill was a whole lot more headlong than it had been with Julia.

Driving east on Sunset, George again noticed the unusually enthusiastic crowds outside the banks. Idly he wondered why all the banks had chosen to give away dishes on the same day. He also decided to delay his own intention of cashing a cheque until after the excitement had died down.

Horizon had been, until recently, one of the more desirable locations in Hollywood Hills. Now, with the westward trend, prices were dropping. There were some great homes for sale up here at half what it had cost to build them eight or nine years previously. Turning into Wilbur's street George considered that his own buy in Beverly Hills might have been a mistake. He could have bought better and cheaper in Hollywood. Bitterly, he reflected that, depending on how bad this news turned out to be, he might have to!

Wilbur's house was surprisingly modest compared to its neighbours. It was also blocked by parked cars. George parked further up the street and walked back.

Turning into the steep drive that led to the house he saw Hollister come out and make towards his parked Pierce Arrow. George called out to him and Hollister turned back.

'We'd better make this quick, George. All hell's breaking loose!'

'You going to stay long enough to tell me what's going on?'

Hollister gestured aimlessly and blew out his cheeks. 'It's all so terrible, isn't it?'

'What is?' asked George doggedly.

'*This!*' emphasized Hollister. 'I mean, a thing like this comes out of nowhere and flattens everything!'

George completely lost his patience. 'Hollister! My wife's having a baby, Golda's hysterical. The studio's closed and I've driven all the way over here to find out what the fuck's going on! Guessing games with you, I don't need!'

Hollister started holding up placating hands before George was halfway through. He glanced furtively towards the house before leaning in confidentially towards George. 'Listen,' he said, as if afraid he was going to be overheard. 'You know about Wall Street, right?'

'It's in Manhattan. What else?'

This flat response caused Hollister to straighten up in surprise, his eyes widening. 'You mean you *haven't heard*!?'

Any minute now, thought George, I am going to take a swing at this guy. It was only Hollister's stricken, bloodless face that stopped him. Struggling to keep his voice even, George managed, 'You going to tell me what's happening with the studio or not?'

Hollister let out a soundless whistle and spoke like a man starting on a long speech. 'One thing at a time,' he said. 'The first thing is that Wilbur's had a stroke.'

'A stroke! Wilbur?'

Hollister nodded towards the house. 'He's lying in there like a vegetable.'

'Has he seen a doctor?'

'There've been four doctors here since dawn. Wilbur is totally rigid and unresponsive. I don't think there's a whole lot they can do for him. Mind you, it's a miracle we got a doctor here at all considering all else that's happening!'

'What else?' demanded George.

Hollister hesitated. He had the bearing of a man with bad news looking for the gentlest way of telling it. 'How extended are you, George?'

'"Extended"? What does that mean, "extended"?'

'I mean,' said Hollister with irritated patience, 'how much paper do you have in the market?'

George's anger broke through in one piece. 'What fucking market?' he yelled much louder than he'd meant to.

'The stock market!' Hollister yelled back. 'Don't tell me you haven't heard about *that*! Christ, George, where do you live? In a cave?'

George's expression showed that he felt he now had no alternative but to punch Hollister out. Hollister, reading the warning, stepped back and once more held up hands to ward him off. 'OK, George. Listen to this. This morning Wall Street fell off its perch. It's crashed, George. The party's over. The US of A just went flat broke. It started badly but by lunchtime, New York, it was a disaster! They being three hours ahead of us Wilbur got the news over breakfast. That's when he went catatonic. He's wiped out, George. He owes more millions than he's ever seen!'

George felt hollow. 'You mean he's bankrupt?'

Hollister snorted dismissively. 'If it were only *that* I could, maybe, save him something. This is a whole lot more serious, George.'

'The studio?'

'The studio, his house, his car, his spare pair of shoes and,

294

for all I know, the cook's cat! It's all gone, George. Everything!'

The thumping that had started in George's chest had, by now, worked its way up through his choked throat, into his head to set it, visibly, shaking. 'What about my contracts with Galaxy?'

'Toilet paper!' snapped Hollister. 'The banks have got everything Wilbur owned four times over!'

George couldn't comprehend it. 'But the studio, the equipment, the people. They're still there. *Salome* is out making money! How can something like this happen?'

Hollister took a deep breath as if about to explain some elementary facts to a backward pupil. 'Because Wilbur, like everybody else in America, was buying in millions on margin.' Hollister looked at George's blank face and knew he would have to explain further. 'Wilbur was buying on a ten per cent margin. That meant he only had to put up one-tenth of the value of the shares he was buying. With the stock market going up the way it was, it made a lot of sense. He could resell his margins, at a profit, before the full price became due and payable. What has happened is that the market has nose-dived leaving Wilbur, and millions like him, over-exposed. His notes have been called in and the banks are running for cover and snatching back whatever collateral they can lay hands on!'

George was struggling to assimilate one-half of Hollister's diatribe but finally managed to articulate a response. 'What the hell are the banks going to do with a movie studio?'

Hollister sighed. 'I doubt they know the answer to that one themselves. Look, George, nobody's being rational. The banks are headed for the life-boats along with everyone else! You must have passed some banks on the way over here. Didn't you see the depositors fighting to get their money out?'

'I thought they were giving away dishes,' murmured George miserably.

Hollister let out a sound that was part groan, part laugh. 'You, George Schapner, are a true original!'

George ignored the patronizing tone. 'Listen, there's one question you didn't answer. *Salome* is making money, right? How come they won't hold off till we get some returns in?'

'Because, George, you will recall that we took in a whole lot of advances on *Salome*. We haven't worked them off yet but thank God we did, because I doubt many of the people owing us money could come up with it. They been playing the market the same as everyone else.'

George stood there helpless and feeling the ground shift under his feet. All those sweaty days and nights getting Aileen made over into Velma had been for nothing!

Hollister misread the misery in George's face and clapping George on the shoulder asked, 'How much *did* you have in the market, George?'

George shook his head. 'Nothing. I had some RCA stock but I sold out months back.'

Hollister's admiration shone in his voice. 'George, you're the luckiest son-of-a-bitch! You know something, if your bank holds up, you could be among the richest men in America this morning. You and Al Capone!'

George looked up, sharply alert. 'Al Capone?' he asked.

'You don't *know* him, do you?' asked Hollister half seriously.

George shook his head. He was trying to understand why the mentioning of Al Capone had set off such a reverberation in his head. Hollister, meanwhile, was blethering on. 'It's guys like him – mobsters – who couldn't put their money into anything legitimate that are laughing today. Do you realize that, if they knew it, they could buy up half of America this morning? We could end up with Al Capone as president!'

George still wasn't listening. He was struggling to catch the train of thought that Hollister had somehow set in motion.

Hollister was still talking. 'You know something? If I could lay my hands on a million dollars cash money today I could do such a deal! I could gear it up to, maybe, buy back four – maybe five million, of Galaxy's paper!'

Now George was interested. 'Would that save the studio?' he asked.

'Save it? Hell! I could *develop* it! You any idea what's going on out there? The banks are bleeding to death. Anybody with cash money today is going to be able to work himself such a corner as you wouldn't believe.' Hollister became aware of George's quiet, thoughtful expression. 'You wouldn't know where to get that kind of money, would you?'

George kept him waiting a minute longer. 'I might,' he finally said.

Hollister's eyes looked into the face of the Messiah. His voice trembled with excitement. 'George. If you have the least idea of where to find cash money . . .' Hollister's voice trailed off with emotion. 'George, I could buy you half Hollywood.'

George held up a hand to stem the flood of emotion he feared might engulf him. 'It's only a thought. It isn't even an idea yet.'

Hollister was fumbling out a visitor's card. 'Take this. It's my home number. I doubt they'll let me back into the studio. Call me any time, George. I mean it. Even half a chance!'

George nodded but wished he hadn't said anything. The light he'd lit in Hollister's eyes could hardly be justified by his half thought. George promised to call the shaken Hollister.

He watched him walk away to his Pierce Arrow where Hollister turned to call back, 'Even if it's just someone to buy my car!'

George watched Hollister back his car out into the steeply sloping road, and drive off.

George looked towards the outwardly calm house and knew he didn't have the strength to face the drama being played inside.

He walked towards his car guiltily aware that he should go

297

in and console Golda but, right now, he had other urgent business.

13

'Well,' said Madame Gregory. 'I'll say this for it – it's a nice round figure!'

George was nervously perched on the edge of one of Madame Gregory's parlour chairs. He'd just told her he was out trying to raise a million dollars – and why.

Madame G. took her time pouring herself a drink. 'You don't imagine I have that kind of money, do you?' she asked.

'No,' conceded George, 'but what you *do* have is a common interest in seeing that Galaxy survives to honour its contracts. I thought, maybe, that you might know somebody.'

Madame G. came back to the couch wearing her poker face. 'I've taken a beating in the market myself.' She paused a moment for reflection. 'My information is that things will pick up. I'm holding on. You think that's the right thing to do?'

George leaned back in his chair on the point of scornful laughter. 'You're asking *me*!? Listen, when I saw the run on the banks this morning I thought they were giving away dishes! My financial advice isn't worth spit!'

Madame G., looking directly at George, held his gaze for some time. 'Tell you what you do have, George. What you got is luck. Don't put it down. You could be a genius, but without luck you're going nowhere. Now a man who's got it gets a following. I'm superstitious. I'll tell you, when you first came in here, all those months ago, with your crazy schemes I went along with you for the laughs. All I wanted was an inside track on the story when the men in white coats came to take you away. I watched you duck and weave your way through that one and come out smelling delicate when all the brains in this town were shitting their pants. It's a quality I got to admire. Could be I know someone that'd share my opinion.'

George felt the blood starting to move again in his veins. Madame G. hadn't laughed in his face. Maybe she did know someone! George held on silently while Madame G. turned things over in her mind. He knew she wasn't going to speak until she was ready. Finally, 'Let's suppose, for a minute, I have got someone in mind. What would be in it for them?'

George leaned forward again. 'I got to be honest. I haven't the least idea. The only thought I got in my mind is to save Galaxy – if that's possible.'

Madame G. nodded. 'And Wilbur Sterne's out of it? I mean, is there any chance he could recover?'

Again George could only shrug. 'I don't know that either. My information is that even if he made a complete recovery tomorrow it would be too late.'

She let more time pass as she looked directly at George. 'These people I have in mind represent some interests back east. They might just have the money and the inclination to put it into a movie studio. The only thing I got to tell you is that they ain't going to like the time-scale you're indicating. You smell desperate, George, and desperate people get screwed.'

'Look, so far as I'm concerned they can write their own ticket. The studio is up for grabs. If the banks get it they'll just destroy it. If there's any way to keep it going as a functioning studio, with the contracts it's got, it'll come through. Bear in mind that if Galaxy goes under you and I are out some serious money!'

Madame G. nodded at that. 'You understand, I'm not unsympathetic to the idea. What I'm saying is that someone will have to present a better case than you are doing right now.'

'I got the guy!' cried George with enthusiasm. 'Hollister. He's been running the finance and legal departments at

Galaxy since it started. I got him waiting on the end of a phone. Anything these people want to know he can tell 'em.'

Madame G. took this approvingly. 'There's something else, George. If I make an approach to these people I'll be calling in a lot of favours. You cross these guys and they can play rough. I want to be sure that the studio is worth saving. You follow my meaning?'

George was nodding. 'Listen, you think I'd be running around if I didn't think so? We got *Salome* out and it's a smash hit. If Galaxy stays in business long enough the profits are going to be enormous. There'll be plenty for everybody. Their money would be safe.'

Madame G. laughed sourly. 'Nobody's money is safe, George. Nobody knows what's going to happen. A week from now US currency could be worthless. That's one reason why they might just be interested in shifting some cash into bricks and mortar.' She paused and added, 'Who knows?'

George's first excitement at not being turned down flat was starting to ebb. Now he wanted desperately for Madame G. to come up with someone. 'What chances do you think we have?' he asked her.

Madame G. didn't know and told him so. Feeling somewhat deflated George walked to the door. 'Just stay by your phones. If there's anything worth talking about I'll find you.'

As they crossed the hall George was aware of the prevailing silence. 'How's business?' he asked her for something to say.

Madame G. laughed. 'What do you think? A crisis like this comes down on the guys like castration.'

'Things are tough all over,' murmured George, finding himself reluctant to leave the one person he thought could save Galaxy. 'Well,' he finally was forced into saying, 'the best of luck – for both of us.'

George left with Madame G.'s assurances echoing repetitively in his ears and drove back to his office.

When he got back he found his harem sadly depleted.

There was just the one girl there, and when she looked towards him he could see that she'd been crying.

'Something wrong?' he asked her, only to find he'd set off her sobbings again.

Sybil came bustling out of the inner office to elbow him to his own office.

'Best leave her alone. She was down to her Savings and Loan and they've put up the shutters. She thinks she might have lost her savings.'

'And the others?'

'Same thing. They're out chasing their money.'

'And you?'

'I always kept my money where I could see it. Everybody's been telling me I'm crazy. I'm asking, who's crazy now?'

While nodding in agreement to this it occurred to him that he ought to check out his own account. He asked Sybil to get the First National on the phone.

George sat alone in his office and thought about what was happening. If people like his girls were in trouble then the country was surely doomed. He needed the First National to survive or he was doomed himself. Maybe, he considered, the gods had seen it as a good joke to toss him some favours only to snatch it all back when they thought he'd had enough. He'd sat in this same chair and contemplated his share of disaster in the past few months. Familiarity had done nothing to brighten its face.

Sybil came in pinning her hat to her hair. 'They've shut off their phones,' she told him. 'I got a friend works down there. She'll tell me what the chances are. I want to be sure,' she added, 'that you're going to be able to pay me my salary cheque!'

Mention of her cheque inspired George to detain her while he wrote out a cheque of his own.

'See if you can get them to make this good,' he told her.

Sybil was impressed. 'Two hundred dollars?' she asked.

'Don't worry. I'm not planning to leave the country!'

301

Sybil laughed cynically. 'For two hundred dollars you could probably *buy* the country!' She looked up at him. 'By the way the phones you hear ringing are your clients ringing in to ask that all future monies due are paid in cash. Nobody trusts the banks any more.' Sybil smiled thinly. 'Can't imagine why!'

George watched her go confident that, if anybody could Sybil would find out what was happening.

After Sybil's departure he realized that his clients were probably blocking the lines. Madame G. had his personal and private numbers but just to make certain he went through to tell his one remaining assistant that they should give priority to 'Mrs Battershaw' should she ring.

The girl smiled and nodded. George patted her encouragingly on the shoulder. 'It'll work out,' he told the tearful girl. She didn't look convinced.

George had just got back to his own office when the extension rang. He reached over his desk in his anxiety to answer it. It wasn't Madame G., it was far more shocking than that. Von Muller was almost incoherent with grief. He told George that he'd lost 'everything'. George winced remembering that only a few short weeks before he'd handed over the last instalment on Von Muller's payment against *Salome* – almost a quarter of a million dollars!

'Everything?' asked George in a hollow voice.

'Everything!' shouted Von Muller as if it were George's fault. What Von Muller wanted to know was that the balance of his contract was safe and that Galaxy would be in a position to pay it. George didn't have the heart to do anything but lie. He told Von Muller that everything was fine.

This call filled George with a deep depression. He found it hard to contemplate someone receiving and losing that amount of money in just a few short weeks. Had the world gone crazy? He tried to dismiss Madame G.'s chilling comment about the value of money. It seemed diametrically opposed to Hollister's claim that he could work miracles with a million dollars. George was no economist but he hoped there was still some logic out there somewhere.

Sybil returned triumphant from the bank and laid two hundred dollars on the desk. 'Your cheque's still good!' she told him. 'My friend told me that they're getting federal funding to tide them over.'

The relief George felt at this was the first indication of how tense he'd been. Weighing the dollar bills in his hand he felt that he'd been refunded ten years of life. It was while he was still enjoying the fact of having some cash that Sybil casually told him that a 'Mrs Battershaw' was on the line.

George grabbed up the phone.

'Your luck is holding out!' she told him. 'There's a guy in town who happens to be interested in meeting you. His name is Raymond Lewis. He'll be at your house at six.'

'My house? Why not my office?'

'He doesn't like offices and considers he can tell more about a man in the surroundings of his house. You want to argue with him?'

'No,' said George, 'but I got nobody there to entertain him. Julia's in the hospital.'

'She's sick?'

'No, she's having a baby.'

'At a time like this?' asked Madame G. with unconscious humour. 'OK. Listen, you're in luck. Ray Lewis happens to be a great fan of Velma Torraine's. The *one* and *only*, if you get my meaning. He knows nothing about anything else. Now here's what you do, you have Velma there when he arrives. And, George, have her be "friendly". You know what I mean?'

George was appalled. 'I can't just call up Velma and ask her to – '

Madame G. cut him off. 'George! This is "me" you're talking to! You tell that girl what's at stake. She'll be flattered.'

'I'm not so sure that's true any more,' George murmured, feeling slightly sick.

'You want me to call her?'

George hastily told Madame G. that he'd do it and hung up feeling deflated. The thought that someone, anyone, was interested enough to come out to his house to talk should have elated him. The thought that it might all depend, again, on two bare bellies in a bed was demeaning.

His other problem was Hollister. He would need him there to present any kind of reasonable case but he didn't relish him witnessing George in the role he couldn't seem to escape – pimping. A million-dollar pimp, maybe, but still a pimp.

How would Ailleen react if nothing came of the deal. She'd hate him. Or would she? His eye fell on the bundle of notes in his hand.

He'd bought her once and, by the time he picked up the phone to call her, he'd convinced himself he could do it again.

Two hundred dollars was a familiar sum between them.

A million was everybody's friend!

14

George got home just before six to find Ailleen anxiously awaiting him.

'How do you want to play this, George?' she asked as he came through the door.

'I have no idea!' he told her. 'I'm just embarrassed at you having to be here.'

'Don't be stupid, George. If these people can save the studio and our necks then we're here to help.'

'Who's this "we"?'

'Hollister got here half an hour ago. He's by the pool with Nadine.'

'Nadine? Who brought her into this?'

'Madame G.!'

George stared at Ailleen, then moved to the garden window which looked out over the pool. Sure enough, there was Hollister with a drink in his hand and a stupid grin on his face. The grin was caused by watching Nadine swim up and down the pool in athletically eased rhythms.

'She trying for pneumonia or what?' he asked of Ailleen.

'It's still warm for us Europeans. Listen, George, we don't have much time to talk before they come in here. Now what we girls want to know from you is do we play it low necklines leaning over or little Miss Butter-wouldn't-melt-in-her-mouth?'

George looked into Ailleen's eyes and was confused. 'How the hell would I know? Listen, you'd better get Nadine out of that pool before they get here.'

Ailleen was shaking her head. 'No, no! We worked that bit out. Nadine stays out there for five or ten minutes after they get here, then she comes out, wraps herself in that linen wrap she's got out there, and comes in surprised to find you have visitors with the wrap clinging to everything she's got.'

George stared at Ailleen. 'What the hell are you talking about?' he finally asked. 'This is supposed to be a serious business meeting, not a number from the Ziegfeld Follies!'

Ailleen sighed patiently. 'Would you believe me when I tell you that I, Madame G. and Nadine know a whole lot more about men than you do? You and Hollister talk the business, let me and Nadine take care of the decorations. OK?'

George stared at her, stupidly unable to reply. His feelings about the meeting had become progressively more intense the more he'd thought about it. All afternoon he had heard story after story about people who were going down in flames all over Hollywood. People were talking about an avenging visitation by God. First the coming of sound and now this earthquake on Wall Street. It seemed that the parameters had been totally redrawn. He'd begun to believe that his visitors tonight might be his last chance to get into a life-boat of his own. Now, having got a life-saver in sight he found the crew throwing a cocktail party! This meeting was far too vital to be confused by talk of wet wraps and low necklines! You had to maintain a semblance of sanity even in an insane world!

'Ask Hollister to come in here, would you?' he asked Ailleen.

Ailleen nodded and started for the open garden window.

George went through to his den which was where Hollister found him. 'I got out a game plan, George!' he told him.

'I'm glad to hear it,' said George. 'When I saw you out at the pool just now I thought you might have forgotten all about it!'

Hollister seemed to be brought up short by George's sharp tone. 'I was just passing the time of day,' he murmured.

'Do we have that much time?' asked George, keeping the edge to his voice. In truth that 'edge' was generated more by George's own nervousness than anything else. Hollister's attitude, however, became a mite more deferential.

'I'm sorry. I assure you that even before your call I was working on the figures.' George enjoyed the note of chastened apology in the way Hollister spoke. He felt it gave him back something of the initiative that the easy disposition of the girls had taken from him.

'You want to take a look at them?' asked Hollister offering up several sheets of heavy cartridge paper that he'd taken from his case.

George nodded and Hollister spread the sheets out before him on his desk. George had always suffered from a form of numerical blindness. Movie budgets, especially, were the bane of his life. The bottom line never seemed to be the final total – it was always hedged around by supplementaries and exigencies. This spread sheet was no different. Columns of figures all nicely symmetrical and, to someone like George, almost totally meaningless.

'Just run through the headlines for me,' he told Hollister.

'Basically, Galaxy is in a very healthy condition . . .'

Hollister started. 'Almost all our capital equipment is bought and paid for with the exception of certain items of sound equipment which we have on lease. The building and lot are leased but very secure long-term low cost . . .'

George's mind was just beginning to glaze over when the door flew open and an excited Ailleen stood there.

'They're here!' she said. 'Two big black Cadillacs . . . !'

George got to his feet. 'I hope you know what you're talking about,' George told Hollister. 'Because I sure don't!'

George went out into the main room just as the door bell was sounding. He turned to say something else to Hollister but found him gazing trance-like towards the front door as if expecting God to walk in. Maybe, thought George, he isn't far wrong!

Ailleen was doing the door chores as George and Hollister waited for their first sight of Madame G.'s business partners. George had expected almost anything but the slim, shyly smiling, quietly-dressed man who came in, gushing about having been met at the door by his 'favourite movie actress of all time'. Ailleen was playing Velma for all she was worth. She already had a comforting arm squeeze on Lewis as he came in. George judged it was quite an effort for Lewis to tear his eyes from her as she made the introductions.

Lewis shook George's hand. 'This is an unexpected pleasure!' said Lewis. 'I mean, meeting Miss Torraine quite like that!'

George found himself standing there smiling and more than a little lost. Lewis's accent had thrown him for a start – it was English. His vocabulary was not one he would have expected from any friend of Al Capone's.

'Are you British by any chance?' Ailleen was enquiring.

Lewis pointed a friendly finger at her. 'You noticed!' he smiled, then turned to George and said in almost deferential tones, 'I have some associates with me. They're waiting in the car. I didn't have them come in immediately since this *is* your home. May I invite them in?'

Bemused, George just stood there nodding and smiling.

'Would you like *me* to invite them in?' asked Ailleen.

Lewis seemed delighted. '*Would* you, Miss Torraine? I'm sure they would be thrilled!'

Ailleen gave a quick look at George and, turning, ran off about her errand.

Lewis walked forward to the centre of the newly furnished house. 'What a delightful place you have here, Mr Schapner.'

'Yes, we moved in just a few months ago.'

'How very fortunate you are out here in California. So much light and air.' Lewis had moved to the garden window. 'And such a delightful view!'

George looked past Lewis to see that Nadine had climbed out of the pool and was reaching, totally nude, for the promised linen wrap. George glanced at Lewis, worried that this was the wrong approach to take with this surprisingly well-educated man. He needn't have bothered. Lewis had sparkling eyes avidly fixed on Nadine as she made her way round the pool towards the house.

'Isn't that another of your stars, Mr Schapner?'

'Yeah. That's Nadine Bourdon. She featured in our last picture . . .'

'*Salome!*' cried Lewis. 'Of course!'

'You've seen it?' asked George.

'Twice!' murmured Lewis. 'I am a great fan of Miss Torraine.'

Lewis turned expectantly towards the garden window as Nadine came through. She played the scene to perfection. First she stopped, fixed her eyes on Lewis, let them open in a momentary flicker and then half turned as if to run away in confusion before 'gathering' herself up and smiling.

George introduced them while Nadine continued to excuse herself. 'I am so sorry. I had no idea anyone was here but Velma.' She took a coy hand to her mouth. 'Oh, *mon Dieu*, but I am practically naked!' She started to run on tiptoe towards the stairway that led to the upper floor. 'Please forgive me!' she trilled back at Lewis.

'No apology necessary, Miss Nadine!' Lewis called after her.

George looked down at Hollister who had his mouth open staring after Nadine. George realized with a start that he hadn't yet introduced them.

He brought Hollister over to Lewis. 'This is the man you need to talk with. Hollister's been with Galaxy from the start. He is the numbers man!'

Lewis shook hands with Hollister and then held up both hands. 'Numbers are not for me,' he said with a chuckle, then as Ailleen returned with three tight-suited men in tow, Lewis pointed to the fattest, meanest-looking one. 'That's my numbers man.'

George looked into the smallest pair of eyes he had ever seen. Here was a man who had seen a lot of crooked books in his time and looked as if he could spot them a mile off. He did nothing but grunt, twice, as he was introduced first to George and then to Hollister.

Ailleen meanwhile was floating about the room playing the gracious hostess. The two bulky-looking men watched her every move. Obviously they were fans too! These two looked like the 'protection'. The kind of men who felt uncomfortable outside of a fist fight. Lewis didn't bother introducing them, but Ailleen seemed to be making a special point of fussing round them. Her reward came when one of them broke into a smile.

'Tell you what, Mr Schapner,' said Lewis. 'Why don't we let the people that understand these things, my Mr Collellea and your Mr Hollister, talk while we take our drinks out on to your delightful terrace?'

George followed Lewis outside. Off to their right there was the beginning of a beautiful sunset. Lewis took a moment to admire the reddening sky before sitting himself at one of the white iron tables.

'What a delightful business you are in, Mr Schapner. You are probably quite accustomed to the company of such ladies, but I must confess myself somewhat overwhelmed! Velma Torraine and Nadine Bourdon both under the one roof! Goodness me!'

George found himself disconcerted by Lewis. He wasn't anything like he'd expected and he began to wonder if this wasn't some cruel joke thought up by Madame G. It was like a gigantic piece of miscasting; he'd expected Al Capone and got Douglas Fairbanks!

'I just thought you'd like to see Galaxy's most attractive assets,' said George trying to match Lewis's buoyant mood.

'Attractive they are, Mr Schapner, but unless my information serves me wrong they are more *your* assets than Galaxy's . . . ?'

Lewis's smiling amused tone hadn't dropped one whit but suddenly George found himself face to face with 'business'.

'Well, it's true that both ladies are handled by my agency, but Galaxy has their contracts.'

'Ah, yes . . .' mused Lewis. 'Contracts. I sometimes think that contracts are much less binding than loyalties. It's quite obvious where those ladies see their loyalty lying.'

'Those contracts are watertight, Mr Lewis. Positively lodged with Galaxy.'

'While Galaxy exists, Mr Schapner,' Lewis quietly observed.

George had the uncomfortable feeling that he was neither saying nor thinking the right things. Lewis had thrown him. A boozy, loud hood he could have handled. Lewis, with his quiet, smiling but well-researched amiability, was a more difficult proposition.

'It is a tenet of faith with me,' Lewis was saying, 'to put my trust in people rather than things. Things can be stolen, burned down and very easily replaced. People are something else. They are, each and every one, unique. Take those two delightful ladies, for instance. Beautiful, talented young women, of course, but I am more interested in the man that found them and developed them than I am in the ladies themselves.' Lewis turned his eyes to George. 'And I am certainly more interested by someone of that kind of talent than by the bricks and mortar of, say, Galaxy movie studios. Do you follow my meaning, Mr Schapner?'

George had a sinking feeling that Lewis was offering him a job rather than thinking of putting the necessary million into Galaxy. That was a flattering enough position for George personally, but what, he reminded himself, he was here to do was make sure that the big money contracts he had with Galaxy went through. No matter how rewarding a partnership with Lewis might eventually prove to be it would be a long time before it matched the huge pay-out he was more immediately due from Galaxy.

'You can't make movies without those "bricks and mortar", Mr Lewis.'

'No, no,' agreed Lewis. 'I understand that. Perhaps I should make myself a little clearer. Who would be placed in charge of the day-to-day running of Galaxy should it survive?'

This question set George back on his mental heels. He had never imagined Galaxy without Wilbur Sterne, but with Wilbur out of the game, it was an immediately relevant question which he had not even stood still long enough to think about. 'You understand, Mr Lewis, that I am not familiar with all the executive talent there may be out at Galaxy. However, I'm sure that the right man could be found.'

Lewis nodded and looked out over the deepening sunset. 'It is a matter of fundamental importance, I should have thought, no matter who, finally, interests themselves in this enterprise.'

George nodded. 'Maybe we should call in Hollister. He knows more about those things than I.'

Lewis smiled, and looked round into the lighted house. 'I would much rather join the ladies,' he said.

George, following his gaze, saw that both Nadine and Ailleen were elegantly seated in the main room, trying to look relaxed under the gaze of the 'protection'.

'Why not?' asked George.

He followed Lewis into the house, suspecting that the ground had shifted in some way he didn't understand. He had a very negative feeling about the possibility of Lewis taking any further interest in Galaxy. George was aware that in some way he had shown himself inadequate.

As they came in both Ailleen and Nadine expertly switched their charm-meters to 'STUN', and gathered Lewis up into a whole round of solicitous enquiries about what he might want. George was content to hang back and let the social atmosphere take over. He was a whole lot more comfortable as a spectator than he was playing blocker for Lewis's rushes.

From his vantage point he was able to watch as Lewis, bracketed by the two lovely ladies, laughed and joked with them. He felt like breaking in and telling the girls they were wasting their time. Maybe he would have been comfortable with some loud-mouthed hoods. Maybe the girls would have been too, but they didn't show it. Nadine especially seemed to be having a wonderful time. She was now walking Lewis around with her arm linked through his. He noticed that Lewis's arm through Nadine's was resting comfortably against her barely harnessed breasts.

He shook himself out of his reverie which was rapidly heading towards jealousy when Ailleen detached herself from the merry threesome and came over to perch on the arm of the chair into which he had sunk.

'How's it going?' she asked him.

'I don't know, but I don't think the show is the hit of the season.'

Ailleen looked round concerned. 'Anything we can do?' she asked.

George shook his head.

Ailleen seemed disappointed. 'Nadine seems to be getting

along like a house on fire.' She looked back to George. 'Hey, you're looking depressed. You want me to fix you a drink?'

'A good strong one,' said George.

Ailleen levered herself off the chair and hip-swung her way across the room. George saw how the silent hoods' eyes followed her every movement. For some reason it depressed him even further.

George had practically forgotten the solid work going on in his study until the door opened and the mean-eyed Collellea emerged. He stood looking fixedly towards Lewis who hadn't yet noticed him. Hollister emerged from the room and George was surprised to see him smiling. Hollister came towards George, carefully keeping his body between himself and Collellea, and gave George the thumbs up.

George switched his eyes to Collellea and was just in time to catch the almost imperceptible nod that he gave Lewis who had finally turned towards him.

Lewis nodded back. The exchange was like that between bidder and seller at an auction. Discreet but positive. George's hopes were suddenly alive again. Had this been a nod of approval?

Lewis, with Nadine tucked under his arm, came towards George who rose to meet him. 'I wonder,' Lewis enquired, 'if I might presume to confer with my colleague in your study?'

'Help yourself,' said George.

The moment the two were out of sight in the study George turned to Hollister. Hollister pulled him out on to the terrace where the watchful protection couldn't hear them.

'I think they've bought it!' said Hollister in an excited whisper.

'The studio? Galaxy? They'll go for it?'

Hollister was nodding. 'Jesus, George, I think you've done it again. I think you've saved it.'

'Yeah, but what did that guy say?'

'Nothing. But I could see the figures got over to him.

Especially the inventory assets. Jesus, he is a sharp one, that Collellea.'

'You should try Lewis. He's dangerous. He comes on like your favourite relative and all the time he's in there digging.' George's excitement was reaching fever pitch. 'You really think so, huh?' he asked, not having to elaborate his meaning further.

Hollister clapped George on both shoulders at once. 'After this people'll be expecting you to walk on water, George!'

George nodded and peered back into the house where he could see both girls were as on edge as he was. Hollister brought him down to earth with a bump. 'There's only one problem, George.'

'What's that?'

'Suppose they were willing buyers . . .'

'We don't know that yet!' cautioned George.

'No, but suppose they were . . .' Hollister let his words trail off as if the next would be too important to put into the same speech.

'What?' demanded George.

'Neither you nor I have title to sell.'

'What does that mean?'

'It means that we're here negotiating to sell something we don't own.'

George was speechless for fully a minute. 'That's ridiculous!' he finally managed. 'There's no way Wilbur wouldn't want to get out of trouble!'

'Wilbur is in a catatonic state. There is no way he could even appreciate his problems, let alone see the advantages of selling off the studio.'

George felt angry. 'Why didn't you tell me this before? I mean, are you saying that all this has been for nothing?'

Hollister placated him. 'I'm not saying that. I'm saying that, even if they come out of the room with a "yes", we still got a long way to go!'

'Why wouldn't Wilbur, or Golda – she's not catatonic –

why wouldn't they want to sell? Would they rather the banks got everything?'

'That's the point. Bringing new money into Galaxy might well save the studio but it won't save Wilbur. He'd be out of the studio and with his personal commitments have to go right into personal bankruptcy.'

'A million dollars wouldn't help him?'

'Personally, not one little bit. Wilbur's finished, George. He might just be of a mood to let the studio go down with him.'

The realization of what Hollister was saying was too much for George. He turned to the wall and started beating the side of his clenched fist against it. 'Holy shit!' He turned angrily on Hollister. 'Why in hell didn't you tell me all this before I got into this stupid deal?'

'It was a question of first things first, George. First we had to have a deal before we could start working on the problems.'

George saw Lewis and Collellea emerge from the study and stand looking round. George hastily adjusted his expression and, smiling confidently, went back into the house.

'I hear good, positive things, Mr Schapner,' Lewis greeted him. 'However, I understand from my colleague here that time is of the essence. That being so I must confer with my partners back east. I think I shall have a more positive response for you tomorrow morning. Shall we say ten at your office at the studio?'

George was confused by the speed of events. 'Er – I don't have an office at the studio, Mr Lewis . . .'

Hollister stepped in. 'I'm sure we could use Mr Sterne's office, though.'

Lewis nodded. 'Fine. Well I'll be there at ten tomorrow morning. Thank you very much, Mr Schapner, Mr Hollister . . .' Lewis moved away towards the girls. His goodbyes to them lasted longer and contained much hand-clasping and cheek-kissing before they started for the front door. George, with Hollister's latest bombshell weighing him down, tried hard to rally a bright smile as he followed them towards the door.

Both he and Hollister were brought up short by the two protection men. George's heart leapt into his mouth as he saw one of them reach inside his bulging jacket pocket. George nearly collapsed with relief when the man brought out nothing more threatening than a small notebook.

'You think the ladies would sign my book fer me?' the heavy-built hood asked.

George almost broke into a hysterical laugh. 'I'm sure they'd be delighted!' he told the man. 'Girls . . . !' he called, summoning them both forward.

He went on to where Lewis and Collellea were waiting just inside the front door.

'The appeal is universal,' said Lewis, smiling as George joined him.

'Seems like it,' said George.

They stood there exchanging courtesies while both the hoods got their books signed by both girls. He was somewhat relieved when they rejoined their bosses and were waved away.

George turned back into the main room to see Nadine, Ailleen and Hollister standing all in a row. As if on cue they raised their hands and started applauding George as he came back into the room.

'I need a drink!' he told Ailleen who happily scooted off to fetch it.

Hollister slapped George on the back. 'You heard him. "Something more positive" by ten tomorrow!'

George nodded. 'Let's hope we have something to sell them by that time.'

Hollister raised an approving finger. 'That I'm going to get right on.' He started for the phone and, while waiting for his number, turned back to George. 'Don't expect to get too much sleep tonight,' he called cheerfully.

Ailleen handed George his drink. 'Sounds exciting. What does it mean?'

'I wish I knew,' said George.

15

'There is only one candidate,' said Hollister. 'You!'

The single syllable ricocheted round George's skull, leaving him momentarily stunned. 'Me?'

'Certainly you,' said Hollister as if George's objections were an annoyance. 'Who else is there? You have practically single-handed put Galaxy in the position it's in today – creatively speaking.'

George stared at Hollister. He had never in his wildest imaginings seen himself as the head of a studio. The thought was frightening. In his own mind he was the product of a series of stumbling accidents, disasters circumvented or simply postponed. He'd known that his bluff had worked, but this was ridiculous!

Both men were standing in Wilbur Sterne's house. It was past midnight and the doctors were again examining Wilbur.

George's first sight of the prostrate Wilbur had been traumatic. He had gone to Wilbur's house immediately after the meeting with Lewis. George had been hoping that there might have been some dramatic improvement but his first sight of the tableau at Wilbur's bedside had dispelled any such hope. Wilbur, that once vitally energized living man, had been laid out like a prone statue, his open eyes apparently seeing nothing, his brain stilled in shock. Golda had stared at George from the bedside, her eyes eloquently pleading for miracles, her hands clasping Wilbur's as if trying to transmit her own life force into him.

'I think he can hear us, George,' had been her only words.

George had come up to the bedside and not known what

to say. Looking down into Wilbur's eyes was frightening. There was a vacancy there that he'd never seen before. It was like a waxwork representation of the man he'd known. It didn't seem possible that this Wilbur lived and breathed. Finally he'd just stood there and repeated Wilbur's name a few times. Golda's sobs indicated that this was less than inadequate. George looked across at Golda's head bowed in misery on to Wilbur's still clasped hands and wondered what she had expected of him. This wasn't something he could bluff or lie or cheat his way through. He was grateful when Hollister pulled him gently away and out of the room.

'That was the most scary experience of my life,' George told him. 'I never imagined a thing like that could happen. What is it exactly? I mean, what is this "stroke" business?'

Hollister shrugged. 'I'm no medical man. The doctors gave me so many different interpretations I don't know which is the most important. Seems it's some kind of emotional seizure. Total failure of the brain to cope. It just stops working.'

'It's like some monster is out there waiting to grab us. Jesus, a thing like this could happen to us all!'

Hollister shrugged again. 'Right now we've got to concentrate on matters in hand – like Lewis!'

George couldn't see any answer to that. 'There's no way we can get through to Wilbur in this state. It's like he's dead.'

'Thank God he's not,' said Hollister. 'I happen to know that Wilbur's will is a mess. It's set about with all kinds of family commitments. It would take us months to get it through probate.'

'What's the difference in this situation?'

'Simply this. We get Wilbur declared incapacitated. There shouldn't be any trouble with that one! Next we get Golda given power of attorney. We get that endorsed by a judge and hopefully we'll so gain power to negotiate.'

George had stared at Hollister. 'All this before ten tomorrow morning?'

Hollister had nodded. 'We don't have any choice but to try, George. Apart from satisfying Lewis and his associates, I have to be in a position to hit the banks while they're still reeling. The day after tomorrow the government may have come up with some rescue package and calmed them all down.'

'How the hell we going to do it?'

'First thing is to get Golda's approval to *try*!'

George had been happy to leave it to Hollister. A reluctant Golda was persuaded away from Wilbur's bedside and subjected to a wheedling argument that seemed to George to be exploiting her confusion and misery. Golda had stared at Hollister throughout this painful process through tear-filled, grief-stricken eyes and with only half her mind engaged. At the end of it all she had asked, 'You say this could save Galaxy, Mr Hollister. I ask you, will it save my Wilbur?'

Hollister pleaded that this way there would be something tangible for Wilbur to come back to. His fate was in the hand of God, his business they could, mortally, save.

George had grown increasingly uneasy about putting this kind of pressure on an already disturbed and confused mind. He'd kept at a distance, both literally and figuratively, throughout, but he couldn't escape Golda's final appeal which was addressed directly to him.

'George?' she called to him. 'You tell me, George. What should I do? Is this the best for Wilbur?'

George had nodded, knowing that he was not equipped to decide one way or the other. He felt, somehow, that they were looters at the scene of disaster. He suspected he was lying both to himself and Golda, but he re-emphasized it. 'I can see no other way, Golda. Whatever happens this is a long way from the worst.'

Golda had nodded. Obviously she had as little idea as George of what they were about. Finally she had agreed to recall the doctors. They were with Wilbur now.

'There can't be any doubt about their verdict, can there?' George asked Hollister.

'No, but they have to cover themselves. My worry is how Golda will stand the strain.'

'What "strain"?'

'Having to appear before Judge Neuerling. She hasn't slept or eaten since this thing happened. She's not a young woman.' Hollister paused. 'Maybe I can get the doctors to give her something.'

George stared at the windows of Wilbur's house, startled to realize that the Los Angeles basin was lightening again. He himself hadn't slept through twenty-four hours. He couldn't remember eating either. Sheer momentum had carried him this far, but now he felt suddenly drained. His eyes hurt and he felt light-headed. 'Maybe they could come up with something for me, too,' he told Hollister.

'Good idea,' said Hollister. 'We've still got a long day in front of us. You want me to make some coffee?'

The thought of coffee made his stomach heave. He wished he'd missed out on some of the drinks he'd been taking. They now lay like a heavy weight in his stomach. The spectre of what had overtaken Wilbur grew in his mind. Maybe this is how it started? 'Maybe we ought to catch a little sleep,' he suggested to Hollister.

'No time,' snapped Hollister as, at that moment, the bedroom door opened and the two doctors emerged in murmuring conference.

'Well?' asked Hollister directly.

The two glanced at Hollister and, walking round him, crossed the room to a table where their murmuring continued.

Hollister turned on Golda as she came out of the room, her face buried in a handkerchief and sobbing. She looked at Hollister but addressed herself to George. 'God forgive me,' she said, moving to George and putting out her arms. George took her into a faintly embarrassing embrace. 'I know that Wilbur never will.'

Hollister came close, excited. 'You mean you've got power of attorney?'

Golda, her head buried in George's chest, simply nodded.

Hollister reacted as if it were New Year. George pulled Golda tighter against him, fearful that she would turn and see Hollister's silent grinning joy.

'It's OK, Golda,' George told her. 'I'll see neither you nor Wilbur have cause to regret this. You have my word!'

Golda held him tighter, while Hollister was briskly crossing to the doctors. They were completing some kind of legal document which Hollister had earlier drafted. The moment it had both their signatures Hollister whisked it from the table and hastily scanned it. He had some comment to make and the form of words was amended and initialled by both doctors.

Hollister's suddenly breezy mood made him insensitive to Golda's feelings. 'OK,' he cried. 'Next stop Judge Neuerling's.'

Hollister crossed to the phone and asked for a downtown number, but had to break off as he saw the doctors preparing to leave. After a quick consultation one of them produced some pills from his bag and handed them to Hollister. Hollister nodded his thanks and resumed his telephone call.

George watched all this, immobilized by Golda's desperate hold on him.

Hollister came back to George and Golda. 'Seven-thirty at the judge's office. It's all fixed. We're on the last lap.'

Golda finally turned out of George's embrace. 'Whose last lap?' she demanded. 'Yours or Wilbur's?'

'Believe me, Golda, this is for the best!'

'To you,' she told him with sudden fire in her voice, '*Mrs* Wilbur Sterne.' She turned to George. 'You I trust. To you, Golda.' She turned back to Hollister. 'Another thing. I'm not going anywhere. This judge wants to see me he comes here!'

321

Hollister started protesting. 'He can't do that, Mrs Sterne. This is like a hearing in court. It has to be done formally.'

Hollister looked at her a long moment. 'I'll get you a glass of water,' he told her.

Hollister hurried off to the kitchen while Golda turned to George. 'A glass of water?' she asked.

Hollister came back with the pills in one hand and the glass of water in the other. 'These'll make you feel better,' he told her. 'The doctors left them for you.'

Golda looked to George. She was obviously intent on doing nothing unless George approved.

'It'll be all right, Golda,' he told her.

Golda shrugged, and flushed the pills down her throat.

Hollister beamed approval.

Judge Neuerling scanned the papers. They were all seated in his chambers. 'Seems to be in order,' he said looking up at them. 'It falls to me to satisfy myself that you, Mrs Wilbur Sterne, understand fully the implications of passing power of attorney to these gentlemen . . .'

'Not "gentlemen",' snapped Golda, pointing to George. 'Only *him*.'

Neuerling nodded and looked down at the papers before him and made a marginal note. 'Well then, if I give effect to this proposal it means that all rights to dispose of the property and commitments of the Galaxy Motion Picture Company pass to Mr Schapner, who would, in effect, be acting in your place. You do understand that, Mrs Sterne?'

Golda nodded. 'Him, I trust!'

Neuerling nodded. 'You will need to, since Mr Schapner will be free of any obligation to you except to account, at some future date, solely for the financial distribution of the assets of the company. Do you understand the implications of that, Mrs Sterne?'

'I only know that I trust Mr Schapner. That's all I need to know,' Golda said emphatically.

George found that the struggle to present an amiable face to the judge under the weight of Golda's constantly reiterated protestations of trust was weighing heavily. He had deceived Wilbur, Galaxy and Hollywood. He'd ducked and twisted, lied and prevaricated. He was exploiting the name and reputation of a dead girl and now was looting the trust of a living, confused older woman. Somehow he was sure he was doing the right thing, but he couldn't shrug off the tainted means by which he was doing it. He could only console himself with the thought that without him there would have been only a pile of ashes to sift through.

'In that case,' Judge Neuerling was saying, 'and giving due weight to the urgency of the matter, not without some reservations, I approve this order.'

In the absence of a gavel the judge knocked on his desk with an ink bottle, counter-signed the order and handed it to the attendant clerk for the official imprint.

'We did it!' exulted Hollister as the cab drove them from the court building. George, busy waving away the cab that was carrying Golda back to Wilbur's bedside, turned back to Hollister.

'If anything happens out of this that hurts Golda or Wilbur I will personally choke you to death!' George told him.

Hollister looked at George, momentarily startled. 'Hey, come on, loosen up! Sure, drop something their way, but you do realize what's happened here, don't you?'

George put a weary hand to a confused head. 'What?'

Hollister slapped George on the shoulder with delight. 'You son-of-a-bitch! You own Galaxy Studios!'

'In Golda's name,' said George.

'Technically,' grudged Hollister. 'The point is you own the rights of disposal – that's *ownership*, old buddy! I'll bet you didn't count on that when you woke up this morning, huh?'

'*Yesterday* morning,' said George.

16

George came awake to find Sybil shaking him. It took him a moment to register that he was in the office. He remembered coming back here after leaving Hollister to go off and start negotiating with the banks. He tried to shake his head clear but it only made it worse.

'What time is it?' asked George.

'Eight forty-five, Mr Schapner. Are you all right? When I came in just now I thought you were dead!'

'I'm just about alive, Sybil. Thanks. I've had about thirty minutes' sleep in the past twenty-four hours. Look, we've got to get organized. I've got a big meeting at ten. Can you find me some breakfast, also a clean collar and maybe even a soap and towel?'

Sybil was nodding throughout this. 'Yes, but where have you been? Everyone's been trying to reach you.'

'They'll have to wait. Get me some coffee at least, would you?'

Sybil hurried off and George tried to collect himself. Big meeting? He couldn't get it straight in his head. He just wanted to lie back down and sleep some more. He knew he couldn't. He knew he shouldn't, but it was too easy just to close his eyes again.

The next time Sybil shook him awake she had a man with her. 'Who's this?' asked George.

'I got him from the barber's shop,' she told him. 'You need a shave!'

George let himself be cosseted by Sybil. He sat with his collar off and shirt open while the barber struggled with the problems of shaving a man eating bagels and drinking coffee. Further complications arose when he took a call from Hollister. He was anxious to know if George had heard from Lewis.

George told him 'no'. Hollister chuckled. He was about to go into a meeting at the bank. 'We're going to look pretty stupid if they don't show,' he told George.

The call did nothing to improve George's frame of mind, but the shave and the fresh collar worked wonders.

'Where is this meeting?' asked Sybil.

'At Galaxy but no one's to know about it. Tell any callers anything you like except where I really am.'

'Sounds intriguing,' said Sybil.

'It's more than intriguing but don't ask me what it's about because I'm not sure myself.' George looked at his watch. Nine twenty-five. 'I'd better get over there,' he told Sybil.

He had a full trio of girls in the outer office but instead of his usual morning chorus of greetings he got curious looks. It seemed that his coming *out* of his office when he would normally have been going *in* had destroyed their routine.

George got to the gates at Galaxy to be confronted by a highly suspicious newcomer. 'I got no orders about a Mr Schapner,' the man said dubiously.

'Then ask someone,' George snapped. He sat fuming in the car while the gateman went off to consult on the telephone. George wondered what sort of impression he would make on Lewis if he couldn't even get in the studio he was purporting to sell.

The gateman returned after an interval. 'They getting on to the bank,' he said. 'They gonna call me back.'

George sighed and sat there. He couldn't see much else to do.

'Things is bad all over,' the gateman confided to George. 'I hear they closed the Beverly Hills Hotel, even.'

Absorbed as he was in his own problems, this was nevertheless startling news. 'Why'd they do that?'

The gateman shook his head. 'Ran out of money same as everyone else, I guess,' he murmured. The telephone in his hut sounded and he went to answer it. George saw him nodding into the telephone several times before coming back.

'Seems you got the OK. Anybody's name you want to leav with me to let through, Mr Schapner?'

George gave him everybody he could think of, but wa finding it increasingly difficult to function with people wh had had a night's sleep. It was like trying to talk through a fish bowl. George couldn't decide if he was inside talking ou or outside talking in. He knew if he could only believe i what was happening he might find a shot of adrenalin from somewhere.

The furtive feeling started when he parked his car in Wilbur's slot. Going into Wilbur's office only increased it. I was several minutes before he could bring himself to si behind the desk and, when he did, all he saw was the accumulated dust. Had they even fired the cleaners?

George was still flicking the dust layer off the polished wood when Hollister came in. He didn't comment on George's domestic chores but launched directly into an excited recounting of his first skirmish with the bank.

'We got 'em, George!' Hollister told him excitedly. 'When I started to outline what we had in mind they opened their mouths and kept them that way! They want that cash money so bad! Look, it's not going to bail us out altogether but enough to get the studio open again before anyone notices too much.'

'With me running it?'

Hollister nodded. 'I got the impression from Collellea that his people had that very much in mind, George.'

George sat behind Wilbur's desk. 'I don't know that I could handle it.'

'You have to make up your mind to it. This business isn't about four walls, George. It's about people. Don't you realize you're the hottest property in town right now?' Hollister broke off laughing. 'Anyway, the place suits you.'

'Well, I'll tell you. If it makes the deal work – OK, but there's no way I could run an operation like this.'

'You think Wilbur was a genius? Look, George, *you*

brought Velma Torraine here in the first place. All that other talent you brought in lately? Wilbur had eight years till now. He never got another Velma. You did! Everything that's any good about this studio has happened in the last year.'

George nodded. 'Maybe we've been lucky.'

'That might have something to do with it, but my bet is that you're the kind of guy that *makes* luck. You can do it, George. I know it.'

George looked at his watch. It was past time for the appointment. '*If* there's going to be a studio to do anything with.'

Even as George spoke the telephone on his desk buzzed. It was the gateman telling him that 'a Mr Collellea and colleagues' had just been passed through.

'They're on their way up,' said George suddenly terrified. 'Funny thing is, Lewis doesn't seem to be with them.'

This news seemed to disappoint Hollister. 'Dammit! You think he's come to say "no"?'

George shook his head. '"No" they say on the phone.'

Hollister and George both stood practising their grins and wishing away the interval between gate and office. Finally they heard voices at the far end of the corridor. They exchanged crossed fingers as the footsteps came closer, clearly heard in the otherwise deserted offices.

Finally there was a tap on the door and the gateman was there showing in Collellea and the two protection men. They exchanged handshakes and George couldn't stop himself asking after Lewis.

'Mr Lewis had urgent business this morning, Mr Schapner,' Collellea told him.

George invited Collellea to sit down and, as he walked round the desk to take his place in Wilbur's chair, he caught Hollister's disappointed gaze.

Collellea came right to the point. 'We've spent some considerable time on your proposals, Mr Schapner, and I

327

have here two copies of the terms and conditions under which we will consider taking a part of the action.'

George's spirits soared out of his boots. They'd come back with something! He and Hollister scanned the two separate pieces of paper. Neither had got beyond the introductory paragraph before Collellea interrupted.

'One moment, please,' he said. 'There are some preliminary questions that I have for you.'

'Can't we read this first?' asked George.

'There is little point until after my questions have found satisfactory answers,' said Collellea.

'OK. Shoot.'

'We understand that Galaxy Studios is one hundred per cent owned by Mr Wilbur Sterne?'

Hollister came in quickly brandishing the various documents that they'd got through the night. 'If you care to glance through these I think you'll find all your questions answered, Mr Collellea.'

Collellea scanned through the papers and then settled down to study them in more detail.

The three read silently for the next two minutes. George, who understood less about what he was reading than Hollister, finished first. He sat watching Hollister's reaction as he read more carefully.

Finally, Collellea noticed that both Hollister and George had finished reading. 'If you gentlemen wish to confer separately, please do so. I shall be another few minutes.'

Hollister and George took off to the far end of the long room where Wilbur kept his conference table.

Hollister was excited. 'They'll go for it, George. You've done it! Another goddamned miracle!'

'But they get control. They take fifty-one per cent!'

'What the hell did you expect? The only reason they're taking *that* little is because they don't know the leverage I got on the bank. Don't you understand? They're putting in a million . . .'

'It doesn't say that on their draft!' George protested.

Hollister shrugged that off. 'They know the amount we're asking. So far as they know we have to raise another two million to pay off Galaxy's debt. Don't you see? If they knew about my ability to gear their money for a near complete settlement they'd take everything but a few crumbs!'

George knew he was floundering way out of his depth. He just wished he wasn't so damned tired!

'What happens when they find out? You do realize who it is we're dealing with here, don't you?'

'Sure I do! I knew that from the first moment. The fact is we've got a chance to save something from this mess. Believe me there's nobody else who'd be willing or able to move this quick – and if we don't move quick we're dead!'

George took a long deep breath. 'You know, this is all happening too damned fast. Hollister – promise me you know what we're doing!'

Hollister nodded vigorously. 'I *know* what we're doing, George! Trust me!'

'Gentlemen?'

Both turned to find that Collellea had laid down his papers and seemed to be waiting for them to rejoin him.

'I think I can say that, in broad terms, we can come to an agreement this morning. There are some matters of detail which we can safely leave to a later date. However, on the main point – the saving of Galaxy Motion Picture Studios – I think I can say that we are in accord.'

Collellea reached down into his bulky briefcase, giving George and Hollister time to exchange triumphant grins.

Collellea resurfaced with copies of a short agreement. There is one major condition to all this, however, and that concerns Mr Schapner personally.'

Collellea handed George the top copy of the agreement.

'As you will see, this calls upon Mr Schapner to agree to become president and executive in charge of production for the newly formed studio corporation in exchange for substantial benefits in both salary and stock options. Prior agreement to that is our one condition to proceeding further.

George looked at Hollister. He suddenly saw how careful he had been conditioned for this move – something that would have been unthinkable twenty-four hours before. He also saw that he had little option. George turned from Hollister's encouraging head-nodding to the sober face of Collellea.

'No problem,' he told Collellea, and, taking up a pen hurriedly furnished by Hollister, signed.

Collellea then pushed several more one-page documents before him which, in effect, gave control to Lewis and associates.

George signed one after the other, initialling some, with a feeling of unreality. Had he really, during that long, barely understood night, acquired the right to sit here in Wilbur's office and dispose of his assets? Was it possible that he was going to walk out of this office as head of production?

From the congratulatory hand-shakes that Hollister kept thrusting on him every time he signed it seemed he was, yet he couldn't escape the feeling that he'd fallen among self-deluding lunatics. It might, for differing reasons, suit those present to go through this farce, but would the rest of the world take it seriously? It didn't seem possible.

With light-headed reflexes George signed where he was told, and tried to believe he understood. It wasn't easy. His one thought through all this unreal authorization was that when this came before 'real' lawyers they'd pick to pieces his legal right to do what he was doing. In a way that would be a relief.

'When and how can we expect the money?' asked Hollister in what, to George, seemed indecent haste.

'Immediately,' Collellea told them calmly. Turning to the two protection men he gave a nod. Both the men immediately turned out the door and their feet could be heard echoing down the strangely quiet office building.

330

Hollister watched their departure and turned back to Collellea. 'Is it a draft or what?' he asked.

Collellea shook his head. 'Much more straightforward, Mr Hollister.'

George waited uneasily, starting to suspect that with their signatures already locked away in Collellea's briefcase they were about to get machine-gunned. As insurance he moved himself imperceptibly in line with Collellea.

The two protection men returned, each carrying two large suitcases which they ceremoniously placed dead centre of the carpet.

Hollister, mouth open, turned to Collellea. 'In there?' he asked.

Collellea stood and, reaching a set of keys from his pocket, started unlocking the cases. The lids opened one after the other to reveal serried ranks of impeccable bank notes. 'So that's what a million dollars looks like?' breathed Hollister.

'You should count it, Mr Hollister, because that's what *two* million dollars looks like.'

'*Two* million?' asked Hollister.

Collellea nodded. 'It was Mr Lewis's opinion that you had grossly miscalculated the amount you would need to clear Galaxy's present indebtedness. You have one million in stock purchasing and a further million which you may consider as an undated loan.'

'Undated?' asked Hollister.

Collellea nodded. 'That doesn't mean unaccountable, however.'

Hollister seemed silenced by awe.

George was shifting his thoughts around uncomfortably. 'You mean we have to sign personal notes for this money?'

Collellea allowed himself his first smile. 'That will not be necessary. We might call this a gentleman's understanding.'

Hollister recovered his voice. 'Look, this could lead to problems with the bank's examiners. I mean, how do we explain all this cash money appearing out of nowhere?'

'Proper and sufficient paperwork will be supplied by us, Mr Hollister. You may rely on our judgement for that. In the present state of confusion reigning in the banking system I doubt that any such question will be asked for some months. By that time all will be in place.'

George, watching Hollister, saw that he was accepting this. George had a feeling he might easily end up in jail trying to find out what it was he was doing right this minute.

'Well, gentlemen, I think that concludes our business for the time being.' Collellea extended a hand to George. 'May I wish you well in your new responsibilities, Mr Schapner.'

George shook Collellea's hand but couldn't escape the feeling of dread which had descended on him.

It wasn't until Collellea and his two heavies had left that the reality of being in an unprotected office with two million dollars in bank notes dawned on George. 'What happens if they come back and rob us?' he asked Hollister.

Hollister, kneeling in supplication at the cases, was flicking through wrapped brick after brick. 'I don't think they'd do anything like that, would they?'

George picked up Wilbur's private line. It was still alive. He asked for the First National. Connected, he told them he wanted an armoured car and four armed guards to come to the studio. George hadn't completed the call when Hollister took the phone from his hand and asked instead for his contact there.

Covering the phone, Hollister asked George to leave it to him.

George was only too happy to crash into Wilbur's chair, and stare into space. Hollister completed his call and started a lunatic dance round the office crying: 'We did it!'

George watched him with detachment. He found it hard to see what there was in all this for Hollister. George knew one thing for sure – Hollister was dangerous and George didn't like him.

Hollister had no similar feelings about George. He dragged him to the window where they could see the gatehouse and a panorama of the entire lot. 'All that out there, George. That's all yours!'

'Until Wilbur finds out what we've done!'

'Forget it!' crowed Hollister. 'It's all sewn up and legal. Now, what's your first executive decision?'

George didn't need to think about that. 'I'm going to get some sleep,' he told Hollister.

17

George left his car at the studio and took a cab. His problem was knowing where to go. His brain was shuffling through concrete and he wanted to hide. He knew he ought to go back to his office. He felt he ought to call Madame Gregory who had set all these events in motion. He thought about going home but knew that when news of this leaked out – and you couldn't keep a secret in Hollywood – his phone wouldn't stop ringing for a week. That left a hotel. The Hollywood Hotel would be like taking an ad in the paper. They'd find him at the Alexandria, or the Ambassador. The Beverly Hills was closed. That left a flop-house or the newly opened Beverly Wilshire.

It was then he remembered Julia!

'*Mister* Schapner!!' the mountainous nurse greeted him. 'We have been trying to contact you all night!' The nurse's narrow eyes were boring into him. Her whole expression was of disapproval.

'Is everything all right?' he asked her.

The nurse hesitated over answering and seemed to be considering withholding information she felt he no longer deserved. 'Mrs Schapner was having a difficult time . . .' she started and paused.

'Me too!' said George.

The nurse's frown intensified. 'But was safely delivered of a baby girl at one thirty-seven, this morning!'

Delighted relief all but overwhelmed George. 'A girl? You mean I'm a father? Can I see her?'

'The baby or your wife?'

'Both!'

'If you will wait here I will go and see.'

George watched her walk away and turned to scan the lobby for someone to congratulate him. There was only one sorry-looking man whose head was downcast. He kept murmuring to himself: 'Never again. Never again!' George thought it best not to intrude.

He turned this way and that before realizing that the ache in his face was due to the fixed grin he'd acquired. Impatient to see Julia he started taking a few tentative steps down the corridor in pursuit of the nurse. He must have missed her because she spoke from behind him. 'Mr Schapner?'

George turned to see her standing halfway out of a door. 'Your wife will see you, Mr Schapner.' The nurse made it sound as if it had been a close-run thing.

George reverentially stepped through the held-open door.

Julia lay in the bed, her head turned towards him. George was shocked at how pale and drawn she was.

'Hi, George!' she greeted him.

George went to her and buried his face against her throat. 'I'm sorry about not being here,' he told her.

'I thought you'd left town,' said Julia quietly.

'When you hear my news you'll maybe think I should have!'

'What's happened?' asked Julia.

George told her about Wilbur, about the studio and the night-long paper chase culminating in the meeting with Collellea. Julia listened carefully but silently throughout and when he'd finished, gently turned her head away on the pillow and started to sob.

334

'Hey!' George chided, 'being made head of a studio is bad news?'

Julia was obstinately resisting his attempts to turn her head back towards him. 'No! Being married to you is the bad news!' She suddenly turned to him of her own volition. 'How could you miss the birth of your own daughter?'

'But I just got through explaining it all to you! Julia, I've been up all night with this thing! There's no way I could stop it!'

Julia looked for a moment as if she were trying to decide whether to laugh or cry. 'Neither could I!' she finally said, and the lip-trembling became a positive laugh as she threw out her arms and pulled George to her.

'Did you see her yet?' asked Julia.

George shook his head against her hair. 'I got the rest of my life to see her.'

'You know I'm never going to forget this, don't you?' she asked.

'I know,' groaned George.

They held each other in happy silence for a moment longer before George felt brave enough to ask: 'Is being married to me *really* bad news?'

Julia shook her head. 'The really bad news is that I love you!'